M000281607

SHE

is

HERE

GINA MARTIN

WOMANCRAFT PUBLISHING

Copyright © 2022 Gina Martin

All rights reserved. No part of this publication may be reproduced, distributed, or transmitted in any form or by any means, including photocopying, recording, or other electronic or mechanical methods, without the prior written permission of the publisher, except in the case of brief quotations embodied in critical reviews and certain other non-commercial uses permitted by copyright law.

Published by Womancraft Publishing, 2022
womancraftpublishing.com

ISBN 978-1-910559-76-5

She is Here is also available in ebook format: ISBN 978-1-910559-75-8

Cover design, diagrams and typesetting by Lucent Word, lucentword.com
Cover art by Iris Sullivan
Author photograph by Lisa Levart, goddessonearth.com

Womancraft Publishing is committed to sharing powerful new women's voices, through a collaborative publishing process. We are proud to midwife this work, however the story, the experiences and the words are the author's alone. A percentage of Womancraft Publishing profits are invested back into the environment reforesting the tropics (via TreeSisters) and forward into the community: providing books for girls in developing countries, and affordable libraries for red tents and women's groups around the world.

Printed in Ireland by Carraig Print Litho Press, Cork.

A percentage of profits made with this book will be shared with the following charities and organizations that are doing the good work to protect marginalized peoples, our planet, and the life on Her. Living Stories Landscape; Kunsikeya Tamakoce, Redes Ecovillage and the Cork Traveller Women's Network.

PRAISE FOR
GINA MARTIN

Epic and intimate, mythic and maternal. Reading this book feels like re-membering a legend I've known all my life, buried deep in my bones, but like the thirteen sisters themselves, long ago forgotten. Martin breathes narrative details into the embers of this story that make it crackle to life.
Jeanine Cummins, bestselling author of *American Dirt*,
A Rip in Heaven* and *The Outside Boy

Author, teacher and priestess Gina Martin has woven together visions of the mysteries of the Sacred Feminine from the past, present and future, with an evocative and sensual urgency... Lush with rich, descriptive lan-guage that carries the reader into the cultures and rituals she dreams into being, one has only to let oneself be carried deeply into the heart of these rites and the important spiritual messages they contain.
Sharynne NicMhacha, scholar and author of *The Divine Feminine in Ancient Europe*, *Celtic Myth and Religion* and *Queen of the Night*

Gina Martin weaves a magical tale of possibility. Parting the tides to bring forth a new/old understanding of our shared past; A past in which the goddess – and therefore all life – is held sacred. And that is exactly what we need right now.
**Jessica M. Starr, author of *Waking Mama Luna*
and *Maid, Mother, Crone, Other***

WHO'S WHO

IN THE NOW	IN THE BEFORE
Sally Standing Bear Portreaux, born Kakehtaweyihtam, of the Cree	*Atvasfara, High Priestess of Egypt*
Frances Standing Bear Portreaux Fletcher	*Celebi, High Priestess of Brig, the Brighid of the Mystery School at Calanais*
Walter Little Thunder, of the Cree	*Tiamet, Priestess of Lhamo at the Roof of the World*
Michael Pádraig Francis Kenneally, aka Malcolm Reynolds	*Malvu, Chief Observer at the Mystery School at Calanais*
Bartholomew Winslow	*Eiofachta, devotee of Nematona of the Great North Woods*
Magdalena Kenneally	*Ni Ma, of the Seven Sisters*
Old Shelta Kenneally	*Misi, of the Sea of Grasses*
Sally Standing Bear Fletcher Kenneally, known as Sassy	*Dalia, Priestess of Nut and She who was Pharaoh*

Sally Standing Bear Kenneally Boadu, known as Sisi	*Domnhu, attendant to Badh of the Cailleach*
Young Shelta Kenneally	*Ndeup, of the Goddess Yemaya*
Mame Khadi, priestess of Yoff	*Ni Mu of the Seven Sisters*
Alaman Sulaman, of the Tuareg	*Pel, Dedicant of Artemis at Ephesus*
Kahina, his grandmother	*Yollo, of the Sea of Grasses*
Agnes Weapon Maker, of the Lakota	*Smith the Younger, of the Sea of Grasses*
Ulapi, Elder of the Anangu First Nations People	*Talo, twin brother of Uxua, High Priestess of Ix Chel in Yucatan*
Ele, High Priestess of the Bantu	*Smith the Elder, of the Sea of Grasses*
Great Shaman, of the Goddess Myoungjinguk	*Feyl, of the Goddess Seal Woman*
Wise Woman, of the Yazidi	*Alama, First Among Equals of the Goddess Nematona in the Great North Woods*
Bon Shaman	*Yan, devotee of the Goddess Lhamo*
Michael Francis Kenneally Boadu, known as Mick	*Malvu, Chief Observer of the Mystery School at Calanais*
Hopi Grandmother	*Ni Mo, of the Seven Sisters*
Senior Maori Priestess	*Ni Mou, of the Seven Sisters*
Elder Stregha	*Ni Mae, of the Seven Sisters*
Sally Standing Bear Boadu Tjia	*Atvasfara, High Priestess of Isis*

CHAPTER 1
SASKATCHEWAN, 1928

S ally Standing Bear Portreaux was preparing to die. Known as Kakehtaweyihtam, She is Wise, by her people, a medicine woman, widow, mother, and shaman, she had arranged everything to her satisfaction. Yesterday she had said goodbye to her brother, Walter. She had given him a letter to deliver to her daughter from whom she had been estranged these last ten years. Next to her was the beaded belt that had belonged to her husband Louis. Beside that, the photo of her grandson Tom. In her hands she held the medicine bundle she had sent with Tom when he went off to war and that had been returned to the family with his belongings. She lay down, surrounded by these treasured objects, listening to the double hoot of the great horned owl outside her cabin, and waited to be taken.

Sally Standing Bear, Kakehtaweyihtam, she who had been Atvasfara, High Priestess of Isis was ready to die. More than ready. Eager, in fact. This lifetime had had its joys, to be sure. But the sorrows had mounted until Sally didn't want to stand up under them anymore. Everything she had tried to do, to protect her people, the Cree, to protect their wisdoms, to guide and mold Tom – everything was proving impossible. Her people were restrained on reservations. Their precious children were forcibly taken from their families to residential schools, their hair was cut, and they were punished if they spoke their own language. Traditions were more and more hidden and then forgotten. And Tom...Tom was lost on the battlefield of Ypres. Sally had never recovered from his death.

So, she waited for death to take her. Erratic heartbeats gave her hope for quick release. Liminal light faded, darkness descended…still she lingered. The owl song gave way to the coyote chorus. And then, much later, the serenade of a lonely wolf matched her mood. Sally drifted off to sleep against her will. She had wanted to face this death with eyes wide open. But dreams dragged her down.

$$\mathD \bigcirc \mathC$$

The swell of morning birdsong and the light of dawn pressing against her eyelids brought her awake.

"Damn it! I'm still alive!"

Later that morning Sally had left her bed and was sitting out front of her cabin, disgruntled at the failure of her planned exit, but enjoying the slanted sunshine coming through the cedar branches, in spite of herself. Birds flew up into the trees and the goats gave a bleat of warning. But Sally already knew someone was coming. She had felt the fall of swift, light footsteps before she saw her granddaughter Frances come around the bend in the path.

Sally smiled so hard her eyes almost disappeared. "Does your mama know you are here?" she asked.

"What do you think?" Frances replied, and Sally barked a laugh.

"I think she is unaware that you have headed out into the 'wilderness' to associate with 'savages.'" Sally and Frances looked at each other in complete agreement that Hannah Fletcher, the daughter of one and the mother of another, would be best served not knowing of Frances's whereabouts.

Frances, to her mother's constant irritation, looked a lot like Sally Standing Bear. Her brother Tom, whom Frances had never met because he had died in the Great War the year she was born, had looked like their mother. Tall, fair-eyed, and sandy haired, Tom and Hannah had taken after Louis Portreaux, fur trapper, fiddle player, and their granddad and father. But Frances, the daughter of grief, born ten moons after the telegram had arrived telling of Tom's death, was a throwback to Sally's people, the Cree. Her skin was dark honey, easily deepened in the sun, and her eyes were the brown of buckeye conkers. No matter how hard her Ma tried, and try she did with rag curlers and curling tongs, Frances's hair was as straight and as slippery as a waterfall. She was nine years old, small for her age, and light on her feet. Frances slipped away whenever she could to spend hours with her Grandma Sally and Great Uncle Walter. She stoically accepted the punishments that followed when her mother found out.

"I ran here 'cause I was afraid I was too late," Frances said in an accusatory tone.

"Too late for what?" Sally replied.

"I don't know – but I woke up last night and felt like you were going away somewheres. Are you, going away somewheres?" Frances looked like she might cry with a wobble in her lower lip.

"Looks like not," Sally said with tenderness, and opened her arms and Frances ran into the embrace.

Sometime later, after both had a bit of a cry, Sally settled in to tell Frances about what she had planned. "And so, I figured I could go easy. But Creator has decided that that is not to be my story."

"Maybe Creator is hearing my prayers, and they are more powerful than yours," Frances said, only slightly joking.

"What are you praying for, may I ask?" Sally whispered.

"I feel like you aren't telling me something important, Granny. So, I've been praying real hard that you start talkin'."

Sally threw back her head and laughed till tears, this time tears of joy, rolled down her cheeks. "Maybe it is the right time to be tellin' my story. Is it you who needs to hear it?"

Frances got that stubborn look on her face that drove her mother mad. "I am the only one here, ain't I?" she said with asperity. And Sally laughed even harder.

They sat together through that morning and ate strawberries from the garden, warm still from the sun. Around midday, Sally's brother Walter came through the woods and up around to the front of the cabin. He had expected to come and find Sally's body to set her to rights, but the smile that split his face when he heard their voices was mingled relief and pure happiness. Even now as an old man he walked without

3

making a sound, but Sally had been alerted to his coming by the shift in birdsong and the chatter of the squirrels.

"Lookey here, my two best girls!" he said in his soft slow way.

"Two best 'cause you only had but the one sister and had nothing but sons," Sally retorted with a hint of a smile. This was a gentle ribbing that was almost as old as they were, and Frances giggled as they poked at each other to express their love. Walter lowered himself onto the log that right-angled their seats and watched as Frances settled deeper onto Sally's lap.

The girl turned her bird-bright eyes to her great uncle and said, "Uncle, Granny is getting up her gumption to tell me her story. Can you give her a nudge? She's been a'circlin' round for some time now."

Walter looked hard at his sister. "Her story? And what story would that be?" he asked Frances without taking his eyes off Sally.

"The child has been praying to Creator to know what I know, and I'm thinking that this is why I'm still breathin'," Sally replied.

"And why is she needing to hear it?" Walter prodded gently.

"'Cause I think this is the last circle of the Wheel but one for me, and I think the whole story can be safeguarded till it can be used."

"You feel the end of the cycle comin'?" he asked with a bit of awe in his voice. Sally nodded slowly and Frances busted in.

"What in tarnation are you two talkin' about?"

Sally cleared her throat and when she spoke her voice sounded different, lower, filled with richer tones and sounds. "The world is a big spider web, lovey girl. You know how the web has many spokes, and how it all feeds back into the center? Well, creation is like that. And our lives are the threads of the web. And some threads are our family lines, our ancestors, our foremothers. And some threads are our soul journey, the ways we have been in the world and the lessons we have learned. I think you are destined to see my entire web."

"Who is the spider?" Frances asked, hushed and a little afraid to break the spell of Sally's speech.

"She of a Thousand Names, the Source of all Life, The Maker of Heaven and Earth, She Who Weaves the Worlds," Sally answered.

Walter began to hum softly, a tune that Frances had heard before, heard in her dreams. Sally joined in with words in a language that

Frances thought she ought to understand. The girl felt peace ooze through her like warm molasses, and she drifted off to sleep in her grandmother's arms.

"So, you plan to tell her the whole story, all the lifetimes?" Walter asked after a bit in Cree, their preferred language. "You think this child can hold the memories of the Roof of the World and Egypt and our time at the Abbey in Rupertsberg? That's a lot to grasp. You figure Frances can handle that?"

Sally nodded.

"You want it to be written down?"

Sally nodded again.

"How are we going to do this, Sally? You and I can't write. Frances here can though. But we got a big problem. The girl's mother will pitch a fit if she keeps coming here all summer."

Sally gave a dry chuckle, careful not to waken Frances. It was something that Walter always did, he refused to say Hannah's name. It was like if he didn't name her she wouldn't be real. So, he had referred to her as "Tom's mother" or "Louis's daughter," never by her name. Sally had suffered the estrangement from her only child, had felt, always, the distance between them, but she had never stopped hoping for some opening, some connection. Walter had never wasted any breath on that hope.

"She does care what people in town think of her. Maybe if you let it be known that I am ailing, and suggest that Frances could be my helper this summer, maybe the fear of being seen as petty would let her free the girl up," Sally suggested with a small side smile.

"You are now and always have been the best person I have ever known for moving people where you want them without their even knowing you're doing it." Walter's face lit up with amusement.

Sally's smile now took up her whole face. "I cut my teeth at the court of Pharaoh, remember. Small town Saskatchewan is a piece of cake."

So, these two, friends from ages and lives past, sister and brother of their beloved mother in this lifetime, sat through the afternoon, taking in the smell of wild roses and phlox at the wood's edge, and strategizing on how to best transmit the story of the Thirteen, the lives of Atvasfara, and the destiny that awaited them to this small child, this precious child of their hearts.

Sally was clear now that it would be the sacred mission of this motherline to carry the story forward and reveal it at the appropriate time. Frances would be the story holder. And perhaps her daughter and her daughter's daughter and so on until the time was right.

Ages ago back in the Land of Chin, Sally/Atvasfara had incarnated as Li Er. This Li Er, who became known as Lao Tsu, had been able to codify the wisdoms of the grandmothers, and those wisdoms had been able to be accepted and revered because people believed that they had come from a man. In other lifetimes Sally, as Hildegard of Bingen and as Palle Pelhutezcan had entrusted wisdoms to beloved descendants of her body. The success had been mixed as Hildegard's writing had been decently preserved, but the writings of Palle's great-great-granddaughter, Sor Juana de la Cruz, had been mostly burned. This time though, she planned to tell the entirety of her story, the truth about her multiple lifetimes and the mission of the Thirteen to hold the Goddess safe. To tell it all without obfuscation, and then demand that it be kept protected. This was a challenge. But Sally had a knowing that this girl, Frances, and the daughters in her line that followed could protect the knowledge. This was the motherline to keep the secrets. Now, how best to get around Hannah?

After a long deep nap, Frances stirred in Sally's lap, blinked twice, and sat up. Walter stood, creaking a bit at the knees and back, and reached for the child. She eagerly let him lift her into his arms, and then they both turned their heads to look at Sally, identical pairs of liquid brown eyes.

"I'm gonna take this little one home now, and then have a good talk with her mother." He sounded a bit grim about it and Frances gave him a worried look. "It's all right, lovey girl. Your Grandma and I have it all figured out."

And with the trust born from being a well-loved child, Frances looked pleased, and ready to proceed. She settled like a broody hen and rested her face in her uncle's neck, loving the smell of safety, tobacco, and the deep forest. And because she knew how the old ones loved it, she responded in Cree, "Here with you is home for me, but you can take me back to town if you need."

Sally made figures in the air with her hands, and it looked like dancing. Frances could almost see the shapes float toward her on the afternoon light, and they settled on her gently like kisses. Walter gave that sound deep in his throat of agreement and contentment and turned to walk back into the white man's town.

Sally resigned herself to staying alive a while longer, fed the chickens and goats, scratched the cat's ears, and settled into her deep prayer practice.

"Beloved Mother Isis
Maker of all things
Protector of the children
Guardian of the morning and night
Fill me with Your peace
Fill me with Your peace, oh Great One
Fill me with Your sacred peace."

She sat thus as the evening fell, and the stars came out like mica flecks in the black stone sky. She would live to see this task finished. And then, the Wheel would turn, and she would prepare for the final events in their mission – to re-kindle the Goddess flame, to re-birth Her name, to see Her reborn.

$$\mathbb{D} \bigcirc \mathbb{C}$$

"Uncle?"

"Yes, lovey girl."

"What you gonna say to my Ma?"

"Gonna tell her your Granny is poorly and that she needs your help."

"Is Granny poorly?"

"Not so's you need to worry about."

"So you're gonna tell my Ma that why?"

Walter just rumbled deep in his chest. It was not really a laugh, not really a signal of agreement or denial. It was a sound peculiar to him and Frances giggled, then asked, "So, we gonna fool Mama into letting me be with you in the forest?"

Walter just kept the easy pace of his footsteps heading down the dirt road back to town. The corn in the fields alongside the road was knee high, and swallows, flashes of iridescent green catching the sun, flew high and swooped down into the plowed furrows. This was about as civilized a landscape as Walter could stomach, and he gripped his inner resolve to face the noise and clutter of the town. Frances was thinking hard with her eyebrows drawn together. She spoke carefully.

"And it's not really a lie, cause Granny was thinkin' she was dying, right?"

Again, Walter made that deep sound, and Frances could feel it tickle her cheek that rested against his chest. In that safe space she could voice her worry.

"The priest says lying is a sin."

Deep rumble.

"You don't much like that priest do you, Uncle Walter?"

"I think he is a mean and small man who professes to know the mind of god," Walter replied. "And I know he listened to your Ma and wouldn't let Granny Sally come to Tom's funeral. So, no, I don't care for him much. Do you, care for him, lovey girl?"

Frances was quiet. Walter waited.

"He smells funny, and sometimes he gets close and…hurts me," Frances said so softly that Walter wondered if she had even spoken aloud. But he could hear her and hear the fear in her spirit. He decided right then and there that Father Macky needed some lessons delivered.

"Well, lovey. I'm thinking he won't ever hurt you again. Alright?"

Frances nodded and Walter felt her small head bump up and down and jostle his chin.

Walter didn't take the main road into town. He walked around back behind the houses that edged onto fields and came up to Frances's house by the back door. He wanted something from Hannah, and it would rile her if he was visible to all and sundry coming up to the front of the house. Chickens scattered across the yard as he approached, and Hannah appeared at the door. Walter came to a stop and Frances peaked up at her mother through her eyelashes.

"Hey Mama. Uncle Walter carried me home 'cause I was ti…"

"Frances Anne, where have you been?"

Walter spoke softly "I'd think that was fairly obvious, niece."

8

Hannah bristled at his mentioning of their relation. "Get inside and wash up for supper, young lady." She held the screen open for Frances to enter but didn't invite her uncle inside. The girl scampered into the kitchen, and Walter and Hannah remained in their places. He stood as solid as a beech tree, and Hannah looked away first. "Are you wantin' something?" she asked churlishly.

"A drink of water would be good," Walter replied, and he heard Frances giggle from the shadow just inside the door.

Hannah snapped her head around to glare inside. "I told you to go wash up!" And then she turned back to her uncle, her face beet red from having had her inhospitality pointed out by him, albeit in his not-very-pointed way. Walter could hear Frances dragging her feet across the kitchen floor as she reluctantly walked upstairs.

Hannah stepped out onto the back steps and let the screen door smack closed behind her. "Help yourself then…" she gestured toward the pump.

Walter walked over, pumped the handle vigorously a couple of times and filled his palms with water, taking deep drafts of the cool liquid. He took his sweet time 'cause he knew it would irk Hannah who just wanted him gone before any of her neighbors saw him. At last, re-freshed, he lifted his gaze and looked at her, Sally's daughter. She was still a handsome woman, but bitterness had etched harsh lines that ran from her nose to her mouth. Her sandy hair was as much ashy gray as yellow these days, but she still reminded him of her father, Louis Portreaux whom he had called friend.

Walter couldn't help but think that if Louis had lived he might have softened his daughter, he might have been a bridge between her and her mother. But he died when Hannah was but two years old, and Hannah had seemed to turn against Sally. It never made any sense, and they never talked about it.

For Hannah, the memory was fuzzy and nightmarish. She could al-most recall seeing her beloved Papa on the bed and seeing her moth-er give him medicine from a glass. And then Papa had thrashed and choked, and Mama had held him down, and then he had died. Han-nah kept the memory shoved down so deep that it only burrowed under her skin. The thought that her Mama had killed her Papa…it was so slim as to be a fragment of a dream, but it acted like poison in Hannah's heart. So, from the day of Louis's funeral on, Hannah had carried anger toward her mother, and sought only the company and comfort of Louis's sister, Meredith. She had pushed her mother away, and Sally, mourning in her own way, had let the child find solace where she could. Hurt had been piled atop hurt that made a solid wall until Sally had moved back out to the woods, and Hannah had remained in town so she could pass for white and go to the town school.

It was true that Sally didn't want Hannah to be carried off to a residential school, for that was beginning to happen to First Nations children. Much had been changing since this land had become part of the country called Canada. The freedoms that First Nations peoples had had under the Hudson Bay Company's *laissez-faire* approach had become curtailed. Children were taken, and many never came back. It was a true and growing fear among the First Nations. But the sourest truth was that Hannah didn't want anything to do with her Ma, and Sally let her have her way.

"It's your Ma, niece," Walter finally said. "I thought I was gonna lose her today." And of course, that was the truth 'cause Sally had planned to die.

Hannah paled, and then looked, not at him but sideways over toward the woodshed. "Is she sick?" she asked.

"Not to look at her, but she is slipping away. That I know." Again, Walter spoke truth, without telling the whole story.

"What does she want, what do you want? I can't bring her here. What would people say?" Hannah spoke hard shards of words, and any hope Walter had still carried that she might be redeemable flew away.

"Well, I figure she knows that. She hasn't asked to come here and have you tend her," Walter said with asperity, his feelings about Hannah's position evident in his tone. "But she will need help through these next few months. I was thinking maybe Frances, since school is out, could come and be a helper for her granny."

"Oh, I don't know. What will people think? I can't tell folks where she would be!" Hannah sounded panicked, like she could see her entire life construct crumbling.

"You tell folks she has gone to tend a sick relative in Nova Scotia, somebody from your husband's side."

Hannah was thinking hard. If she said no, she feared that Frances would spend the summer sneaking away to the woods to be with Sally, and for sure, people in town would get wind of that. Walter was right – saying she was 'away' was best. "Well, I suppose that would be alright. I will miss her help around here though," Hannah said with a whine in her voice.

"Think of how much less laundry and cooking you'll need to do without the girl here," Walter slid in.

"That's true," Hannah replied. She suddenly had visions of an entire summer where she didn't have to be concerned over her daughter's escapades. Her relief showed in a flash across her face.

Walter hid his disgust and laid out a plan for Frances to be brought to the station very early the next day for the first train east. He would be waiting in the shadows and help the child off the train at the far side of the passenger car to see her out to Sally's without anyone the wiser.

"Don't you worry none, niece. Your dirty secret is safe with me," Walter said.

Hannah felt some shame, but she took him at his word. Maybe Frances would get this fascination with her grandmother and the Cree out of her system this way. Maybe she, unlike her brother Tom, would want the life Hannah offered. Hannah shuddered at the thought of the smell of the Indian camp, the scent of tanned deer skins and bear grease. *How could anyone want that?* she thought. Without another word she turned to go back into the house, leaving her uncle alone in the yard. He looked up and spied Frances's little face at her bedroom window. He smiled and brought his hands to his mouth to make the cry of the red-tailed hawk. Frances's face lit up, and she knew her uncle had outdone her Ma. She started to tremble with anticipation. She would get to be with Granny Sally! She would hear the story. Granny had promised. The summer held freedom and love.

Uncle Walter made the hawk cry again and waved gently as he turned and made his way back, along the field edges, back toward the woods. Frances watched him as long as she could, and then held the sweetness of the days to come close to her heart as she answered her mother's call to come down and help with supper.

$$\mathbb{D} \bigcirc \mathbb{C}$$

The next morning, before first light, Frances was up and dressed, clutching her satchel tightly, standing on the train platform with her father at her side. Samuel Fletcher was a man worn down by life. The loss of his son Tom in the Great War had almost bent him double. He loved his little girl Frances, the surprise baby born of a frantic coupling fueled by grief, but he had been afraid to ever give her all of his heart. He was kind, yet distant. And he never seemed to be able to get in front of his wife's moods. He hadn't found the energy or wherefore to be a buffer for little Frances. So it was, with some relief that he was waiting there on that platform to send Frances 'away' for the summer. Maybe there could be a little peace in his home.

As the train pulled into the station, Samuel handed Frances the box of food that her mother had prepared to complete the façade of a long train journey.

"This may be for the best, daughter. You like being with your Granny, don't you?"

"Oh yes, Pa! I love it there!" Frances felt a twinge of guilt at her eagerness to be gone. "But I will miss you, Pa."

They both knew that that wasn't the fullest truth, but they let it lie. Samuel helped Frances up the steps and watched as she sat down at a seat just behind the exit door. She was following Walter's instructions, and she waited until the hoot of the train whistle sounded its last call. Checking to make sure no one else was in the train car, she slipped out the door on the far side of the car, ran down the steps, and up to her Uncle Walter, half hidden in the shadows of the sycamores that ran along the tracks. They disappeared into the trees, and when the train pulled out of the station, Samuel looked and couldn't find them. He wound his way back home to his breakfast in the now mostly silent house, only punctuated by the sounds of Hannah's grumbling and clanging pots in the kitchen.

The pre-dawn bird chatter had stilled into the raucous screech of jays and the sweet trill of the cardinals by the time Walter and Frances made it to Sally's place. She was stirring a pot of corn porridge over the outside fire and looked up with a wide smile to see them walk into the clearing. Her color was better than it had been yesterday, and she even seemed to be sitting more erect.

"Well done, you two! Right sneaky!" Sally dished up some porridge for Frances, and they all smiled.

Frances dug in. These early morning adventures brought on quite an appetite! Sally watched her fondly, and with a pang remembered how Tom had also eaten her corn porridge with gusto. She reached down and gently tugged on the ears of the dog at her feet, Tom's dog as she always thought of him. Tom had written from Belgium, missing home, and aching for a pup of his own. When word had come of Tom's death, Sally had walked, half blind with grief, to the Cree settlement farther north along the river. A bitch had had a litter six weeks past, and Sally aimed to get one in Tom's memory.

She had found herself on the ground next to the pups without any real recollection of how she had gotten there. One of the puppies, the oddest-looking little thing, ambled over, crawled in Sally's lap, and fell sound asleep. He was spotted, white with amber, gray and black spots the size of pawpaws, and one ear that pointed off to the side like he was always listening for something.

"I guess you picked me then, little fella," Sally said. She tipped her head down and let her hair fall all around her face, sheltering her from view. Then, and only then had she let herself weep.

She called him Atim, Cree for dog, and he had been her constant companion these last ten years. Sensitive to her state of being, an excellent watchdog, constant in his desire to catch a fish in the river, and still to this day a failure in that endeavor, he was a balm to her sore heart. Today, his tail swung vigorously, pleased at their company, and Sally felt like a bit of Tom was with them, sitting by the fire, enjoying the morning birdsong.

The day progressed in a pattern that would be theirs for this golden summer. Chores, animals fed and watered, firewood chopped and carried, and then the trinity of woman, man and child would settle, outside if the sky was fair, or inside Sally's cabin if there was rain, door open as always for the air and the freedom and the chance to see the clouds.

Sally would place some poplar buds she called Balm of Gilead into the fire and cleanse herself with the smoke. Uncle Walter would smudge, then Frances. The scent was multi-layered, and Frances began to develop the ability to feel the layers of her energies as they were washed clean by the sacred smoke. Sally would draw sigils for protection in the air, sit herself down, and then rest in silence until she found the right place to dive into the river of her story.

Frances had brought a small leather-bound diary, a gift at her birthday from her Pa, and several composition books from her last year at school. She would have one of these on her lap, pencil in hand, head tipped to the left to catch everything Sally would tell her.

That story began in olden days in a land called Egypt, a place that Frances remembered seeing on the map that had hung on the wall of her schoolhouse. On that it was colored a soft pale green because it wasn't part of the British Empire but was a Protectorate. Frances wasn't sure what that was, but Sally talked about a different kind of Egypt, as a mighty land with a powerful ruler, a woman who was called Pharaoh. Sally said this was long before there even was a British Empire.

Frances wrote down all about the vision that thirteen women had received. They had wonderful names and she would lie awake at night and repeat them over and over to herself like a song until she drifted off to sleep: Atvasfara, Io, Awa, Badh, Kiyia, Tiamet, Maia, Parasfahe, Silbara, Autakla, Eiofachta, Ni Me, and Uxua. Wondrous sounds their names made in the ether. And as Frances slept she could feel sweet presences coming close, whispering around her with tenderness. She had never felt so safe, or so loved in her life.

Page after page after page, Frances filled them all with the stories of far-off places and a multitude of lives. Sally was specific about each place, about what the lessons were from that lifetime, about what had been her regrets.

"About a hundred some years ago in solar counting, I worked hard to rescue the enslaved. My name was Alexander Farley, and I found some refuge in the Quaker traditions. I don't know why so many of the Thirteen had chosen to suffer that fate of slavery. To experience the fullness of man's inhumanity to man? I would'a thought we'd had plenty of chances to do that. Sometimes the big pattern is all a mystery to me. I did what I could, one person at a time. But it never felt like enough."

Frances wrote and wrote, afraid to break the flow of information as it poured out of her Granny. Only occasionally she would peek up to ask a question.

"Granny, why were you sometimes a woman and sometimes a man?"

"That's a good question, lovey girl. Why do you think?"

"I think that boys have more fun than girls. They can run outside and nobody fusses at them. They can ride horses without gloves and silly hats. They can be loud and wander the woods and go to the stream and don't have to be stuck in the kitchen when it's hot."

Sally laughed, and Walter chuckled as he responded.

"Yes, lovey, that is the way it mostly is, especially with white boys and men. Our ways with the Cree use to be different, but these days the women have less freedom than before. "

"So why, Granny? Why choose that?"

Sally got real still, and her voice shifted into that echoey place when she spoke and afterwards didn't remember what she'd said. "Life is light and shadow, yin and yang, female and male principles. All is designed to be in balance. The ways and laws of humans have lost the balance. To bring it back the souls must know all the light and all the shadow."

The three sat in silence then, and Sally gradually opened her eyes. They were filled with unshed tears. She looked at Frances. "To be human is to experience it all, lovey. Pain and bliss, loss and love, power, and subjugation. That has been the journey."

And Frances wrote and wrote. One day the need to know burned right up her throat and out her mouth. "Granny, have I been one of the Thirteen? Have you found me before?"

Sally's breath caught in her throat. She had both hoped and feared that someday Frances would ask this question. And she had learned over and over again that the revelations of former identities could be quite difficult, sometimes harrowing for the person to whom they are revealed. Honesty was demanded of her with this beautiful child, but Sally was aware of the need for surgical precision in the delivery of those truths. She reached forward and took Frances's hands. As she looked deep into the girl's eyes she waited until the words felt just right. "What do you remember, lovey girl? Do you have memories or dreams that keep comin', pokin' at you?"

15

Frances shook her head, like she had just come up from being underwater. "I feel like I ought to remember, you know? Like when you wake up and know you had a great dream, and you ought to own the details but then they seem to belong to someone else."

"Sometimes, the knowing of the time before can be a burden," Sally said thoughtfully.

"I do have one dream, over and over. There are giant stones in circles, and I am singing and swaying with others and watching the moon. The stones are talking to me, talking straight into my head like they are my friends. It is always lovely, even though sometimes it is raining, and we guess where the moon is, and sometimes it is cold. But there is always a sense of peace in the dream, like I belong there." Frances sounded half in the dream as she recalled it.

"What do you think, lovey? Of the times Before?" Sally asked ever so gently, so as not to startle a knowing away.

"I think I have known you before, Granny. And Uncle Walter. I think I came into this world now so's I could help you. And that may be enough." Frances looked far wiser and sadder than any nine-year-old had any business looking. She seemed content with the non-answers to her question and tipped her head back down to the notebook.

Sally took a deep breath and started telling the story of a Mystery School called Calanais, and the wise High Priestess, the Brighid, named Celebi who had abandoned her role and title to travel to Egypt and support the work of the Thirteen. Highly educated and capable of guiding an entire Mystery School, she had been loyal and constant. She, perhaps more than any of the other Companions, had the deepest sense of what they were all facing. And yet she had stood strong and eternal in her devotion to her Goddess. As Sally spoke, Frances kept her head down, but small silver tears ran down her cheeks and made tiny drops of remembrance on the page. Sally saw the tears and left the process of knowing and remembering to the patient Ones who held them all.

Throughout that summer, members of the Cree nation would arrive to see Sally, express their respect, and say goodbye. Frances didn't know how they knew that Sally intended on leaving her body soon. But they came in twos and threes with gifts of summer berries and snared rabbits. They would sit for a while, sometimes speaking, but mostly in silence, and then, with some kind of mutual awareness, they would stand, bow their heads to Sally and turn and leave. Walter and Frances would take the gifts and use them for supper or store them for another day, and Sally would sit staring at the fire, absorbing the goodwill and energy that the visitors had brought.

Frances had always known that the Cree thought Granny Sally was special, but this parade of tribute showed her exactly how special Granny was. To Frances, Sally was her Granny. To the Cree she was Kakehtaweyihtam, She is Wise. Frances had always felt a weird battle within herself, to love her Granny without reservation, or to absorb and abide by her mother's disdain for Sally and the Cree. Hannah Fletcher had spent her life denying any association with the Indians, but Frances saw the beauty of their culture and the dignity of their lives, lived in spite of the prejudice that surrounded them. And it was in these visits from the Cree that Frances left the child's automatic belief in the parent behind. She grew up in an eye blink, and in consequence, saw her mother's biases and hatred as the weaknesses that they were.

"Granny? Why did you come to this life this time? There had to be easier and fancier places to be," Frances asked, in what was a moment of acute insight as to the workings of reincarnation and choice.

"Well, lovey, these people, our people, the Cree and the other First Nations, they hold some of the most potent wisdoms. And it is so that the outside world wants to wipe those wisdoms away. So, I came to help hold onto what I could," Sally said.

"What do they know, Granny?"

"That the Earth and all that dwell on Her are equal. That respect for life means all life, even the creepy crawlies. That the stones are the ancestors, and that the measure of a person is in how they treat the generations that came before and the ones that will come after. These are the wisdoms from the times before, but the world has spun crazy and is in danger of forgetting it all."

"I won't forget, Granny. I promise." Frances was fervent.

"You won't. I know that, lovey. And you need to make sure that your daughters and their daughters and on and on won't forget neither. We are all gonna be counting on you."

And Frances, who had been the Brighid, The High Priestess of Calanais, again picked up the familiar mantle of responsibility and wore it well.

By summer's end, Frances had filled her diary and four composition books with the stories of Granny Sally's lives. In the garden the three sisters, the corn and beans and squash, had come in with abundance, and Uncle Walter was spending much of his days fishing and then preparing the fish to be smoked and preserved. Frances noticed that each day Granny grew tired a little earlier than the day before. By mid-August, they were only spending a couple of hours each day in the dictation, and Sally was nodding off in front of the fire more frequently. Frances felt her heart tear inch by inch with each passing day.

One afternoon, Uncle Walter stayed with them and began to tell of his recollections from the times before. He talked about his home in a temple built into the side of a mountain in a place where the air is so thin that light can seem solid. He also spoke of the journey to Egypt and the cataclysm that had swallowed the Thirteen. After a long pause he began to speak of his time in a place called Rupertsberg, and his voice got higher and younger. He smiled as he told the story. It had been a magical place there where a Mother Hildegard had made such safe sanctuary that many of the Thirteen could come and be and live together in peace. His life then had not been long, but he had felt loved. As he finished the telling he turned and looked at Sally.

"You can never be given enough thanks for the making of that blessed oasis. That was the very best of all the lifetimes I can recall." Uncle's voice was back to his normal tone.

"Even better than the Roof of the World?" Sally asked with skepticism.

"Even better, for the time spent with you. But this lifetime has surpassed even that, my beloved sister and friend." He cleared his throat of the sudden tightness there and stood quickly to go turn the fish grilling on the fire spit.

For the next several days, Sally was recalling bits and pieces of information and demanding that Frances not forget.

"I won't, Granny. I swear!"

And then one day, Sally and Walter, solemn and quiet, motioned for

Frances to come and sit with her notebook. The day had come to talk about Frances's brother Tom.

"Lovey girl, you need to know that our Tom was one of the Thirteen," Sally began.

Frances gasped. "He was? Why him and not me?" She sounded hurt and tears pooled in her eyes.

Uncle Walter reached over and took her hand. "Sweet girl. None of us knows the whys and wherefores of all this. What is, is just what is. But we couldn't love you more if you were twelve of the Thirteen all wrapped up in one." He shook her hands a bit, as if to emphasize the truth of his words.

Frances tried to calm her mind and hear what needed to be told. But she was thinking, *what was so special about Tom?* Tendrils of jealousy whipped up in her. All her life, everyone had been all torn up about Tom. Well, dang-nabbit, she was here wasn't she? She was, and Tom wasn't. She wished she could be mad at him, pop him in the eye, and be done with it. But she couldn't. He was the phantom perfect child. So, she took a deep breath and lifted her eyes to Granny. "So, who was Tom?"

"There was a place called Sumeria and a city called Babylon."

"I heard of that in the Bible," Frances interjected.

"Yes, the Bible folk got there later. But this is a Babylon from the Before. A powerful Goddess, the Queen of Heaven and Earth, was worshipped there. Her name was Inanna, and her Temple was vast and glorious. There were two sisters, twins, who were Her priestesses. But one of them had been ill, had suffered for much of her life with pain. And her name was Parasfahe…" Sally continued with the events that led to Parasfahe traveling to Egypt, and the work they did together, and the end.

"So, when Tom was born and I recognized him, I had to try hard to placate your Ma, just like I did with you. She didn't like it none, still doesn't, that you and Tom sought me out. But she just can't know, can't understand how powerful the bond is, the belonging. There is such sweet tender joy in the seeing you in the now." Sally stroked the girl's cheek with her warm calloused fingers.

"So why did Tom want to leave? Why would he want to join up and leave you and Uncle Walter? That doesn't make no sense to me!" Frances sounded distressed.

"Well, you see, lovey, Tom carried the wisdoms of ancient Sumeria, but he was also a seventeen-year-old boy. And teen-aged boys are some of the stupidest creatures on the face of the Earth. Look how many of them are eager to go off to war, if you don't believe me!" Sally's voice rose as she was swept up again in the frustration and pain of Tom's decisions.

"We bring who we were with us, but we also need to be who we are," Uncle Walter continued. "It is the way of learning. And for your Granny, the source of some of her deepest pain. She has had to watch us all do stupid things and make even stupider choices for about five thousand years now. I reckon she's about fed up with us all!" Walter smiled to let Frances know he was kind of kidding, and then shot a glance to Sally whose lips turned up in a bemused grin.

"See, lovey girl," Walter continued, "Our Tom, when he was Parasfahe, lived a life of great physical handicap. So, in this life, in this body he had strength and power in his physical form, he loved to run, and he was fast! It gave him a sense of freedom, of control. And that need to run, to move, added with a young man's impatience with restrictions, well it just made him a bit crazy, I think. He wanted so bad to *go* somewhere. And he ended up on the killing fields of Belgium."

Sally sniffed. Walter was quiet. Frances got that fierce look of deep thought that drew her eyebrows together.

"So, who we are now is *not* just who we were then?" Frances said, in a statement of understanding, not posing a question.

"Absolutely right, lovey!" Sally beamed.

"So how much of me is *me*?" Frances asked.

Sally paused. She seemed to gather all her reserves of energy, and then spoke slowly. "You are the girl child of an angry bitter mother. You are the beloved grandchild of my heart. You are a girl who is considered a white person, can grow up to vote, and be a citizen of Canada. You are a child who speaks English and Cree, so knows the world of both. And you are all the talents and inclinations and character strengths and flaws of all those times you have lived before. In my eyes, you are a brave, smart, inquisitive, and compassionate soul, as you have always been."

Frances blushed. Praise from Sally was precious and not liberally doled out. "Granny, what am I to do with these stories?"

Sally and Walter shared a look. And then Sally proceeded. "You are to keep them safe. I'm thinkin', a smart one like you, will go on to more schoolin', maybe college even. And most important, you are clever and have the instincts of a chameleon. When you go with white folks, be more white than them. It won't be any ways you a'turnin' your back on us. Be better at being them than they are. You will find your life and your loves, I see that for you. And I'm thinkin' you will find a way to put all these stories together into a book. And when you have a daughter…"

"I'm gonna name her Sally Standing Bear!" Frances interjected.

Sally swallowed hard and Walter's lips turned up in a smile. Sally continued. "And when you have a daughter, named Sally Standing Bear," Frances nodded her head vigorously, "you will give her the book for safe keeping, and she will give it to her daughter…"

"And her name will be Sally Standing Bear too!"

This time Sally and Walter laughed.

"And *that* Sally will pass it along to her daughter…yes, I know, also named Sally…until the world needs the book."

"When will that be?" Frances and Walter asked, at the same time.

"There is the end of an epoch coming. Our Mayan sisters and brothers of the south tell it so. It will herald the return of the Divine Feminine. And the world will see tremendous upheaval. And the planet will be burning. And we, the Thirteen, will return, together again at last, and that will be the time." With those words, Sally seemed to run out of steam and fold in on herself. She sat, small and still, eyes tipped down. Frances and Walter watched her with concern. Sally reached out a hand to Frances and Walter and squeezed them hard. Finally, she spoke, "And now, I believe my work here is done."

Frances discovered that tears were streaming down her face. She looked at Uncle Walter, and he too was weeping. But Sally lifted her eyes to the west, where the sun was resting on the tops of the trees, and her face was joyful. It was as if she saw old friends and was delighted at the reunion. She took one final breath and spoke on the exhale.

"Beloveds!"

☽ ○ ☾

As darkness fell, members of the Cree nation began to slip into the clearing silently. Walter and Frances had prepared Sally's body, removing all her clothes and possessions, and wrapping her in a blanket. This was to be a blending of customs. Sally had made it known that, contrary to the Cree practice of burying the body, she desired that her body be burned.

"When I lived in the Land of Qin so many years ago we knew how the buried body anchors the corporeal soul to the land, to the family. I'm gonna need to fly freer in the coming years, my loves. I am gonna have to fly free."

Walter agreed to arrange the cremation, and Sally knew he would. But to honor the lifetime with these people, and to acknowledge their wisdoms she would accommodate the needs of her family and kin to follow Cree customs and burn all her possessions. Walter had begun to pile up firewood, and the men and women who slipped into the glade helped him as he dismantled Sally's house. Frances helped distribute the livestock to folks, and Walter knew he was going to be taking Sally's dog, Atim, with him as Frances's mother wouldn't countenance a 'dirty Indian dog' in her house. The stored and harvested food was parceled out, the fencing pulled apart, all Sally's clothes and shoes and blankets were packed around her body on the pyre.

And when all was finished, and they couldn't find any other reason to tarry, Walter and Frances did as family was supposed to do, and took off their own clothes and shoes, until they were naked and shed of anything that Sally might have touched. They added them to the stack of belongings. Together they lit a rush to put it under all the planks of wood and tools and baskets that had held Sally's life together.

The fire lit quickly, and folks had to back up fast. Everyone stood there in silence, watching the flames engulf all that had been Sally Standing Bear, until the women began to ululate, voice after voice rolling in pain and praise. They wailed until a specter of presence, something seen and yet unseen, lifted up, hovered, and then disappeared. Atim howled once, and then all was quiet.

)〇(

The moon was tilting toward the west when Walter and Frances quietly dressed themselves with the bits and pieces of donated garments that had been left for them by the Cree. The clearing was empty of people and animals and buildings. All that remained was the last smoldering bits of wood and iron, and the man and child and dog who watched the smoke spiral upward. A solitary owl flew into a nearby tree, watching them and saluting Sally Standing Bear with a series of plaintive hoots.

The three left to walk back toward town before dawn. Frances was carrying her satchel that held all the notebooks as well as a stone that had been part of what was left of the foundation of Sally's cabin, which she had slipped into her pocket. Walter carried the photograph of Tom. They held hands, and Atim trotted along beside them.

First light saw them standing in Frances's backyard. They could hear the noises from inside the house, the clatter of wood being put into the stove, the harsh sound of cast-iron skillet hitting stove top, the murmur of voices. They waited in silence until Hannah Fletcher opened the back door to come outside for water. She pulled up short, startled at the sight of her uncle and daughter in the dim.

"What?" Hannah said in a bark of sound.

"She's gone, niece" Walter replied with kindness in his voice.

And they were all surprised when Hannah Fletcher crumpled to the steps and began to weep as if all light had gone out of the world.

CHAPTER 2

For Frances the next years required an exquisite balancing act. She did what Granny Sally had told her to do, and when with the white folks she became a model of good behavior. She dressed and talked and walked like the girls around her, and she broke ranks in only one regard: Frances wouldn't, couldn't dim her intelligence. She excelled at school, skipping grade levels, and passing exams with ease. And this caused her mother to chafe.

"Frances! Lift your head out of those books and come look at this pretty material I got to make you a new dress for the Spring Dance."

"Mama, I've got to study for these university entrance exams. And besides, I look dreadful in pink."

"I don't know why you want to go away to school. It ain't natural. All the other girls in your class are staying here and finding beaus. Why do my children always leave me?"

Frances gritted her teeth and counted silently in her head in Cree, till her mother's whining voice drifted off.

)○(

Toronto, Ontario, Canada, 1939

When Frances Fletcher had arrived at university four years before, alone, and still wearing the battle scars of getting her mother to agree to higher education, she had found her people. She loved school, always had, and now she was surrounded by others who shared her love of academia.

The college was still set up as it had been in the past, with separate dormitories and residences for female students, but the rigid proscriptions of past decades had softened. Now men and women could socialize, study together, and even be romantic with one another. Frances had dipped her toe into romance once or twice, with women and men, but found it to be distracting from her first love: learning. What she was going to do next with her life after this she had yet to determine, but that she would conquer after this week's exams.

Frances, at twenty-one years of age, was poised to be the only female graduate of her department in the university, with her degree in linguistics. Always adept at languages, Frances now was fluent in six (English, Cree, several dialects of French, German, Irish and Italian), able to muddle along in four others (Swedish, Japanese, Lakota and Polish) and capable of counting and asking for the facilities in several others. Her skills had been noted by her professors, and one in particular had been quite curious.

"Miss Fletcher, I have been going over your German final exam. It is...flawless!" He had looked at Frances, sitting perfectly poised in the chair before him, ankles crossed and tucked neatly to one side. She was as placid as a lake.

"Work this perfect might raise suspicions of...shall we say... extra-curricular support?"

Frances remained still and unreadable.

"Miss Fletcher, perhaps you don't understand me. This exam feels... unnatural."

At that, Frances gave a single bark of a laugh. She swung her legs to the other side and settled her ankles accordingly.

"Miss Fletcher, I must ask you outright. Did you cheat on this exam?"

Frances replied softly, so softly that Professor Griffin needed to lean forward to hear her. "Sir, is it my gender or my heritage that causes you to doubt my academic abilities?"

Griffin, a man of unexamined middle-aged comfort, had never been so stopped in his tracks. "I...uh...no, of course, not!"

Frances looked at him implacably. "Is my excellence so far beyond the bounds of credulity then? Is it impossible that a girl from the prairie, a girl with a *squaw* for a grandmother, could outshine the private school boys with fine pedigrees?"

The professor took a big swallow and re-assessed the young woman before him. He seldom found himself on the back foot.

"Miss Fletcher, who are you?"

And Frances graced him with one of her rare smiles. "Whomever is needed."

Later that same day, Professor Griffin wrote a letter to his university flatmate who now worked for the British Home Office. *"You asked me to keep my eye open for 'talent'. Well, I have been near-blinded by some."*

$$\mathllap{)} \bigcirc \mathrlap{(}$$

Frances stood on the steps of the university library, holding a hand to shield her eyes from the glare of the afternoon sun and fingering the stone in her pocket. Her last exam finished, she stood poised for whatever the next step would be, literally and figuratively. *Granny Sally? I could use a tiny bit of guidance here. What path next?*

"Excuse me? Could you direct me to the McCarger women's residence?"

Frances looked down into the eyes of the man standing two steps below her in half shade. He appeared to be in his thirties, hair a soft caramel brown, well enough dressed to not be a student but also not so well attired as to be a toff. A professor? No, she decided. He looked too brisk, too *aware* to be a man of books. He was no laborer though. She saw hands that were well manicured and smooth. He looked like someone you could see and then not be able to describe later. Except for those eyes, those turquoise eyes. Intrigued, Frances answered his question with one of her own.

"And why would such an address interest you, sir?"

"I am looking for a woman."

Frances couldn't help herself. She laughed aloud in her characteristic single bark. "Then that women's residence would suffice, I suppose," she replied.

The man's lips lifted in a quirk, and he responded quickly. "A particular woman, not just any woman. You see, I am looking for a certain Frances Fletcher." His eyes never left hers, and the gaze was an interesting blend of curiosity and warmth. Like he was scouting a litter of pups and was sort of hoping she was the right dog.

Frances was startled but didn't let it show. That was a big part of her heritage from her Cree family. That opaque face had driven her mother crazy and kept friends and acquaintances guessing. This man though seemed to appreciate her unreadable demeanor. Frances got the distinct impression that she had just passed some test.

"And why would you be seeking a certain Frances Fletcher, may I ask?"

"I am wondering if she would like to be of service to His Majesty's government," he replied quietly. And now Frances did look astonished. It was the man's turn to laugh. He offered her his arm. "Could I interest you in a cup of tea?"

Frances tossed a quick thank you to her Granny Sally, took the fellow's offered arm and walked down the steps into the afternoon's mellow light.

"I have sought you out at the recommendation of several of your professors." The fellow blew on his tea to cool it and took a sip.

Frances watched him without responding. It reminded him of the way a predator – a fox, or an owl maybe – would watch their prey, content in the power of stillness. He, however, was determined to not be the mouse in this scenario.

"You have prodigious talents that are of interest to us," he continued. *What woman could resist that bait?* he wondered. Her only response was a very slight flush rising up her neck. And still, she said nothing. The fellow laughed again, to his own surprise. "Are you ever going to speak?" he asked.

Frances gave a Mona Lisa smile and replied, "When I have something worth saying."

"My name is Malcolm Reynolds," the fellow offered.

"That will work for now," Frances replied. She knew for sure that wasn't the whole truth, but it would suffice. "Why don't you tell me exactly how His Majesty's government plans to use my 'prodigious talents' then."

27

"It would appear that you have a preternatural proficiency with languages."

When Frances remained silent, he chuckled.

Frances tilted her head to the left and posed a question. "You have a melodious voice, Mr. Reynolds. Do you sing?"

He sat back a bit and smiled, "Why yes, yes I do."

"And how do you learn a new song or piece of music?"

"I listen to it, and I …" He looked fractionally embarrassed.

"You what?" Frances urged.

"I *feel* it"

She nodded. "And any language is like music, patterns and pitch. I too *feel* it."

He took a pause, then asked, "So then – how do you feel about secrets?" He sounded blasé, but the look he gave her was a threshold.

Frances thought she felt the cool touch of Granny Sally's fingers on her shoulder giving her a gentle push. "Love 'em!" she said.

$$) \bigcirc ($$

Bletchley Park, Milton Keynes, United Kingdom, June 1942

"McGovern, fetch me Fletcher!" bayed Ralph Simpson, a small-boned man in his mid-forties. Dark circles pooled under his eyes and his thinning hair had a tuft on the left side that he tugged when in frustration or distress.

Within minutes, Frances Fletcher stood at the door to Simpson's office and knocked softly twice.

"Fletcher! Come in, come in, don't hover!" She walked in and sat down across the desk from him.

"Someone has been asking for you, Fletcher," Simpson said while shuffling papers on his desk. Those words, and the fact that Ralph Simpson hated giving bad news and tended to avoid eye contact whilst doing so, had Frances on high alert. The last time someone had come looking for her had resulted in her being here at Bletchley, deep in the eye-crossing and nerve-stripping work of decoding enemy dispatches in a frantic attempt to get ahead of the Nazi juggernaut. Everyone here was stretched to their limit and then beyond. Frances braced her hands against the armrest of the chair. Now what new fresh hell?

She was the only Canadian posted here, but she had found friends among the "Uni women," the female students from nearby Oxford and Cambridge who were astute and quick and had been deemed useful for this part of the war effort. Frances was not the only polyglot, but her command of the more outlier tongues of Cree and Lakota had proven helpful in the creation of codes. She had heard of some Navaho speakers who were serving in the American forces in a similar way. Frances thought it sadly amusing how when the chips were down, they decided that they needed the Indians.

"May I ask who?" she said.

"Some fellow. Says he knows you. Malcolm Reynolds, I believe." Simpson ruffled some more papers and Frances knew good and well that Simpson knew exactly who had come looking for her, and why.

"And what does Mr. Reynolds want?" Frances asked.

Simpson actually harrumphed. "Not sure. Not sure, old thing. Better ask him yourself. Meet him today, 17:00, at the gazebo."

Frances masked the erratic thump her heart gave. The last time she had seen Malcolm Reynolds had been over two years ago. It had been the last day of her orientation and she was set to catch a train up to Bletchley House. Desperate for some minutes of solitude with the sharp autumn wind she had raced out of the non-descript building, a war-requisitioned house that faced Hampstead Heath. As she reached the sidewalk he materialized, seemingly from thin air, and she had heard his voice from behind.

"Fletcher?"

She had turned to face him. "Reynolds."

"Making your escape?"

Frances had softly chuckled. "Taking last gasps of fresh air before I face a crowded railroad car."

"May I accompany you?"

Frances had nodded. As they had walked and found their rhythm together they had begun to play a word game that had become pop-ular in the Intelligence set – the "when this war is over" game. It was a test of wits and also, if one made careful choices, how *not* to reveal anything truly personal about oneself.

"When this war is over I shall have an...apple," Frances had begun. And Malcolm Reynolds was presented with an 'e'.

"When this war is over I shall have an egg." A 'g'.

"When this war is over I shall have a glass of milk," Frances had re-torted and had lifted her lips in a small grin of victory.

"Drat you, Fletcher. What begins with k?"

They had both been laughing as a sudden gust whipped leaves into a tiny tornado, and they had run toward a gazebo for some shelter. Fran-ces was ahead and had stopped up two steps so that they were eye level.

"So? Do you concede defeat?"

Malcolm had shaken his head slowly and walked up those two steps to be standing right beside her. A strand of her hair had blown across her face, and without thinking he had lifted his hand to brush it away. As the back of his fingers touched her cheek he had frozen and felt his truth rise to the surface.

"When this war is over I shall have a ...kiss." He had been focused on her mouth and couldn't break his gaze.

"Why wait?" she had whispered. And as if moving under water he had lowered down until cool lips met cool lips and the rest of the world fell away.

The sound of church bells had been a cold splash, and Frances had exclaimed, "My train!"

They had each taken a step back, stared hard at the other, then she had turned and run across the Heath toward the station.

☽ ◯ ☾

And now, two plus years later, another gazebo. Malcolm Reynolds, as was, had an interesting sense of humor, she would give him that.

So, at 16:45 Frances donned some sturdy boots and her raincoat and took off through the gardens to the gazebo at the edge of the lake. She was of two minds about the soon-to-be reunion with Malcolm. Frances hadn't heard a peep from him in two years. Not a letter, not a coded message, nothing. People in his line of work did frequently go to ground, and it was war. He might well have died, and she never would have heard a thing. But here he was again. Or, she reminded herself, someone saying they were Malcolm Reynolds was here.

She saw the outline of a man atop the highest of the three steps that led to the inside of the gazebo. The sun was behind him so she couldn't see his face but could see the line of the coat and the definition of the fedora. He was leaning against the railing, and she felt his eyes upon her. She stopped on the grass about fifteen feet away and waited.

Finally, a deep male voice, "Are you ever going to speak?"

Frances laughed in relief and replied, "When I have something worth saying."

The man's voice got noticeably warmer. "You really are inscrutable!" And Frances could hear the smile in his words.

She began to walk closer and up the gazebo steps. When she came eye to eye with him, she answered, "So I have been told." They seemed caught in each other's gaze for a second, a minute, an hour. And the two years and the unanswered questions between them melted away and they fell into each other's arms.

At last they broke apart.

"Fletcher," he said with a dry husk in his voice.

"Reynolds," Frances replied. "I hear you have summoned me."

"How's your French?"

"Quebecois? Parisian? Burgundian? Occitan? Alsatian?" she asked. "All better than yours, I wager."

"My clever, clever girl," he replied.

She let that pass and waited him out. It started to rain lightly and Malcolm Reynolds pulled her under the roof of the gazebo and led her to a bench, chivalrously wiping it down with his handkerchief.

"Simpson says you have done well for yourself here," he said. Frances held quiet but watched him with a kind of hunger that took her by surprise. She had barely allowed herself the mental space to think of him these last two years, and the rigors of her work had kept her busy and challenged. But seeing him here now, she realized that she had truly missed him, the sight, the sound, dare she say, even the smell of him. *Oh dear,* she thought, *I might lose my head over this one.*

He held himself very still, as if he were hunting and poised in the bushes, cautious in his body, as if he needed care in his movements.

"Where are you injured?" she asked.

He looked at her sharply for a moment. He reached out his hand, palm up on the bench, and looked ready to wait till she took it. So, she did. His palm was slightly cool, and she realized that he must have been out here for some time as he had waited for her to arrive. And she noticed odd callouses at the base of his fingers. *Farmers hands,* she thought.

"What have you been doing, Malcolm?"

"You have signed the same Official Secrets Act that I have, so I know that to be a rhetorical question," he chuckled.

"Well at the least you must tell me if you are in pain. Do you need a doctor?" Frances asked, and she was all seriousness now for he looked paler than a few moments before.

"I think it quite likely that I have pulled some stitches loose. Must have been the fervor of our reunion!" he jested, but now had a line of sweat across his upper lip. "Perhaps I will just lie down here for..."

With that he tilted into her shoulder and slowly slid down prone. Frances put her fingers to his wrist and took his pulse. Rapid and light. She pulled his raincoat open and saw the slow spread of blood across the front of his abdomen on his left side. Her fingers shook only slightly as she undid the buttons of his shirt and found the bandage that was soaked and falling off. She gently pulled it back and took a quick gasp at the sight of a wound, about four inches long that ran on the diagonal from his upper belly to the bottom of his ribs. A quick count gave her about ten stitches, and indeed, several of them were torn loose.

"Stupid man," she muttered under her breath as she pulled her scarf off and held it to the bleeding wound. In a few moments his eyelids fluttered open and locked on hers.

"See the effect you have on me. Knocked me quite senseless!" he said, and his breathing was labored.

"We are going to see this looked after, and when we have you sorted,

I will truly knock you senseless!" Frances retorted to cover her relief that he had come to.

"A man can dream, Fletcher," he chuckled. "A man can but dream."

Frances quickly mentally flashed through her options. One, he had asked to meet her away from Bletchley House, so he must not wish to be seen by all and sundry. Two, her boss knew of Reynolds and his request to see her. So, it was an officially cleared visit. Cleared but circumspect. Three, the bleeding had slowed but he still was white as milk with a stuttering breath, so there was pain. Four, she knew what to do.

"Can you walk a bit?" she asked. He nodded, struggled to lift his head, and she ran an arm cross the back of his shoulders and helped him to sit up.

"About a hundred yards to the northwest there is a gardener's shed. We are headed there." She had drawn him to his feet and put his good side arm across the back of her neck to support him as they walked.

She helped him down the back steps of the gazebo, away from any view from Bletchley House. He took in her direction and appreciated her quick grasp of his situation. And as always, he admired the precision of her mind. "I can do a hundred yards for you, but not one more."

"Then lucky for you I have it measured off," she muttered under her breath with the effort of keeping him walking forward.

$$) \bigcirc ($$

The shed of soft rose brick was low and long with three small windows across the southern side. Frances had only ever seen one of the three gardeners come in here, the oldest one whose service to the estate had preceded the wartime usage of the house and grounds. Bartholomew Winslow had been connected to the owners here all his life, and his family had served the estate since before the Hanovers sat on the throne.

This shed was Bartholomew's domain, but he had let Frances use it as a quiet space, when she needed the smell of earth to still her mind. So, like a rabbit running to its warren, she took Malcolm Reynolds there.

For his part, Malcolm Reynolds had allowed himself to trust – trust Frances, trust her plan, trust his fate to another, an altogether novel experience for him. Granted, he was bleeding from that gunshot that had glanced off his ribcage two days ago. And also he was, as ever, tilted off his axis by the blinding combination of spirit and intelligence that was Frances Fletcher. He always quoted Shakespeare when he thought of her, *"Though she be but little she is fierce."* With her he knew that this level of surrender was unlike any other experience in his lifetime. And for now, that knowledge would suffice until he had the wit and wherewithal to figure it out better.

Frances helped Malcolm down onto the bench and found some old toweling to make a pillow for his head. His former paleness now verged on translucence. Frances ran to Bartholomew's first aid box.

She pulled out the yarrow powder used to stop bleeding, and a box of bandages. With a tender efficiency she removed the existing bandage, and bathed the wound with witch hazel water, then sprinkled on the yarrow powder. Frances began to sing softly in Cree, a healing song she had learned from her Granny Sally. She focused on her breath, and the rhythm of the song, and she could feel her ancestors enter into the shed and stand at her back. With one final full-bellied breath she bent to her work and quickly anesthetized and then stitched the wound. Malcolm drifted into a kind of sleep that felt warm and protected. He came to again as the sound of Frances's song ended, and he could feel her hands reach under his back to finish the bandaging, bringing the cotton strip around to the front of his body and tying it off. He heard her say something, like a prayer, in a language he didn't know. The pain along his belly had lessened considerably, and he felt bathed in an overall sense of well-being.

Frances sat on the floor by Malcolm's side, holding his hand. "You are safe to sleep here, but I do need to go back to the house for dinner or I will be missed," she said finally. "I know how to circumvent the security alarms though, so I will be able to come back and check on you after lights out. Do you need anything before I go?" she asked.

"Water?" he said.

Frances rose soundlessly and went to the pail of fresh water over by the door. A tin cup hung on a hook there, and she filled it to the brim and brought it back to him. When he had finished he looked at her with a world of meaning in his eyes.

"What a red-letter day it was that I crossed paths with you, Frances Fletcher." In his fatigue his careful Oxbridge vowels slipped, and Frances caught more than a hint of an Irish accent... *You are no more a 'Malcolm Reynolds' than I am Marie of Romania,* she thought to herself, and smiled the small smile of victory. He saw it and let her have the win as his eyes drifted shut, and he fell into a pain-free sleep.

☽ ○ ☾

Several hours passed in excruciating slowness. Finally, at some point past midnight Frances eased out of bed, wrapped her raincoat around her nightclothes and carried her wellies to the door. She knew that the spotlight outside made a forty second sweep of the perimeter of the cabins, so she waited till the light swept just past her feet, then ran silently through the cloud-covered night toward the shed. There was a second light sweep around the main house, so she paused, waited for the arc of light and then sprinted again. It felt good to run. It made her feel connected to her brother Tom, the brother whom she had never met, but who had lived, just the same, in the minds of all her family. As she ran, she heard the hoot of a barn owl off to her left. Then she heard two hoots up ahead and slightly to her right. She froze. That wasn't a barn owl response. With her will she quieted her breathing and listened to the night the way Uncle Walter had taught her.

"I figured that the visitor in the shed had something to do with you," came a soft rumble from the dark. Bartholomew! Frances let her breath out in a rush.

"I should have known that you never miss anything," Frances replied. Bartholomew chuckled.

"I found the scarf in the compost. Is our visitor hurt bad?" the gardener asked.

"Weak, but infection free when I last saw him. Do you want to come with me as I check now?" Frances thought, *"In for a penny, in for a pound."*

"I think not. Plausible deniability. Isn't that what the spooks say?" he replied.

"I'm sorry to use your shed. It was the safest place I could think of." Frances said with some contrition in her voice.

"It be your shed too, little miss. Don't you forget that." Bartholomew said over the sudden lump in his throat. He had found such sweet friendship with this girl. "It be yours too."

"You are my guardian angel. You know that, don't you?" Frances asked. And Bartholomew decided that she deserved to know something then and there.

"Your Granny told me to keep a look out for you, little miss." He almost whispered the words like a prayer.

"I am, strangely, not surprised, my friend. We shall have much to discuss then, eh?" She reached out and clasped his hand. It was gnarled and ropey from years of work in the earth. It felt like sanctuary to Frances. Like her Uncle Walter's hands had always felt. Like home.

Frances jogged over the remaining lawn soundlessly and used her key to unlock the door to the shed. The well-oiled door swung open, and she turned on her torch pointing it down to the ground. From the spill of light she could see Malcolm's eyes, opened and alert, staring at her.

"I think we might forgo that illumination," he said in a low tone. And she clicked off the torch. She took a minute to let her eyes adjust to the darker dark inside the shed, then moved across the floor to come by the bench where he was sprawled. Reaching a hand toward his forehead she felt him – normal adult male warm. She slid her hand down his arm to his wrist and took his pulse – slightly rapid, but not alarmingly so.

"I see you haven't managed to throw yourself into more desperate straits since I saw you last then," she said.

"I have managed to muddle along without you," he replied, again with the smile in his voice.

She sat down on the ground next to the bench, and felt his hand come to rest lightly on her head and slowly stroke her hair. It was soothing, and familiar, and with the promise of tenderness. Frances had the oddest sensation that they had done this very thing before.

"When are you going to tell me why you needed to see me?" Frances asked. He didn't respond for a while and she wondered if he had dropped off to sleep again.

"Not in the darkness, Fletcher. It can wait till light." he said. And his hand kept up the slow and rhythmic stroking. He peered at her in the pie wedge of moonlight that had sliced into the shed windows. She felt seen, truly seen, for the first time in years.

She held his hand to her cheek. "I truly am glad to see you again, Reynolds. And most agreeably pleased that you will live through the night. The disposal of your body would have been problematic."

He pulled one strand of her hair through two fingers as if he were testing fine silk. "I am glad to oblige, Fletcher. And I too am most pleased to see you again. I am hesitant to admit it, but I did miss you and your sparkling wit." She turned her head quickly and bit his finger, not hard, but with purpose. He laughed out loud. "Hungry? Oh, I have indeed missed you!"

"I should go back," she said.

"Next time, come after you've eaten," he said, again with the smile in his voice.

) ○ (

"Thanks to your ministrations, I think I will survive to fight another day." Malcolm Reynolds was sitting up in the shed the next morning with color in his face and armed once again with his quick wit and arms-length astuteness.

"Perhaps you can now tell me why you needed to see me," Frances said, hiding her disappointment in his change of demeanor. *This is safer,* she told herself.

She poured coffee for them both and gave him a small bowl of porridge she had brought. As he ate and drank, she sipped her coffee and purposefully didn't look at him. *Two can play at the cold north wind,* she thought.

"You have a particular quality, Fletcher that I find both annoying and damned attractive," he said, as if in spite of himself. She chose not to look at him but did grant him a glimpse of a small smile. "Where did you learn to be so enigmatic? You can be as still and as unreadable as a rock."

"I find that rocks are quite communicative," she replied. "If you know how to listen."

And with that unanswerable set-down they looked at each other for a moment or two, or a thousand years. Hesitancy evaporated. Pretense dissolved. Truth rose to the surface as it always would with them.

"When this war is over, Fletcher..." he said from his heart. And she nodded: it was a vow.

The details of the mission he had for her were indeed urgent. A British agent, working with the French Resistance was in Tours, and had been betrayed. Malcolm had intercepted a signal being sent from a Nazi agent in London that would have identified the Brit. Hence the gunshot wound that he was, thankfully, recovering from. The Nazi agent would be sending no more signals.

Malcolm needed Frances to infiltrate behind the enemy lines, find the British agent and facilitate his safe return to England.

"Why me?" she asked. "There must be plenty of others who are better trained for this kind of mission."

"You are quick, your French is impeccable, and you are dark and small," he replied.

"I agree to all of that assessment. But why, may I ask, is being dark and small of use in this circumstance?" Frances sounded sincerely curious, and also miffed. Her coloring and size were always a bit of a sore spot for her when surrounded by the tall Nordic immigrants in Saskatchewan and the pleasantly pale Englishmen and women here at Bletchley. She did seem a bit out of place to others, an oddity, and it invariably led to questions about her heritage.

"We are sending you into France in a caravan of gypsies," Malcolm replied. He looked as if the idea had been sane when first developed, but now, as it was coming out of his mouth, was appearing less sound. She looked at him, startled, and a slightly mad giggle escaped from his lips. "You know, gypsies? They are small and dark." He seemed to want to let the floor swallow him up as she continued to stare at him. "For god's sake, Fletcher. The plan was devised on the fly. It has some flaws, I admit. But we think it will work."

"You *think* it will work?"

"And can you dance?" he sputtered, "and play the tambourine?" At which point he dissolved into a fit of giggles at the look on her face. Frances stormed off and went back to work.

$$) \bigcirc ($$

The next day, Frances received a transfer that would take her to London. Once there she was to take the train to Plymouth where a boat would be waiting to carry her to Biarritz on the southwest coast of France. The journey gave her time to reflect on what had been...and prepare for what was to come.

"The gypsies are able to traverse the borders in the Pyrenees," Malcolm had explained the night before, as she cleaned his wound. "They move back and forth from Spain to France to Andorra, then complete the circle. You will meet with a small family band, the Levevres, on the coast, just north of Biarritz. It is dangerous for them to travel too far into Nazi occupied territory. The Führer doesn't like gypsies much."

"Then why are *they* taking me north?" she asked, applying a fresh bandage.

"Because," he replied. "Hitler doesn't like gypsies much, and they *really* aren't fond of him. But they will take you as far as they possibly can."

The return extraction would involve traveling overland, without the help of the gypsies, to Brittany and the little town of Vannes.

"You will need to travel only by night and avoid all roads. Our network in Vannes will help the two of you get to the coast and a fishing boat can get you back to Plymouth. Oh, and in Brittany you will need..."

"I know, I know. To use a Breton accent."

"At which you are adept," he said.

"But of course," she replied in perfect Breton French.

They had drilled the details over and over: her assumed name, back-story, contacts, where the agent was to be found, and how to traverse the countryside to get to Vannes. Frances had finally yawned so wide-ly that Malcolm could see her back teeth. He reached forward and grabbed her hand.

"Frances!" he sounded different, and she was startled by his use of her first name. "You must know this information backwards and for-wards. Your life depends on it. If there was any other way..." his voice drifted off.

She leaned forward and kissed him hard on the lips. "When we meet again, and we *will* meet again, I demand a forfeit."

"When that blessed day occurs, you may have anything at my dis-posal to give you," he replied, still feeling the bruise of her lips on his.

"I shall demand to know your real name," she said defiantly.

He chucked and said softly, "Well, you will need to know it to take it when we marry."

She stared at him fiercely, as if she was memorizing every detail. And he imprinted her as well.

"I'll be gone on the morning before first light," he said gravely.

"As will I." She kissed him once more, and ran from the shed.

Biarritz, France, June 1942

The people clustered around the three fires of the Romani camp felt and then heard the sound of boots marching long before they saw any-one. They were farther north than was prudent, and had set up camp far off the road hoping to avoid detection. But, damn the devil to hell, this was the sound of soldiers, German soldiers on a night patrol who would most certainly see the light from the fires.

"Quick! All the children, inside the caravans, and hide!" Marguerita Levevre, the matriarch of this band of Roma, sounded stern and fierce. "And the young men – disappear into the woods! Don't come back till it is safe!"

People scurried and did her bidding. By the time the patrol had worked its way down the slope of brush and thorns, they arrived, sweaty and annoyed, to find a few women and three old men stirring pots over the campfires.

"You! Gypsies! What are you doing here?" The officer in charge was young and sounded full of bravado, but underneath one could hear the whisper of uncertainty.

Marguerita Levevre stepped forward so that her face fell out of the firelight. "Oh sir, I am so glad you found us! We must have gone awry back at the river and headed in the wrong direction. Please, come and have something to eat, and perhaps you can steer us right." She was calm and earnest, and still lovely and round-breasted in her late middle age. She offered a maternal yet sensual invitation to forget about the war. To the officer she was non-threatening, and yet exotic and a bit feral. He softened his tone.

"Well, there should be no harm in some food and a rest. But come morning I'll need you to clear out. Your kind have no place here."

Marguerita showed none of her disdain or fear and gestured to the soldiers to come closer to the fire. "Of course. It shall be as you say. And while you are with us, we may share some music and dancing with you too? I am sure you would enjoy the talents of my niece, Margret." At that a small, dark young woman stepped forward, head tilted coyly to one side, flashing the Germans a smile.

Violin music, laughter, lechery and a pretty girl who they had been led to believe had loose morals. A tried-and-true recipe for confounding the enemy, if the enemy is male that is. Margret, aka Frances Fletcher, petticoats hiked up to her waist and tambourine flashing, was dancing farther and farther away from the fire. With every pirouette she steered the gaze of the German soldiers into the dark beyond. And with every deflected glance the men and women of the Levevre family poured more of the potent liquor of their own distilling into the cups of those same soldiers. Between the intermittent glimpses of calves and a smidgen of thigh and the high alcohol content of the Romani home-brew, those German soldiers, were so mesmerized and sufficiently inebriated that they didn't notice the caravans loading up behind them in the shadows. While the officer had said he would let them clear off in the morning, come the light of dawn he could very well have changed his mind. It was far safer to never trust a Nazi. Best to be off and let the Germans awake to find them gone.

As the music finally wound down Frances was sitting on the lap of a boy so young that his cheeks barely revealed peach fuzz. He had tried to kiss her, but his aim was off, and he missed her mouth and landed on her cheek before passing out. Frances walked soundlessly back toward the caravans.

"They are all out cold," she whispered.

"You are a natural, Miss!" replied the short compact man tying up the last bundle on the side of his caravan.

Frances gave a sharp bark of a laugh and then covered her mouth with her hand. "Well, that beats being called unnatural. Most folks say that of me."

"Gorger people?" he asked, with a smile in his voice.

"Yes, Gorger!" Frances said.

"Fools!" he retorted, and the company of Romani slipped off into the night to get Frances closer to Tours.

$$\text{☽ ◯ ☾}$$

Three weeks later, Frances and her rescued British agent, Edward slipped into the old walled city of Vannes after dark and made their way to the overhanging balconies of Cathédrale Saint-Pierre de Vannes. They waited in the shadows for their contact. Since Frances had found him in Tours ten days ago, they had been on the move, avoiding roads and villages, making a wide circumference around Nantes, sleeping and finding sanctuary in the woods. He was terse and nursing a sprained ankle that he had suffered in a frantic dive into a ditch to avoid detection yesterday before dawn. She was dirty, exhausted, and at the edge of nerves.

From the dark streets came the faint sound of whistling as someone walked along the cobblestone road. As the person drew closer the tune became clearer, and Frances had to stifle a laugh: "Oh, Canada!"...that was the signal.

Frances tossed a pebble from the darkness into the middle of the road and the whistler halted ever so briefly, and then proceeded toward them. He spoke in Irish.

"Bandia dhaoibh!"

Frances felt her heart leap. *Malcolm!* She hadn't thought he would be their contact. She had a momentary flash of self-consciousness. She must look a fright and smell even worse!

She replied in that language, low and barely keeping the joy from her voice. "And a thousand blessings upon you."

He slid into the shadows next to them and rapidly gave directions. Edward was to walk down the street toward the south of town. A farmer's cart would be there awaiting him to take him to the departure point. She was to come with Malcolm, who was calling himself Michel Didier, and they would, in the manner of a courting couple, walk in the opposite direction and circle around to meet up with Edward and the extraction boat in the early hours of morning.

"The guards have been doubled in the last week. We don't know if the Krauts are worried about invasion or if they are hearing of our network. Either way, we split up and distract."

Edward gave Frances a quick hug and then walked silently down the street, clinging to the fronts of buildings, letting the shadows be his friend. Malcolm and Frances stood still for more minutes, watching to be sure Edward had not been followed. She realized that Malcolm smelled strongly of cow and took pleasure in imagining him spending the night with one. Her own ragged appearance seemed less dire. They slipped arms around each other's waists and walked north and west, following the road that led out of town.

"Where are we headed? And why are you here?" she asked, again in Irish.

"There is a tiny fishing village called Quiberon at the end of a spit of land. They will wait for us till the next tide turns. If we miss it we will need to hide until the tide returns in our favor," he whispered in her ear. She giggled coquettishly for any observers and then asked again.

"That's one answer. Why are you here?"

"I wanted to see you."

"That is gratifying. But a reunion also could have taken place back in merry ol' England. So, I ask again, why are you here?" He didn't answer and they walked on out of the town.

As they came around a bend, Malcolm tucked her more firmly

against him. Frances gasped at the towering shadows in the field ahead. Were they discovered?

She froze. But he beckoned her on.

The shadows came not from soldiers, but stones. Hundreds of tall stones, throwing long shadows in the half moonlight.

"What is this place?" she asked in awe.

"It is called Carnac," he replied. "It belongs to the Old Ones."

"It looks like a battalion!" she exclaimed.

"Can you hear what these stones are saying? You did say you enjoyed conversing with them," he asked, only slightly facetiously.

"Can I hear them? How can you not?" she replied. "They are singing!"

Frances broke from his embrace and ran into the field of standing stones. She raced from one to another, touching them with reverence, muttering under her breath. Malcolm saw her move in and out of shadow, looking for all the world like she was in a joyous reunion with beloved family and friends.

Although he felt the pressure to speed on and deliver her to the rendezvous point quickly, he couldn't help himself from luxuriating in the pleasure of her nearness. Above all others in this wide, wide world, he wanted to spend his minutes with her.

"We can rest here a bit," she said. "The stones will warn us if anyone approaches."

"What else do they say?" he asked, now completely serious.

"Volumes! It is wonderful! They ask me to remember Calanais. I have heard the name. Does it sound familiar to you?"

He searched his brain. There was a tickle there, a wisp of memory. And in that instant he thought he could listen to the stones too. "Ah yes. It is a group of standing stones in the Hebrides," he replied. "Why do they say you should recall it?"

Frances was silent, stunned. And then she spoke carefully. "They say we herald from there, you and I. That we have been together before."

He walked forward and took her hand. "That feels more right than anything I have ever heard."

She leaned in and up and reached his mouth with hers. It was a kiss that took its time, a kiss of reconnection and reunion. It was a kiss that held the promise of vows taken, in this lifetime and the lifetimes that preceded.

Their two bodies melted to the ground. Neither knew how clothes were removed. They melded flesh so swiftly that the choreography seemed to be immediately forgotten. It was a meeting of souls and bodies that stretched over thousands of years. At times, Frances felt herself different, older, taller, and she could hear the reverberation of sound as if they were in a cave. Malcolm had flashes of them, different, the same, on a cold stone floor, matched together by the Goddess for all time. Their lovemaking was fluid and expansive and vast. It was urgent and immediate and eternal. His body knew hers, and she his. The joy of reconnection exploded in their hearts as their bodies reached climax under the canopy of stars.

In the floating haze that held them both they could see the spool of time, rolling backwards like a beautiful golden ribbon. Over and over again they had been together, in different places on the Earth, and in different circumstances. But always as lovers. The memory of the Sacred Marriage that they had performed, thousands of years ago, the ritual that had hidden and protected the people deep within the mountains now called the Pyrenees, that ritual had granted them grace. And that grace had allowed them to always find each other, and always be together. They saw themselves as East Indians and Chinese and Aboriginals and European peasants and courtiers. They had forged a life from the wilderness of New France, and had penned letters as Eloise and Abelard. They were bound together in love and bliss throughout all time.

And then, at the very end of the unspooling lifeline ribbon, they saw how they had been as Celebi the Brighid and Malvu the Chief Observer. They felt the presence of their stones, the circles at Calanais. And there, in the flicker of an instant, like the flash of fish scales in a sunlit pond, was the memory of the first time they had ever seen each other. New students of thirteen years of age at the Mystery School of Calanais. She of the blazing intellect and gooseberry green eyes. He of the untamed thatch of black hair, sapphire eyes, and the confidence of twenty boys. They paused in that first glance and cherished that memory, and then, with some regret, knew themselves to be drawn quickly yet smoothly forward into the present.

Stars swirled and sang overhead. Frances and Malcolm came back to themselves and felt the shift of awareness from the always to the now. Around them the stones stood sentinel, and they felt the pieces of the machinery of time click into place once again.

"Beloved," she whispered.

"My Goddess," he replied.

They were silent as they dressed in the half-moon light. Malcolm stood near her as she said a formal and tearful goodbye to the stones. He whispered a prayer, asking the stones to see her safe. They linked fingers as they started back to the road, and along the way to Quiberon and the boat for England.

About two miles farther on, she asked him, "Now will you tell me why you are here? Surely someone else could have come to facilitate our extraction."

His voice was so low she could barely hear him. "I am not coming back with you. My war takes me farther into France now. But I wanted to see you again." He cut himself off abruptly. The unspoken "one last time" hung in the air like thick smoke from a house fire. She clung to his hand tighter, and they walked on.

About an hour before dawn they arrived at a small stony beach at the end of a long deserted narrow road with deep cart ruts that had made the walk treacherous. They hadn't talked, just tried to navigate the road and avoid wrenching an ankle. And really, what needed to be said between them? They were who they were now, and the war demanded them to go and do what needed doing. But now they were also fully aware of who they had been, and that nothing would ever break that connection.

Ahead a small hut seemed to tilt to one side and threw a long moon shadow toward the water. Two men moved forward to help Frances into the boat that rocked in the shallows. She had one foot in the boat and turned frantically to reach for Malcolm. "What is it? Your name! I demand my forfeit!" she said in a hushed voice.

He slung an arm around her neck and whispered in her ear, "Michael Pádraig Francis Kenneally of Ballinskellig, County Kerry."

They turned their heads and gave each other a bruising kiss. Then he put his hands on her waist and lifted her the rest of the way into the boat. The two other men took to the oars, and Frances sat down hard on the bench next to Edward. who patted her thigh but said nothing. She never stopped watching as Michael's silhouette grew smaller and smaller on the shore, and she clung to the memory of the sensation of his hands on her waist.

London, United Kingdom
October 1, 1942

The afternoon sky was overcast, and little light came through the high clerestory windows crisscrossed with tape, that faced out into an alley. Frances was sitting on a bench in the hallway at the non-descript building that held the offices of Secret Intelligence Services (SIS). The place smelled of carbolic and wet wool, and Frances used all the techniques she had ever learned from her Granny Sally and Uncle Walter to calm her mind and still her urge to twitch. After an interminable wait a young thin man in a smart suit approached her.

"Frances Fletcher?"

She nodded and stood quickly.

"The Deputy Director can see you now." The young man turned and walked back the way he had come, and Frances hurried to keep up with his long strides.

He knocked twice on a battered-looking door and ushered Frances inside, leaving her alone with the Deputy Director for Observational Technologies, as his title officially ran.

He was a man in his early fifties with salt and pepper hair that still held a fullness other men envied. He stood as she entered and held himself with the erect posture that spoke of a military past. Everything about him, his smug safeness, his assumption of authority, his very position of power behind his desk was like splinters under Frances's skin. She kept her bristle in check, for she needed something from him.

"Miss Fletcher, please come in and take a seat. Shall we have tea?" he asked. He didn't wait for her to respond, and he pushed a button on the wall.

"Now, how might we help you?"

"I understand the need for secrecy, Mr..."

"Turnbull," he inserted. "My apologies for my lack of manners. So much goes by the wayside in times of war," he said with only a waft of sincerity.

"Mr. Turnbull, I am hoping that I might have some word on the status of Malcolm Reynolds. There is some personal urgency, you might say."

Turnbull looked at her for a moment, his gaze softened, and then took on a condescending air. "Personal urgency, you say?" he replied.

Frances refused to blush and simply nodded her head. A sharp knock on the door, and a middle-aged woman entered with a tea tray, placed it on Turnbull's desk, and then quickly left the room closing the door with a snap.

"Shall you be mother?" he asked, indicating the teapot.

"No, I don't believe I shall," Frances replied, keeping a tight grip on her temper. *Let him pour his own damn tea!*

Turnbull was momentarily taken aback, then wrapped himself in his upper-class aplomb and reached forward to pour them both a cup. "You Canadians find us hidebound in our customs I assume," he chuckled, glossing over her resistance.

He sipped his tea and looked over the cup at her. Making some decision in his own mind, he reached into a desk drawer and pulled out an envelope. He held it between two fingers and extended it to Frances.

"Agent Reynolds left this for you, in the event that you ever came asking for him. Understand, this letter in no way gives confirmation of his status or whereabouts, nor does it make any determination to whether he is in any position to be in communication with you."

Frances held the letter close to her chest but didn't open it then. She, and Michael, deserved privacy for that. "Thank you, Deputy Director. I will be leaving service at Bletchley in the next week. I shall give notice of my whereabouts and would appreciate it if that information could be extended to Agent Reynolds when possible." She stood to leave.

"Miss Fletcher, His Majesty's government appreciates your service. Oh, and congratulations on your engagement!"

Frances caught her breath, smiled politely and walked at a brisk clip out the door, down the stairs and out into the cool early October air.

She rolled over in her mind what the Deputy Director had said. He had congratulated her on her engagement. That meant that Michael, before he came to find her in France, had left this letter and the news that they were to be married. *Cheeky man!* she thought. *I hadn't officially said 'yes' yet!* But she smiled at the feeling of understanding and belonging that existed between them.

She shouldered her way down the sidewalk. London looked ragged and beleaguered. Some blocks were intact. Then you would turn a corner and blasted buildings left gaping holes where the sky poured through. People walked with a stubborn determination, though everyone looked grey and wan. The Blitz was one year past, but no one even gave a thought to rebuilding until the war was over. Frances saw an exposed kitchen perched out at second floor level, like a bird's nest way out on a limb. She gave a small prayer for extra grace for whoever had lived there.

She came upon a small church that sat back from the road. It had survived the bombing, and despite the sandbags piled high against the walls looked lovely and peaceful in the dimming light. She walked through the ornately carved wooden door, and immediately felt peace descend. "Ah, this was one of the ancient sacred places then," she muttered. She walked halfway down the nave and sat in a pew that was smooth from hundreds of hands over hundreds of years.

Talking a deep breath, she slid a fingernail under the wax seal and opened the letter.

7 June, 1942

Frances,

If you have received this letter it is because of one of two reasons. Either, I have died, and this letter goes to you as my receiver of final notice. Or, you have need of me, and I am nowhere to be found at present. In either event, if you choose, there will always be a home for you amongst my people in Ballinskellig. My mother lives there as well as my brother and his family. I recently purchased a small cottage in your name near them.

It is yours to live in, to sell, to throw wild parties in...

Two sisters of mine are in the States, and can be of service to you, if you feel the need to cross the pond. One is in Boston and one in New York. My mother can provide you with their details.

Our time together has been brief, but for me, profound. I meant it when I said it, Fletcher. When this war is over, if we both shall live, I shall find you.

MPK

Frances read the letter three times through. One hand drifted to her belly where new life stirred. She made up her mind in an instant. She would away to Ireland and Ballinskellig in the back of the Celtic beyond. She would burrow in till this blasted war was over, and she would will Michael to return to her and their child. She would will it so.

Frances had one more train trip to Bletchley to retrieve her clothes and the all-important book of Granny Sally's lives that she had given into Bartholomew's safekeeping. She went looking for Bartholomew. He was, as she had hoped, alone and amongst the strawberry beds. She smiled at the sight of her friend. He was rising seventy now, but still tall and upright with weathered skin that encompassed a life of sun and laughter. His eyes were a peculiar shade of green. Sometimes they looked grey, sometimes like new spring leaves, but always crystal clear and focused.

"How did my Granny tell you to look out for me?" she asked without preamble.

"She says you have a book," was his cryptic reply.

"I may have," she said slowly.

"And if you do, you may have heard of a place called the Great North Woods and a young foolish girl called Eiofachta."

"And if I have?" Frances continued.

"Then you will know that she had a particular affinity to trees."

"Many love trees." Frances was still cautious.

"But can many do this?" he asked and waved a hand toward the small clutch of alder trees at the edge of the garden. They waved back. He waved again. The trees waved back. Frances noticed that no breeze was blowing at the moment. She stood transfixed. "That is, indeed, a most unusual talent."

"And can many do this?" he continued. And he cupped his hands around his mouth and made a sweet call, almost a bird song. Frances felt like she should be able to identify the sound, but it slipped just out of her grasp. She felt her breath catch when, at the woods' edge, she saw an assemblage of forms, like people, but tall, and shimmering, beautiful in an awesome way.

"Who are they?" she gasped.

"The ancestors, the Fey, my friends," he replied in an emotion-choked voice. "You are the first person I have ever been able to show them to."

"May we talk with them?" Frances asked, awestruck.

"Sometimes they allow it. Shall we go and see them?" he asked.

Frances took the hand he offered and the two walked slowly toward the edge of the woodland. The forms, the Fey, stayed motionless, but the same no-wind that had moved the trees caused their robes to float and sway gently. Bartholomew and Frances came to a stop once they were fully in the shade of the trees.

"My Lady," Bartholomew addressed the Fey woman who stood at the front of the grouping. She appeared to be made, not of flesh, but of rainbow light with dewdrops and ice crystal strewn through her hair. Her eyes, those astonishing eyes, took on every hue in a constant floating drift like clouds moving smoothly across the sky. She was taller than Bartholomew by about a foot, and her beauty was a constant shift and shimmer from young maiden to old, glorious crone.

"Old friend," she responded, though Frances would later be hard pressed to say if she heard or felt the words. "And our new young friend." The Lady turned her eyes to Frances who felt/heard the comfort of the word "welcome" in Cree and English and French and a hundred other tongues. Frances's eyes filled with tears of an inchoate happiness and sense of having come home.

"My Lady," Frances responded and placed her hand over heart and gave a slight bow.

"Ah!" came the trip of laughter that was like the sound of swift running water over smooth brown stones. "This one has been well brought up I see. She is the descendant of Atvasfara, yes?"

"I am the granddaughter of Kakehtaweyihtam, known as Sally Standing Bear, she who was Atvasfara, High Priestess of the Goddess Isis, yes," Frances replied.

"The rumblings in your world tell us that your life has times of danger, daughter of Atvasfara. As the Wheel turns you will have important work to do, for these times and the times to come. We shall be looking over you and protecting you. When you have need, go to the trees, go to the trees…"

The Lady's words came clear and with a sense of urgency. Frances nodded that she understood. The Lady reached forward and touched Frances's belly about an inch below her belt. Her eyes focused there and Frances felt a warmth building, like a small sun glowing. The Lady raised her eyes, smiled at Frances and Bartholomew, and then seemed to evaporate. There one moment, and then in an eye blink, gone.

Stunned, Frances placed her hands over the spot on her abdomen as if to keep the warmth there. Bartholomew knuckled a tear away from his cheek and looked at Frances. "A miracle, you think?" And Frances nodded. "And a blessing, little miss. A royal blessing."

With the wind of that blessing at her back, Frances was to Ireland, to birth a child and await her soul mate, her Malvu, the man currently wearing the life of Michael Pádraig Francis Kenneally.

7 July, 1942

Mammy,

Since the moment when you opened your door and your heart to a wet and sobbing little boy and his distraught father you have been the bulwark of my life. The truest mother, the constant comfort, the North Star.

I may be out of communication for a piece and have another favor in an unanswerable list of favors to request of you. The law offices of Connelly and Cavanagh located on John Redmond Street in Cork City are in possession of several vital papers. They know you to be my executrix and will make all assistance available to you.

My last will and testament is there. In it I have made arrangements for the deposition of monies for you, Malachi and the girls. You have consistently rejected any offer of financial assistance from me up until now, but I am counting on the fact that you may not refuse my offer if I should be deceased. Maggie and Stella can use the help to establish their lives in America, and perhaps Malachi would like to expand his land holdings. And you, a new coat and a tighter roof?

I can see you making the sign to ward off evil, and, by the Lady, I hope we shall be together in days to come and joyfully burn this letter in your hearth as we sip our tea.

Also included in the documents held by Messrs Connelly and Cavanagh (old man Connelly is worth a look see — he is ninety if a day and has the most prodigious eyebrows) is a deed to the Scannell cottage and land. I know it has been empty since the old ones passed away. Their son Paddy has expressed no desire to return from Chicago and has made the place available to sell. You will note that the new owner is listed as a Miss Frances Fletcher, with yourself and Malachi as co-beneficiaries in the event of her demise.

If Miss Fletcher should find her way to you, please be advised that I intend to take her as my wife, should the gods allow. She is extraordinary, and she has my heart.

I know I can count on the generosity of your spirit to see her safe and welcome, just as you did for me all those years ago.

I remain in all the ways that truly matter, your devoted son,

MPK

Ballinskellig, Kerry, Republic of Ireland, 16 October, 1942

Magdalena Kenneally woke with a start. It was just shy of dawn and the chorus of birds outside was deafening. The preceding week had been constant rain, but today looked fair and hopeful.

"Something is about to happen," she told herself with the certainty that her fifty-two years of possessing second sight gave her. "Something that will change everything."

As she went about her morning, Magdalena drew water from the well and put a pot on to boil. She stoked the fire and added three bricks of peat. Chickens were fed, the goat was milked, and the soft cheese was strained. As she mixed the dough for her soda bread she felt her pulse quicken, and she made fast work of the bread so she could get to washing the front windows.

An hour later Magdalena was arranging a vase with blossoms from the hedgerow when she heard a pony cart coming down the road. There were only three houses along this road that led to the sea, so carts and company were rare. She brushed her hands on her apron and went to the front door.

A small girl descended from the cart and said farewell in excellent Irish to the driver, Tommy Óg. He winked at her and told her he'd be back in a week to see how she was doing, then turned the cart around and headed back up the hill toward the main road.

Magdalena saw the girl adjust her scarf and then turn to face the cottage, startled to see someone standing there watching her.

"Hello," the girl said in a surprisingly deep and rich voice. "I am Frances Fletcher."

"Frances…" Magdalena replied. "I've been expecting you."

At the sight of Magdalena's opened arms Frances walked forward, and fell into an embrace that, for the moment anyway, solved all ills.

February 1, 1943

The first caravan arrived on Imbolc Eve and pulled into the fallow field just uphill from Magdalena's cottage. The Travellers set up camp, hobbled the horses, and walked in family procession up to Magdalena's front door.

They didn't knock, just stood outside and waited. Frances, inside the cottage and tucked into a blanket, was so deep into her book that she would never have noticed except that Anu, Magdalena's red terrier, gave a single woof, stood up creakily with tail wagging, and went to wait at the closed door.

Frances was alone, but not concerned so she went to see who the dog was eager to see. As she stood, she placed a hand in the small of her back and let out a little groan. The baby was getting bigger, "growing like gorse" as Magdalena liked to say, and Frances was finding the new girth problematic in her little body. Sometimes she wondered if the baby would be born as tall as she, the eternal self-conscious curse of the short in stature.

As she swung the door open, she was surprised to see strangers. So few people came down this dead end lane that Frances thought she knew everyone in the area. But the folks here were new to her.

"A blessing on this house," the man said. He was holding his hat in his hands and small ice crystals had formed in his chestnut hair.

She responded in the same language. "And a blessing on all who cross her threshold. Won't you come in out of the cold? Magdalena will be here shortly, and I can set up a pot of tea."

She stepped back and swung her arm out, gesturing them inside. As they walked into the cottage she could see that their manner of dress was as unusual as their accent. They wore a combination of modern garments and old-fashioned pants and skirts with what looked to be several layers of multi-colored petticoats on the women. Shawls of floral patterns were draped over shoulders and heads, and their shoes looked to be handmade and of fine quality. The man was followed by a woman – his wife? – and another woman with much the look of the first – her sister? – and three children ranging in age from about fourteen to six. The eldest, a boy, held the hand of the youngest, gender indeterminate. The middle child, a girl stared openly at Frances as she passed with an abundance of self-confidence. Frances came from peoples for whom a direct stare was a sign of hostility, but this gaze, while piercing, didn't feel aggressive. The girl's eyes reminded Frances of someone, but she couldn't think who.

The family settled by the fire as Frances put the kettle on to boil and added a brick of peat to the hearth. All were silent, and only the tick of the mantle clock gave sound in the room. Anu leaned against the man's leg, and he petted her gently.

Within moments the door flew open, and Magdalena swept in with the icy air at her back. Her face was lit with delight. "Bartley! How wonderful! But you are early this year, no?" She gave the man a fierce hug and went on to embrace the others with equal fervor. With the greeting made, she turned and practically sang out the introductions. "Frances, I want to meet...did you introduce yourselves?" she asked the man. He shook his head and she laughed, "Of course not, you mystery man. Frances, I want you to meet Bartley Kenneally, Michael's cousin and the King of the Travellers in the West."

Frances gave a start of surprise, and then stepped forward and extended her hand. "It is a pleasure to meet you, Bartley. I am Fra..."

He interjected. "You are the famous Frances Fletcher, the woman who has captured my cousin's heart. And I hear...you're fierce handy with the tambourine!"

Frances was startled and speechless. How did he know of her? No one outside the intelligence agency knew of her foray into France, and Frances had certainly never broken the Official Secrets Act. Bartley laughed and in that laugh Frances saw the resemblance. He threw his head back just as Michael did when he was truly amused. "Don't be concerned, wee Frances," he said. "Word spreads like sea mist amongst the Travellers and Romani."

The evening progressed with Frances meeting the women and children. Magdalena served up a stew that she had magically been able to increase in volume, and everyone relaxed and told the tales of their travels since last spring.

"But really, Bartley. Is anything wrong?" Magdalena sounded concerned. "Why are you here, moving about in winter? We usually see you in May."

The middle child, the girl with be familiar eyes answered. "Word was on the wind that a child of Michael's was to be born, and we knew his people needed to be here." With that she walked over and placed her hands on Frances's belly with a royal air. The girl, whose name was Young Shelta, stood very still and listened. When she spoke it was in a rough hush, like the voice of a very old woman. "Ah, a girl, one of the Old Ones. And one you have known before," she said to Frances. Everyone in the room nodded their heads solemnly, and Frances felt goose-flesh run up her arms.

More caravans arrived over the next few weeks. The Travellers were welcomed and brought their skills to the work of preparing Frances's cottage. It had seemed like an overly ambitious dream to have the place ready for her before the baby was due in April. The Scannells, the old couple who had lived there, had passed away a few years back. Their children had all emigrated and the couple hadn't been fit enough to keep the place up in their last years. Then it had sat empty, and birds and other creatures had taken up residence. Now, with all the extra hands available, the Travellers set about to repair and replace, to paint and furnish a new home for Frances and the baby. She realized that as much as she had appreciated the sanctuary with Magdalena, this would be her first home of her own. The fact that Michael's family were all helping to make it fine made her heart sing.

By the full moon on the twentieth of March a settlement of nineteen caravans filled the fallow field. Frances was moving slow, only reading and sleeping those days, but between Magdalena and the Traveller women she wanted for nothing.

As the moon rose in the sky, they sang songs of blessing as Frances placed coins under the hearth stone, lowered it down, and Magdalena and the oldest Traveller woman each brought a small piece of peat from their own fires as seed. Frances then built her first fire in the hearth. It brought back sweet memories for Frances of the Cree weddings where the woman and man each had their own fire and then the two were combined to become one. The alchemy and the transformation. She felt even more at home seeing the connections between her culture of origin and the one she was adopting.

Bartley raised his arms and boisterously shouted, "It is right and truly done!"

She was home.

The music went on far into the night and the dancing spilled out into the yard. Malachi and his wife were cuddled on the settle with their youngest, little Pádraig, stretched across their laps. Magdalena's laughter rolled on and on as she was swept from one dance to the next. Frances walked out into the night, bright as day with moonlight giving the dancers huge shadows. She took it all in, the cottage, the community, the joy, the love of all these people who cared for her and Michael and their child. She let all that seep into the stones and mortar of her home and the muscle and blood of her heart. Home.

April 2, 1943

The day began with a low wet clouded sky and the pain in Frances's lower back that matched. It felt like the weight of rocks pressing in, pressing down, dull and inescapable. She didn't immediately associate it with labor, for the baby wasn't due till the full moon and the waning crescent had been but a tiny sliver in last night's sky. As the day wore on the clouds hung lower and lower and the back pain got stronger and stronger. Magdalena had come by with a basket of still-warm bread, and Bartley's wife Sophia had brought some lamb stew that filled her cottage with all the smells of comfort and safety. Frances hadn't told either woman how she was feeling, but it also didn't surprise her when, by late afternoon, the Traveller women had arrived with baskets of herbs and a birthing stool that had been the location of the birthing of "seven generations of Kenneallys." Frances chuckled to herself, that whether or not this baby was timely, it appeared she was to be born shortly, if the Kenneallys had anything to say about it.

As darkness fell, the Traveller women lit candles and began to brew teas and decoctions that made the cottage smell like summer. The heavy overcast sky cleared as the first stars broke through. Frances had been walking and moving most of the day as that seemed to soothe both her and the Turnip, as she had taken to calling the baby. She made her way outside and leaned against the stone wall, tipping her head back and watching the pinpricks of light spark and glitter. The dark moon meant those stars had no competition tonight, and their display was dazzling.

Frances felt a pull down deep within her, and the sensation in her back shifted to some undefined location, a place she could only identify as her 'center.'

"So, it is to be tonight, eh?" she asked. The startling flood of bright sharp pain in her lower abdomen seemed like the baby's response. Frances stood, face skyward, then turned to face the stone wall, leaning her elbows on the solid presence of the ancestor beings. She kept up this dance, looking at the stars between the pains, and turning to press forehead to the stones during them as the women inside the cottage made all right and ready.

Frances lost all sense of the passage of time. She was in the pull of the tides, yanked back and forth with each new contraction. All of her being was focused on the rise and fall of the river of birth. At some point she heard herself moaning and wondered in a vague way if she had been doing that all along.

Magdalena came down the path from the road followed by her faithful Anu. She stood on the other side of the stone wall, sending Frances waves of love, watching carefully as several contractions surged through Frances's body.

One rolling crashing pain after another. One tiny island of quiet, then the roar of muscle and bone being pried apart for life to emerge. Then, something changed. The rhythm was broken. The waves that Frances had come to listen to and respond to became staccato and unpredictable, and she felt panic rush in.

"I can't do this!" she cried to Magdalena and the stars and the Old Ones and to anyone who would listen.

And being beyond hearing or knowing or sense, she felt the reply like the stones were talking and the ancestor bones long buried were talking and the voices and hearts of Magdalena and the Traveller woman were joining in.

"Yes, you can!"

Magdalena came in through the gate, held Frances around the back of her shoulders and helped her inside. From that point on, all was soft voices and tender hands. Warm cloths and slightly bitter teas. Flickers of light and faces in candle shadow. Frances felt invincible and then fragile, fierce and then frightened. She walked and then fell into waiting arms, then walked again.

One of the Traveller women was their respected midwife who had seen three generations of babies safely into the world. She placed her hands on Frances's belly and waited through two contractions. "These be doing the good work," she said in their language and gave Frances a nod of approval and encouragement. She was doing alright, this tiny dark thing that their Michael loved. Her little body belied her powerful determination, and the midwife felt that rightness that comes with knowing that all would be well.

Sometime later, after minutes, hours, eons, Frances said, "I need to sit down." Women rustled about bringing the birthing chair into the space set out before the fire. Frances threw off her sweater and dragged at her shift. "It's so hot! I am so hot!"

Cool cloths were draped on her forehead and soft sweet hands rubbed them down her back. The oldest of the Traveller women, wizened and nut-brown sat in the corner and began a low chant in their language. It was a lineage story, a series of the tales of the previous generations and their lives and losses, so that this babe would be hearing the path of those who had walked before as she came into the world. Magdalena threw mugwort onto the fire, and the almost sweet smell seemed to Frances to waft through her skin and into her bones.

She rocked forward and back, pulled by the overwhelming need to bear down like she was a mountain that needed to thrust up from the Earth's crust. The old woman in the corner was talking faster, and now the lineage tale was a prophesy, a foreseeing of this child's life. A word here or there came through to Frances who had been learning the Travellers' language these last few months. "Bold. A healer. A keeper of the bloodline." The very tiny portion of Frances that could hear and process this information was amused. Their child, hers and Michael's, bold? That would be no surprise.

Another sensation of mountains being born and the earth being torn asunder. The midwife was kneeling in front of Frances and her voice penetrated the fog of pain.

"There's a girl, let it come. There's a clever, clever girl." And it was as if Michael was in the room saying those very words, and Frances gathered all her strength and all her courage and pushed through the wall of fire. It was like the beginning of the universe, the explosion of creation, unique in itself, and identical to every other birth. With a whoosh, the room was filled with another life, another spark of the divine. Frances was a million miles away, but she heard the high wail of first breath and the exclamations of delight from all the women in the room. The midwife's hand rested at Frances's bottom and within a few short minutes the afterbirth fell into the waiting hands with only a slight feeling of contraction.

The baby was wrapped in the warm toweling and all the women be-gan a soft trill of welcome. The oldest woman held the baby and whispered her Fey name in her ear. The others lifted Frances, helped her to her bed, and gently bathed her legs and torso. When she was clean and dry, propped up on pillows and tucked into blankets that helped calm the shivers and trembles that coursed through her legs, Frances was given her girl child into her arms. They locked eyes, and the first words Frances said to her daughter were, "There you are! I've missed you!"

The oldest Traveller woman beckoned to Magdalena who was wiping tears from her face. She came over to the old one and crouched down before her low chair. The old woman clasped Magdalena's hands in a bone crushing grip.

"He needs to know that his daughter has been born. Together, you and I, we can reach him."

Magdalena nodded, but didn't know exactly what the old woman meant. But anything felt possible after the miracle she had just seen.

"What do we need to do?" Magdalena asked.

"We need to go to the faerie ring." And with that the old woman stood with surprisingly little difficulty, wrapped numerous shawls around her shoulders and bustled over to the door, looking back in some impatience for Magdalena to follow. Granting herself another lingering look at the sight of Frances and baby, snug and safe in the bed and surrounded by smiling faces, Magdalena slipped outside and hurried to catch up to the old woman, who was walking at a much younger woman's pace.

The faerie ring was about half mile to the north-east, up a hill and circled with hawthorn trees. It had been known as a place of the Good People for as long as humans had lived here, and everyone knew not to tarry there at night and to never under any circumstances cut down those trees or even use their fallen branches for a hearth fire. It was a mark of some courage for Magdalena to follow the old woman up that hill and walk into that circle of trees.

All sounds stopped once inside the faerie ring. No wind, no night birds, no sound of the not-so-distant sea. The Traveller woman stopped in the center of the circle and began to strip off all her clothes. In an instant she was naked and unabashedly so. She made clear, with some irritation, that Magdalena was to do the same. Quickly following suit, soon the two women stood in the blackness of the night, and Magdalena could see nothing and only hear the other woman breathing.

The old woman said, "I am Shelta, the mother of Michael's mother, she who was known as Bridie."

Magdalena was startled. She hadn't known of the connection but felt she had been granted a great treasure in this information, for the Travellers seldom mentioned those who had passed over, and even less frequently shared that knowledge with the "settled people" such as herself.

The old woman continued, "Bridie was to be the Wise One of her generation. But she, in her labor with her second child, was denied care by the hospital in Killarney. By the time her husband got her to us, it was too late, and she and her babe died. But her son, her Michael, and her grieving husband came to you for shelter, and you cared for them, and you loved them. You became the only mother that Michael ever knew, treating him the same as the children of your body. And you were a loving wife to Pádraig. So, you are the mother of Michael's heart. He will hear us, his bloodline and heart-love mother."

The two women took hands, fumbling only slightly in the dark.

"What do I need to do?" Magdalena asked.

"Think on him," the old woman replied. And so they did. They thought of the small boy he had been, the ravenous hunger for knowledge and daring that he had displayed. They remembered the sound of him singing, the sweet-honeyed warmth in his voice as he sang the old songs. They recalled how he had been spotted as a brilliant scholar, given the chance to study in Dublin and in Oxford. They remembered his sense of humor in the absurd, and his fierce sense that evil must be faced down. And it was if he joined them on that hill, in the enfolding velvet darkness, surrounded and protected by magical trees. He was real and as palpable to them as they were to each other. They told him of his daughter and felt the jolt of surprise, joy and regret that rushed through him. They told him that mother and child were well, and held, and loved by all who loved him. So, wherever he was, he heard them, and deep within himself he vowed to try and stay alive. The cold and illness and danger that had plagued him had begun to feel like burdens too heavy to bear. But he vowed to try. And his bloodline and his mother of the heart heard him and prayed to every goddess and god in all the world that their beloved one would come home.

Back in the cottage, Frances had the baby to her breast and was being shown how to encourage her to nurse. She and the child had still not broken that deep timeless gaze between them. The baby started sucking and Frances laughed at how strong and fierce her little girl was. In that instant, as all that was important was finished, as all that needed to be done had been done, Frances felt herself slip into some sort of dream state. She thought she saw Magdalena and the oldest Traveller woman, naked as the day they were born, standing atop a hill holding hands. The sight seemed so absurd as to be ridiculous, and then she heard Michael's voice, clear as day: "I will try." And then Frances felt the brush of a kiss across her forehead and the slight smell of book leather and persimmon that was Michael's scent.

"Your daddy loves you, little Turnip," Frances whispered to her daughter. And as one single tear rolled from the outside of her eye, she slipped gently into sleep.

May 1, 1943

They had been up before dawn and made the journey in the back of Malachi's pony cart. Frances had the baby snuggled tight against her chest, and Magdalena sat at her shoulder to share the warmth under the blanket. For the first of May it was chill, and the moon was setting in the west in a cloudless sky as they came to Kenmare and the stone circle at the top of the hill. Frances could hear the stones, even from a distance. They sang welcome to her, and she responded with a silent, "I am coming to you!"

They were all silent, even the baby, as the full weight of the sacredness of the place descended on them. To be here, on this morning, was to be in the lineage of the thousands of people over thousands of years who had acknowledged and honored this energy vortex and this turn of the Wheel.

The three adults walked up the hill, still in darkness, and asked permission of the stones to enter. Permission was granted, and Frances could feel the stones stirring, waking, coming to attention at the request to hold ritual within their circle. They walked the outer circumference three times sunwise, entered between two stones, and then Malachi placed the basket of ritual items directly in the center. Magdalena stood, feet planted, and anchored herself there in that time and place. She had her head thrown back and her arms were extended out to her sides. As her hands lifted skyward the first light began to leach apricot from the eastern horizon.

"Come the Light!
Come the Sidhe!
Come to greet the new life!
Come to hear her name!"

The air around them became heavier and yet filled with an almost discernible sparkle. The Sidhe, the Fey, the Old Ones had heard the clarion call from the stones and from the priestess Magdalena, and they encircled the group, leaning in. Birds swooped and fluttered and landed on the stones. A hare came up close poised between two of the outer stones and watched. It was as if the natural world was held in an expectant hush, like an audience waiting for the curtain to rise on a performance about to begin.

After the baby's birth, when Frances had first spoken of the desire to have a naming ceremony, she had been emphatically clear that it was not to be a baptism.

"I'm sorry if that offends you, Magdalena, but I am not letting a priest put his mark on this child! She is of me and Michael, of my people and of his. I don't think Rome and her church has any claim here."

Magdalena, who had come from a line of women who had needed to placate Rome for centuries, was secretly thrilled at her daughter-in-law's defiance. "I think we can blame it all on your Protestant people back in Canada." She chuckled at how the local padre would sputter about that. "And I am far from offended, child. My people hold to the Old Ways, always have. We can do whatever form of ceremony you wish, and it will be right and truly done."

Frances herself, having lived with a foot in two different worlds, had also learned how to accommodate the expectations of the society around her. She had told Magdalena how she had been christened in the local

Anglican Church, and then how, some months later, her Granny Sally had carried her off into the woods and done ceremony with her people, the Cree. For the Cree, a child was given a baby name, and then when somewhat older, around three or four, their character had been revealed and they were given their true name, their power name.

Frances's own power name had only been known by her Cree grandmother and great uncle. And there had not been time yet to tell Michael what it was. She stood alone in the world, the only one in possession of her power name. So, she decided to share it with Magdalena in exchange for her support of the ensuing ceremony for the baby.

"Wiskicack. It is a small fierce little bird. The English call it a whiskey jack. My Granny gave me that name, and now only you and I know it."

Magdalena took a moment to repeat the name several times, and then smiled, giving Frances the fullness of her generous smile.

"Welcome to our home and family, Wiskicack!"

And now on this Beltaine morning they stood ready to present this new baby girl to all the assembled personages, and to remember all those who could not be with them in a ceremony that melded their traditions and forged new ones. Frances unwrapped the baby from her many shawls, and Magdalena placed the circlet of spring flowers around her tiny head. She took a small silver dish from the basket and walked widdershins around the inside of the circle, gently brushing dew from the stones into the shallow container. Malachi stood guardian as Magdalena approached the mother and child. She dipped two fingers into the dew and washed the baby's face declaring, "Now you shall see beauty all your life."

Frances held the baby higher, so that the first bit of spilled light coming through the spaces between the stones moved across her face. "Blessed child, you are the daughter of Wiskicack, the granddaughter of Hannah, the great-granddaughter of Kakehtaweyihtam, the great-great-granddaughter of Misimohokasiw. You are the daughter of Michael, the granddaughter of Magdalena and Bridie, the great-granddaughter of Shelta, and the great-great-granddaughter of Mari. Your ancestors see you. They claim you. They shall watch over you every day of your life."

The baby watched all of this with wide eyes. Malachi stepped forward to be in place of his brother. Magdalena was at his left shoulder, and Frances at the far side of their small sacred circle. The three placed their hands under the baby and lifted her even higher. Frances sang a song of blessing in Cree, Magdalena chanted an old Irish prayer, and Malachi pledged the protection of his name and body. With that Frances began to ululate and the sound rang around the stone circle like the very first song ever sung.

"Welcome to the world, Sally Standing Bear Fletcher Kenneally!"

CHAPTER 3
DECEMBER 21, 1943

F rances put the finishing touches on her letter to Michael, hoping
to wave down Tommy Óg tomorrow on his way to Killarney so
he might post it for her. She had been writing every week without fail for over a year now, sending off missives to the post box at SIS
allocated for agents in the field. She had had no response in that time,
except for the one cryptic letter from Deputy Director Turnbull which
read: "The agency has lost contact with the person in question. They are
officially listed as missing/presumed dead." That had caused Frances to,
overnight, develop a stark white streak in her black hair that shot straight
up from the center of her forehead. She had refused to share that piece
of official judgment with Magdalena and Malachi, insisting to herself
that D.D. Turnbull was a pompous squirt of goose shit. She simply had
a knowing, and in her heart, she felt that Michael was still alive.

*Sally pulled herself up today, hanging onto the arms of the rocker that
sits near the fire. She looked like a drunken sailor as her 'safe hold'
rocked rather vigorously back and forth. I must say, I believe our daughter has a future as a circus performer. If you could have seen the delight
on her face as her little body tipped right and left. If I were an artist, I
would capture it for you.*

*Your mother and Malachi and his family are arriving later tonight
for a feast to celebrate Yule. Magdalena is supplying the food, but Bartholomew, having risen from his sick bed, has undertaken making pies.
He seems better, and I am praying to all the gods and goddesses of this*

place that it was only bronchitis and not something worse.

I have been teaching Malachi's girls a winter song in Cree, and we will be performing it tonight. Molly has a good ear, and Theresa has gusto. I want you to picture us all here in the light of the fire with the good beeswax candles in the windows to show you the way home. Feel the love we send you as we sing and tell stories – a true céilí – to keep company on this longest night. If there is a beneficent Being, one day you will be here with us. Your mother tells me you had a fine voice as a child so I shall make you sing as well.

Always,

Frances

She folded the pages of onion skin paper and carefully wrote the circumspect address. Frances didn't know if Michael even received any of these letters, but her faith sent them across the sea to the waiting receptacle in London where hope was buried deep like daffodil bulbs.

She could hear Bartholomew telling Sally a fairy story in the other room. Her cottage had, after much scrubbing, fresh whitewash, new thatch, and some smudging, become a tidy and snug home for the three of them.

Bartholomew had arrived in September, finally acquiescing to her persistent appeals for him to retire and come keep her company. When she had seen him descend from Tommy Óg's pony cart a cold shiver had come across her. He hadn't been well, the summer heat had worn at him, and he needed more rest and care than he had been willing to admit. His connection to little Sally whom everyone called Sassy, had been immediate and eternal. They became constant companions, and Frances could often hear them speaking in a language she almost remembered.

Two weeks ago he had developed a fever with a bad cough. Magdalena had swooped in with her herbal remedies, and Frances had fussed over him so much that he asserted that they had nagged him back to health.

It was all here in her home: love and family, illness and decline, war and fear, and hope. But for now, Bartholomew was here, and Sassy was here, and Frances believed that Michael was somewhere on this side of the veil. So, tonight she would gather the family under her own roof, to hold the old feast and lift a glass to those not present.

August 12, 1945

The dogs were barking, all of them. Frances had acquired two wolf-hounds over these last years, and they had names appropriate with the ruckus they were raising now. Cú Chulainn was the elder by a year, and Fionn Mac Cumhaill still had the gangly long-limbed, big-footed looks of a giant puppy. In normal times they would alert Frances to company or a stray bird overhead with a few choice chuffs. Today though they were braying like they were headed into battle. Malachi's sheep dog joined in, and all three raced up the road to be joined by Magdalena's ancient terrier who met them at the garden gate and followed along.

The hullabaloo ratcheted up a notch into a kind of hallelujah chorus. Frances put down her pen and found Sassy amongst some wild angelica. She took her daughter's hand as they walked their path to the road, and her heart was running a triplet. Frances spotted Malachi coming over the top of the rise to the south alerted by the dog chorale. Magdalena appeared in her doorway wiping her hands down the front of her apron.

A figure came over the hill from the main road and the dogs reached him. They circled and jumped, and the barks became yips and howls of joy.

The man, for it was a man, began to walk slowly down the lane with the canine procession racing forward and back, circling him in excitement.

Frances felt her heart stop. The man, so very thin and limping wore a brown slouch hat and had a rucksack over one shoulder and walking stick in the other hand.

She felt his eyes on her and Sassy, the heat of that gaze like the sun, and she knew. She knew that her intuition had always been correct. She had never lost faith. And now her faith had been rewarded.

It was Michael, or Malcolm or whatever he called himself these days. He was hers. He was battered and weary in body and soul. But it was he. He was home. Home from the war. Home to her.

October 31, 1953

Bartholomew's voice ran down like an old phonograph. He had been telling his stories to Frances with an urgency these last few months and she had been assiduously taking down every word. She was adding his recollections of lifetimes to The Book, the one she has first started while sitting in Granny Sally's cabin so many years ago. Over the years she had transcribed those words, taking the details and meanings and emotions that Sally had gifted to her and giving it a tidiness her nine-year-old self had not been capable of.

The Book had gone with her to university, then on to London and Bletchley House, and then finally to Ballinskellig and the home she had created here. When Michael had returned after the War, she had found that the two of them would have dreams that matched and mirrored one another. The dreams were like doorways into their past. When they shared these dreams, the memories came flooding back in, so she had made addendums to Sally's Book, the lives of Celebi and Malvu, as had been.

Frances had also begun to write the essence of these lifetimes as fictional stories. At first, it had just seemed to be a way to tickle the minds of any who might be inclined to enjoy them. As time wore on, Frances found success as an author. Her books appealed to many on many levels. For some, they were rich and well-researched historical fiction. And for others, they were a telling of a history that was a mere gossamer form. For some the stories woke memories and brewed a hope for what might be. Frances took the *nom de plume* of Frannie Portreaux, and from her sanctuary in Kerry she connected with the world.

Even though she had always known that Bartholomew had a history that was interwoven with theirs, he had never shared the details. Until recently. Now the floodgates were opened and he raced time to tell about all he had been. They jokingly called these addendums to Sally's history "The Lives of the Apostates."

"After Comté de Foix and the massacre of all the sisters in my care, I felt so burdened by failure. I chose lives where I could be of service, make some difference in the sufferings of others," Bartholomew said softly.

"Did those lifetimes assuage the guilt?" Frances asked.

"A bit, and at times," he replied. "Let me tell you about the one they called Joan of Arc." He had made fateful meetings with some of the Thirteen occasionally. "I was able to offer some comfort to Joan, she who was Maia, and I saw Atvasfara there at the burning! Did Sally mention that in her story?"

"Yes, she did," Frances reassured him. "But she said you did more than offer some comfort. She said that the two of you stood by Joan as she burned, and that you asked the trees to ignite more fiercely to speed her journey and alleviate her suffering. That was no small thing."

Bartholomew was quiet for a while and then continued. "I saw Kiyia once too. On a slave ship. I was able to secrete her some water and food. Only a tiny thing, but again, I tried."

"That was you? Sally said that a kind boy had saved Kiyia's life on that ship, and had given her hope when she had none. Kiyia was known as Khadee then. She went on to live a full life and have several children and become the matriarch of her community. And you did that, you made that possible!" Frances grabbed his hand and squeezed hard. "You may have felt like these were only small insignificant things. But fates are changed by small gestures of kindness. Lives are retrieved from darkness by acts of generosity. And courage, my friend, courage to act in whatever ways we can, that courage is the stuff of greatness!" Tears fell from Frances's eyes as she looked upon her dear friend. And his eyes filled and overflowed as well.

"You have given me peace of mind, my sweet girl. Perhaps doing what we can is the very best we can do." Bartholomew closed his eyes and sighed. "I am so very weary, but I feel as if the weight of guilt has been lifted. You have done that for me."

Frances put down her pen and stood to draw the blanket up around Bartholomew's shoulders. "Rest now, dear one. I will be heading up to the Samhain fire, but the night is cold. I don't think you should attempt it this year."

He nodded in agreement but held her hand for a moment longer. "Thank you for these years with you, Celebi. Tell Dalia that I will always watch over her." He drifted off to a sleep so deep that it frightened Frances. And why did he refer to her as Celebi, and to Sassy as

Dalia? Those past identities were known to them but seldom referred to. Had he slipped his anchor in this time? She stood and watched him for a few minutes until Sassy and Michael came to the door, eager to be out to the fire. Frances bent down to whisper in Bartholomew's ear. "All your debts have long been paid, Eiofachta. Travel well and swiftly."

She turned to face her husband and daughter, and the sight of them made her heart spill over. It was all here. Life, love, loss. All to be treasured and all perfectly revealed, exactly as it was.

"It is on we go then, yes?" she said to her beloveds. The three made their way out of the cottage to join the families gathered on the nearby hill for the celebration of the thinnest veil. As they walked, Frances could see the shades of beings, the Sidhe, float past her to gather and surround her cottage. It was a parade of gossamer and faerie light, a display of the Shining Folk to honor one of their own. His beloved Fey were coming to see Bartholomew home.

June 5, 1964

Cú Chulainn the Third, otherwise known as Hoolie because he was his own party all by himself, stood abruptly and bayed. Frances had been working and was so deep into the text that she jumped in alarm. Then, resting her fingers on the typewriter keys, she stilled her heart and listened. Hoolie, braw and golden, clawed at the closed bottom half door, and Frances quickly went to let him out.

Malachi's three sheepdogs came barreling over top the hill and raced down into her yard. The dogs had a quick conference and then ran pell-mell down the path and up the lane to the hilltop. Frances put a hand to her heart. Could it be? And then she started to run. She was a healthy, spry forty-six years old, and she was keeping pace with the dogs when Magdalena came to stand at the door of her cottage.

"Is it?" she cried.

"My heart, and the dogs say yes!" Frances replied. Magdalena had broken an ankle in the spring and still used a cane, but she too was making remarkable time as they made their way up the lane. Just shy of the crest a woman appeared. She was tall, like her father with his dark honey hair that caught the light. But this woman had seen tropical sun. She was as brown as a nut, and she vibrated with good health and vigor.

"Mama! Grammy!" the woman, Sally Standing Bear Kenneally exclaimed.

The women and the dogs made a jumble of happy tears and embraces and silly yelps. They were soon joined by Malachi and his son and youngest daughter who had put down the shearing tools as soon as they heard the commotion. Malachi grabbed her duffel bag and the group made a chaotic procession down the lane toward Frances's cottage with dogs tripping feet and voices flowing over each other like the river after the snow melts.

"We didn't expect you!"

"Look how shiny your hair is!"

"I missed you!"

"Are you hungry?"

"Are you back from Ghana for good?"

Everybody was laughing and no one truly expected any answers as they pushed open the gate and made toward Frances's door. Mother and daughter had their arms around the other's shoulder. Sassy had fulfilled her mother's prophecy and become taller than she. Long at birth, she was always lanky, and had at the age of eleven had a growth spurt that had shot her up above her mother. Now she towered ten inches taller, but they had their easy way with one another and their arms knew their paths.

"How is he?" Sassy asked quietly, for only Frances's ear.

"Sleeping now, but he will be so much better for the sight of you," Frances replied, not really answering her daughter's question.

The family stood just outside the door, waiting to allow Sassy to enter first. She took a moment and looked at her beloveds. Magdalena looked so happy as to burst. Malachi was grinning ear to ear and her cousins mirrored his joy. She took a deep breath and walked into the cottage, pausing a moment to let her eyes adjust to the cool dimness. It smelled like home, fresh flowers in a pitcher on the table, peat smoke, and the ever-present smell of her mother's passion, coffee. Her eyes moved to the left and the entrance to the bedroom. Sassy felt the pain in her heart and went to see her father.

He was, by some miracle, or some deep illness, still asleep even with all the noise their coming had made. Sassy walked quietly over to the bed and sat in the chair that was pulled up close. She slid her hand into his. It was warm and dry, and Sassy was flooded with a lifetime of memories of that hand holding hers. Her eyes filled but she willed them to not spill over.

"Da, it's me, your sassy girl. I've come home, Da." She spoke quietly, but her voice reached him, and he worked to open his eyes. They drank in the sight of each other, like thirsty folk who have crossed a desert.

With the muted sounds of family chatter and laughter filtering in through the door, Frances came to the bedroom sometime later. "Tea?" and walked in with the tray overflowing with soda bread and fresh butter, last year's elderberry jam and this year's first honey. To Sassy, this was the best idea any one had ever had, and after two years of fish and lentils and chicory coffee, it was heaven. She slathered a slice of bread and her eyes drifted shut in bliss as she chewed.

"So, besides the obvious desire for good Irish butter, what brings you home, my darlin'?" Michael's voice sounded scratchy and tired, like an old record that had been played a million times. He looked at Frances and she simply gave a small shake of her head in negation. No, she hadn't written to their daughter and asked for her to return. But Sassy had known, able to read between the lines, and feeling the urgency crest within her, had returned of her own volition.

It had always been thus with the three of them. Vows of friendship and love forged in ages past and now given their opportunity to flourish again in this lifetime, they felt the rhythms of each other with unerring accuracy. Their trinity was eons old. As Celebi and Malvu and Dalia they had, as a unit, helped to rebuild the honor and viability of an Egypt ripped asunder by planetary and social catastrophe. The flooding, the loss of several years of crops, the severe weather changes that had occurred when the earth had ruptured and the Thirteen had disappeared, it had been a supreme struggle to feed people, to restore order, to maintain a sense of safety and justice in the face of the fear and panic that spanned continents. But those three, the most profound of friends, had clung together, had done whatever they could to repair and restore the world.

Now, in the twentieth century, they had come together again, and the preciousness of these years had been beyond measure. When Sassy had gone to Montreal for university, and then to Ghana for service with CUSO, they had still, regardless of oceans and miles between them, been able to 'hear' each other. Just as when Michael had been in a forced labor camp those last few years of the war and Frances had always 'felt' him. Just as he had received the news of Sassy's birth, sent via love and energy from the faerie ring, their connection defied geography. It was made of sterner stuff than mere distance in feet and miles.

But Sassy could not deny that the sweetest thing of all was to actually be here, to feel the warmth of her father's hand, to see the white widow's peak that graced her mother's forehead. Time and distance might be meaningless to such as they, but proximity was precious.

"I needed to be with you," Sassy replied, and with those simple words they knew that she understood that Michael's days were limited. "And, I have some important news," she continued.

The air suddenly seemed charged, and Frances filled the moment by pouring tea for her husband and daughter.

"Well, don't leave me hangin', *mo chuisle*," Michael said with a smile, the Irish deepening in his accent.

"I have met someone," Sassy said almost shyly. And she stopped.

"What sort of someone?" her mother asked with a tinge of asperity.

"A someone that I love," she replied, and sat somewhat breathless, waiting for her parents' response.

"Are we to know this person's name?" Michael asked. He grinned and Frances chuckled.

Sassy felt her mouth split into a smile. This was going to be all right. These were her parents after all, not like the rest of the world.

"He is called Kwame Adusa Anto Boadu," she said proudly. "And he is amazing!"

Sassy settled in with another slice of soda bread, this one with honey and butter to tell her folks all about the dazzling Kwame, physician, humanitarian, son of a Senegalese freedom fighter. She painted a picture of him with her words, and Frances and Michael watched as their beloved daughter's face lit up as she described this remarkable man. "And he loves me too!" she finished with some astonishment in her voice.

"He would be a fool not to!" her mother retorted. Michael laughed and the laughter turned into a cough that wouldn't stop. Frances simply stood and added more pillows behind his back to prop him up, acting as if nothing alarming was going on. Some minutes later Frances continued, "And where is the amazing Kwame?"

"He is still in Ghana. He is running a medical clinic in the Ashanti region. That's where we met, when I came in to do field nursing. But he will be coming to England in the Fall. He has a fellowship at Oxford, Da, just as you did."

"Yes, but which college?" Michael said, his voice faint but his eyes bright.

"All Souls," she replied, knowing full well what would come next.

Michael sniffed as if in some discernment of a bad smell. "Well, I suppose that isn't too bad. Not as top drawer as Balliol, of course!"

Frances and Sassy nodded their heads in unison, seamlessly moving into this long-lasting family trope. "Of course! Nothing tops Balliol!" they replied.

"And," Sassy slipped in, "I will be there as well."

"For what purpose, *mo ghrá?*" her father asked, suspiciously. "You wouldn't do something as foolhardy as move country to be with a man, now would you?" His eyes sparkled and he and Frances shared a deep, long gaze that might have been embarrassing, except Sassy had seen them in such gazes all her life.

"No, of course not, Da. What self-respecting woman would do such a thing?" she asked in jest.

"The bravest kind," he replied, and Frances leaned forward to give him a gentle kiss. "What will occupy you then in the wilds of Oxfordshire?"

"I have enrolled at St. Johns. I am going to become a doctor!" Sassy announced, and finally she had knocked her parents speechless.

"Sassy, my sweet chick, are you sure?" Frances asked, and she and Michael began to laugh until both had tears streaming down their faces. Sassy blushed and tried hard not to smile. It was legend in their family that Magdalena tended to physical wounds, Frances nursed the sick of heart and the ailing plants, Malachi took care of the animals, and that Sassy couldn't bear any suffering at all. She wept herself ill at the loss of a lamb. She ran and hid in the hills when one of the family dogs passed away. She trembled and cried when her cousin had a run-in with some barbed wire fencing. Her, a doctor?

Face flaming, Sassy held her head high and pronounced, "Yes! An obstetrician! And I am going to become a pilot too!"

"In the air?" her father squeaked out the question. And when she nodded defiantly, both her parents succumbed to peals of more laughter as they recalled her historic fear of heights. Every time the laughter started to die down Frances or Michael would catch the other's eye and they would swoop up again into their hysteria. At long last, wiping eyes and noses, they muttered apologies to Sassy and tried again to ask the questions.

"Precious, why are you aiming for these professions?" Frances was able to squeeze out.

Sassy sighed, smiled, and proceeded to tell them why. The Ashanti region was desperately cut off from the major towns. Healthcare of even the most rudimentary kind was scarce. So, she and Kwame had a plan. She would pursue her studies. He was coming to England to become a surgeon. And then they intended to run a bush plane operation, able to drop deep in the back country, bringing medicine and care to the most isolated, and able to fly the seriously ill or injured back to a hospital in a larger population area.

Frances nodded and Michael looked more and more concerned. *Mo chroí,* what of the political situation there? I have heard things…" And, indeed, he had. He had maintained an ongoing correspondence with several members of the former SIS, now divided into MI5 and MI6, his colleagues from the war. He might be tucked in the back of beyond and be ill unto dying, but Michael Kenneally still had a finger on the pulse of world events. The agencies had availed themselves of his expertise and insights over the last two decades. He had been asked to analyze and assess various potential hotspots and emerging political trends.

His health had never fully recovered after the years in the camp. The 'putrid throat' one old leftist there had called it. The result had been his weakened heart. Life had become narrower in the physical sense. He didn't travel, and a journey even as far as Killarney was taxing. But his exquisite mind could roam the Earth, and his boundless love for Frances, Sassy, and his adoptive mother and siblings had given him wings. Old Shelta, his mother's mother had come to see him not long after he had returned to Ireland.

"You should be a ghost, Michael, but her love brought you back." Shelta gave a nod toward where Frances had been standing at the stove. "That one is fierce." Michael had laughed and thanked all the old goddesses for his brilliant good fortune in finding his clever, clever girl in this lifetime. His was a life of great joy after enormous sacrifice, but he could feel the minutes running short.

So, when his colleagues had sent him reports about possible military unrest in the newly formed country of Ghana he had kept the troubling news to himself and hadn't shared all of his information with Frances. Now she started, aware that he must have kept something from her to save her some worry while Sassy had been in Africa. Sassy looked deep into her father's eyes and quoted John Wesley.

"Do all the good you can,
By all the means you can,
In all the ways you can,
In all the places you can,
At all the times you can,
To all the people you can,
As long as ever you can."

Michael and Frances joined in quoting what had been their family motto. And they, her parents, guilty of having followed the same directive in all of their lives, could only open their arms and hold their precious girl.

CHAPTER 4
OCTOBER 31, 1966

Frances planned to sit by the fire until dawn. It was a sharp, cold night and the stars were muted by swiftly moving clouds. A perfect night for the thinnest veil. She and Young Shelta had been the scryers for the last few years since Old Shelta had passed over, and the task was both an honor and a hard piece of work. For both women the messages had come fast and furious on this Samhain; concise, terse directives from the beyond on what to do and what to not do in the next year. Folks went away happy or shaken, or both. When the last person, Tommy Mór, had come to see his future for the new year, sometime long past midnight, Frances had found herself traveling more deeply into that between, that liminal space where all the ancestors could speak and be heard. In that space she heard Sassy calling to her. "Mama! Please come! Kwame is missing!"

Frances broke clear, as if rising swiftly from deep water, and let go of Tommy Mór's hand abruptly. "I'm sorry, Tommy. Ask Young Shelta for your reading. I must away!" She rose and ran back over the hills, past the faerie ring and down to her cottage.

By daylight she had packed her belongings and gathered the Book to take with her as far as Dublin. There she planned to store it in a safe deposit box and catch a plane, first to London, then on through to Senegal. Her Sassy needed her!

Yoff, Senegal, November 3, 1966

Frances emerged from the plane, stepping onto the tarmac at Dakar Airport and walked into a wall of heat. She was exhausted and yet every nerve was on high alert. French and Wolof and several other languages swirled around her, and she caught bits and pieces of phrases and the odd word.

"Stupid man!"

"…he has a car waiting…"

"Trouble in Accra…"

Frances heard that last one and tried to zero in on the speaker. Kwame was last seen leaving Accra. What sort of trouble was brewing there now? She found her bag in the pile next to the plane and followed the river of people heading into the building that served as a terminal. It had a metal roof and was open on all four sides. The sounds under that roof were amplified and bouncing. Frances felt like she had fallen into a vast echo chamber, and her head began to swim from the pounding sounds and heat waves.

"Mama!" Sassy's voice rose above the cacophony, and Frances saw her daughter, bronze haired and taller than most all the other folks around her. She was like a beacon in the maelstrom, and Frances and she fell into each other's arms.

"Thank the Goddess you're here!" Sassy exclaimed, and she let herself weep for the first time since the news of Kwame's disappearance.

Frances leaned back to look up at her only child. Sassy had deep worry lines between her eyebrows and she looked worn and thin.

"Where is Sisi?" Frances asked.

"She is back at the house in Yoff with Kwame's sister. She still naps in the middle of the day, all saints be praised," Sassy replied with a small hint of a smile and a broad swath of Kerry in her speech.

They began the serpentine path through the throngs of people meeting and greeting in the terminal and made their way to a line of small three-wheeled rickshaw-like vehicles with the driver in the front, and the small, raised seat for two covered by an awning of bright patterned fabric.

She stood as Sassy negotiated with the driver in Wolof, repeating "mama" until the driver succumbed to the combination of charm and guilt and agreed on a smaller price. Sassy and Frances clambered up onto the seat and the driver stowed Frances's bag under the bench. The tuk-tuk moved faster than Frances expected and navigated the seemingly unorganized traffic like a fish moving through the shoals. She clung onto the side of the bench as Sassy slung an arm around her shoulder.

"Jesus, Mary, and Joseph!" Frances muttered.

Sassy threw back her head and laughed, just as her father had done. Frances felt something in her simultaneously break in grief and relax from worry.

The airport was close to the fishing village of Yoff, and their journey, whilst harrowing, was short. The driver turned down a dirt lane that quickly became sand, and he started muttering what were probably curse words under his breath. He stopped when he could go no further. Sassy thanked him profusely and Frances touched her heart and then his with her right hand. He was surprised and then moved by the blessing, and as he turned to drive away he shouted a blessing in return.

"What did he say?" Frances asked.

"He called all of Allah's blessings upon you. He said you were a holy woman!" Sassy replied.

"Well, we will take all the help we can get!" Frances retorted, and Sassy laughed again. They made their way farther down the lane, and Frances could feel the hot sand filling up in her shoes. She noticed that Sassy wore woven sandals and a loose cotton tunic in brilliant sapphire and made a note to herself to acquire some as soon as possible. Frances, like her husband Michael, had always been a chameleon, able to blend into whatever land they found themselves in. Senegal would be an interesting challenge for her in that regard: the heat, the colors, the sand, the smell of fish. Well, fish, at least that felt familiar, like Ireland.

She had begun to soak in a bit of Wolof on the flight here. She had always been a magpie for languages, but the music of the language here in Yoff was different.

"What do the people here speak?" she asked Sassy as they walked closer and closer to the sea.

"It's Lebu," Sassy replied. "And they are very clear that is isn't Wolof. Theirs is a complicated history"

"Shall I resort to French then?" Frances asked, and Sassy nodded. Frances sighed in relief. At least something wouldn't be an uphill battle. She shielded her eyes against the sun that felt piercing, almost loud within her head, even though the sky was overcast. Goats and sheep wandered the lane, and Sassy pointed out which was which, for they looked very different from the animals Frances was used to.

They arrived at a door set within a wall close enough to the sea that Frances could hear the waves just beyond. They sat on a bench just there and removed their shoes.

"Kwame's sister is distraught since we have had no further word from him. Just be prepared. She tends toward the dramatic." Sassy said.

She opened the heavy outer door and led the way into the cool, dark hallway. They walked past a series of rooms that opened off the hall, and then they flowed into a larger central room, opened to the sky, with covered seating areas and a fountain in the center. To Frances, in her travel-beleaguered state, it felt like she had walked into a story from *One Thousand and One Arabian Nights*. The tinkle of water, the cool shadows around the circumference of the room, the scent of coriander and pepper, all as she had imagined from reading such tales.

"Sister!!! Thank the Prophet you are back!" Kwame's sister, Ami, wailed. Her hair looked like she had been tugging on it and her face was wet with tears.

"What is it? Is there news?" Sassy asked hurriedly.

"Yes! A man came by and dropped off a satchel. He said it was from Kwame and it is for you!"

"Did you open it?" Sassy asked.

Ami looked horrified. "Of course not! The man said it was for you!"

Sassy bit back her frustration. Ami was two parts whiny and eight parts fearful, and it, even on good days, drove Sassy mad. In this moment Frances stepped forward and spoke into the fray.

"Let us see the satchel now then." As Ami scurried away to fetch the bag, Frances led Sassy to the divan, and held her hands in a tight grip. "Courage, my sweet girl. We shall deal with whatever we find."

It was at that moment that little Sally Standing Bear, known to one and all as Sisi, came into the room, rubbing the sleep from her eyes and blinking hard at the sight of her mother and the small dark woman sitting with her. The child stopped and waited until the women turned their gazes to her. At eighteen months of age, she was precocious in speech and demeanor. She still carried the wisdom of the ancestors with her into her waking hours. So, it was with no true surprise to anyone that the first word from her mouth on seeing her grandmother was, "Celebi?"

Frances and Sassy were struck breathless, but what else was there to say but, "Yes, it is I. And I am your Grammy now, my lovie."

Little Sisi nodded her head, for of course she had been correct. "Long time!" She came toward her mother at a run and hurled herself into the laps of the two women. "Good sleepy, Mami. See Papi. Me fly. Me is bird."

Sassy was afraid to ask the follow-up but Frances couldn't wait. "What did you see, little bird?"

"Green trees. Papi happy." Sassy stroked her daughter's curls, swallowed a sob, and replied, "You are the smartest little bird I have ever known."

At that moment Ami came rushing back into the room holding a worn leather satchel at arm's length. "Sister, here it is! It is heavy! What is in it? Oh please, by the Prophet, blessed be his name, may it not be a head!"

"Ami!" Sassy stood abruptly, rolling Sisi into Frances's lap. "Control yourself! That is crazy talk!"

Sisi was watching all this with wide eyes, and Frances bent over her granddaughter and whispered in her ear, "We only hold the good thoughts, little bird. All the other thoughts just go away."

Sisi spoke into the shocked atmosphere of the room, "Me brave!" And she clamped her lips hard and nodded her head fervently.

Ami broke down into torrents of tears and hurried from the room. They could hear her cries gradually diminishing in volume as she ran to the farthest room of the house.

Sassy and Frances held a look over Sisi's head that expressed volumes. "Maybe you would like your Grammy to get you a wee snack, Sisi?"

But Sisi just shook her head hard and said, "No! Me look in samchel! Papi say look in samchel!"

There was something in that stubborn set of the child's jaw and her courage in the face of the unknown that struck a memory chord in Frances. Who had this little girl been? The memory was right there, tickling the back of Frances's brain. Who had been so brave and stalwart and faithful? Ah, Domnhu! That was who she had been. Domnhu! Besotted companion of Badh, from the land of Eiru in the long ago. How wonderful to see him again in this perfect little girl, with the same copper curls, then as now.

All this recollection happened in an eye blink as the three, connected by blood and fate, set the satchel onto the ground. Frances held Sisi tight, and Sassy bent to undo the catch and open the leather flap. She looked inside and let out a huge sigh of relief. Thanks be to the Goddess, it wasn't a head!

Sassy breathed out, and she reached in to lift out a metal box with a combination lock, and placed it on the small table.

"How will you open it?" Frances asked.

"If Kwame sent it to me then I know the combination," Sassy replied. "We always use the same code whenever we need to keep something from prying eyes." She fingered the lock and began to turn the dial. "Seven… to the right. Eleven… to the left. Three… to the right." The lock clicked open.

"Seven, eleven, three?" Frances asked quietly.

"We met on the seventh of November at three in the afternoon." Sassy replied, halfway between a smile and a sob.

"Perfect." Frances said. *"Allons-y, courage mes chères!"*

They paused, suspended, then little Sisi reached forward and lifted the lid. "Open, Mami!"

Frances and Sassy let out tiny nervous giggles and then did, indeed, look inside. There was a folded piece of paper with *"Ma femme"* written in a bold, deeply-slanted script.

"Kwame's handwriting?" Frances asked. Sassy nodded assent. She lifted the paper out, unfolded it and began to read aloud.

My beloved Sassy,

I so hope that you have not been frightened by the recent turn of events. I was all ready to leave Accra as planned, with the medical supplies for Ashanti. Right before take-off several gentlemen with large guns forced their way into the plane and made a cogent argument that I should divert the plane to an area where they felt the supplies would be more needed. I was in no position to disagree with them.

I may not disclose to you where I am at present, but I need you to do something to help facilitate my return to you and Sisi. In this box you will find bonds. How they came to be in the possession of my acquaintances here I cannot say. But it is to suffice that they require these bonds to be cashed, the money deposited into the Attijariwafa Bank account listed below, and this satchel then placed (with the deposit verification information secured within the metal box) outside our door at 2:00 AM. Someone will look for it each night until you are able to complete this task.

I have been assured that I may return to Senegal, and you, my love, when this is done. It is most likely that I will be coming overland, as the men have claimed ownership of our airplane.

What these funds will be used for, I cannot speculate. But I do believe that my new friends here believe their cause is just. I am concerned that there might be suspicion that would circle around you in these actions. I would advise that you tell no one of what I am asking of you.

Be confident that I am well treated here. Being a physician makes one's continued existence more likely in conditions such as these as I am a valued commodity.

Until I hold you in my arms again,

Kwame

Frances and Sassy only looked at each other without speaking for a long moment until finally Frances said, with a tinge of laughter in her voice, "Your father would have loved this!" And with that it was as if the spirit of Michael Kenneally flew into the room. They could feel the touch of his kiss upon their foreheads and could smell the tang of persimmon.

Sassy reached out and clasped Frances's hand. "With you here in the flesh, and Daddy in spirit, we shall not fail! Now, how, my mother the spy, do we go about this caper?"

"Me? A spy!" Frances responded with a bit too much astonishment in her voice.

"Oh, Mama. I know all about you and Da and your escapades!" Sassy said fondly.

They spent the rest of that day planning. At one point at about four in the afternoon, the fatigue of travel caught up with Frances and she fell asleep with her head resting on her elbow and her granddaughter heavy in her lap. She woke with a momentary sense of dislocation when Ami came into the room with a tray of tea and sliced mango. Upon tasting the fruit and asking its name she exclaimed, "So this is mango! Truly a divine fruit!"

Sisi, whose mouth was full of same fruit began to laugh and the high tripping sound lifted all their worries.

The next day the plans took action. Frances took a *car rapide,* which was more substantial than the conveyance she had ridden in yesterday, again with the negotiations handled by Sassy. She rode in a higher style to the downtown Dakar building of Société Générale. Her hair was upswept in a twist, her traveling skirt and coat had been pressed, and she had assumed the demeanor of a very rich and very bored woman. There in the bank lobby, with her handbag bulging with those spurious bonds, she asked to speak to a manager in the most impeccable Parisian French. Though a small woman, Frances had the ability to look imperious, and she was received with a kind of obsequious courtesy that would normally set her teeth on edge. However, in these circumstances it worked in her favor for them to assume her of the highest status and wealth. The manager was a thin man in his forties with wire-rimmed glasses and a good suit. Though he had gone to university in France, and though he was a liberationist at heart, the long-ingrained pattern of deference to the white person took over and he felt nervous.

"*Madame,* welcome to Société Générale. How may we be of assistance?"

Frances proceeded to unfold the story she and Sassy (with ghost-whispered assistance from Michael) had concocted. She was, she told the manager, a widow traveling in Senegal (true enough, stick to the truth whenever possible, so said Michael). Her late husband, she elaborated, had been an investor in several mining operations in West Africa and the Congo. "I have been advised by our business people to transfer these bonds into liquidity." Frances finished with a sniff, as if even discussing filthy lucre was beneath her.

"But of course, *madame*. May I see these bonds so as to begin the processing?"

Frances lifted the stack of bonds, now encircled by a red ribbon from her handbag and lowered them to the surface of the manager's desk with a small moue of disdain. "I am engaged to luncheon with *Madame* Senghor at the Presidential Palace today, so if you would be so kind as to expedite this transaction," and here she gave a little shiver, "I would be most pleased." She sat back, rested her hands in her lap, and looked as if her supply of patience would be finite. The manager hurried away, with the name *Senghor* buzzing like a hive of bees in his head. *The president's wife! Mon dieu!*

Frances willed herself to stillness, not allowing herself a look over her shoulder to see if this request was indeed being expedited, or if they had called the police on her. Her entitled demeanor had, like a tidal wave, pushed aside most normal procedures. The manager hadn't asked for her papers, he simply assumed she was who she said she was. What if, as he stepped outside the fog of confusion she had created, he began to wonder and insist on documentation? She drew upon her SIS training and began to calm herself by reciting Yeats' poetry, in Irish, to herself. That almost always worked. She could hear snatches of whispers, the sound of feet moving rapidly over marble floors, and in a remarkably short amount of time the manager returned, quickly returning to his pocket the handkerchief with which he had just wiped his brow, and placing a bank check before her.

"*Madame,* here are the funds from the bonds. I apologize for the wait."

Frances stood, calmly placed the bank check in her handbag and clicked it shut. "Thank you, *monsieur*. The service has been adequate. I will be telling *Madame* Senghor of the acceptable work that you do." She put out her hand, palm down, so that he was only able to squeeze the ends of her fingers, and then she turned and elegantly walked across the lobby and out the giant double doors held open for her by the manager as he raced ahead to assist her.

"*Au revoir, madame!* Société Générale appreciates your patronage." The manager actually bowed as she swept by.

Frances turned at the last moment and smiled at the man, granting him a genuine smile that reached her eyes. He felt the warmth of that and was taken aback. Then she proceeded down the wide front marble steps and into the waiting car. As the *car rapide* sped away she allowed herself the first deep breath in many minutes.

"It is to the Attijariwafa Bank then, *madame?*" the driver said, turning his head to look into the back seat at Frances and causing her to gasp as he barely missed three pedestrians.

"*Oui, monsieur, allons-y!*" Frances stifled a giggle and let herself rest back against the seat.

Ten minutes later the *car rapide* pulled up in front of the bank.

"Pull around the side please, *monsieur*." Frances directed. He did so and the cab came to rest under a small stand of trees that offered a hint of shade. Sassy was waiting there and let out a huge sigh of relief at the sight of her mother. As they had arranged, she nonchalantly walked by the cab, and received the handbag out the window. Without a word of acknowledgment, she walked back the way the car had come, and turned the corner to proceed to Attijariwafa Bank. Frances watched out the cab's back window until Sassy was out of sight, saying many prayers to many goddesses, then directed the driver to pull around the block and wait near the side street that was the entrance to the outdoor market.

Minutes ticked by with exquisite painfulness. The waiting, the waiting and not knowing! "I should have done every step of this myself!" she muttered under her breath.

"*Madame?*"

"It is nothing, *monsieur,*" she replied. The waiting!

Finally. Finally! Frances saw Sassy walk down the street and enter the market, looking for all the world as if she had nothing on her mind.

"Thanks be to Brig!" Frances said, aloud this time with so much joy in her voice that the driver's face lit up with a big smile. "Now, *monsieur,* if you would be so kind, I would like to return to Yoff."

Frances let herself enjoy the trip back to the village. She watched the streets fly by and soaked in all the color and life on the streets. The driver made good time since he obeyed no known traffic regulations, and Frances left the cab with a lightness in her step after leaving him a very generous tip.

"*Merci, madame!*" he called after her, and shouted out the same blessing in Wolof that the tuk-tuk driver had given her the day before.

"We will take all the help we can get!" Frances responded in Irish, waving and smiling brilliantly at him as he sped away.

An hour later Frances had shed the traveling suit and donned some of Sassy's cool clothes. Since her daughter was a good ten inches taller than she, Frances had had to roll up the waistband on the trousers and tuck the tunic hem up as well. She was sitting in the beautiful central room, playing finger games with Sisi when Sassy ran in, face flushed, and triumphant.

"We did it, Mama! We did it!"

Frances stood, holding Sisi in her arms and the three hugged and laughed and danced around in celebration until Ami came into the room.

"Please! Please! The noise! I have a headache!"

Frances and Sassy shared a look and then burst out laughing. Sisi joined in, thrilled to see her Mami and Grammere having such fun. Ami walked away in disgust, holding her head in her hands.

$$\text{☽ ◯ ☾}$$

That night Frances sat in the dark, tucked small on the floor in the hallway just inside the door. She had placed the satchel with the required bank information out in the sandy lane. She had made a bit of a show of it, breathing audibly, placing the bag with a bit of a thud, and then pushing the door to with a clear click. Then, like the Cree hunters she was descended from, she had silently gentled the door open a crack and settled down to wait. Instead of retreating to her bed, she sat, still as a sentry and quieting her own breath. After about twenty minutes she heard the almost indistinct sounds of hesitant footsteps in the lane. She rose, soundless, and peered out the small crack she had left at the door. As the person leant over to pick up the satchel, Frances slid out the door like a shadow and, whipped an arm around the fellow's neck while holding a knife to his throat with the other hand. The man was so startled he froze.

"Know this," she whispered in his ear. "If Kwame Boadu is not returned to his family with nary a scratch upon him, the entire might of the intelligence services of France, Great Britain and the combined wisdom of all the nomads on the Earth will find you and your fellow thugs, and we will make great pleasure in your destruction. Is that perfectly clear?" She spoke in French, and then repeated the entire message in English, just in case.

The man squeaked an affirmative response. Frances purposefully nicked his neck and he squawked. She drew an audible sniff of air and continued in Cree, "I have drawn your blood and will forever be able to find you, no matter where you hide. I smell you and your fear."

He couldn't understand the words, but he clearly understood the sentiment as Frances could smell the sharp tang of his urine as he wet himself. She pulled the knife down his back to the level of his kidney, and said, with the deepest gravel in her voice, "You have been warned!" And then she evaporated, back into the house. The man heard the click of the door, and he turned and ran like demons were chasing him.

$$\text{☽ ◯ ☾}$$

The next two weeks were a study in suspended torturous waiting. They attempted to do normal things, with one ear tilted to hear any sounds that would signify Kwame's return. Early morning would find Frances in the central courtyard saying the morning greeting prayers that she had learned from her Granny Sally. On the third day Frances felt eyes upon her and gave a small inner smile. After a while, little Sisi spoke.

"What doing, Grammere?"

"I am praying, little pearl."

"Aunt Ami pray."

"It is different, and yet the same. Would you like to join me?"

Sisi walked from the shadowed doorway and came into the new dawn light that now filled the courtyard. She still had sleep in the corners of her eyes, and she was trailing a quilt that gave her comfort.

"What I do?" she asked as she planted her sturdy, chubby little feet in the swept sand.

"Well, first, we listen, and then we stand like this." Frances turned to the east and stood with her feet hip-width apart and her knees slightly softened. She then lifted her arms to her sides and above her head and brought the palms together, letting the right hand slip down to rest halfway down the left palm. Sisi mimicked her, still holding on tight to her blanket so that it draped over her face.

"What we do next is a tradition from our foremothers. From my Granny and from her granny and all the way back. We say it is the work of the women to open their hearts to the world each day."

Little Sisi nodded solemnly, one eye peaking around the drooping blanket.

"And we begin by being grateful for our life, for this day, and we bring the sun down into our hearts."

Step by step the two danced through the morning prayer, the work of the women of the Cree, keeping the people's hearts and the world connected. They looked to the four directions, they gave their hearts out to the world, and welcomed the world back into them. One complete revolution around the four directions and then Frances came to a stop.

"We done?" Sisi asked.

"You may be," Frances answered. "But I will continue."

Sisi nodded again jutting out her chin in the way that gave Frances shivers of recognition, and said, "Me too!"

Another complete sequence all around the four directions, and Sassy, rubbing her eyes and yawning until her jaw cracked, came into the courtyard and picked up the prayer as they began again in the east.

Their routine was evolving into a semblance of normality: morning prayer, breakfast, chores and then the market.

Ami and her band of women from the village insisted on doing the cooking and cleaning, and Frances had to wrestle with them to make her own bed. Finally, after she literally had to clasp her sheets to her breast and refuse to give them up, she was able to give Ami an explanation she could understand.

"It is my tradition," she said. "My people, we clear our spaces from the night time to make open space for the day."

Ami tilted her head to the side as she mentally chewed on this, and then nodded. Tradition was to be allowed then. Sassy, listening from the hallway smiled and thought about how clever her mother was. Da had always called Mama his clever, clever girl. Sassy was swept to tears with the memories of her father. She said her silent gratitudes. Ever since he had passed to the Summerland on the very day that Sisi had been born, Sassy had continued her conversations with him in spirit. And now she told him, "Da, Mama is being clever once again."

Frances, always a magpie for languages, walked a half step behind Sassy and soaked in all the sounds and rhythms and music being spoken around her. She marveled at the fruits, the stacks of vegetables that she had never seen before. The people were loud and friendly and so very pleased when she attempted to converse with them in Lebu or Wolof. They laughed with her when she made a remark that went astray. Frances felt more alive than she had at any time since Michael had passed.

One morning, a full ten days after the events with the satchel, Frances was standing at a stall and being given a tutorial in the different varieties of mango. The fruit vendor was a woman about Frances's age. She was dressed in vibrant scarlet and lime green with a matching head wrap, and she gesticulated wildly, waxing poetical in Wolof about the ripening schedule of the fruits. Frances got about half of it and smiled broadly. Just then, in her ear she heard a man ask in English, "Frances Fletcher?"

In the space of two heartbeats Frances recalibrated. Without turning to look at the man she responded, "Not for a very long time."

He chuckled and then said in perfect Oxbridge English, "Shall I call you Mrs. Kenneally then?"

Frances whipped around drawing the small knife she had worn on her waist since the war. She pointed the tip just under the man's breastbone.

"Who is it that wants to know?"

The fruit seller felt the danger in the air. "*Madame,* do you need help?"

The man, about fifty years of age and astonishingly non-descript in appearance whispered softly, "MI6."

Frances lowered the knife to her side and looked over her shoulder at the fruit seller, "Thank you, *madame,* but for now I am fine."

As she maneuvered though the crowded market Frances saw Sassy negotiating for a quarter section of goat. Sassy spotted her mother and started to lift her hand and call out, but Frances gave her head a small almost indiscernible shake and turned to go down an even narrower alley that led to the fabric stalls. It was difficult to walk two abreast, and overlapping awnings kept the sun muted so it allowed Frances to duck, shift and slip into an empty stall to stand motionless behind a stack of bolts of fabric. The man walked past, went about ten feet farther, and then made his way back. By then Frances was standing at the entry to the stall watching his return.

"Your skills still appear to be operational," the man said. She said nothing. They stared at one another for a long thirty seconds. "Are you going to speak?" he asked.

"When I have something to say," she retorted.

"Her Majesty's Government has need of you," he said very softly.

"Her Majesty and her Government can stick their need up their arses!" Frances said venomously. "You left Michael Kenneally to rot in a labor camp for almost three years. He gave his health to your Majesty's Government, and it wasn't even his country. And it sure as hell and the devil isn't mine."

The man flashed a look of chagrin across his face. He had perspiration breaking out across his upper lip. He replied, "It was war, Mrs. Kenneally."

"When isn't it?" Frances asked. She pushed past him and walked back the way she had come, back into the sunlight, and found Sassy waiting in the center of the market scouring the crowd for her.

"Mama? Is it about Kwame?"

"No, my sweetness, it is just old ghosts come to haunt." The two made their way back home and spent the remainder of the day attempting the head wrap that Frances had found so fetching on the fruit seller.

"I am less than dazzling," Frances remarked after they both wiped tears of laughter from their faces.

"It's just that the head wrap is as tall as you are, Mama," Sassy said, bursting out laughing once again.

"Oh, it's short jokes again, is it?" Frances exclaimed in mock anger.

"Grammere little like me!" Sisi crowed, and they swooped up the little girl and sandwiched her between them.

"My Granny Sally use to say that everything is perfectly revealed, exactly as it is." Frances smiled into her granddaughter's neck.

$$\text{)} \bigcirc \text{(}$$

They went to bed that night with still no word of Kwame.

Sassy came in and sat on the edge of her mother's bed.

"How did you do it, Mama? How could you bear to wait and not know about Da for years?"

"You keep faith, my sweetness. You keep faith that love will survive. And then you hoard and polish the kernel of revenge that rests deep within you. You keep it for the day, perhaps, when you can let that seed blossom, and extract a payment of equal punishment for any who dare to hurt the ones you love."

Sassy saw her mother with fresh eyes. "Mama, I wouldn't ever want to be your enemy."

Frances grinned. It wasn't a smile. It was more like a baring of teeth. And she told Sassy about the MI6 operative who had found her in the market today.

"What do they want, Mama?"

"Whatever they want, my sweetness, is most certainly not what they are going to get."

$$\text{)} \bigcirc \text{(}$$

The next day at the market another man talked quietly into Frances's ear. This time she stepped back hard onto his toes and walked swiftly away. By the time she let herself be found he was sweating and limping slightly. This fellow was in his late thirties, with brown hair thinning on top and an oddly endearing smattering of freckles across the bridge of his nose brought out by the tropical sun. His eyes, a pleasing chocolate brown, looked earnestly into hers.

"Mrs. Kenneally?"

She stared at him. His accent was American.

"Miss Fletcher?"

She continued to stare. He looked flummoxed.

"The government of the United States of America wants your help."

"Why?" Frances lifted an eyebrow.

"If you could come to the Embassy tomorrow and ask to see Sheldon Stewart in the USAID office, he will explain it all to you," the man said.

"Why?" Frances asked again.

"Ma'am? Why what?" the man asked. He was sweating more profusely now and pulled a handkerchief out of his pocket and wiped his forehead. Frances had a moment of private delight at how many men she was making sweat lately.

"Why should I come talk to this Stewart fellow?"

"We might be able to assist in the return of your son-in-..." he started to say. Frances again pulled out her knife, and this time she pushed the tip past the fibers of his shirt until he could feel the sharp prick of steel at his diaphragm.

"Do not *ever* presume to barter my family's welfare for my assistance. Kwame Boadu returns home healthy and whole, and then, and *only* then, will I consider talking to your Mr. Stewart. Are we clear?"

A tiny dot of bright red emerged on the man's white shirt. "Crystal clear, ma'am," he said. Frances turned, went back to the center of the market, found Sassy and they returned to the house to wait out the day.

$$) \bigcirc ($$

On the next morning, while sorting through a pile of fruits that she had discovered she loved called papayas, Frances felt a person close behind her and on her right. That person said, "*Madame,* I beg you not to hurt me." It was said with sincerity and some humor. Frances simply turned her head and replied, "All right, for now, but no promises."

The man standing there was stunningly handsome. He was tall, and lean, with deep sun-darkened skin and a turban of vivid blue wrapped around his head and across his chin. He wore the robes of the desert and held himself with a certain kind of stillness that reminded Frances of her great-uncle Walter. It was difficult to ascertain his age. Frances thought he might be slightly younger than she. He smiled at her, and it was mesmerizing.

Frances swallowed and retorted, "That works for you often, does it?"

The man laughed, placed his right hand over his heart and bowed to her. "With the less stalwart, *madame,* yes?"

Now it was Frances's turn to laugh. "The day is exceptionally warm. Shall we find some cool fruit juice?" She said it loud enough for Sassy, two stalls down, to hear. The man agreed that that sounded delightful, and he and Frances made their way to a small outdoor café. He was the only man dressed as he was there, but he seemed to own the space and they sat and sipped their hibiscus juice, another new-found treat for Frances.

"My name is Alaman Sulaman of the Tuareg people. I bring greetings from Django Levevre, King of the Romani in the part of the world some call France. He says you knew his mother. There was evidently a rather memorable dance that you performed – something to do with a tambourine..." His French was oddly accented, the consonants soft and the "r"s rolled like a Scotsman.

Frances looked at him hard. This was information known only to Michael and her. And of course, to the Romani family she had traveled with in the War. "Did he tell you, perchance his mother's name?" she asked.

"Stalwart and suspicious," he replied and looked at her with approval. "Qualities that I'm sure held you in good stead when you danced with Marguerita."

Frances felt herself relax fractionally. "What precipitates this message from my Romani brethren?"

"I believe you have been approached by emissaries from the British and American governments. Am I correct?"

Frances said nothing and gave nothing away. The very same expressionless face that had driven her mother crazy was still hers to use when needed.

"*Monsieur,* I have almost finished my juice. And when it runs out so does my patience." She stood and placed coins on the table. "Please extend my best wishes to the Levevres." He watched her walk away and smiled to himself. That one was a lioness, a worthy mate of his friend Michael Kenneally.

) ○ (

The next day Frances found herself looking for the Tuareg man. She and Sassy had done their homework, learning all they could about the nomads of North Africa. Frances thought to herself, *Well, I did summon the wrath of all the nomads, didn't I?* Now she was eager to see this particular nomad again.

She and Sassy had gone to the market earlier than was their routine. Frances wanted to be able to see his approach, should he return. She was standing under a yellow and emerald awning, making a faint attempt at perusing tomatoes, when she saw a flash of that vivid blue he wore. He spotted her watching him, and he smiled that weapons-grade smile of his. The smile grew even brighter as he approached.

"*Monsieur* Sulaman," Frances said politely.

"*Madame* Kenneally," he replied, again placing a hand over his heart and bowing slightly. "Well met."

Frances fought hard to keep the corners of her mouth from stretching into a genuine smile.

"I neglected yesterday to ask after your husband," he said.

Frances eyes filled and spilled over. He immediately took her elbow and walked her into deeper shade.

"*Madame,* I am concerned. Is something wrong?"

Frances, head tipped down and to the side, blinked hard twice and lifted her eyes to his. "My husband is deceased." she said quietly.

"Allah yarhamo!" he replied, and he looked stricken. "Michael was my friend, and I owe him my life."

Frances reached out and took his hand, squeezing it hard. "*Monsieur* Sulaman, would you like to come back to our home and have tea?"

He could only nod. Frances and he walked back out into the stunning sunlight. She placed a hand above her eyes to look for Sassy who was pretending to inspect a rug. She signaled to her, and when Sassy approached she said loud enough for anyone to hear, "Sweetness, I have found a cousin of your father's. Shall we scoop him up and bring him home?"

They made their way through the crowd and back down the sequence of lanes leading them closer and closer to the ocean. At the house they went directly to the central courtyard. Ami came rushing out when she heard them, took one look at the tall berobed and turbaned Alaman Sulaman and beat a quick retreat into the kitchen. Sassy followed her to order up some tea and juice, and Frances and Alaman sat down on the cushioned bench near the fountain.

"My daughter's husband's sister," she explained with a wry look and a wave of her hand as the sounds of raised voices came to them. "She tends toward the histrionic." Alaman smiled in return and adjusted his head covering so that his face was fully revealed. Frances had a chance to look at him carefully as he stared into the fountain. He had a sharp bridged nose and dark lashes and eyebrows. Across the lower portion of his jaw, a faint indigo hue spoke of the brush of vivid blue fabric against his skin. His was a face that had seen and felt much. There were laugh lines and sun lines and worry lines. And for some reason Frances wanted to trust him.

"Tell me how you knew my husband," she said into the silence.

Just then Sassy returned with a tray that held teapot, juice carafe and several small glasses. She set it down on the small low table and took a seat on the edge of the fountain.

"*Monsieur* Sulaman, this is my daughter, Sally Standing Bear Fletcher Kenneally."

Sassy nodded in greeting and waited.

Alaman looked at Sassy and then gave her one of his knock-out smiles. "I see so much of your father in you," he said with affection.

"You knew my Da?" Sassy asked eagerly.

"We were just getting to that," Frances interjected. "Perhaps some liquid refreshment, and then you must tell us your tale." Frances said this with all politeness, but Alaman and Sassy heard the core of steel in her voice. Her daughter looked quickly at Frances in surprise, but Alaman simply nodded, and replied, "It is a tale that needs telling."

"In the spring of 1943 I was working with the Free French Resistance. I was eighteen years old and looked younger. My people are slow to grow beards, much like your Cree people I understand." He looked at Frances and she gave a nod of assent.

"I had been educated in monastery schools and my French passed muster, so I was recruited to infiltrate areas of Vichy France to collect information from the Romani camps. By then, the Roma had been the victims of much oppression by the Nazis, but some remained in the eastern edges of the Pyrenees and they had been instrumental in assisting Allied pilots and others who had ended up behind enemy lines in escaping into Portugal.

Frances interjected. "Is that how you come to know the Romani king?"

"Yes, *Madame* Kenneally. I met them about six months after your foray into France in their company."

Sassy looked at her mother in some alarm. "You went into Nazi occupied France?"

Frances lifted one corner of her mouth in a kind of smile and only said, "I had an appointment with a tambourine. Continue, *Monsieur* Sulaman."

"Django Levevre, he who is now King of the Caravans, is a few years my junior. When you traveled with his family he had recently gotten married and established his own caravan. Perhaps you recall that?" he asked Frances.

"There could have been a young couple much occupied with their newfound intimacy, so much so that we rarely saw them out of their caravan," Frances replied with a slightly bigger grin.

Alaman laughed aloud. "You knew them in the summer. I met up with them in the hard end of the following winter. Django and I traveled north to Tours to gather information. We were escorting a downed Canadian pilot back south when we were discovered by a Nazi patrol. We split up – Django and the pilot escaping – and me providing excellent distraction, if I do say so myself." At that he paused and looked down to the ground. Memories of horrors flashed behind his eyes.

"I take it that the next bit doesn't need re-hashing," Frances added quietly.

"*Oui, madame*. No re-hashing is necessary." He looked at her, and his eyes spoke volumes.

"Eventually, the Gestapo determined me to be, not a spy, not an enemy combatant, but merely a gypsy." He said this with a wry tone and then pursed his lips. "The soldier in charge of the relocation orders had an 'other than conventional' inclination, if you get my drift." He looked up at Frances under lowered lids. She felt embarrassment for him, but she kept her gaze steady.

"Did his 'inclination' contribute to your survival?" she asked with a calm tone.

"Most fortuitously, *madame*. Because of his 'curiosity' I missed the train sending undesirables to the camps in Poland, and I instead was carried by truck to a work camp in Germany. Later, of course, we learned about the destinies of those sent to the camps in Poland." Alaman swallowed and took a sip of tea. "It was in that work camp that I met Michael Kenneally."

Sassy and Frances gripped each other's hands. Here was some bit, some morsel of connection to Michael, perhaps some information that they had never known. Or maybe, just the joy and pain of being able to discuss him with someone who had known him.

"My first night in the camp I was battered and exhausted and…terrified, to be truthful." He stopped again, as if he had made a confession.

"*Monsieur* Alaman," Frances demanded that he look at her. "Only the insane do not respond with fear to fearful situations. We may then assume you to be a sane man. Continue." He flashed that high wattage smile, and Frances and Sassy both felt the impact.

"As I lay shivering and trying not to weep, I heard the most melodious voice. A man was reciting poetry in a language I didn't know, but the entire barracks was hushed, listening to every sound. It was beauty. It was a reminder that beauty still existed somewhere in the world. It got me through the night. I found out later that it was Michael, reciting Yeats in Irish. No one knew what he was saying, but we all knew what he meant."

"Michael used to say that Yeats was proof that there was a divine being," Frances said softly with the barest hint of a sob in her voice.

"Your Michael was the strongest man I have ever known. His was the magnetic moral center that held us all together in that place," Alaman added. "The combination of Yeats and Michael Kenneally, and most of us survived. *Madame,* you said that he had passed. Recently?"

At that moment little Sisi ran into the courtyard and hallooed to her mother and grandmother. "I made *pish-pish* in the potty!" She hurled herself into Frances lap and then caught sight of the strange man sitting there. She sat up straight. "Mami, who blue man?" She never looked away but gave him a stare that might have made lesser men quake.

Alaman placed his right hand over his heart and bowed at the waist. "My name, fierce one, is Alaman Sulaman, but I would be honored if you called me Blue Man."

There was a long pause, so long that Frances was quite tickled at her granddaughter's stoic response. But some knowledge, some vital quality of his nature must have been communicated, for Sisi nodded her head and replied, "We know you...Before, *oui?*"

Alaman felt a deep stirring within his memory, like a hint of a remembered scent or flavor. "Perhaps, little warrior, perhaps. But for certain I knew your Grand Da. And you are truly of his blood."

Sisi leaned back onto Frances's chest and reached one dimpled hand up to reach her grandmother's cheek. "We keep him, okay, Grammere?"

The adults laughed and Sisi jiggled up and down on Frances's lap.

"It shall be as you wish, little pearl. Just as you wish," Frances said through her laughter.

They settled down to tea and juice and generalized chitchat about Alaman's home and people. After she had consumed a biscuit, Sisi clambered down from Frances, and crawled into Alaman's lap. He was startled into silence, but bit by bit he relaxed and allowed himself the pleasure of the weight of the child, trusting and sacred. Sisi, having found her preferred napping spot, let her eyes drift shut and began to snore softly.

The adults picked up the tale of the labor camp in hushed voices.

"You said that Michael saved your life..." Frances stated.

Alaman took a deep breath and asked, "*Madame,* may I ask of what accident or malady our Michael died?"

Frances looked at him and saw pain and guilt. It puzzled her, but she responded calmly, "His heart was damaged by a fever he contracted in the labor camp. After the war, his health was never robust, but he found joy and purpose, and we found happiness and peace together. His beautiful heart gave out eighteen months ago. He was but sixty years old."

Alaman's mouth twisted as if in torment. "*Madame,* I need to confess something to you. If, at the end of my tale you wish me to leave I will comply without hesitation."

Frances and Sassy exchanged looks that held an entire conversation. They nodded in agreement. No matter what information was coming, it would be better to know it, they concurred.

"It was December of 1944, and it was bitter cold. The Germans were planning what for them were reduced Christmas festivities – by then the Allies were causing them some pain. We, the inmates were always hungry, always cold, always exhausted. A fever and a bad throat ran through the camp, and several men died of it. I was ill, Michael was ill, by Allah, we all were ill. My fever made me mad and I decided to sneak into the soldiers barracks and steal some food that they had in their personal cabinets – they had received Christmas packages from home and had been bragging to us about how their families loved them and how our people were garbage. Michael grabbed me by the shoulder and tried to stop me from going. He tried to reason with me, but I was beyond that. I can hear him pleading. He called me all kinds of fool and told me that the guards would kill me for Christmas sport. I was hungry beyond description. I was sick and tired, and tired of being sick and tired. I felt something in me snap. Who was this man to tell me what to do? I felt like we were all going to die anyway; I wanted to have some say over when. I pushed Michael aside and ran out the back door of our barracks. I felt like I had lost my mind.

"I was almost to the guard's barracks when I heard Michael out front, singing the 'Internationale.' His cover identity in the camp was as a communist called Michel Didier. They would have killed him long before if they knew he was a British agent. He was so very good at subterfuge he had them completely fooled as to his true identity. But the Nazis hated the Reds too. He had run out front and was singing to provoke them. He was pulling their attention away from me. He must have seen the guards coming back to the barracks. Two minutes later and they would have found me in there. I froze in that shadow.

"The soldiers stopped in their tracks and watched Michael as if he were an exotic animal in a zoo. Slowly they began to walk toward him and one shouted, 'Shut up, you commie!'

"Michael kept singing. I saw him slide his eyes toward the shadow and I could tell he saw me there. I started to sneak back toward our barracks and I watched what happened next."

Alaman's voice dropped, and he hung his head down, staring at his linked hands. He told them how Michael kept singing as his voice was cracking, but he kept it up as they approached him, and one guard swung a fist into his jaw. He nearly toppled, but straightened and resumed singing, switching into 'God Save the King.' The soldiers seemed confused but started taking turns slugging Michael until he crumpled onto the ground and couldn't get to his feet. They delivered multiple kicks to the gut and one particularly vicious boot to the kidney. One guard spat on him as he lay there, and the another shouted, 'You'll stay there all night, you piece of shit!'

"We all watched out the front windows. When we tried to go retrieve Michael, a guard saw us and threatened to kill us all if we moved him before dawn. As night fell a sleety rain began to cover Michael's body. We would call to him, and sometimes he could respond, but as the night wore on we heard him less and less."

Michael had felt the boot in his back, and then blacked out. When he came to he was shivering violently and there was a fire in his chest. He could hear some fellows, yes there was Pointpierre the Belgian anarchist, calling to him. "Michel! Stay with us! Don't give up!" He kept drifting in and out of awareness. He began to long so powerfully for Frances that he could feel her near. She always smelled of the woods to him, new leaves, moist soil, old wisdom. She was so very, very near that he smiled at how pretty and keen she was. "My sweet clever girl!"

Her form grew even closer. "Don't you dare die. Do you hear me? You promised to make an honest woman out of me, and I am holding you to that."

He felt her fingers, cool and smart, brushing across his forehead, easing the fever that raged there. "This is a tough spot, beloved," he confessed. "It may not be up to me whether I live or no."

"Unacceptable!" Frances sternly replied. "Completely and totally unacceptable. This entire war was your idea, you know. I could have remained safely on the other side of the Atlantic, but no. I had to follow some rascal who called himself Malcolm Reynolds into the valley of death!" She sounded truly angry now, and Michael wished he had the strength to chuckle. "If you leave me widowed before I have a chance to be a bride, I will haunt you forever!"

"There are worse fates I could imagine," he replied. She made a concession of a slight smile and handed him a shimmering golden globe about the side of a rugby ball. It tingled in his hands and felt like summer and falling in love and hope. He clutched it to his heart.

"I'll try," he said. With that he went more deeply into the realm of the unconscious.

Alaman told them how at first light they had swung the door open, and several men lifted and dragged Michael back into the barracks, stripped him of his clothes and rubbed him down with the tatters of blankets that they had.

"Michael's fever worsened and we thought he would die. The other men were furious with me. I had been rash, stupid, selfish, they said. And now Michael, our lodestone, had sacrificed himself for me. We had been given days of rest over Christmas, so one of us could be with him at all times. We kept constant vigil. He was delirious, kept calling out for Celebi. Is that you, *madame*?"

Frances was stark white with tiny tight brackets around her mouth. She could only nod in assent. Alaman continued.

"His fever finally broke after six or seven days, but we still feared for his life. His breathing was so labored. He was as weak as kitten, he said. For the rest of our time there before the Allies liberated the camp, we all took turns doing his work so that he wouldn't be considered dead weight and shipped away or shot. It took months, and then he started to get stronger.

"We had been an odd jumble of leftists and communists and clergy and homosexuals – all the odd bits the Nazis wanted to clear away from society. But Michael's weakness made us all stronger. We became cohesive, a true clan of survivors. From that night on, no one gave up, no one fell to despair. We all vowed to live and let our survival be the best revenge. But our Michael, he was damaged, and that was all my fault."

Alaman's last words were so soft that the women had leaned in to hear them. He finally lifted his eyes to look at those women, Michael's wife and daughter, and the granddaughter he had never seen, still asleep in Alaman's lap. He knew they must hate him, for he still hated himself.

Frances stood abruptly and a white cloth napkin fell from her lap onto the floor. She rushed out the doorway, blinded by her tears. Sassy stood to follow her, but Alaman said urgently, "Miss Sally, please let me." He indicated the sleeping child in his lap and Sassy came and gently lifted her daughter into her arms. Alaman walked, like a condemned man, out the doorway to catch up with Frances.

She had raced down the hallway and out into the odd milky white sunlight of midday. Her feet took her toward the ocean, until she came to stop with her toes at waves' end. Alaman came up behind her on her right and waited about a yard away.

"*Monsieur* Sulaman, what do you believe about our lives after death?" Frances asked, tossing her words toward the waves. He hesitated, not quite sure he had heard her correctly.

"After death, *madame*? What do I think happens?" he queried.

"*Oui.*"

"The Prophet, blessed be his name, tells us that we may approach an eternal paradise, if we have lived as one should," he replied.

Frances chuckled at the obtuse response. She had lived her entire life fluent in obtuse response and she recognized in him a kindred spirit.

"The Prophet, and Jesus Christ, and Joseph Smith, and a host of others say the same thing. But what I asked you, *monsieur,* is what *you* believe." Her voice was thick with tears, but she spoke deliberately.

He walked up slowly to stand next to her and together they watched the sea.

Frances spoke, "The people here worship Mame Ndiare. She was a warrior who came with magic horses to save the people when they were under attack. Or, She is the Great Mother. Or, She is the ocean itself."

"What do you worship, *madame*?" he asked quietly.

Frances laughed. "No wonder Michael cared for you. You answer one question by asking another."

Alaman shook his head hard, like he was shaking off a stinging fly. The notion that Michael had cared for him, and that Frances thought it true was too much.

Still staring straight ahead she spoke, "There was time when Michael risked himself to take care of me as well. And I know this to be true, *monsieur*. There is no force on Earth that could stop that man when he decided to rescue someone. You must lay down your guilt. It doesn't serve you, and it does not honor his memory." Frances reached out and took Alaman's hand. "We have much to discuss and discover, *monsieur*. If you will allow?"

Alaman looked at this woman and saw someone small in stature but fierce in spirit. He thought, for a moment, that he saw her face shift and change shape. It was as if he saw a dozen faces, one after the other, each with the same undying loyalty shining out of the eyes of each visage. "I am your servant, *madame*," he finally whispered.

Together they turned and walked silently back to the house, Frances, still feeling the stinging sleet of that night some twenty years before on her skin.

$$\text{☽ ◯ ☾}$$

The rest of the day passed without incident. Alaman sat on the floor of the central courtyard and showed Sisi how to make shadow animals with his hands. Sassy looked up at every sound, hoping beyond hope that Kwame would be coming through the door. Frances sat near the fountain and trailed her fingers through the water, deep in memory and recollection. Suddenly it occurred to her that she had no idea why Alaman had come to them. Breaking from the peacefulness of the mid-afternoon, she asked, suddenly, "*Monsieur,* how did you know to look for me here? And why now?"

Sassy looked up from the accounts she had been doing, startled. Yes, it had blown by them, what with the connection to her Da and all that taking the foremost spot in their brains. But why was this man here now?

Frances's voice took on a steelier tone. "You mentioned the Americans and the British. How did you come to know about them as well?"

Alaman looked up quickly and then lowered his eyes to his hands. Sisi grabbed his fingers and began to manipulate them and talk to them with her own special language.

"*Monsieur?*" Frances said in that voice that Sassy remembered from her childhood – the voice that brooked no dissent.

"*Madame,*" he said and lifted his eyes and then shot her to the backbone with that smile of his. "*Madame,* there appears to be a competition for you?"

"What sort of competition?" Sassy interjected, but Frances said nothing, just kept looking at him with an unblinking gaze. And then she spoke with a voice dripping in contempt.

"What our friend here means, my love, is that some governmental bodies would like me to engage in acts of espionage on their behalf. Am I correct, *Monsieur* Sulaman?"

"Alaman, please. Call me Alaman," he implored, while admitting nothing.

"There was that pompous product of Oxford or Cambridge, then the sweaty young American from…Indiana or Illinois if I correctly heard his accent. Then you. For whom do you stand, Alaman?" Frances said his name with painful emphasis.

"Mostly, I stand for myself and my people," he replied. Frances only glared at him. "But on occasion I have worked for the benefit of the French and DGSE."

"And in this instance?" Frances asked, each word slipping out like mercury.

"Would you believe…Interpol?" he asked with a bit of a flirtatious gleam in his eye.

Frances couldn't help herself. She laughed outright, and then brought herself under control. "No, actually, I would not believe that. But for now, it will suffice."

Two days later Kwame Boadu finally walked in the front door and into his wife's arms. He was hale and whole, but tired and dusty from making his way back from the Congo via, bus, tuk-tuk, ox cart and, at one low point, bicycle. His wife Sassy wept, his daughter Sisi laughed and pulled his beard, his sister Ami wailed and threw her apron over her head, and his mother-in-law Frances felt herself relax for the first time in three weeks. His relief at the sight of these women he loved was so huge that he kissed and hugged and exclaimed over them all again and again.

They helped him settle for some food and drink after he had bathed the dust of the road off, and he gave them all the details. His story was as they had suspected. He had been kidnapped at rifle point, made to fly his plane east to the Congo, and then had his ransom negotiated and delivered by Frances and Sassy. He was sitting on the floor with Sisi in his lap and his arm around Sassy when he looked at Frances on the divan and said,

"The man who retrieved the bank information told an interesting story."

"Oh really?" Frances replied nonchalantly.

"Yes, evidently, he had been accosted by a six-foot Amazon who pinned him to the ground, held a giant knife to his crotch, and threatened his manhood. She was accompanied by a host of other Amazons. Truly a frightening sight, he said."

Frances's lips twitched as she fought the grin that threatened to spread wide across her face. But all she said was, "Yes, he was right to be truly afraid."

Kwame looked at his mother-in-law and responded in his native language, "A woman of valor is a formidable thing."

Frances lifted an eyebrow at him, and he responded in kind.

108

It was late that night and Frances had awoken drenched with a hot flash and still pulling the cobwebs of her dream with her. Michael had been in the dream, trying to tell her something, something about Alaman. She stilled her breathing and spoke aloud into the velvet dark, "Beloved? Come to me. Talk to me. I miss you so!" She could feel a tiny breeze come in through the high window and hear the swoosh of the waves on the shore. "Should I trust or fear this Alaman?" Frances felt a warmth, like a man's hand atop her heart. Was it truly Michael, or her branded memory of his touch? And then she felt the whisper of pressure on her lips and recognized that kiss. "So, I trust the desert man then?" The breeze intensified and the curtain moved at the windows. "Could you be more cryptic?" she said with asperity.

She took herself out into the courtyard, to listen to the sounds of the fountain and regain her equilibrium. She had only been there a few moments when Kwame came out as well. He had on the loose white tunic that Senegalese men wore, and his bare feet were soundless as he walked toward her.

"Couldn't sleep?" he asked.

"Some, and then not," Frances replied with a smile in her voice. "And you? I would have thought you would be dead to the world after the journey you've had."

"I was, but something woke me," he answered. "*Mame* Frances, Sassy mentioned some European agents, that they came to find you? Are you troubled by that?"

"Exceedingly," Frances said softly. "I thought that I had left all that far behind."

"Can you ever tell us what transpired for you there, then?"

She only shook her head, and he could see the motion faintly in the glimmer of starlight that fell into the courtyard. "I can only tell you that nothing glamorous took place, and that the stench of war soaked into every pore. I have no wish to wade into such waters again."

Just then they both heard the door pull, the tiny tinkle of the bell at the outside door.

"Were we expecting company?" Kwame said as he stood and headed toward the door on high alert.

"I have discovered that Senegal is not a restful place," Frances replied as she followed him. He motioned a hand to stop her, but she ignored him and kept on his heels. As they reached the door the bell rang again, just one light tug on the rope.

Kwame spoke through the closed door. "Who is it at this hour?"

A deep male voice replied, "I am Alaman Sulaman. I come in peace."

They could hear a small chuckle as he said these last words. Frances stiffened and whispered to Kwame, "It is best if we let him in before he wakes the whole neighborhood."

Kwame unlatched the heavy wooden door and swung it open, only wide enough for the man outside to slip in. Then he locked the door again, and as they stood in a clutch in the hallway said in his most formal tones, "And to what do we owe the honor of this visit, Mister Sulaman?"

"I come seeking your and *madame's* help."

Frances pulled at Kwame's arm to stop him from replying. The silence held until Alaman chuckled. "*Ma lionne.* That is what Michael used to call you. I have a healthy appreciation of your fierceness, *madame,* but as I appear to be bleeding, I was hoping I might be invited in." He pulled his robe away from his chest and Frances and Kwame heard a sucking sound.

"Holy Mary, Mother of God!" Frances retorted. "Is it always so dramatic around here?" And she turned to walk back into the central courtyard, allowing Kwame to help Alaman enter and then rest down on the divan with a groan.

As if she had heard a summons, Sassy spoke from the shadows, "I believe we need water, medicine and bandages," and she left quickly to go back into the house to retrieve those things.

Frances and Kwame set about lighting several lamps and positioning some pillows behind Alaman's back. With the lamplight they could see that his robe and tunic were drenched with a spread of blood that looked black in the dim. His face was tight, and he held his lips pressed firmly together. The occasional groan slipped through though.

"Stoicism is as stoicism does," Frances muttered to him, and his laughter rode atop a moan. "What are we dealing with here? Knife? Bullet? Cannon ball?"

Alaman laughed again and moaned even louder as he said, "Bullet. Small caliber. From behind." And with that he passed out.

Sassy brought the medical supplies and hurried back toward the kitchen to fetch hot water. Frances pulled Alaman's robe aside and used her knife to cut the fabric of his tunic, gently drawing the cotton away from the raw wound just below his ribcage on his left side.

"We need to see if the bullet passed through," Kwame said. Frances held a lamp high so he could see better and she looked at Sassy with relief when the young woman re-entered the courtyard.

"This is one of those times it's good to have a doctor or two in the family," Frances said wryly.

Kwame and Sassy set about discovering the extent of Alaman's injuries, working swiftly without even needing to speak. Frances watched her highly competent daughter and son-in-law and felt a rush of pride. Here were two who were, indeed, doing all they could, whenever and however they could.

Kwame looked up at Frances and motioned for her to lower the lamp closer to Alaman's body. "It looks like the bullet went clean through, and by the grace of God, seems to have missed his spleen. I'll make some stitches and we can pack the wound. *Mame* Frances, do you think we need to be concerned that his enemies may have followed him here?"

Frances shook her head. "No. I believe *Monsieur* Sulaman to be quite adept at deception, even while bleeding. But it would be best if we can move him out of the common area before the village women arrive. The fewer who know of this, the better."

Kwame and Sassy bent back down to their work, and in short order Alaman was trussed up and ready to be moved. Sassy and Kwame each put one of his arms over their shoulders and hoisted him upright. He was surprisingly heavy and still unconscious, so they needed to drag him toward the back bedroom where Frances had been sleeping, the most private of the rooms in the house. She slipped around them and raced to her bed to pull back the light blanket and laid some towels over the mattress.

Frances said, "There's two hours before dawn. I'll sit with him. You two go back to bed. Sisi will be in to pounce on you before long." She smiled at the two before her and felt the rush of joy and love that is the visitation of grace at the most unexpected times.

"You will call for me if something changes with him?" Kwame insisted, "If he spikes a fever or the wound breaks open?" Frances nodded and gave a small smile. In this light Kwame's skin melted with the shadows in the room, and it was only when he smiled back that she saw the flash of his teeth and the warmth of that smile.

"Please, Kwame, don't worry. I have done such as this before."

He looked at her sharply but decided not to pry. He left the bedroom and softly closed the door. When Frances heard the gentle click she reached forward and rested the back of her hand against Alaman's forehead. Normal.

She sat silently through the pre-dawn hours, letting her mind drift back to the night she had tended to Michael's gunshot wound, the night he had appeared at Bletchley and caught her up in the mad escapade to France. She had known him as Malcolm Reynolds then, but in her heart she had known that she had always known him, whatever name the world chose to call him.

Frances was deep in the recollection of those hours, remembering every detail as clearly as if it had all happened last night. The owls calling in the nearby woods. The smell of soil. Her awareness of that man on that bench before her. She was so deep into her memories that this man on this bed before her needed to call her name several times before she came back to the present.

"*Madame? Madame? Madame* Kenneally?"

Frances started, and then leaned forward to hear the raspy voice.

"What do you need, *monsieur?* Water?"

He nodded and she could see the movement of his head in the thin silver light seeping into the window. Frances brought the cup to his lips and gently lifted his head as he swallowed. When she had rested him back down, he said, "I thought we had agreed for you to call me Alaman, *madame.*"

Frances snorted. "Well, Alaman, since I have had the privilege of seeing the inside of your guts, perhaps we should agree for the formalities to cease, and you to call me Frances."

She smiled and he felt himself forgiven for something he couldn't even name. They sat for some minutes before Frances spoke again. "The time has come for you to tell me why you have sought me out, Alaman."

There was a long pause of silence. Frances thought that he had fallen back to sleep. But then his voice, firmer now, came to her in the half light.

"I came at the behest of the Grandmothers. They wish to call you into the service of the Goddess."

Of all the things he could have said pertaining to his purpose, this was the one Frances did not expect. She had spun many ideas about his agenda in her mind. In service of the British? That seemed unlikely, but then Michael had worked for the Brits, and that was passing strange. He had mentioned that he sometimes worked for DGSE, and the French had many fingers in many pies here in Africa, still trying to exploit and control their former colonies. So that alliance was possible. And then, his familiarity with the Roma, that seemed a plausible motivator, but for what reason she hadn't been able to ascertain. But to serve the Goddess? And whose grandmothers was he referring to? She decided to give nothing away as yet.

"Are you delirious from pain or fever, Alaman?"

"No, Frances. I am *compos mentis*. And I ask you again, who do you worship?" His voice had taken on a quality of solemnity, as if he were asking her to declare herself in some ritual or initiation.

Frances knew this tone. She had heard it from her Granny Sally when she had declared Frances to be the keeper of the Stories. She had heard it from Magdalena and Old Shelta when they had shown her the mysteries of the standing stones in Kerry. And it plucked a chord in her, some subterranean vibration that shifted time and space, leaving her exposed and porous. Frances felt herself in the now and the then, standing tall to declare her alignment with the divine. She felt Granny Sally beside her and felt Michael's hand resting on the back of her neck as he had so often done.

"My soul has pledged itself over and over to the Great Mother, the Maker of all Things, to She of a Thousand Names," Frances replied.

"The Grandmothers wish for you to make the way ready for Her return," Alaman continued.

Frances felt the weight of that request and felt the rightness of it as well. Granny Sally had said, forty years ago, that the time was coming. So now, she, Frances, was to help all come to fruition. She felt the power of that soul contract, and something clicked within her. She had been making herself ready for this task all her life.

☽ ○ ☾

An hour later, Sassy poked her head into the room to discover her mother and the wounded man both sound asleep with hands clasped. Nothing could have surprised her more, for Frances, while a warm and generous soul, was slow to make physical contact outside her small family circle. Yet, here she was, palm to palm with the wounded Tuareg man. Sassy backed away and went into the kitchen to warn her sister-in-law to avoid the back bedroom and aim to keep some quiet in the house today.

A short time later Sassy went back to that bedroom, making a noticeable amount of noise in doing so, with a tray loaded with tea and porridge. She shouldered the door open and saw her mother at the window, pulling back the shutters and letting the marigold light flood into the room.

"Good morning! How's our patient this morning?" Sassy sounded a bit too bright, and Frances shot her a curious look.

"I am much improved from when you saw me last, *Madame* Sally," Alaman said, aiming for a vigorous tone and managing one substantially less than stentorious.

"Sassy, please. I think we are on a first name basis, yes?" And Sassy gave him a full-faced smile that lifted the corners of her eyes, a trait that she had inherited from her father. Alaman's breath caught short at the sight of it. Seeing Michael in his daughter was both a sweet pleasure and sharp grief.

Frances came to help Sassy set out the breakfast, putting some more pillows behind Alaman's head, and checking his bandage.

"We'll need to change that dressing this morning, but for now, let's see if you can eat something," Sassy said gently. She felt her mother's gaze upon her. It was always like sunshine when Frances looked at her, warm and encompassing. She turned her head to look into her mother's eyes and was startled to see tears there, pooling but not falling.

"Sassy, my sweet chick. When you and Kwame are available, we need to discuss what Alaman has shared with me, and to figure how to deal with the foreign agents interested in my cooperation." Frances looked settled in herself, and Sassy knew that look. Frances was rock solid and implacable. Sassy called it the 'Injun look,' and that always made Frances laugh.

"Ok, Mama. I can tend to our friend here if you want to go lie down for a while." Sassy thought her mother looked a bit pale.

"I don't want to sleep, but as your father would say I wouldn't say no to a *taoscán* of *uisce beatha*. Yes, a good dram or two of whiskey would fix me right up. But, this being a Muslim country, that may be out of reach at the moment." Frances shook her head a bit to sweep away the cobwebs. She brushed her hands down over her clothes as if dusting herself off. Sassy recognized the motion as what she had learned from her Grammy Magdalena to 'clear the pixies away.' "Most useful at the moment would be a bath," Frances said, and Sassy left well enough alone.

The morning progressed with frequent bursts of laughter rolling through the house as Sisi, now fully awake and reveling in her father's return, hung on him like a limpet and demanded the telling of the "stowey" at least a dozen times. Frances, after having bathed and put on one of the loose flowing house dresses that she had purchased in the market and had needed to savagely hem, walked into the courtyard to hear Kwame in the midst of the "stowey" once again.

"Papa was far away, little monkey, and some people wanted to get a present from me. So, I gave them the present and then I took a ride on a truck. It was through the jungle. Then I took a ride on a bus to a city, then a ride on a motorcycle to another city, then a ride on another bus to get to Senegal. I was on a little bus – like a tuk-tuk – when it broke down. So, your Papa was smart man, and I traded my watch for a bicycle and rode it home to you!"

Sisi crowed with delight and patted her father's cheeks with her dimpled hands. "Smart Papi!"

"Yes, littlest monkey, I am smart, but in truth your Mami and your Grammere are smarter by far. They made sure that those men got the present they wanted so badly. I think your Mami deserves a big kiss, do you?"

He reached over to grab Sassy's hand and pulled her to him. They kissed and made a big smacking sound that sent Sisi into more paroxysms of giggles. Frances stood and watched, sending prayers of gratitude again that Kwame had been safely returned to them. And an even deeper gratitude that her beloved daughter had found a partner who was worthy of her. They were both healers, Sassy and her Kwame, and the bonds of love and respect between them made everyone they came into contact with feel held and cared for. *Michael, you taught her well what to look for in a man.*

Sassy spotted her and began to laugh. "Mama! You look proper Yoff now!"

"A Yoff woman who needs to cut a yard of fabric away at the hem, you mean?"

Kwame came forward and took Frances's hand, lifted it and kissed it gallantly. "Good things come in small packages. That is the saying, yes?"

"Did they teach you that chivalry at Oxford, son-in law?" Frances asked gaily.

"No, mother-in-law. This is my natural born manner of being. It's a gift!" He smiled and then laughed and Sisi joined in laughing too, swept away by the enormous relief amongst her grown-ups.

Frances sat with them by the fountain and accepted a glass of peppermint tea. As she sipped it, she firmed her resolve and spoke. "Our bandaged friend is not amongst us by happenchance. He came looking for me and managed to end up between some battling factions. Hence the bullet wound which you two so skillfully took care of. Seriously, Sassy, you astound me. Your capacity to care for others has overcome your empathy with their pain. Brava, my sweet chick. Brava!"

Sassy blushed and swept Sisi's hair back off her forehead. "Thanks, Mama. But it doesn't feel like courage when in the middle of things. It's just what needs doing. Now – quit stalling and tell us what Alaman is here for."

Frances took another deliberate sip of tea. "This tea is really quite good. Ami does a wonderful job…"

"Mama!"

"All right, all right." Frances laughed softly. "Unto the breach, then. Our friend, Alaman, has been sent to find me by a group he calls The Grandmothers. They have work they wish for me to do. As things would have it, the British and American intelligence services also have tasks they wish me to take on. Hence the competition."

"What tasks?" Kwame asked quietly.

"And who are these Grandmothers?" Sassy asked in a less dulcet tone.

"I believe that Alaman is best suited to answering your questions," Frances replied.

Kwame stood and lifted Sisi, to carry her into the kitchen to be minded by his sister, but Sisi put up a squawk. "I want see blue man!" she insisted, and after they exchanged looks Frances nodded, adding, "She is in this too, then. Let us all go see the Blue Man!"

As they entered the bedroom they could all see that the Blue Man looked enormously better. He had been sleeping, but his eyes fluttered open as they came through the door, and he looked at them all with that direct and penetrating stare that held no sign of fever or distress. A remarkable turn-around from last night.

"Well done, man. Your recuperative powers are impressive," Kwame said.

Alaman smiled a sly smile and replied, "I have many guides and guardians."

Sassy felt the end of her patience tether and said sharply, "Shall we get on with this? What do you want of my mother?"

Frances snorted, and Alaman's eyes widened a fraction. "*Absolument, Madame* Sassy. We shall 'get on with this.'"

Kwame perched on the window ledge. Frances and Sassy took the two chairs. Sisi clambered up on the bed.

"Careful, little pearl! The Blue Man has a booboo." Sisi just nodded and crawled a bit more slowly until she came to rest at Alaman's hip. She leant back against him and looked at all the adults with wide eyes and a twitch of the impatience her mother was feeling.

Alaman took a deep breath, let his eyes come to half-mast and began. "The time of the Great Mother is returning. You all know this, yes?" He waited for the four to nod before he continued. "And there is a Book, yes?"

The three adults went stone-faced, but Sisi began to chant, "Grammere has book! Grammere has book!"

Alaman chuckled and said, "Out of the mouths of babes!"

Sassy began to speak, but Frances reached over and took her hand to stop her. Frances spoke in a tone that lifted the hairs on the back of the neck. "Friend, Alaman. We do not speak lightly of any Book."

He had the grace to look chastened, and then continued, "My apologies. It is just so very exciting to be in the presence of the motherline of Atvasfara, she who has been Sally Standing Bear."

"Supposing that there is a Book, why do you know of it and what do you want with it, friend?" Sassy sounded less than friendly.

"Well, that is why I have been sent to seek out your mother." Alaman cleared his throat and stroked Sisi's copper curls. His long fingers swept through her hair like water weeds at the shore. They all watched, mesmerized, as the emotional temperature in the room began to fall.

"The ways of the Goddess have gone underground for a thousand years or more. There have been sanctuaries of her knowledge and esteemed memory holders who live in every corner of the globe, women like the estimable Sally Standing Bear," he said.

"And like your grannies Magdalena and Old Shelta," Frances directed this to Sassy who looked momentarily stunned and then focused.

"These Wise Women have a council, and they meet in their dreams and in their visions and in their sacred medicine journeys. Of this council there is a central group we simply call The Grandmothers who speak and make decisions for what action can be taken in the greater world. My own *grandmère*, my *jida*, is one of these. They have decided that the seed of Goddess knowledge must be planted now, to come to fruition at the time of Great Change. And for this task they have selected Frances Fletcher Kenneally of the clan of Kakehtaweyihtam, Sally Standing Bear Porteaux, she who had been Atvasfara, High Priestess of Isis." Alaman finished with a flourish and an arm gesture toward Frances like a courtier making a gracious bow. The room sat in a frozen silence. Even Sisi didn't have anything to say in response to Alaman's pronouncements.

Finally, Sassy in a strained voice, queried, "And my mother is to be a seed planter? What in the name of the sweet Christ is that?"

Frances could tell that Sassy was close to some breaking point. She only sounded like the old men of Ballinskellig when truly flustered. "What it means, my darling, is that I am being asked to stir the pot, pull back the curtain, spread the Goddess gospel like some twentieth century John the Baptist."

Into the frisson of the room that was littered with Frances's metaphors and similes, Sisi spoke up. "I come too?"

$$) \bigcirc ($$

Later that day Frances walked along the beach, mulling the new information about The Grandmothers and their summoning of her for their purposes. Still persisting was the need to deal with, avoid or circumvent the intelligence agents that wanted something of her. Too many needs… Frances couldn't clear the threads of thoughts.

She turned to the scene before her to find her center. She saw that the fishing boats had been pulled up high on the sand above the high tide line to rest. They were brightly painted, vivid turquoise and orange, some with eyes at the bow. They looked jolly, lined up like birds on a telephone wire, all down the shore. The day was hot and the sun was cloudy, but Frances began to enjoy the heat and the water tickling her feet. She found herself praying to Domnu, the Irish goddess of deep water. *"Great One, She beyond the ninth wave. I seek your wisdom. The way before me is obscure and stormy. Help me sail through these waves."*

A song that old Shelta had taught her came into her head and she began to sing softly.

"Raindrops fall into the streams
Rivers flow into the seas
Domnu lives beneath the waves
Holding all the world

She says 'I am the Ocean
I am the Mother's Waters
I am the Heart's Blood
Holding all the World.'"

Over and over she sang until that feeling happened, that shift that meant the veils between the worlds was lifted, and conversation between the worlds could flow easily. Frances stood looking out at the ocean and was one with that ocean and with all oceans and with all water and with…

"Mame?" The voice was liquid and musical. Frances took a moment to realize that the voice was coming from the every day world. *"Mame!"*

"Greetings *Mame,* my name is *Mame* Khadi. I have been observing you, and I think perhaps there is something here that might be of interest to you…would you…" She gestured for Frances to follow her.

Frances took her in for a moment: another stranger looking out for her! She was a woman of middle years with an absurdly colorful and beautiful dress and matching head wrap. Frances took in her compassionate smile, her open gesture and fell in line behind her up over the dune to a small clay building adjacent to a well.

Mame Khadi paused at the well and turned a spigot on the outside wall gesturing to Frances to take a drink and wash her hands and feet. The water was cool and tangy with a hint of iron and Frances drank deep, filling some thirst she hadn't known she had. When she was done, *Mame* Khadi led her into the small building.

Inside was dark and cool. It took several seconds for Frances's eyes to adjust to the dim light. *Mame* Khadi walked ahead of Frances down a corridor into a room that was divided in two by a half wall. Light came into the room from a few high small windows, and the space had the feeling of a cave. The first half of the room was sparse, with only a low wooden bench running along one wall. As the two women walked into the back half of the room Frances saw bowls of water gathered in the center on the floor. Between the bowls of water were bundles of grain and nuts and fruits. It reminded Frances of the holy wells in Kerry, where people would leave offerings in honor of the spirits that dwelled there.

"This is our shrine," said *Mame* Khadi, "the place of the helpful spirits. All people need the help of spirits, ancestors, guardians. But sometimes those helpers become too entwined with people. So, we do ceremony to separate the person from their spirit helper, and the spirit is given a home in the bowl of water. People, families, come here to talk to their spirit, make offerings, connect to the ancestors. Here they get help."

"I need help," Frances said very quietly.

"I know," smiled *Mame* Khadi, squeezing her hand. "We were told in a dream that you would come and that we should be ready to assist you. I have been keeping my eyes open for you. And when I saw you singing down at the shore, I knew it was you."

"Can you help me trick MI6 and the CIA?" Frances asked, half-jokingly.

"Yes, *Mame* Frances, we can!" She called out in Lebu, and almost immediately women poured into the small shrine room, so many that Frances couldn't count them all. They ranged in age from the shine of early teens to white-haired and bent.

Mame Khadi motioned for them all to sit upon the ground and said, "Let us begin!"

That was on Tuesday.

On Wednesday, a small woman wearing the traditional dress and matching headwrap of Yoff went to the market. That woman was Frances. She made a quick survey of the stalls, haggled good-naturedly in her beginners Lebu with the woman selling mangoes, made sure that the people around her heard the joking and joined in, then exited the market down a side alley and disappeared.

On Thursday, a small woman, wearing the same dress and head wrap as yesterday wove through the market and purchased rice. Again, there was easy negotiating and laughter. The mango seller spotted a white man on the far side of the market watching. She signaled to the small woman, Frances, who immediately evaporated into the crowd. Thirty minutes later a small woman, dressed exactly the same, re-appeared on the opposite side of the market, walking quickly through the crowd. As she exited the market she was followed by the white man. That woman was a thirteen year-old girl and Frances's height, the niece of *Mame* Khadi. The young one easily evaded the man, and he stood in the middle of the busy road looking sharply from side to side. In frustration he wiped his face with his handkerchief.

On Friday, Frances, in that same outfit, circled the market and slid behind the mango stall, crouching down. The same white man, still dressed for Whitehall, not for Yoff in November, began to search the crowd. A small woman of Frances's height with the signature headwrap suddenly appeared at the rice stand, then went out of sight. Ten minutes later the same dress, same headwrap, same height popped up at the entrance to the alley where fabrics were sold. This time the man didn't hesitate, but instead began to push through the crowd rudely and followed her. She too was like fog and disappeared. The man was seen storming out of the market. Frances stood from her hiding place, *"Merci, madame."*

"No problem, *Mame* Frances. *Mame* Khadi says the priestesses are working to confound your enemies. It is our pleasure to assist." As Frances walked out of the market she was hailed and smiled at. The people of Yoff seemed to all be in with the game afoot.

On Saturday the market was overflowing with people from the countryside. It was the busiest day of the week. A large pen of goats and sheep took up much of the center of the courtyard. It was noisy and pungent and crowded. A small woman, same headdress as the days before, entered from the east. The white man started after her but was stopped by a cluster of men who descended to argue about a goat. Then he spotted her walking west and again tried to pursue her. This time a wagon of watermelons blocked the alley. He turned and saw the woman on the far side of the market on the northeast, looking through the piles of tomatoes. The crowd was pushing against him as he tried to backtrack. By the time he reached the tomato stall, the woman was long gone.

"That woman, very short, where did she go?" he asked in British schoolboy French, marking height at about his shoulder level with his hand.

The man at the stall looked at the white man uncomprehendingly with a shrug. He answered in Lebu. "Nowhere you will ever find her." The he smiled and gestured to his tomatoes. "You want?" in purposefully bad French.

The white man was heard to say, "No! I don't want your bloody tomatoes!" in English as he shoved his way out of the market. After he left, three young women, all dressed in the same head wrap and of similar demure stature, met in the center of the market and took a bow as the crowd around them cheered.

As this was all transpiring, Frances Fletcher Kenneally, cool and calmly appointed and dressed as a proper European matron was seated in a *car rapide* with the same driver, Ousmane, who had been behind the wheel when she and Sassy had pulled 'the big bank caper,' as they liked to call it. Ousmane had declared himself Frances's major-domo and had been able to make all sorts of arrangements for her with the villagers. With his help and the power of the priestesses, Frances had been adopted into the fold of the inter-related families of Yoff.

Ousmane wove through the traffic and, after several hair-raising minutes, he safely deposited Frances at the entrance to the American Embassy. She asked him to wait, and he grinned widely, pulling out his lunch wrapped in brown paper, and replied that, "No force on earth could get me to move, *Mame* Frances."

Frances sailed up the wide shallow steps to the front door and announced to the Marine standing there that she was expected at the USAID office to see Mr. Sheldon Stewart.

"Of course, ma'am. Right this way." The Marine swung the heavy door open for her and walked beside her as he led her up the central staircase and then along the long corridor to the right. Sunlight spilled into the hallway from the bank of windows that graced the outside wall. Their footsteps echoed down the corridor. "Where are you from in the States, ma'am," the young man asked with a hint of homesickness in his voice.

Frances made her split-second assessment of his accent and replied, "Kansas, Sergeant. And you?"

"Oklahoma, ma'am. A long way from here."

"Yes indeed, A long, long way. Is this your first tour overseas?" And as they walked Frances learned much more than the young man intended, including the number of Marines stationed at the Embassy and the fractious relationship between the Ambassador and Mr. Stewart, the titular head of USAID, but, as her young Marine told her, "Everybody knows that his department are really here as spooks."

Frances nodded, as if she did indeed, know this, thanked the young man sincerely as he directed her to the appropriate office. He left her, feeling better than he had in weeks, like the Midwest plain's breezes had just blown through the Embassy and brought the smells of home.

Frances was ushered into an inner room where Spencer Stewart was seated behind an enormous desk. He stood as she entered, and she got a good look at him. He was about forty with the paunch that so many

American men got as they aged. His hair line had receded, but he had made no tacky attempts at a comb-over for which Frances issued a small sigh of relief. He was sharp eyed and deeply tanned. *An outdoors man, a hunter? Not tennis or squash, not with that belly. No, a golfer! That was it.* He walked around his desk, extended his hand, and gave hers a firm shake. Frances was again relieved. She detested weak-handed men.

"Mrs. Kenneally! What a pleasant surprise! My man had said you might be coming by, but when the weeks passed, I confess, I had given up hope."

Frances looked at him with some amusement. Americans were so refreshingly forthright. She had almost forgotten that lack of subterfuge that was their *modus operandi.* Even, it seemed, in their covert services. She decided on the spot to meet his frankness with her own.

"Mr. Stewart, I have come to offer my services to the Central Intelligence Agency."

"I beg your pardon?" he almost sputtered.

"You know. The Company. The folks at the Farm."

"Mrs. Kenneally, I assure you, I don't know what you are talk..." And he caught look of her face and the barely suppressed grin he saw beneath those knowing eyes. He took a breath and then said, "Well, alrighty then!"

This, their first conversation lasted an hour and a half. Frances had, of course, come, as her new American friend said, "loaded for bear." She had a list of the stipulations needed for her cooperation with the Americans, and as one would expect of Frances, the list was extensive and multi-faceted. She intended to undertake this new chapter in her life with "all the bases covered" as Sheldon Stewart exclaimed. Frances felt awash with American aphorisms but persevered.

"My daughter and her husband have had recent obstacles to their humanitarian work," Frances had said mildly, referring to the theft of their transport plane, Kwame's kidnapping and the subsequent extortion of blackmail funds as if they were potholes on the road to a society luncheon.

Mr. Stewart *("Sheldon, please!")* replied in kind. "We had become aware of some unpleasantness in the Congo that resulted in Mr. Boadu's discomfort."

As if being kidnapped and threatened death by machete was merely unpleasant. And, of course, he had known Kwame's name. Frances wondered if he was letting her know that he knew, or if he had slipped up. His face was unchanged in its guileless demeanor, but Frances decided he was more clever than he appeared. She countered with blunt honesty.

"Their continued safety and ability to do the doctoring they desire is a prerequisite of my cooperation with you and yours...Sheldon."

"Agreed, Mrs. Kenneally. Now, how do we go about doing that?"

They hammered out a plan in which Sassy and Kwame would become the directors of a "USAID program designed to reach far-flung communities and deliver medical services and supplies to the needy," as Sheldon phrased it. The fact that no such program had existed – or even been thought of before today seemed to be of little concern to Sheldon Stewart. Frances found herself warming to this fellow who presented with an amiable and slightly bumbling personality. *Kind of like a retriever puppy,* Frances thought. But he clearly moved mountains with a stroke of his pen, and Frances was beginning to like the momentum he created.

"In addition, it will be necessary for a free clean water source to be constructed in Yoff. The village has had its traditional access to the wells and aquifer cut off by development in Dakar. That, of course, is undesirable," Frances explained calmly.

"It is quite a coincidence then that I can tell you about a new engineering program that USAID is undertaking to extend well access and establish water purification centers throughout the coast and in the village of Yoff in particular." Sheldon was also beginning to enjoy this.

After several more items were satisfactorily covered, they got down to the true business at hand.

"The world and the map are changing rapidly, Mrs. Kenneally. The Company is finding that information about radical movements and domestic upheavals in certain parts of the world is becoming harder to come by with our 'traditional methods'."

"Spies, you mean," Frances said, dropping the word like a hot stone in the middle of Sheldon's lap. He had the grace to look ever so slightly chagrined.

"Yes, if you must, spies."

"I do think it is best to begin as we intend to proceed, Sheldon, and say what we mean…and mean what we say." Frances was really starting to have some fun now.

Sheldon cleared his throat and began again. "We feel that you are particularly well-suited to being able to visit and observe some areas that are becoming more difficult for us to…infiltrate."

Frances's face went blank, and she felt that inner calm that came with danger. "And how might that be?" she asked.

"As you travel to research your next series of novels. Your publisher is especially excited that you are going to undertake this new line of books."

"Oh, they are, are they?"

"Yes, indeedy. In fact, your advance for this new series is the biggest they have ever extended to any of their authors. Your already comfortable financial situation is poised to become quite cushy." Sheldon looked very pleased with himself, then paused as he realized that Frances was as still as stone.

When she spoke, after several long and tense moments, she spoke very, very softly. "A new series of books…about which I have had no knowledge. You pitched this to my publisher?"

Frances's face began a transformation into something Sheldon Stewart had only seen in his most frightening dreams.

"Do you mean to tell me that you conspired behind my back and without my permission? That you co-opted the approval of my publisher with whom I have, or thought I had, a relationship of confidentiality, and that you arranged for what sounds like a substantial sum of money to be allocated to me in order to pressure me into working with the Company?"

Sheldon looked at her and the façade of sweet mediocrity fell away. The man who looked back at her was razor sharp and fixed on his purpose. Frances mentally acknowledged the new man across the desk from her, and she met metal with metal.

"What if I had decided to go with MI6 or forget the whole lot of you?" she said even more softly.

"Well, then, we would have lost this roll of the dice. The new series of books is a green light whether you work for…"

"Work *with!*" Frances interjected.

"Work *with* us or not. Obviously, I would be much happier if you decide to join in alignment with our goals. But the choice is all yours."

Frances looked down at her hand, fingers tightly linked together. This was the tipping point. *Could she use the Company? Could she align her goals and the goals of the Goddess by manipulating the CIA?* Frances, she who had been Celebi, the Brighid of the Calanais Mystery School, she who had navigated the choppy waters of brilliant minds and enormous egos in that school and kept all harmonious – she thought this challenge before her now sounded like child's play. And, the money, so generously provided by the CIA, would fund her journeys to go where the Grandmothers needed her to go. She loosened her laced fingers, lifted her eyes up to Sheldon and began to laugh. "Well, alrighty then. Looks like we have ourselves a deal!"

Sheldon internally uncoiled. Frances asked for coffee, and they got down to "where the rubber meets the road."

"Would you like to have an American passport, Mrs. Kenneally? We would be able to arrange one."

"It's Fletcher. My surname is Fletcher. Or so it says on my Canadian passport."

"Oh, I'm sorry, I assumed you traveled under an Irish passport with your married name."

Frances laughed again. "No, you didn't. You knew very well how I traveled and under what name – or you wouldn't have been able to track me to a market in Yoff." She waited, saying nothing else.

"Well, alrighty then!" And Sheldon Stewart had himself a new agent, albeit one he was never really sure if he controlled her, or she controlled him.

$$) \bigcirc ($$

When Frances returned to Yoff that afternoon after her first meeting with Sheldon Stewart she found Sassy and Sisi playing in the central courtyard.

"Mama, you look like the cat that ate the cream!" Sassy said with delight.

"Do you remember Aoife, our cat that guarded the chickens?" Frances asked.

"Of course I do. I saw her standing up on her hind legs fighting off a fox," Sassy laughed.

"Well, my little pigeon, your mama is now going to do exactly that! I intend to fight off some foxes."

☽ ○ ☾

Some more meetings at the US Embassy, new documents to acquire, and several long nights with the priestesses of Yoff, and Frances was ready to begin her new chapter.

Before she left, the priestesses arranged a special ceremony for her. It was an initiation into their tradition and a weaving of protection for her as she undertook her new life. It was called the *Ndeup,* a ceremony of cleansing and protection, that required that multiple lineages of priestess lines come together. All the drummers of the village gathered on the beach near the shrine, and the lines of women, each line adorned in their own special fabric pattern, began to dance. It was that liminal time, neither day nor night, when the light was pearlescent, and the spirits began to roam. Frances was ushered out of the shrine and given a special seat to watch the dancers. *Mame* Khadi placed a strand of carnelian beads around Frances's neck and whispered a prayer in Lebu.

Before long she felt the drums permeating her skin and beginning to set up vibration in her bones. Without her making any conscious decision she stood and was folded into one of the dancing lines of women.

The sun set, making a flash of crimson along the horizon, and the drumming and the dancing continued. Frances felt outside of herself, woven into the larger organism that was this community of women, part of something grand and ancient. The movements, not familiar to her, were spontaneous and of a piece with everyone else. From time to time the drumming would shift to the next song, the rhythm would alter, and the dance organically changed as well. Lines of women, like wild birds in flight, making shapes and symbols in the sand for hours and hours. Time became a mere notion, the physical body stretched beyond its normal capacity, the spirit soaring.

With the dawn the drumming came to an end, and the lines of women, melted down onto the beach like individual flowers that drooped with grace and fatigue. Sassy and Kwame came and brought water and juice along with platters of fish and vegetables. The women ate and talked softly, replete in all the ways that matter. When Frances stood to take her leave, she felt such an ache in her muscles that she laughed. She was surrounded by her new spirit sisters, those of the flesh and those of the ephemera.

$$\text{)} \bigcirc \text{(}$$

Two days later Frances and Alaman entered Dakar airport ready to board a flight to Morocco. They had displayed their passports to the airline agents, and Alaman carried their bags as they prepared to walk out onto the tarmac and get on the plane. Suddenly a voice shouted, calling Frances's name.

"Mrs. Fletcher! Mrs. Fletcher!"

She stopped and turned, immediately spotting the MI6 agent rushing toward her. Alaman immediately moved to stand between Frances and the man hurrying in her direction. The agent stopped short at the sight of the robed Tuareg who looked as if he would be most at home with a knife between his teeth.

"Mrs. Fletcher! You have been most difficult to track down," the man said, breathing a bit with difficulty.

Frances smiled that Mona Lisa smile of hers and replied, "I am always easily spotted by those whom I wish to find me."

"Ah yes, quite." The fellow looked flustered, and Frances almost took pity on him. Almost. Until he waved a hand at Alaman to dismiss him so that he could talk directly to Frances, as if he were a fly. Frances felt every slight that her Granny Sally and Uncle Walter had ever been subjected to. She heard the metaphorical slap of presumed superiority, and any pity she might have felt for the perspiring British agent evaporated.

"You, sir, are impeding our progress. Don't ever do that again!" She said it quietly, but Alaman smiled as he saw the British agent take a step back automatically. Sheldon Stewart, seated nearby with a newspaper held up before his face, smiled too.

And so it began that that Frances Fletcher Kenneally, known in twenty-three languages as Frannie Portreaux, author of twelve highly successful historical novels, started her research into a new series of books, set in far-flung corners of the globe.

Morocco, 1967

Their first trip was to the deserts of Morocco. Alaman arranged for them to have the use of a Land Rover, battered and missing a fender, but trailworthy. After a day and half they arrived at a Tuareg camp where Alaman was to introduce Frances to his grandmother.

The camp was what looked to be a random cluster of tents, as if someone had thrown down a handful of jacks like the ones Frances had played with as a child. When they stepped down from the Land Rover, Alaman was greeted with ululations from the women, and rifle shots into the air by the men. To Frances, it all felt very much like a Cree village with different clothes and much more sand. Greetings and embraces were exchanged, and Frances was given shy smiles and the pats of small children.

Kahina, Alaman's grandmother, was sitting on cushions in her tent, wrapped in a beautiful shawl of magenta and sapphire. Alaman stooped to enter and made the formal introductions in Berber, then repeated them in French for Frances's sake.

"*Jida,* I bring to you the one you requested, the granddaughter of the Memory Holder, she who was Atvasfara. This is Frances."

Kahina motioned for them to come closer and to sit down. The sun came into the tent through a small slit on the opening and filtered down between the tent poles. Frances saw the old woman in the speckled light. Whatever she had expected it was not this glorious creature. A laugh of delight shot out of her.

"Revered One, I wondered where your grandson found his physical beauty, and now I see that it is but a mere diminished form of yours."

The old woman understood enough of the French to begin to smile, but she laughed aloud when Alaman finished his translation of Frances's comment. She had most of her teeth and they looked surprisingly white and sturdy. Her eyes were the same as Alaman's, almond shaped, hazel and astute. She could have been forty or four hundred years old, so clear and unlined was her face. It, simply put, was the face that could have launched a thousand ships.

"My grandson creates enough havoc in the world with his diminished beauty. It is best I kept most of it for myself."

Alaman shook his head good-naturedly and relaxed, knowing that these two remarkable women now were fast friends.

For three weeks Frances settled into the life of the camp. The Tuaregs rose with the sun and followed the ancient rhythm of tending animals, preparing food, feeding children and singing together as they worked the tasks of life. Again and again, Frances found the similarities between these people and her Cree family, and there was great comfort in that.

Her research notebooks were filling up with the sounds and smells of these nomads. The laughter that spilled out from the weaving tent. The shared pipes and stories around the goat flocks. The smell of animal dung and campfires. And the scent of the resin incense that wafted from small devotional urns night and day.

She spent some of each afternoon with an uncle of Alaman's, named Igidir. His name meant 'eagle' she learned, and his eyes were a light hazel with gold rings around the pupils that gave him the look of his namesake raptor. And like Alaman's entire family, he was stunningly good looking. He taught Frances how to ride a camel, and together they spent hours riding the dunes and exchanging poetry, hers in whatever language spoke to her at the moment and his mostly in Arabic.

"My husband loved Yeats. Do you know him, W. B. Yeats?" Frances asked.

"Our Alaman quotes the man sometimes," Igidir replied. "And when he does, he, like you, looks most sorrowful."

"My late husband Michael's place in our hearts is vast," Frances said through tears.

"Does that preclude any others to reside there, do you think?" Igidir asked, innocently enough.

Frances shot him a suspicious look, and only shook her head in reply. But yet, the question niggled at her.

Alaman was always waiting when she returned, helping her dismount and walking with her back to camp. He was ever courteous, ever patient and helpful. Frances found herself looking for him then, or across the campfire, or as he finished any work. And she was surprised that her heart sparked a bit of joy each time she saw him again.

$$\text{☽ ○ ☾}$$

Mornings and early evenings Frances spent with Kahina. In her role as Grandmother, Kahina was teaching Frances what was to come and how she was to facilitate the future.

One night they sat together outside the tent, wrapped in blankets, looking at the diamond-filled sky. Several campfires were crackling, babies were snuffling and rooting, animals bleated. Life.

"There is your map, daughter," Kahina said. "It is like the pattern of a weaving of cloth, or the ley lines that criss-cross our Mother Earth. Or like the interwoven threads of time that brought you and me together again."

"When I first saw you, in your beautiful shawl, I thought I remembered you, but I couldn't quite..." Frances quietly replied.

"And I you. It has been many, many lifetimes since I have seen you, Celebi of the Goddess Brig," Kahina reached out her hand and clasped Frances's.

"And it is a treasure to see you again, Yollo, master weaver of the Goddess Epona."

"This is our best gift to those we followed into danger in the Before. In this life we prepare the way for them, for the Thirteen. And we hold the bloodline for their next incarnations. This is our gift to them, and the Goddess's gift to us."

"Are you saying that the Thirteen will arise from us?" Frances stumbled over the thought.

"They will be born from the Companions, yes. We Companions are scattered all over the planet now. Your Grandmother, she who was Atvasfara, the Memory Holder, she has come in visions to each of us to awaken our memories. She has unfolded the past for us Companions, and has shown us the way to the future. These memories of what was, they are bittersweet and precious, and they reveal our mission. So it will be that the Thirteen will emerge from all parts of this world and do the work they set out to protect all those thousands of years ago."

Frances turned her eyes back to the velvet black. "My Michael was one of us, a Companion. He had been Malvu, the Chief Observer at the Mystery School at Calanais and my beloved. My daughter Sassy was Dalia, Priestess of Nut and she who became Pharaoh of Egypt after the cataclysm. Her daughter Sisi was Domnhu, the devoted servant and lover of Badh of the Cailleach. And you, you were Yollo. Now you tell me, all of us, the Companions, we are all on this Earth at the same time to prepare the way! This is wonderful…incredible! So, when comes the return of the Thirteen?"

"With the turning of the Wheel, and the beginning of a new epoch, they will all be born again and find their paths. And you, beloved Frances, are to illuminate their paths and ignite the connections between them."

Frances swallowed a laugh, "So, no pressure then?"

Kahina smiled and began a song that was picked up all around the camp, women adding their voices to the eternal tale of women.

"I am the vessel of creation
I am the mother of the Earth
In the darkness always spinning
Always spiraling into life."

"What do you want me to write about your people, Grandmother? I have the disguise of authoring a new series of novels. My publisher thinks I am going to be writing fiction about 'the forgotten peoples.' I will do as the Goddess asks, but I do also need to write some books." Frances chuckled ruefully. "In this one year I have gone from having no purpose, no job, to having too many to contemplate. Did Alaman tell you that I am also pretending to work for the American spies, or working with them in a fashion that suits me?"

"The Celebi I knew was adept at juggling many tasks. You will thrive with the work before you, daughter. And as for the Tuareg, tell of our dignity, our honesty, our desire to harm none." Kahina looked gravely at Frances. "But you must leave us soon, after the Solstice I feel."

Frances felt tears rising. "Will I ever see you again, Grandmother?"

Kahina laughed from deep in her belly. "Don't you see me every time you look upon my grandson?"

Frances felt herself blush. "Does that mean he will travel with me?"

"If you will allow," Kahina replied. "Are you able to allow?"

Could she? Could she allow for her bruised and scarred heart to soften and expand? Could she forge new connections without denying those that had come before. Was love finite?

Frances spent the next few days learning all she could about the Grandmothers and their network of knowledge holders around the planet. She was awash in information and glasses of peppermint tea. Kahina taught her the meditation techniques to travel on the astral plane and communicate with these women. They made forays together so Kahina could help Frances learn to navigate the expanses of physical space and distance. After a successful trip to Mount Kailash in Tibet to meet with a Buddhist nun, Frances found herself more full of questions than ever.

"How will I know where to go and when?" Frances asked. "And how will I know if astral travel is sufficient or if I need to be there in the flesh?"

"How do you ever know?" Kahina replied. "In seriousness, daughter, how have you known in your life when to take a step, which turn to make, which way to jump?"

Frances chuckled. "Well, usually, I do a thing and then look back and see that I did it."

"Like you did as Celebi of Calanais, jumping into that boat to travel to Egypt? Or, in this life, accepting Michael's offer to work behind

Nazi lines? Or how you ended up here!" Kahina's face had an expression of deep compassion and amusement.

"Yes," Frances smiled ruefully. "None of those decisions were ones I actually 'made'. That quality, or fault of character as my mother would have described it, has always moved me. My Granny Sally said I was an expert at jumping and then seeing where to land."

"Well, daughter, I don't think now is a time to change your basic nature. Best to work with what you have, eh?"

"Michael always said that if you must sing off-key, just be louder than all the rest." The two women leaned into each other, resting shoulder against shoulder.

Kahina took a thick stick of sandalwood from the bundle of incense and began to draw in the sand. "We are here," and she drew a five-pointed star. "And here is your Irish home." Another star. And here is where we traveled in our spirits to that high holy mountain." She scratched another star far over to her right. And another, and another, and another, until the ground before them look like a constellation map. Kahina asked Frances to imagine that map as if it were on a fine parchment, and then to drape it across a globe. "And there you will find them, the Companions, the ones who will be the foremothers of the Thirteen."

They were silent for a long time as Frances filed the image into memory. "And where to start?" she asked.

"Jump, daughter, jump!" Kahina said joyfully.

)○(

That night Frances walked away from camp, leaving the warmth and companionship around the fires and leaning into the silence and solitude of the desert. It was an astonishingly quiet place. No sounds of rustling birds as she had heard in the Canadian plain. No trickle or gurgle of water in streams as in Ireland. Not even the burr or whistle of insects. Just the celestial songs of the stars filling the space between her heartbeats. She asked and listened. Like a gentle click, the answer came to her.

She heard the almost sound of footsteps behind her. She could feel Alaman's presence, even though he stood a respectful distance away. She turned and reached out a hand, a faint white shimmer of movement in the moonlight.

"Would you like to go to the Pine Ridge Reservation in South Dakota? With me?" she asked him.

That question held profound layers of meanings, and he understood them all. Repercussions for the now and the future. She was asking for more than a fellow traveler. She was asking for a true companion of body, mind, and spirit. Her heart had opened and made space. And she waited for him to decide. The drums began in the camp in the distance, the drums of family, and history and the heartbeat of the Earth. The open silence between them stretched, and yet she waited in patience and in longing.

"With all my heart." He clasped her offered hand. Warm palm met warm palm, and a new kind of rightness whispered through Frances and settled along her bones.

Alaman felt the subtle softening between the bones of her hand that came with her acceptance of what might be. He tugged gently and drew her near to him. She nervously anticipated a kiss. It had been decades since she had kissed anyone but Michael. Twenty-five years of only knowing his body. Twenty-five years of her body changing and aging. What if this kiss didn't meet her expectations? And perhaps worse yet, what if this kiss didn't meet Alaman's expectations.

But Alaman pulled her in front of him so that her back nestled against his chest. She was of such a height that the top of her head fit right under his chin. They rested like that for precious minutes, poised at the beginning of their being together in this new way. Frances's heartbeat slowed down and came into synchronicity with his. They began to breathe together until, with a gasp, Frances spotted a flurry of falling stars in the blackness overhead.

"It's the meteor shower," Alaman said in her ear. "It's most brilliant here in the desert, yes?"

"Oh, my Goddess, yes!" Frances said on an exhale.

They watched the scattershot of falling stars, dozens of them, flash across the expanse of dark. The meteors fell in clusters over a period of minutes, fifteen, twenty, long enough for Frances to lose all self-consciousness pressed against Alaman's body.

"This feels quite wonderful," she said at last.

"Mmmm."

"Is that an affirmative 'mmm'?" Frances asked with a bit of tetchiness in her voice. "I think I need a bit of confidence boosting here. I am a bit long in the tooth for new romance, you know."

Alaman began to rumble. She could feel his chest vibrate and then feel the bubbles of laughter rise. Before he could actually laugh aloud she spun around in his arms and reached up to grab his face between her hands. With a not-so-gentle tug she pulled his head down and kissed him, hard. That kiss shattered her into pieces of light and star matter like the meteors overhead. They kissed like starving people, voraciously aiming to get closer, be closer. Constellations whirled.

Long minutes later, "Frances, my queen, what does 'long in the tooth' mean?" he asked before descending to envelope her again. He could feel her lips lift in a smile. They slowly cascaded down to rest on the sand, Frances stretched across Alaman's chest. All the world fell away as they found their pleasure in each other with only the stars as witness.

Frances felt new and alive and awakened as Alaman found her tender places. With each soft moan he smiled, delighted in the learning of her and her body. He could feel her restraint fall away, and as the rhythms built he chose to ride the wave of desire with her. Frances felt that poised moment before all sense deserted her, and then, the universe was born again. Stardust showered them.

$$\text{)}\ \bigcirc\ \text{(}$$

Some timeless time later she was snuggled into his shoulder, and they watched the sky as their breathing slowed. Frances lifted a boneless arm, feeling like she moved under water. She pointed to a particular grouping of stars on the southeastern horizon. "I once knew women from that star," she said softly, almost inaudibly.

"As did I," Alaman replied.

"A Companion, were you?"

"But of course, my queen."

She turned her head so she could see his profile, dimly lit as the moon shifted west. "Let me think. Our salient qualities stay the same. That is what my Granny Sally said. So, if I were to describe you..." She saw his lips turn up and his eyes cut sideways to see her. "I'd say steadfast, and stubborn, brave... And beautiful."

"I am honored that you see me as such," he replied, giving away nothing.

"And dedicated."

"Yes, I am that," he said softly.

Frances remembered back to the days when the Companions and the Thirteen had come together and faced terrifying odds. And then suddenly, it clicked. She saw Alaman as the strong and confident man he was, and simultaneously saw the tall, lithe, young woman he had been when he had been Pel, the dedicant of Artemis who had accompanied the young Io to Egypt. The same steady courage, the same conviction and follow-through, the same iridescent beauty.

"Why didn't I see it before, Pel of Ephesus?"

"Oh, I think you did. You knew you knew me, yes? You knew you should trust me, yes?" Alaman turned his head so he could see her fully. "You did remember me, my little queen. And you also saw the Blue Man. It can be a bit confusing, yes?"

"Very."

She was quiet for a few moments, and he left her to her silence.

"Alaman?"

"Yes, my Frances?"

"I think my brain hurts a bit from all the confusion. And there is only one remedy." She nuzzled her nose against his chest.

Alaman's face lit up as starlight caught in his eyes. "Do you require medicine?" he asked her, his voice lowering.

"The most ancient medicine," she answered and rose above him to lower herself slowly until flesh met flesh and the anchor of his body kept her where she wanted to be.

☽ ○ ☾

"I think we need to go to Ireland before we travel to America," Frances said the next day.

Alaman looked wary. "I shall follow you to the ends of the Earth, my queen," he said, his jaw moving off to one side as it did when he was puzzling something out. "What is it we shall do there, in your Ireland?"

Frances looked down at the ground and then abruptly lifted her gaze to his. "I want to introduce you to Michael's mother."

Alaman was stunned. He looked at Frances for several moments, searching her face for a clue. "For what purpose, my queen?"

"Because I think she will like you. I want to tell her of my missions. And I want her to stop worrying about me."

"Do you seek her approval of me?"

"Good gracious, no!" Frances burst out laughing. "I need no one's approval or permission to love you, Alaman. Don't you know me better than that?" She looked genuinely perplexed.

"Frances, my sweet, my torment, my love, you are not the only one who needs a bit of confidence-boosting from time to time."

Frances leapt at him and he barely caught her in time to prevent them both from tumbling to the ground. She wrapped her arms tightly around his neck and kissed him along the jaw till he giggled. "A smidgen of insecurity is very attractive on you, my Blue Man!"

☽ ○ ☾

After Winter Solstice, Frances and Alaman took their leave of the Tuaregs. As they were preparing to climb aboard the Land Rover, family and clan members were pressings gifts upon them.

Kahina moved from the back of the crowd toward Frances and Alaman. The clan parted like water as she walked calmly with a beautiful amethyst and magenta shawl in her hands. The Grandmother placed the shawl in Frances's hands, looked deeply into her eyes, and said nothing. What could words do at such a time? Frances took the shawl, unfolded it and draped it around her head and neck.

"Now I carry you with me, Grandmother."

"Go with the Goddess, daughter. You carry all of us, and all we hope for with you as well."

$$) \bigcirc ($$

Frances was very quiet as the bus wound south from Shannon airport. Their journey had been long, stretching over two days with bad weather and missed connecting flights making it even longer. The closer they got to Ballinskellig, the farther away Frances seemed to pull. Alaman, dressed in western clothes that they had purchased for him in Morocco, felt the damp chill seep through his wool coat bringing back the unpleasant sensations of the labor camp and the bone-breaking cold of those winters. And he felt Frances's distance, as if the sun that warmed his heart had gone behind the clouds. But Alaman was a patient man. He had waited all his life for a love like this, and he spoke to soothe his inner panic. "Tell me what we shall see when we arrive."

Frances shook herself out of her reverie. "Oh, my dear one. I am so sorry. I was a million miles away."

"Was it a good place, this million-miles-away place?"

"I was remembering when I first came here and saw these mountains. It was in the War. I was pregnant. Michael was missing, presumed dead. And all joy had been scooped out of me and left a hollow husk. But these mountains, they spoke a welcome to me. They were new and strange to the eyes of this lifetime, but I did indeed feel like I was coming home."

"There is much magic here," Alaman said quietly.

"Oh yes! You feel it too?" Frances reached over and took his hand. For the first time in their acquaintance his fingers were cold, and she rubbed them briskly between her hands. "This land will always be a home to me, just as now, your heart is my heart's home too."

Alaman smiled a small, sweet smile and lifted her hands to kiss her knuckles. "And you are a balm to whatever ails me, my Frances."

When the bus pulled into Limerick town Alaman commented, "Where are all the cars? This is Europe, yes? I thought it would be more like Paris and Nice. It feels rather desolate here."

"Ireland is the land Europe left behind," Frances replied.

"And yet, the magic," Alaman supplied.

Frances smiled at him, and his sun was back.

☽ ○ ☾

The difference between Frances's journey to Ballinskellig in 1943 and now was that instead of pony cart, they took a taxi from Limerick down into Kerry. The mountains rose higher and higher, and even with the winter drabness the landscape sang.

"The nature spirits are rising up and calling your name, beloved," Alaman said quietly so that the taxi driver couldn't hear.

"This land, this land…" Frances murmured.

The driver who had tufts of cinnamon hair poking out from beneath his tweed cap spoke. "Magdalena got the cottage all lit and warm for ye, Frances."

"Thank you, Timmy. And how is your da?" For the driver was the son of Tommy Óg who had delivered Frances to Magdalena's doorstep those twenty-odd years ago.

Alaman sat back and let their conversation wash over him as it flipped back and forth between English and Irish, with more and more Irish as they got deeper into Kerry. He was amused at how the land and the landscape seemed to pull a different language, a different worldview, from Frances and Timmy. Before long they pulled up in front of a cottage that faced the narrow road. A woman in her later years stood at the open door, as if she had felt their arrival, and didn't mind that cold air was rushing inside. She had a cane in one hand and was holding a shawl closed at her chest with the other.

At the sight of her, Frances let out a cry of joy and threw herself out of the not-quite stationary taxi. The older woman walked with some obvious pain forward, and Frances met her more than halfway up the path. They embraced and cried and smiled, all in a mix.

Alaman had busied himself helping Timmy lift their suitcases out of the taxi. When he turned back around he found that both women were staring at him, Frances smiling quite broadly and the older woman, Magdalena looking at him with an intense scrutiny overlaid with a polite half-smile. Flustered, he pulled out a wallet to pay Timmy their fare, but the driver waved it away and hopped back into his taxi, shouting something in Irish to the women on the path. Alaman picked up their bags and walked toward the cottage.

"*A mháthair,* may I present Alaman Sulaman of the Tuareg people. He was a dear friend of our Michael, and is now a precious friend to me." She was gripping Magdalena's arm and gripped double tight as she finished speaking.

"My children's friends will always find home and sanctuary here," Magdalena replied. "Please, come in and rest before we settle you into wherever you shall be staying."

Frances shot her a side glance and a twisted smile. Magdalena would be gracious at this new addition to their family circle, but there was still much to be explained and navigated.

"Yes! Tea, please! Good Irish tea!" For Frances had discovered that whenever there was social muddiness, tea solved all things.

They found spots near the fire, and Magdalena set about to brew a pot. The smell of peat was strong as the open door had pulled smoke down the chimney and into the cottage. Frances breathed in, threw back her head, and smiled at the ceiling, drawing in deep drafts. Alaman watched her and couldn't help himself from the pleasure the sight of her gave him. He felt himself relax in the essence of what was Frances, and then started as he found Magdalena looking at him with a disturbing degree of perspicacity.

They drank their tea and Magdalena asked after Sassy, Kwame, and Sisi. Frances talked of the sun and the heat and how precocious little Sisi was.

"And why are we not surprised at that?" Magdalena chuckled. "Acorns don't sprout blackthorn trees."

Frances smiled down into her cup and then lifted her lashes to peer at Alaman. He was his most composed and stoic looking self, but she felt for him. "Timmy said you had my cottage all warm and ready. How did you know I was coming home?" Both women laughed out loud and then shared a secret smile.

"I would imagine that the nature spirits told her. They certainly were loud enough in their welcome to you," Alaman said, and both women turned sharply to look at him. Frances covered her mouth to hide her wide grin, and Magdalena shot him a look of grudging respect. "I can see that Michael would have valued your friendship," she finally replied. And that was all it took. Magdalena's reservations fell away, and Alaman felt himself enveloped in the unconditional acceptance that was the Kenneally family. But as for where he was to sleep, that required an entirely different set of conditions met.

"I am glad of heart to see you home, daughter. But I'm thinking there is more to this story," Magdalena said after some quiet around the fire.

Frances started to respond but was caught unawares by an enormous yawn that felt like her jaw would crack. "I have so much to tell you, *a mháthair*. But it needs to wait till my body catches up to the distance we traveled. I think Alaman and I will go get settled in my cottage. After a good sleep we will tell you all you want to know."

Magdalena's eyebrows lifted almost up to her hairline. But she blinked rapidly a few times and then said, "Of course, *mo chroí*. Shall ye take your bags now then?"

Frances nodded. Alaman stood and bowed to Magdalena with a hand over his heart, and they left the warmth of the cottage to face the January chill. Frances led the way, taking two steps for every one of Alaman's long stride. She steered them down the lane to the next path on the other side of the road that wound up over a slight rise and straight to the home that Frances and Michael had called their own. There was smoke rising from the chimney, and when they entered they saw a vase of winter grasses and vines with dried berries waiting on the table.

Frances went to add more bricks of peat to the fire while Alaman began to walk around the room, looking at pictures and paintings that covered the walls. There were photographs of Sassy at every age. The early ones were clearly studio portraits with fancy backgrounds and tidy clothes. The later ones were taken with a home camera and showed Sassy with the wind in her hair and the sound of her laughter almost pouring out of the pictures. There were family groupings with Frances, Michael, Sassy and all the extended family situated on hillsides and picnics laid out before them. There was Frances's favorite, a snapshot she had taken herself of Michael, head tilted down, deep into the book he was holding, the light behind him outlining his face. Alaman was astonished to see that all the paintings, of wild countryside and cozy domestic scenes, were signed by Michael.

"I don't see a wedding portrait. Do you not do that here? In the desert, newlyweds must have the obligatory photograph in their wedding attire."

Frances straightened from the hearth and said, almost offhand, "Oh, we never married."

Alaman whirled around. "My queen, what does that mean? I assumed…"

"Oh, everyone assumed we were, and we let them. But we just never got around to it. During the War, at first there was no time, and then he was imprisoned. After the War, when he returned, it took time for him to regain his strength, and then, well, who would have sanctioned our union? The priest would be scandalized to know that we hadn't done it before Sassy was born. There was no civil marriage here in Ireland. The Travellers require the bride to be a virgin, and that ship had sailed. So, we just married in our hearts as we had always done, and left the paperwork to perdition. I was his and he was mine, and that was all."

Alaman nodded, absorbing the information and then said, "I can feel him here, hear the timbre of his voice. He is steeped within these walls."

"And does that trouble you, my Blue Man?"

Alaman came forward and gathered Frances into his arms. He kissed the top of her head and whispered into her hair. "On the contrary, my queen. I find it very comforting."

"You are the only man in all the world that would find it so," she said into his chest. "And now, I find myself in need of comfort." She led him by the hand to the bedroom on the other side of the hearth wall. Frances was confident that Magdalena had made sure the bedding was fresh, so she gently undressed Alaman and he assisted her. They fell into the soft bed and in an almost dreamlike state they found their comfort and release in each other until the deep fatigue of travel and emotions pulled them both down into cloudless sleep.

꘍ ○ ꘍

They slept through the rest of that afternoon and evening. At one point Alaman woke to hear Frances stirring the fire and then softly whisking back into the warm bedding. She hadn't known he was awake so was surprised when he drew her to him, reaching down to warm her feet between his hands. She groaned in pleasure as her toes thawed, and then squeaked when his hands rose higher on her legs.

"Again?" she asked.

"Most assuredly, again," he replied.

As his hands rose higher on her thighs he exclaimed, "Even the small beautiful globes of your buttocks are cold!"

Frances giggled and replied, "Only an Arab or an Irishman could make a bum sound poetic!" And then her words were swallowed as his lips covered hers and their breaths became entwined. Touch became the language that wove them together, and he read her skin like braille.

꘍ ○ ꘍

With daylight, Alaman woke with a start, realizing that Frances was not there. "My queen?" he called out.

"She left before dawn to walk the hills," came a voice from the other room. Alaman scrambled out of bed and pulled on his clothes. As he walked into the front room he saw a small woman, ageless but probably in her thirties, wrapped in multiple layers of mismatched clothes, stirring a pot of what smelled like porridge on the stove while wisps of fine auburn hair curled around her forehead.

"Come and sit and eat, Alaman Sulaman," she said, gesturing to the table where a pot of tea sat ready.

"I'm afraid you have the advantage of me here. I don't know your name," Alaman said, hand on heart, making a bow of middle depth.

"I am Michael Kenneally's cousin, who some call the resident witch, and who all call Young Shelta," she said, lifting up the right side of her mouth in a wry smile. "And you are our Frances's lover."

Alaman's eyes opened wide and he gulped. "I am indeed honored to be so."

"That's good," she replied. "If you didn't find it an honor I'm afraid the Kenneallys would have to kill you!"

She laughed out loud showing a mouth of solid teeth, and Alaman knew she was only slightly joking. He slid into the chair at the table and watched her out of the corner of his eye as he poured himself some tea. For only a fraction of a second he wished he was wearing his desert robes with the handy knife attached to his belt.

"Magdalena says you knew our Michael," she said without turning to look at him.

"I did. In the War. He saved my life," Alaman calmly replied.

"Oh, by Bride and all the saints! That means we must adopt ye then!"

"Excuse me, My English is not so…"

"It is the Traveller way. If you save a person's life they become your kin. I best go and get the adoption ceremony organized." Young Shelta spun around and headed for the door, then turned sharply and pinned Alaman with her black, currant eyes. "Don't go thinking of leaving before we get you right and truly blessed as a Kenneally!" And then she was gone, out the door leaving only the smell of slightly scorched porridge behind.

$$\text{☽ ○ ☾}$$

Alaman had rescued the porridge and was halfway through eating his bowlful when Frances returned, her hair wild and wind-tossed with more pink in her cheeks than he had ever seen. She brought the scent of gorse and magic with her.

He drank in the sight of her and felt himself come right with the world.

"A woman was here. A cousin? She wanted to kill me but has decided to adopt me instead!" Alaman's eyes narrowed slightly, curious to see Frances's reaction.

She threw back her head and laughed. "Was she a tiny bit taller than me, with clothes from a rummage bin?"

She floated into the room and placed a small skull – perhaps a vole – onto the table and reached to fill herself a bowl of porridge. Alaman's head tilted slightly as he watched her, and felt warmth spread like honey through his chest. "Ah, so you know this particular bloodthirsty savage?"

"For better and for worse. She is the Wise Woman for the Travellers of Michael's line. And she, as well as Magdalena, are of that network of Grandmothers that you and I now serve."

"I am blessed to be surrounded by magical women," he said with a smile.

"She wants to adopt you, did you say?" Frances mumbled around a hot mouthful of slightly scorched oats.

"She says she must. Something about Michael saving my life and a Travellers' code."

"This should be interesting," Frances muttered, and smiled down into her porridge.

$$) \, \bigcirc \, ($$

The rest of that day was spent in a dizzying array of Kenneallys. Malachi arrived midmorning to meet "Frances's new fella." She opened the door for him, hugged him, and, reaching up on tiptoes, whispered in his ear, "Be kind!" He strode into the room, looking enough how Alaman remembered Michael to be to stop his breath in his throat. Malachi was cut from the same cloth as his brother: lean-bodied, tawny-haired, and with that look in his blue eyes that brooked no fools. He had the calloused hands of a man who worked the land, and the air of ownership that put Alaman on full alert.

"My mother says you are to be welcome here, but I need to make up my own mind about that," Malachi said, with his Kerry accent made thick by emotion. "Who are you exactly and what do you intend for our Frances?"

Alaman stood quickly from his chair, making the wooden legs screech on the stone floor, and Frances stepped between the two men. She placed a hand on Malachi's chest.

"*Your* Frances is standing right here, Malachi, and fully capable of answering any of your questions. Now, can we accord some hospitality to our guest, if you please?"

He came up short, blushed, and moved with reluctance to the chair Frances indicated on the other side of the table. She fetched another cup and poured him some tea, then took the remaining chair, strategically placed so she could see them both.

"Malachi, this is Alaman Sulaman of the Tuareg people. Alaman, this is my brother-in-law, Malachi Kenneally."

Honey hazel eyes met with azure. Neither man gave way until Frances barked a laugh, and then they both turned to look at her.

"You shall be friends. I decree it so. Enough foolishness. I am not a bone to be snarled over."

Malachi looked chastened, and Alaman grinned as he took her hand and lifted it to kiss her knuckles. Malachi bristled at the sight, but when Frances glared at him, he sat back in his chair and took a slurp of tea. It was too hot and burnt his lip. He swore in Irish and then the tension seemed to evaporate in the room. Within thirty minutes both men were deep in a conversation about the differences between sheep and goats and the methods of grazing each. They went out onto the hills so Malachi could show Alaman his flock, and Frances took the opportunity to hurry up to Magdalena's cottage and have the necessary conversation with her.

Magdalena was sitting in front of the fire when Frances entered, and she lifted her beautiful grey eyes and smiled. Frances went to her, knelt by her chair and laid her head in Magdalena's lap. As the older woman stroked her hair, Frances spoke quietly.

"*A mháthair,* I am called to do the Goddess's work. The Grandmothers have summoned me, and I have answered."

"As we always knew you would, daughter."

"Does it tear at your heart that I have found love again?" Frances asked, needing to know.

"I see that this man has brought you joy. I see that you are embracing life fully. And I know that Michael will never be forgotten. But I will miss you, my sweet daughter of the heart."

"I shall return, *a mháthair!*"

"Yes, but not to live here again, not for quite some time. I see that your future is like the nomads, like your Cree ancestors, like this man Alaman's people. You shall travel the Earth and find your home in each other."

"You have been the mother that I always wanted. You have been my truest mother," Frances said whispering past her tears.

"And you, and our Michael, were not the children of my body, but the children of my soul. The Goddess has been very good to me." Magdalena leaned forward, took a deep whiff of Frances, her hair, her scent, and then kissed her gently on the head. She stored that combination of the particular Francesness: forests, books, dried mugwort, and something ancient. It was a precious distillation that she would always treasure.

Magdalena, staring into the low fire, fell into reverie. She could remember every detail of the night in 1908 sixty years ago when a knock at her door had awoken her. It was raining sleet outside and the wind tore at the corners of her cottage. She had wrapped a shawl around her shoulders and opened the door a bit. Peering out into the dark she saw a man and a child, huddled together into one sodden lump.

"Missus, we implore your help. Our caravan has broken a wheel and my son is very sick. Can ye help us?" The man's voice sounded raw and jagged, like words hurt.

"Come in! Come in out of the cold!" Magdalena had drawn them in and set them by the fire which she quickly poked back into a strong blaze, adding bricks of peat generously. She brought blankets and toweling and helped the man strip the wet clothes off the little boy. He was too thin, that boy, all bone and sinew, and burning up with fever. His face was so pale as to be translucent and his hair was cut with short tufts and places close to the scalp, as if someone had done a hurried job with scissors. When they had him naked and rubbed ferociously to bring warmth back into his fingers and toes, they laid him on a pallet close to the fire. Then, and only then, did Magdalena turn her attention to the father. He too looked gaunt and thin, the same auburn hair cut haphazardly, the same protruding cheekbones. He was shivering constantly, and his eyes were red-rimmed.

Magdalena had hurried for more blankets. "I shall bring you some dry clothes. They were my Da's and they should fit you." The man lifted his eyes to react, dull, and yet filled with gratitude.

"You are kindness itself, Missus."

She brought him trousers, socks, a shirt and jumper, then retreated to her bedroom to let him change in the warmth by the fire. When she heard the creak from the chair as he sat again, she came back into the front room and put on the kettle. Neither had spoken as tea was made and drunk. Finally, they had both spoken, overlapping one another and laughing softly.

"You said your wheel had bro…"

"I can never thank yo…."

They had looked into each other's eyes and smiled. He had begun again. "I can never thank you enough for giving us shelter."

Magdalena had nodded. "Tell me about your boy. Has he been sick long?"

As the night had spun on she had heard how the man and boy had come to be stranded on the deserted lane. The story of his life as a Traveller, the death of his wife in childbirth, the anguish of guilt and blame that had driven him to leave his extended family and take to the road with only his tiny son for company.

"Michael has been feeling poorly for about a week, but just today he seemed to fall into some stupor. I took a turn to get to the village, maybe hoping to find a healer, but then the wheel, the rain, and then we found you. I'm thinking that the Good People led us to you, and that we have found our healer."

The days had gone on and little Michael had slowly recovered. His father had made himself useful, hauling and stacking peat, milking cows, taking on a bit of healthy weight himself. And Magdalena found herself with a ready-made family and a rescue from the loneliness she had lived since the death of her parents.

When spring came she and Pádraig had been married in the church in Ballinskellig, and all of that had led to this cluster of her beloveds under one roof, in flesh and in spirit.

She and Frances were in tableau with Frances's arms around Magdalena's legs and Magdalena gazing into the fire when Malachi and Alaman returned. The sound of the front door broke through her memories. As if scripted, the rest of the Kenneallys arrived shortly thereafter.

Malachi's wife, Saoirse, came with a freshly baked loaf of soda bread wrapped in a tea towel. Their oldest daughter, Molly and her husband came, carrying their new baby. Their son, Timothy and his new wife came next, shortly followed by the youngest daughter, Theresa. Everyone crammed into the small cottage and filled the space with laughter and hugs and the smell of baby and fresh bread and love.

As the day wound down, everyone settled in front of the fire and the stories and songs began. Malachi had an impressive tenor, and he and his daughter Molly brought everyone to tears with "The Minstrel Boy." Magdalena told the story of Dermot and Gráinne, and Frances sang a hunting song in Cree. The time came when all eyes turned to Alaman to do his piece. Frances had warned him he wouldn't be let off the hook, so he was prepared. He stood, taking the traditional place in front of the fire and began.

"I will arise and go now, and go to Innisfree,
And a small cabin build there, of clay and wattles made..."

He said it through first in English, then began again reciting in Irish. His eyes were closed, and his head tilted back. He looked totally foreign and completely at home, tall and brown, black hair falling down around his shoulders, hands clasped before him. He looked like a bard of ages past, and they heard the echo of Michael in his voice. It was clear to all gathered there that he was deep in his memory. When at last he spoke the last words, his eyes drifted open and he saw all their faces, Michael's family, watching him with respect and with tears streaming down their faces. They knew who his teacher had been, and they perceived his honoring of that teacher.

In that silence that held, filled with sorrow and sweetness, a sharp knock came at the door.

"Alaman Sulaman, come out!" The man's voice was hard and low, not an invitation, but an order.

Alaman looked at Frances who had stood to intervene and he shook his head. "No, my queen. This battle may be initiation or beating, but it is mine to endure for the honor of your love." He pulled his coat on and went to the door. As he drew it open, he saw the faces of a handful of men, ranging in age from twenty to sixty. He walked out into the

151

night, pulling the door closed behind him.

"Malachi, shall you go with them?" Frances asked in some consternation.

"Sister, he has claimed this as his to do, his alone. I must respect a man like that."

The family settled down like broody hens. The baby, who had fallen asleep in her mother's arms, woke and fussed, quieting only when her rooting resulted in a breast. Saoirse put more water on for tea, and Malachi pulled the bottle of poteen from the loose stone in the hearth, pouring an ample dram for all the adults.

Frances let the alcohol relax her body and her tongue, filling them in on what had transpired with the Americans…and where it was leading them.

"And so, my loves, I will be going on this adventure, reaching out to these Grandmothers, all the while using the travels to research and write new books, all about those peoples that the world is pushing to the side. These Grandmothers speak to one another in their dreams and visions. They hold the pattern for what is to come next."

"And these Grandmothers, will you have known them from the Before?" Molly asked.

"From what I have been given to understand, these Grandmothers are the incarnations of those of us who were companions to the Thirteen. I do hope to remember them. I am eager to see them in these new lives and forms. We – these Companions – are the threads, the warp and weft, the tapestry of bloodlines that will comprise the fabric for the return of the Thirteen."

"There is to be reckoning, an awakening, a rebirth…" Magdalena said, voice roughened by the poteen.

All was quiet except for sounds of the nursing baby. When at last she was replete, her mother lifted her on a shoulder and with some gentle patting elicited a healthy burp. Everyone chuckled and then settled back down into stillness and waiting.

The door to the cottage opened with gusto. The family, who had all fallen asleep in front of the fire, came to with a start at the sound and the sharp, cold air rushing inside. It was few hours shy of dawn, still inky black outside. Frances jumped to her feet and met, embraced, and partially held up Alaman as he stumbled, smiled, and trumpeted a hallo to everyone. Frances put a finger over his lips and shushed. "The baby! Don't wake the baby!" But she smiled at him for he was flush with good humor and what she supposed was not a small amount of poteen.

"I have returned, my Frances! And all in one piece," he said, still too loudly.

Frances led him to a chair by the fire, Saoirse poured him tea, and Theresa brought a shawl to throw over his shoulders, tucking it into his arms.

"Ach! Careful there! It appears that that hurts."

"What in the name of all the saints?" Frances exclaimed, seeing some dots of what looked like blood seeping through his shirt.

"Yes, my queen. I have been marked! I am now officially to be known as Alaman Sulaman Brendan Kenneally, Brendan for the saint who traveled far." Alaman began to giggle, and the sound was infectious. Soon everyone was laughing, but they all gasped as Frances helped Alaman out of his shirt and they saw the tattoo that covered his left shoulder and ran down his arm, ending just above the wrist. It was elaborate and mesmerizing, taking the shape of a dragon with open mouth. Between the front claws the dragon held a circle with the triskele inside. The ink was sharp black and the speckles of blood made the dragon look burnished red.

"Holy Mary, Mother of God!" someone whispered.

"Alaman, why did you let them do this to you?" Frances said between the tears in her throat.

"For you, my queen. Do you not know what I would endure for you? And for him, for Michael. And to make clear to that band of madmen that I will not back down. They call this 'The Dragon Protecting the Goddess.'"

They found salve and clean bandages, and Frances led Alaman to rest in the bed. As she helped him lie down she kissed his forehead, and said, "You beautiful foolish man."

And he replied, half in his alcohol slumber. "I am that dragon, and you are that Goddess." He turned his head on the pillow and sank deep into sleep. Frances took some moments to watch that sharp profile, the hawk nose, the long lashes, the stubble of black beard. His face, on the pillow where Michael had slept, and it all felt right. "The Goddess always brings me exactly what I need," she whispered as a prayer.

$$\text{)} \bigcirc \text{(}$$

They stayed in Kerry for another week. The Travellers arrived in force, needing to meet 'the newest Kenneally.' The wanderers and the settled people, all family, and connected, moved from inside hearth to outside fire and back around again. Meals seemed to be at all unset times, children ran in and out of the cottages and caravans at will, and the stories and laughter and tears were a constant song cycle.

On their last night before the journey to America was to begin, Frances and Alaman stood with arms around each other's waists listening to a lovely, if somewhat disjointed, version of The Wild Swans story, mostly told by one of Michael's cousins with energetic assists from sorted and sundry other Kenneallys. The moon had risen and the cloudy sky let moonlight flood the yard, then hide all in shadow.

Frances took Alaman's hand and led him away from the group, out the yard and up into the hills. He thought about asking where they were headed, and then decided that he didn't really care, as long as he held that small, warm palm.

At last they reached a small hollow, nested between three hills. He knew as soon as they walked down into it that it was a sacred place.

"The Old Ones are here," he said softly.

"Yes. They asked to meet you," Frances replied.

Figures began to emerge: tall and shimmering, woven, it seemed to Alaman, from mist and starlight and something more tangible, like moss. There were three of them, one coming from each hill, and as they approached, Frances placed a hand over her heart and spoke in a language that Alaman almost remembered. Her words made a kind of sense inside his head.

"Most Revered, I bring to you the man called Alaman. You had summoned us, and we listened."

The beings, the Sidhe, replied. To Alaman it sounded like musical tones, all together and yet distinguishable one from the other. Like crystal goblets being struck. It made his sinews twang and his heart race.

Frances let go of his hand, and he felt a momentary panic. She stepped forward and was surrounded by these beings. He could see her through them. He knew them to have form and yet they were unsubstantial. To him it looked as if they were anointing her, waving their hands of light over her body and all around her eyes and ears. The tones got louder, and he watched Frances respond, adding her music to theirs. It was the most beautiful music he had ever heard, and yet he never could replicate it in his own mind.

Frances turned and motioned to him. He stepped forward, and then he also was bathed, anointed, blessed by the light and music and crystalline essence. As Alaman looked up into the sky the constellations swirled and took on another pattern, an ancient star map, one he knew that he knew from the Before.

Frances began a prayer in the old language, the Common Tongue, from ages past, and Alaman added his voice, discovering that he remembered that as well. As he watched the Sidhe they seemed to solidify, as if the prayer, the praying, was giving them substance, until, finally, they stood fully formed and visible to all the ways the eyes can see.

"We have a gift for you, our children," they said.

And there, among them, was the shade of Michael. Frances gasped and reached out a hand to touch him, but of course that was not possible. He smiled at her and Alaman, and then lifted specter arms and made sigils in the air, blessings for protection and long life and love. They felt the magic sift over them like a very fine mist.

"Always," he said, and then he disappeared. The Sidhe began to fade and dissolve back into the hills, until just Frances and Alaman stood in the hollow, clinging together, their faces awash with tears of sadness and joy.

Frances looked down at the ground and saw a small smooth stone where the essence of Michael had stood. She bent down and slipped it into her pocket where it nestled perfectly with the stone from her Granny's cabin that she always carried with her.

"Onward, my Blue Man?" Frances asked.

"Forever and always, my queen," he replied.

CHAPTER 5
BIG ISLAND LAKE CREE
NATION, SASKATCHEWAN,
CANADA, 1968

F ebruary in Saskatchewan was a particular kind of hell.

Frances and Alaman had flown from Shannon to Toronto, Toronto to Saskatoon, then a puddle jumper that rattled like death with wings from Saskatoon to Regina, followed by, and victorious in torture, a bus that had no heat to the Cree Reserve.

Frances and Alaman stumbled off the bus with no feeling in their feet, and were swept up in the arms of uncles and aunties who all smelled of woodsmoke and tobacco and venison. The next two days were a swirl of fry bread and coffee so strong it could hold a spoon upright, laughter and reminiscences in English (for Alaman's benefit), and in Cree when the most painful things were discussed.

In English – "We took down a bear this year! Good eatin'!"

In Cree – "Auntie, where are the children?"

"All taken in September to the residential school."

"All of them? Even the little ones?"

"Yes, Frannie, all of them, as young as six years old."

In English – "Your cousin Walter will be so sorry he missed you! He's gone up north hunting."

In Cree – "He took his son north in August to avoid the government agents, they always come in September: the Crying Month."

"Is he gone for good?"

"Most likely – needs to be."

In English – "Would you like to see your Granny's cabin? We've built it up for you."

In Cree – "The People use it to hide when they need to avoid the government. Walter and his Tommy stayed there most of the summer."

The next morning, after they bundled Alaman up so well that only his eyes were showing, a small group of family walked the distance to the new version of Sally Standing Bear's cabin. Alaman struggled briefly with the snowshoes but quickly found the correct stepping pattern, and they made good time. It wasn't far by foot, but it was a million miles by law. Sally's cabin had come to her upon the death of her husband Louis Portreaux, and Louis being a white man, his land was situated outside the Reserve. It had been Sally's, and then she had left it to Frances, and so, it was a place where Indian Agents had no jurisdiction.

Frances walked out of the woods and into the clearing in front of the cabin. The snow was deep, about two feet, but a path had been shoveled leading up to the door. It looked exactly as she had seen it last, rebuilt to be an exact copy of the original. There were freshly painted shutters at the windows and the old sod roof had been replaced with clay tiles.

Frances stood before it, arms spread wide, eyes closed, trying to breathe in the essence of this place where she had been happiest as a child, where she had found refuge with Granny Sally and Uncle Walter. The stone in her pocket hummed in remembrance.

"This was the home of Sally Standing Bear?" Alaman asked quietly from her left shoulder.

Frances nodded and then turned around to point to an area where the garden had been. "And there was where we burned her remains and all her belongings, all except for her Book."

"Sacred ground," Alaman whispered.

One of Frances's uncles stepped forward, holding a large shell, and lighting some tobacco. He lifted the shell, smoke billowing upward from it.

"Ancestor, we honor you today and all days."

The group was silent, watching the wind pick up the smoke and create a dancing spiral.

Frances turned back to her family and said, "It is good that this place remains a sanctuary. Granny Sally would want it so."

"Should you ever need it, it is yours, niece. We keep it in trust for you."

Frances shot a look to Alaman and then replied, "Uncle, the world is an increasingly dangerous place, and we are embarking on work that may upset the powers that be. Knowing that this hidey-hole exists, is indeed good news."

Later that day Frances asked for a lift into town. The main street looked much the same: shops open, cars and trucks parked on the diagonal. In her youth there had been as many horse-drawn conveyances as gasoline-driven, but now it was all mechanized. Frances found herself a wee bit nostalgic for what it had been like, then remembered how unhappy she had been here, shook her head to shake out the cobwebs of memory, and walked into the hardware store. A bell jangled as she entered. "Be right with ya!" called the white-haired man behind the counter up a step-ladder, with his back to the door.

He descended, turned, and then went pale.

"Frannie?"

"Yes, Pa, it's me."

"Lawsy mercy. I thought you were your Granny Sally standing there."

Frances smiled and took the comment as a compliment, although it wasn't clear if that is how her father had meant it.

"You're here. For a visit? Or are you back to stay?"

Frances watched the emotions roll across his face like clouds on a windy day. Happiness, hope, dread, relief, trepidation, guilt. It was as it had ever been between her and her father. Their love for one another sat behind the bars of expectations and disappointments and an inexplicable gulf.

"Just a short visit, Pa. Can we sit and have some coffee, do you think?"

"Oh, sure, sure! Come on back!" He walked them toward the back end of the store where the wood stove made a circle of warmth and the coffee pot stood ready all day long. He poured them both a mug, adding the sugar and cream he knew she wanted and then sat down on a bench so he could see her, but not too close.

They talked for almost an hour. Frances heard about her mother's last illness, the stomach cancer that had taken her, and how her father had been keeping the store going since then.

"Business is good. Keeps me busy."

"You know you could have come to visit us, anytime, Pa. We asked you over and over."

"I know, but Lawsy! Me…on a plane? I can't fathom that."

And Frances let it go.

She told him about Sassy and her husband and baby. "They are settled in Senegal now. Other parts of West Africa are not safe these days with insurrections and such. But they are happy and doing good work in their doctoring."

"Is he, this Kwame, is he an African then?"

"Yes, Pa, he is."

She saw him grapple with that. He had never gotten comfortable with the notion of mixing the races, despite the fact that he had married a woman who was half Native. Because in his mind, she looked white, so she was. But an African? And a half-African great-grandbaby? No, that was too hard to figure out. She watched as his eyes shuttered, and she felt her heart sink. Then she laughed at her own foolishness. Had she really thought, even for a moment, that he would have changed? She dropped any flicker of hope for a deeper connection. Again, she was struck by the complicated notions of family and belonging. How blood connected us some, and how soul paths connected us in other ways, and how brilliant it was when both things lined up. She said a silent prayer of gratitude for all her beloveds, and, with a gentle resignation, let go of any ties to her father.

They talked for about ten minutes more, general chitchat, and then Frances stood.

"I need to get going, Pa. Some folks from the Rez are gonna give me a ride back. But it has been good to see you."

She gave him a long hug until she felt him pull away and then she dropped her arms. "Take care of yourself. I'll write."

"Where you going, Frannie? Ireland? Or Africa?"

"All over, Pa. I'm headed all over."

At the door she looked back and saw him silhouetted in the sunlight that streamed through the store windows. He lifted one hand in farewell, and she jangled the bells as she left.

The next day, two uncles and Frances and Alaman piled into an old Ford truck that, defying all logic, actually ran, and headed south to the Border. The Border guards gave a cursory look at their passports and waved them across.

"This is an international border?" Alaman asked in surprise.

"This crossing belongs to the white man. These guards know us, know we are First Nation and just let us through. Our People don't acknowledge any border. We live on both sides of this line on a map," one uncle said.

"And we try to avoid and break the laws of both sides too," the other uncle chortled. Frances smiled.

The uncles drove them through North Dakota, South Dakota and down to Pine Ridge with snow piled up seven feet high on both sides of the road. It was a long drive, about ten hours, in that rattly truck. The two men told Frances stories of all the extended family, who had moved to the city, who had died from drink, who left for town and never returned. "Your cousin, Albert, Mina's boy, he left for work in the sugar beet fields and wound up in Minneapolis. Last we heard he was in prison: armed robbery, they said."

The pain of their history wove through their words. Frances knew much of this for she had never stopped corresponding with her family on the Rez. But to hear it in their voice brought a particular searing arrow-like shot to the heart.

"There has been the same car on our tail for about three hours," one uncle said.

"I know," Frances replied.

"Frannie? You in some kind a trouble?" the other uncle asked.

"Not yet," Frances replied, her smile adding smoke and texture to her voice.

The talk wore down and the miles wore on. It was long past dark by the time they got to Pine Ridge and pulled up in front of the Community Center. Three people came out of the door to greet them. They were so bundled up it was hard to distinguish features, but they greeted the Canadians warmly and led them inside.

It was a good size room with a wood stove at the back and a pool table on the right. There were smaller tables, for cards or homework on the left side, and the entire room smelled of chili and fry bread. More folks came to greet them, and Frances found herself surrounded by men, women, and children who all seemed very happy to see her.

"Come in! Come in! We waited supper for you."

Frances, Alaman and the uncles were shepherded to a table and plates of food were placed before them.

"Eat! Eat!"

After the meal the front door to the Community Center opened and a group of people entered, two young men, one on either side of a wheelchair that was being pushed by a very distinguished older man. The person in the chair, of indiscriminate gender, looked ancient with deep creased lines across a nut-brown face. Frances and Alaman instinctively stood as the wheelchair made its way across the room.

The person in the chair had long white braids that fell down past the belt that wrapped numerous layers of sweaters and coats together. Bright black eyes, surrounded by folds of flesh peered out that them.

"You have taken your sweet time. I thought I could die a long time ago, but no, I had to wait for you!" The voice was creaky, but clear and precise.

Frances leaned forward ever so slightly to bring her eyes on the same level. "And hello to you too," she responded with a lilt to her voice.

The aged one cackled and replied, "I heard there would be cake."

Later that night when most had left the Community Center leaving only Frances, Alaman and the aged one with her handsome protector, the introductions began.

"I am Agnes Weapon Maker, and this is my son, Brigadier," the old one said.

"And I am Frances Fletcher and this is Alaman Sulaman," Frances added.

"So as not to waste time, let me tell you who I was in the Before. You knew me, I believe, as Smith the Younger from the Sea of Grasses."

Frances looked hard, then looked soft, and then saw what she was looking for. This woman before her radiated the same stubborn refusal to give up that had been the salient feature of the young Smith. He had stuck by his father and their companions. He had refused to run for cover when things got dangerous. He had outlasted trouble and persistently hung in there, fervent in his belief that good times would come again. That stubbornness stared back at Frances now.

"Grandmother, you know why we are here?"

"Yes."

"Do you have any idea what we do next?" Frances asked with some slight desperation. "For we are here on faith, and as yet, with very little direction."

"Yes. Tomorrow. Tomorrow we will pray and do a sweatlodge. Tomorrow we shall take the necessary steps to do what we are asked to do." The old woman nodded and then her eyes drifted closed. It looked like she was going to fall asleep right there.

"Grandmother! What are we doing?" Frances asked, close to the end of her tether.

"Why, I thought you knew… We are going to open a Portal!" And with that Agnes Weapon Maker waved a hand to gesture and get turned around and taken home to her bed, leaving Frances and Alaman standing in the now empty Community Center, mouths slightly agape.

The two uncles were already settled and snoring in the guest bunkhouse, Frances and Alaman slipped in quietly, took off layers and cuddled together under a pile of thick wool blankets that still smelled rather strongly of sheep. They whispered together for a few moments and then fell into deep sleep, only occasionally ruffled by dreams that were more memory than conjecture.

A gentle tapping on the door woke them before dawn. Hurrying into clothes Frances and Alaman left the room without waking the uncles and followed Brigadier Weapon Maker down the road and then over a break in a fence to an empty field. Horses were corralled nearby and whinnied a good morning. The daylight was weak and struggled to lift the leaden sky. Alaman felt his eyelashes freeze and his breath made tiny weighted white clouds an inch past his mouth.

"My queen, how long till we can get warm again?" he asked with only a tinge of pain.

"Oh, my dear. Soon you will be so hot that you will long for this cold," she answered.

They came up to a small, rounded shelter, covered in blankets and hides, with a fire in front piled high and crackling like lightning in the sharp air. They all stood as close to the fire as they could without getting singed, rustling feet, shifting weight to keep the blood moving, flipping front to back as one side got too hot and the other side got way too cold. Shortly, the entourage of Agnes Weapon Maker and her young honor guards arrived, with the ruts in the field making hard going for the chair.

Her bright black raisin eyes met theirs, and the edges crinkled as she smiled at them.

"Let's go sweat!" she said.

The sweatlodge, as Alaman was to discover, was a four-step ritual. Frances and the others quickly shed their coats and outer clothes and the women donned simple cotton shifts. Alaman couldn't believe that they expected him to do the same, but as the others stood and looked implacably at him, he acquiesced and stripped faster than he believed possible in the bitter air.

They crawled clockwise into the hut saying *"A ho mitakuye oyasin"* and *"Hiya mitakuyasin,"* asking permission and giving respect to "all our relations." When they had all settled, Agnes Weapon Maker entered and got herself situated near the door flap. She asked for rocks that had been heating in the fire to be brought into the lodge.

"Six Ancestors, please."

Offerings of herbs, cedar and sweetgrass, were given to the ancestor stones, and a bucket of water was lifted into the lodge. The Fire Keepers outside lowered the flaps until it was as dark as the womb inside the hut.

Everything became sound and smell and sensation. The heat and moisture rose rapidly as Agnes scooped ladles of water over the stones. There followed a sizzle and the explosion of humid air in the nostrils. Agnes began a drum beat and a prayer song. This ritual, this way that White Buffalo Woman had taught the Lakota to pray, the way to be with Spirit, as all had been with Spirit in their mother's wombs.

Time became only a construct. This was the limitless expanse of prayer, of connection, of the surrender of fear and envy and greed and anger, to just be with the heartbeat, with the wet dark, with the Mother of all things.

Four rounds of prayer. Four pauses where the flaps were lifted and more ancestor rocks were brought in. More. More. More.

Frances asked for guidance in round one. She asked for the wisdom to use this guidance well in round two. She asked for the courage to do what was being asked of her in round three. And then she surrendered in round four.

Alaman, a man of the desert, found this experience of wet heat novel, then uncomfortable, then frightening as his lungs worked harder than they ever had before to draw searing air in. But he too found a state of release and letting go. He let be what was.

When, finally, the ritual came to an end the participants crawled out into the frigid air to find that snow was now falling hard, almost sideways. This rebirth from being held in the dark and wet, into the cold and bright and exposed was brutal and exhilarating. Laughing, Frances and Alaman stumbled into their clothes and then walked in some state of delirium and ecstasy back to the Community Center.

In silence they ate the food placed before them, toweled off their once frozen and now dripping hair, and sat looking into each other's eyes.

"Did you see what you needed to see, my queen?" Alaman asked in an almost whisper.

Frances nodded and collected her thoughts, aiming to find words to match her vision.

"There are places on this Earth, portals, that are like spigots. They have been turned tightly closed for centuries. The time is coming when they need to be opened. But it must be done in the proper sequence, with the appropriate timing, to avoid a dangerous release of energies." She fell silent again.

"And?" Alaman prodded.

"And we need to go to the Wind Cave."

Later that day Agnes Weapon Maker and her son Brigadier came to the Community Center to speak to Frances and Alaman. Agnes looked bright and refreshed after the morning's lodge, younger by a decade. She smiled widely.

"And so, Spirit spoke this morning, eh?" Agnes almost giggled as she asked the non-question.

"Hiya mitakuyasin," Frances replied.

"And when will you be on your Moon?" Agnes asked Frances. "We shall need the power of the blood, eh?"

"Yes, this too was told to me," Frances replied. "But Grandmother, these days my Moons are not regular. I don't know when the next one is to be."

Agnes just shrugged and said, "So, we wait."

The next three weeks were easy and lazy. Frances and Alaman slept in late, as the winter asked of them. They spent hours with elders and youngsters, learning about life on Pine Ridge Rez and the hardships the People endured. Frances filled several notebooks with information. Alaman was impressed that she was so skillful at listening and asking just the right questions to gain the deeper insight into people's lives. Frances's uncles stayed and visited for a week or so and then with brisk hugs and few words left her to return to Canada.

"Don't go looking for trouble now," Frances said with a tightness in her throat.

"Not unless trouble comes lookin' for me first," one uncle replied and the other one simply shrugged a shoulder and smiled.

One night, sitting listening to an elder tell the stories of the Ghost Dancers, Frances felt the tug low in her abdomen, the almost pain, almost desire pull of her own woman tides. She listened deeply and felt the whoosh of release as her womb let go.

Making her thank yous to the elder, she stood and led Alaman out into the night toward Agnes' home. As they entered the dimly lit house they could make out Agnes staring into the flames of her woodstove. She didn't turn to look at them but simply said, "It's time."

The next morning Frances and Alaman joined the group who would be heading toward Wind Cave. They piled into pick-up trucks that pulled horse trailers and made their way down snow-packed roads as far as the roads went. Then the company saddled horses and took off into the deeper wilderness. It was a sunny day and the sunlight on the snow was blinding. The only sounds were the crunch of the horses' hooves breaking through the snow crust, the creak of saddle leather, and the occasional piercing call of hawks overhead.

The landscape was deceptively flat, and yet, as the hours went on, the roll of the Earth would allow them a higher vantage point and then a disappearing horizon. Frances found herself in a state of deep reverie. She felt wide open to the land and the spirits of the land and let herself move into a place where human edges were immaterial.

By the time they arrived at the entrance to the Wind Cave, Frances was beyond words, beyond language. Agnes directed the people to carry Frances into the Cave, but Alaman insisted on doing it himself.

"This. This is what I am for her."

And Agnes nodded and gave a grunt of approval.

They made their way down into the cave with folks lighting lanterns, Brigadier holding tight to Agnes's arm to steady her, and Alaman clutching the now entranced Frances to his chest.

When they came to a large open space Agnes directed them to place a blanket on the ground and motioned for Alaman to lay Frances there. He did so reluctantly, for she seemed so fragile and disembodied.

Agnes began a chant in the Common Tongue, which Alaman had heard in the hills of Kerry from the Sidhe, that forgotten language that spoke directly to the marrow of the bones. The people gathered there in the cave picked up the chorus and Alaman felt the deepening of that quality of energy that heralded the place between the worlds.

"We call the Great Mother.
You are the Source of all life
From before time, till after time,
She is here."

Suddenly the room in the cave became very crowded. The presence of many beings, the Ancestors and the Goddess filled the space. The heartbeat drum quickened. The chanting voices grew more fervent. The ground shook.

And then a shaft of brilliance, wind made visible, erupted from the ground and shot right through Frances's body. It lifted her up from the surface of the cave and suspended her about eighteen inches from the ground. Alaman gasped and tried to race forward to her, but he was pulled back.

The chanting became impassioned and intense.

"Sacred Mother!
Sacred Mother!
Sacred Mother!"

Agnes walked forward gingerly and cautiously slipped into the now expanding vibration that was spreading beyond Frances's body. Agnes visibly shuddered as she walked into that pool of divine brilliance. She reached out and placed her hand atop Frances's heart and the energy magnified and kaleidoscoped into a million shafts and a thousand colors.

All there knew they were witnessing a miracle. Each person felt the heat and the love as vibration, as air made tangible entered their bodies. Their chanting evaporated and was replaced by a sound like a crystal bowl being struck and ringing, ringing, ringing. The strands of visible air began to weave together, and the people there formed a tapestry of witnesses. It was bliss, it was glory, it was...

At long last the Wind presence began to diminish. Agnes motioned to Alaman and he swept in and gathered Frances's body before it came down to rest on the cave floor. She seemed to be in a deep sleep, and her face was peaceful with a sweet small smile lifting the corners of her mouth. Alaman leant over and kissed her, calling her back to the place of the living. Her eyes fluttered and then opened. Her face lit with joy at the sight of him, and she spoke so only he could hear. "Hello, my Blue Man."

The Portal was now opened. The air flowed, invisible yet palpable at a steady stream. And in twelve other sacred spots around the globe, from Uluru in Australia to Jeju Island in South Korea, from Mount Kailash in Tibet to the Isle of Lewis in Scotland, there started a rumbling, a jostling of submerged herstory and suppressed wisdoms. Those positioned to guard these sacred places took note of the stirring, the awakening. They watched as the earth rippled like a bedsheet flapping in the wind. They saw water spiraling on its own accord. They smelled the deep scents of sulfur and manganese from down within the Mother. These were the signs that had been foretold. These were the days they had been taught to watch for. The Grandmothers met on astral planes to swap information. The young stewards of these sacred places reinforced barriers and camouflage to keep the spots hidden from the casual and careless.

$$ \supset \bigcirc \subset $$

Mildred Weapon Maker, a two-spirit woman and granddaughter of Agnes, chose a white man, a pipe-fitter with red hair and blue eyes who had come to work on the oil fields to be her mate. One month after the Portal had been opened she conceived a child who received the spirit of one of the Thirteen.

And it had begun.

$$ \supset \bigcirc \subset $$

Frances and Alaman lived in a small cabin not far from Wind Cave for most of the rest of 1968. The living was sparse, and the solitude exquisite. Both Frances and Alaman knew how to live with little fuss, but these conditions taxed even them. The snow lasted until May, but they were serenaded at night with the songs of wolves. They made love, and talked, and slept, and shared their dreams. But most of all, Frances wrote.

It felt liberating and exhilarating. Frances hadn't written anything new since Michael's death. He had always been such a part of her life and her writing. And without him she feared she had lost her voice forever.

She had crafted her first series of books during her years in Ireland with Michael, and as his health had not given them the opportunity to travel, her books had granted them that exploration of the world. Over the years, Frances had established a golden reputation as an author whose words carried her readers to another time and place.

She had used the stories in The Book from Granny Sally as jumping off places and source material for authentic historical detail. Granny Sally's former life as a Quaker abolitionist had been the springboard for the novel *Friendly Valor* set in the early nineteenth century in America. Sally's past life memories of her meeting with Joan of Arc had been the source for *Mystic Maid*. There were twelve books in all. Each written with him there. Each read aloud to him each night.

Michael and she would be together in the cottage, peat fire going, or when the weather was fine in the gazebo that Bartholomew had built for them behind the cottage, with her clacking away on her Remington typewriter and him reading or napping, waking to gaze at her with his smile of deep and abiding love. On his last day she had been curled up against him in their bed, her nose buried deep his neck, into the very Michael-ness of him, his smell, the texture of his skin. His breathing was very labored, but he insisted on speaking.

"Beloved, do you think we shall find one another again?" he had whispered.

"We always have before," Frances had said, swallowing tears.

"I keep remembering what your Granny said, about how this was her last incarnation in a cycle, how a big shift was on the horizon. Do you think that we too are finishing a cycle of togetherness?"

"That is more sorrow than I can bear, my heart. I think we shall always find one another, somehow, in the 'somewhere'."

Michael had been quiet for a long time and his breath had begun to stutter. Frances had listened with her entire body, hoping beyond hope that the next breath would come. But at last, he had spoken again, so softly that Frances leaned up to almost inhale his words. "You have always been worth all the trouble."

She had looked at him, startled, and then saw the smile that lifted the corners of his beautiful mouth. He had looked at her one last time and then his eyes lifted to the ceiling of the room and his last exhale extended into forever.

When he had died she had put her typewriter away, and spent her days walking the hills, occasionally jotting ideas for poems about loss and loving down in her tiny notebook. She disappeared for days at a time in the bottomless grieving for all the lifetimes when they had lost each other. She would sit with the stones, and they would keen together. Magdalena would send Malachi out into the hills to look for Frances. He would eventually find her, wet through, and bring her back to Magdalena's cottage for warm blankets and hot tea.

Magdalena feared that Frances would simply follow Michael into that 'wherever' he had gone. Without Michael she was rudderless. But then, Sassy had needed her. She had received that "Come quickly" astral telegram from her daughter, and she had gathered her scattered pieces of self and hurried to Senegal. Life had come back into her with a tingle and an almost-pain, like limbs that had fallen asleep and were waking up. But still she had been without her writing. Finally, finally this piece of herself had returned.

Occasionally people would arrive on horseback with supplies and mail and carried back return letters. Spring came and went in the blink of an eye as the words poured from her. Summer was gloriously hot, and Alaman discovered that mosquitoes were the bane of his existence. In September Frances finished her novel, *The Ribbon Dancer*, set on the Pine Ridge Rez. Agnes Weapon Maker's family proudly carried the manuscript to the nearest town to make sure it got sent off to the publisher by certified mail. And Frances and Alaman packed up their belongings, hearts open to see where they would next be guided.

Frances was alive with purpose. She would travel and research indigenous communities. She would connect with those Grandmothers that had sent Alaman to find her. She would be the vehicle by which the long-closed portals would be opened. If the Goddess needed seeds planted, she, Frances, was up to the task. She could write books that might open minds. She could satisfy her American espionage associates with just the information she wanted them to have. But most importantly, she would be serving the Greater Good.

The Ribbon Dancer became the inspiration for a generation of Native women to claim their heritage, to make sure their voices were heard, to demand both an education and a spirituality in order to become whole. On the Pine Ridge Rez, the women started singing louder, dancing more confidently, making the wisest choices for the next seven generations.

Los Angeles, California, USA, 1969

And so it began that Frances found ways to drop the seeds of Goddess knowledge into the ears of those most receptive. While visiting a museum in Los Angeles in December of 1969 she stood next to a woman who had been arranging a diorama of a burial scene. The 'corpse' was laid on its side with knees tucked up in a fetal position and dressed in a beautiful white buckskin tunic, adorned with jewelry. She, it *was* a she, had a knife and spear laid next to her.

"She looks ready for battle," Frances said, seemingly to no one.

The woman, a staff archaeologist, started. "Oh no, they say she is being protected in the afterlife."

Frances laughed. "Protected? By whom?"

"By the spirits of the knife and spear?" the woman answered, doubting her own response for the first time.

Frances looked at the woman's ID tag. "Marija? What a lovely name."

"It's Lithuanian," the woman responded.

"Marija, perhaps *she* is the one who does the protecting." And with that seed dropped, Frances walked away, leaving Marija Gimbutas staring after her while the wheels began to turn in her head, and the memories began to pour into her heart.

Alice Springs, Northern Territory, Australia, January 1970

Frances and Alaman headed to Australia, arriving in Sydney in a heat wave. They were greeted by representatives of Frances's publishing company, delivered swiftly to the hotel that had been booked for them and promptly fell into a twenty-hour sleep. The next day Frances had a meeting with the branch office of the publisher who had efficiently prepared all the travel arrangements that they would need to make their trek into the Outback. Next, she had a seemingly accidental 'sit side-by-side' meeting in a lushly flowered park with the local CIA operative who passed along the 'request' from Langley and the Australian government. They desired Frances to do a what they labeled a 'friendly infiltration' with Aboriginal activists who had been organizing to secure legal justice and reparations for land stolen. Frances nodded and her face demonstrated compliance, but she had absolutely no intention of doing anything to hinder the native activist movement, just as she had not disclosed the organizing by AIM on the Pine Ridge Reservation.

The journey to the Outback and a town called Alice required a small plane, then a smaller plane, then a crop-duster. On the tarmac two groups stood waiting. At the front was a delegation of townspeople including the mayor, the head of the Ladies Guild, and a children's choir from the local school. Clearly all of European descent, they all had red, flushed faces and heavily freckled arms, and were somewhat taken aback when Frances, small and light brown, and Alaman, tall and deeper brown, alighted from the tiny plane.

"Welcome to Alice Springs, Mrs. Portreaux," the mayor exclaimed. The Ladies Guild head handed Frances a bouquet of flowers, and the children burst into song.

Off to the side and standing farther back was a cluster of First Nation People with skin so dark that Frances felt immediately at home and longing for Senegal and her family there. The spokesperson for that group was a man of late middle age with white hair and forearms like anchor cables. He stepped forward and said, "Auntie Frances, we have been awaiting you."

The mayor looked startled, the head of the Ladies Guild looked peeved. Both groups clearly thought that Frances was to be their guest. How to navigate this Solomonic conundrum?

"What a delightful reception!" Frances spoke to both groups, extending her arms wide. "I am excited to see your town and then get to work doing my research for the next novel." She looked at the mayor. "I would be honored if you would give us a short tour." And to the spokesman for the First Nation, "Uncle, I come with the blessings of my people to meet yours."

The First Nations man, who she would come to know as Uncle Tume, lifted a hand to cover his mouth as he grinned, the mayor nodded and looked flustered.

The tour of Alice Springs was indeed short. The main intersection held the bank, hotel, general store, church and the school. A handful of dusty roads spread out from there. Clusters of First Nation men stood in the shade of giant gum trees, and the sun felt like it would bake the brain. Frances and Alaman graciously accepted a light lunch at the town's only hotel, and then went to find Uncle Tume.

He and his small group were waiting at the edge of town and had all of Frances and Alaman's belongings stacked in the back of a pick-up truck. They slid up into the hot bench seat, as the others piled into the back of the truck. The engine started reluctantly, and the truck rolled out of Alice Springs, past the occasional farmhouse that Uncle Tume called cattle stations. The land was baked and beige, with vivid splashes of green trees and shrubs that lined the creeks and tiny rivers that they passed. Cattle and sheep stood in heat-drenched stupor, and Frances delighted in the sounds of foreign birds.

Far off in the distance a rock formation seemed to jut up straight from the earth. It was shimmering gold in the late afternoon sun and shimmering also with some intangible power.

"Is that it?" Frances asked, breathless.

Uncle Tume grunted an assent.

"Oh, my word!" Frances sighed, gripping Alaman's hand tightly. "How can anyone sleep around here with that rock yelling so loudly all the time?"

Uncle Tume shot his eyes sideways to look at Frances. "Not everybody hears as well as you, Auntie Frances."

About thirty minutes later they pulled up to a line of trees that told of nearby water. As they climbed down out of the truck people began to emerge from the shade and surround the truck, greeting Frances and Alaman as long-lost family. They were taken back into the relative coolness of the glade where small low round structures of lattice and woven grasses formed circles around fire pits, three circles in all. Their hosts gently sat them down on low benches and handed them sweet water from gourds.

Frances saw about twenty-five people, mostly women and children. Uncle Tume began the introductions, starting with the youngest up to the most venerated elder. She was tiny, but the brilliant light of her intelligence shone through.

"Grandmother, may I introduce our guests. This is Frances Fletcher from the line of Atvasfara, and her companion, Alaman Sulaman, messenger of the Grandmothers."

The old women peered up at them, her neck arching from her slightly bent spine. She hooked a finger at Frances, motioning her closer, and Frances leant in.

"Welcome to my heart, Celebi, High Priestess of Brig."

Frances looked deep into the eyes of the woman before her, and as if a film on her vision was dissolving she saw the soul of her comrade in the Before. Here was dignity of the first water. Here was loyalty beyond measure, and the arrogance that sometimes comes with excellence. Here was the one who had been Talo, the twin of the priestess Uxua, devotees of the Goddess Ix Chel. The same Talo who had been lovers in the time Before with none other than Pel of Artemis, who now inhabited the body of Alaman Sulaman. Frances's eyes grew wide, and her sense of the ridiculous grew wider. She gestured behind her to Alaman, and drew him forward.

"Grandmother, I have here another old friend. I believe you two knew each other very, *very* well."

The old woman stared hard at Alaman, and then recognition dawned for them both. She started to laugh until tears rolled down her crevassed cheeks. Frances looked at them fondly and then said, "Who says the Goddess doesn't have a sense of humor?"

Alaman stood stunned and more than slightly embarrassed, as if he had been caught guilty of infidelity. And yet, he reminded himself, his love of this other person had taken place over 5,000 years ago. But still...

Frances took his hand and placed it in the hand of the Grandmother, then she clasped his other hand. "Memory can be a blessing and a curse. So, what say we decide to fall on the side of blessings, eh? Reunions such as this can only be a treasure in the realms of time."

The Grandmother, whose name now was Ulapi, took in Alaman's discomfort and gently squeezed his hand. "Love is love is love," she said. "You were once a very beautiful woman, and now you are a very handsome man. I am also very beautiful, yes?"

Alaman saw her through the eyes of today and yesterday. "As always, a beauty that stops the heart."

$$\mathbb{)} \bigcirc \mathbb{(}$$

Later that night Frances and Alaman stood together at the edge of the band of trees watching the sunset splash crimson and persimmon across the horizon. The air was filled with the raucous sound of the day birds coming in to roost and the night birds swooping out to begin their hunt. Behind them they could hear the sounds of the settlement, cooking pots clanging, low voices and the occasional admonition of a child, the repetition of chanting and the low drone of a didgeridoo.

"The inter-weavings of time and soul make me dizzy sometimes," Frances said softly, leaning into Alaman's shoulder.

He chuckled and responded. "I too am feeling a bit vertiginous."

"This woman, this Ulapi, who was Talo, she can be found in Granny Sally's Book, you know."

"Yes?"

"Yes. When Granny Sally lived as the Abbess Hildegard she had a lover, a Cardinal from Rome named Giuseppe. It was a great love, a secret love," she said.

Alaman took a deep breath and drew his brows together. "So, this woman, this Ulapi, she who was Talo, was the lover of Hildegard, she who was Atvasfara, who was your Granny Sally. This woman was also my lover in the Before?"

"That about sums it up, yes."

He threw back his head a laughed from deep in his belly. "In what I had already thought to be a rather interesting life, I find that I am perpetually astounded by life with you, my queen."

"Stick with me, boyo. I think things may get even more interesting!" Frances said with a wide smile.

"Never fear, my queen. I intend to stick like glue."

$$\text{☽ ◯ ☾}$$

Over the next two days people began to arrive by the truckload. Women, men, and children came to be present at the Great Opening that had been foretold and that Frances was to facilitate.

"Where are they all coming from?" Frances asked Ulapi.

"They heard of your arrival along the Song Lines and the Dream Times. Some have been driving for days from as far as Sydney and Melbourne."

Frances had told Ulapi about the Portal opening in South Dakota, so she asked, "Will this be like the Portal at the Wind Cave?"

"Well, daughter. That is a question that no one knows the answer to. The Portals have been closed since the time before time. It may be that they all open the same way. It may be that each one is different – its own Being – if you will. I am guessing that we will just have to see how it goes."

"Grandmother, that is less than encouraging," Frances muttered wryly, and the old woman just laughed.

$$\text{☽ ○ ☾}$$

Two days later, when the moon was dark, the group of ritualists and ob-servers set out three hours before sunset, driving in a caravan toward the sacred mountain called Uluru, what the white people called Ayers Rock. Frances and Alaman held hands as the truck bumped and jostled over the rough track. As had been the case in South Dakota, the journey, the swaying, the blur of the landscape seemed to lull Frances into a trance.

By the time they pulled up on the west side of Uluru, the sun had fallen and left a soft purple gloaming. Everyone descended from the truck in silence and began the walk up into the Rock. It took the better part of an hour, and Alaman struggled to help Frances over the uneven path in the dimming light. It was almost completely dark when they were led by Ulapi and her family into a cave that began as a shallow incline and then quickly expanded into a vast vaulted chamber. Every-one settled down onto the ground in a circle and the chanting began. Frances swayed slightly and then her head began to loll to the side.

"It is time!" Ulapi said in a voice of unquestionable authority.

Several people came and led Frances into the center of the circle and helped her down to the smooth stone. She turned her head sharply upward, as if listening or seeing something descending from above. And then, just as abruptly, she turned her eyes to the stone beneath her and threw her body down, prostrate. She began to contract and release, her spine lifting, arching and then flattening out. It looked to Alaman like something a human spine ought not be able to do. It was powerful and frightening, as if the forces deep within the Earth were pulling Frances and toying with her like a puppet. Up and down, arch and release, like a snake struggling to shed its skin. The didgeridoo and the bone rattles got louder and louder until at last, with one final extreme arching, Frances's body slammed back down to earth and a fountain of painfully bright white light shot up and through her, hitting the top of the cave and cascading back down to the ground. Everyone there felt the light, warm and fluid, flow under their bodies and support them as if they were floating. Frances too was suspended on a bed of brilliant white, suspended and infused with light so that she was translucent.

And then, a subterranean 'click' happened. It was not sound but resonance, not audible but palpable. This Light here, this Portal, connected with the Portal in Wind Cave, and the river of power that ran between them made the earth tremble. Two locks of the thirteen, two vital locks that had held the Goddess down in the subconscious of humankind for thousands of Earth-years were now opened.

After a time, the Light diminished, and all the people there woke as if from a collective dream. They moved slowly, stretching cramped joints, feeling the tenderness in their earthly bodies from the intensity of what they had all experienced. Alaman pulled Frances into his lap. Tears were streaming down his face, and some fell on her causing her eyelids to flutter.

Ulapi came forward and poured sacred herbs into Frances's mouth to return her to herself. When they left the cave, the sun was high in the sky and blazing hot. They walked back to the trucks with only soft and sporadic talking, everyone still pulling the cobwebs of the Great Dream behind them. And the sacred mountain, Uluru, sang so loudly that Agnes Weapon Maker could hear, all the way in the Pine Ridge Rez on the other side of the world.

Later that night everyone clustered around a small fire kept safely contained in a stone pit. Ulapi sat on a low chair with Alaman at her left foot, his head in her lap. With her arthritic fingers she gently stroked his hair while he brushed his fingertips over Frances's face that was resting in his lap.

"Love is love is love," Ulapi whispered.

)○(

The next months gave Frances and Alaman time to explore the Dream Time, the storehouse of myth and history of these Original People. They were each initiated into the societies that held the men's and women's mysteries. The antipodean summer flowed into autumn, and as winter was approaching Frances finished her next novel *Dream Dancer.*

On the day she wrote the last sentence, she went to look for Alaman. He was wrapped in a blanket with Ulapi, sitting in front of her cabin. As Frances approached, she saw how at peace they were with each other, and she felt a momentary twang of guilt that she would separate them. They felt her and looked up from the fire at the same time.

"Is it time?" Ulapi asked. And Frances nodded.

Alaman leant over and kissed Ulapi gently on the lips.

"And you will be going with her," Ulapi said, not asking but declaring.

"She is my home now. And you will abide in my heart always." Alaman answered, words difficult through his tear-choked throat.

"Love is love is love," Ulapi replied, smiling sadly.

That night, Ulapi's granddaughter, Maggie, took her third cousin, Artie, to her bed and conceived a child who received a soul of another of the Thirteen. Two portals now opened. Two souls of the Thirteen now embodied.

CHAPTER 6
NEW HAVEN, CONNECTICUT, USA, 1970

In September of 1970, Frances was sitting in a coffee shop in New Haven, Connecticut. She had been in New York, visiting her publisher and was on her way to Yale to begin the book tour for her latest novel. At the table adjacent two young people were arguing about the place of women in clergy, with the fellow expounding on St. Paul and leaning heavily on the Adam and rib motif, while the young woman was daring to bring up the mention of Mary Magdalene. Their conversation was getting heated, and Frances couldn't help herself from interjecting and planting another Goddess whisper seed:

"And what of Lilith?"

Both young people stopped and stared at her.

"Excuse me?" the man said.

"I said, what of Lilith?" Frances calmly replied.

"She is a temptress demon," the fellow pompously retorted.

"Or, what if she is the true seeker of wisdom? When given the directive to avoid the source of knowledge she demurred. Perhaps, she is most beloved of the Divine. Perhaps she began a lineage of priestesses that the Hebrews feared…"

The young man began to turn a queer shade of purple. He wasn't used to being challenged, and he didn't like the look of delight that had sparked in his friend's eyes. His intentions for Carol demanded that she have that look of delight about him, not this wild theory being espoused by some strange, little, dark-skinned woman.

"There is no such thing as a lineage of priestesses! No such thing at all!" he insisted.

"You may be right, young man. You certainly seem as if you think you are. But what if…? What if you are wrong? What if there were such a thing?"

"I think that would be wonderful," the young woman, breathed. At that the fellow stormed off, leaving Carol and Frances to spend a rich and satisfying hour in conversation about the 'what ifs.' As Frances finally stood to leave for her next appointment, she reached out a hand and said, "I think that the wonder you wish for is right there for you to find. What is your name, dear?"

"Carol…Carol Christ," the young woman replied.

"Well, isn't that a delicious irony?" Frances chuckled, and turned and left the coffee shop with another seed planted.

Yoff, Senegal, 1971

After six months on a book tour, six months of hotels and restaurants, six months of presenting a fresh face to each interviewer, six months of Western civilization, Frances and Alaman were thrilled to be coming back to Senegal.

Sassy and Kwame met them at the airport with their small ambulance truck and drove them back to Yoff. They all sat up long into the night, sharing all the stories of the time apart. Sisi was now five-going-on-thirty-five, so her mother said, and she sat up with the adults until she curled up into her Grammere's lap and went effortlessly into her dreams.

Frances's right leg had fallen asleep, and as she gently lifted Sisi up to be able to stretch out her knee her skirt got caught under her grand-daughter's body and slipped up high on her left calf.

"Mama! What is that? What happened to you?" Sassy gasped.

Frances and Alaman exchanged swift glances, and then he shrugged, almost imperceptibly. Frances took a deep breath and answered. "It is a mark, a sigil. It appeared after the Portal opened in Australia."

Sassy bent down to get a closer look. The mark was dark, like a tattoo. As Sassy stared, she found herself having trouble focusing, and the image changed shape again and again, with shimmering colors like petrol on water. It was a river, or a snake, or an organism from the primordial ooze.

"Does it hurt? Did it hurt?" Sassy whispered.

"Not a bit. But it does tickle sometimes, like now, when someone is really trying to see it. For most folks it looks like a tattoo and is static, but for some, some with the Sight, it comes alive and moves and tells a story of the place whence it derives."

"Tell her," Alaman nudged.

Frances didn't say anything, but lifted the hem of her blouse to expose her lower right ribs. There was another of the marks, the sigils. This one looked as if it spoke a different language from the mark on Frances's calf, but it, too, oscillated and shimmered. It was a figure that moved like a person dancing or a tree blowing in the wind. Or maybe it was a grouping of falling stars.

"And this one? Mama?"

"Appeared the day after the Portal opened in South Dakota."

"What do they mean?"

Frances seemed to draw into herself and Sassy shot a frantic look to Alaman. He replied, "We think, and really, dear girl, it is only supposition, but we think that these marks will show where all the Portals will be." He reached over and gently stroked Frances's head, tucking a stray piece of hair behind her ear. "We think that perhaps your mama will be a living, breathing, walking map, which… presents some interesting concerns."

Kwame and Alaman looked at each other and then back to Sassy who was trying to punch down a rising panic. "What concerns? Jesus, Mary, and Joseph! What does 'interesting' mean?"

"It means that there may be some people for whom the awakening of the Goddess is…a less than desirable occurrence. There may be some…" and Alaman cleared his throat, "some who will do much to prevent this awakening. And such a map as this might assist them in sabotaging Her return."

Sassy blanched. "Who? Who might wish this?"

Alaman shook his head, and Kwame stepped in to answer. "Mining companies...leaders of the Abrahamic faiths...governments with much invested in a militarized world..."

"Agri-business...drug companies...colonizers...Do you see, my chicken?" Frances continued. "Most of the moneyed and powerful in this world will do almost anything to keep what they have."

Sassy looked at her wild-eyed. "Shite!"

"Exactly!" Frances replied with a small smile growing across her face. "So, we need, always, to be several steps ahead and many times smarter. Sound like fun?"

Woleu-Ntem Province, Gabon, 1971

The cave was almost invisible to the eye: a tiny low entrance covered by dense brush. Frances and Alaman were led into it by Priestess Ele, the reincarnation of Smith the Elder. They had to crawl on all fours and wiggle on their bellies to get into the darkness. The cave seemed to hum in expectation of what was to come. The low dome bounced the voices of the rocks and the heart beats of the humans, weaving them into a fabric of organic sound. The priestess began to chant an almost forgotten melody in a language that the cells remembered.

Frances, in the now familiar trance, felt warmth pooling in the small of her back as she lay stretched out on the earth. To Alaman the light that began to flicker in the blacker than black space hurt his eyes, but he stayed focused on the light and on Frances. A flicker. A tongue of flame. And then a spout of searing brilliance. Another Portal opened – this time a Portal of Fire. Another channel of power connecting the Wind Cave and Uluru, and this place. And another sigil emerged and took shape on Frances's left hip.

These people were descended from the original inhabitants of this land, the Baka. They practiced their indigenous spiritual tradition and taught Frances their language while Alaman studied ritual drumming. Her next novel, *Mask Dancer,* was finished as the heavy heat of autumn lifted slightly. After nearly being run off the road by a pick-up truck bearing the logo of Royal Dutch Shell on their way to the airport in Libreville, Frances and Alaman were relieved to take some holidays in Dakar and Yoff.

Frances met with her CIA handler there and was able to give him the names of corrupt officials in the Gabonese government who were bilking Western companies.

"They mean to seize power," Frances told him, mentioning that the solidification of the avenues of control by Omar Bongo Ondimba would result in a dictatorship that might last for decades.

"Oh, well, the devil you know..." Sheldon Stewart replied.

"Is still a devil!" Frances retorted.

And while Frances pointed a finger one way in purposeful misdirection, the priestess matriarch in Gabon selected her sister's daughter to be the keeper of the bloodline wisdom.

On the next lunar eclipse this young woman, after fasting and purifying for three days held space for the Goddess to come through her and participated in the Sacred Marriage. The child conceived that night was the next fleshly vessel for one of the Thirteen. A third Portal opened. A third soul incarnated.

Staunton, Virginia, USA, 1972

In 1972 Frances was giving a talk on her latest book, which included the topic of the destructive repercussions of colonialism and missionaries on native peoples in Africa. While fiction, her book had generated a lot of conversation and controversy, and she had been invited to speak at Mary Baldwin College in Staunton, Virginia. It was a curious mix of traditional Southern 'women's college' with finishing school airs and a history of education for women ahead of its time. Staunchly Christian in its funding and student population, Frances was expecting a lively and perhaps fraught discussion.

"But the message of Christ must be spread to those who haven't heard the word!" one professor almost shouted.

"Would Christ want His message to spread disease and rampant exploitation as well?" Frances asked quietly. Several hands shot up. Frances looked over the crowd and her eyes fell on a young woman with wavy hair the color of fallen leaves and a brightness of gaze that spoke of a burning intelligence. Frances nodded to her. "Yes?"

"Are you saying that the wisdoms of these natives are of comparable value to the wisdom of Christianity?"

"What is your name, dear?" Frances asked.

"Lee,"

"Well, Lee, I deeply appreciate what others may label the 'audacity' of your question. And what I would like to postulate is the possibility that the wisdoms of those we have called 'heathens' is comparable to, and in some circumstances *superior* to, the dominant theology." Frances let that statement sit there as many in the audience looked stunned.

"That just turns everything on its head, doesn't it?" the young woman, Lee, replied. And then she smiled a wide generous smile.

After the lecture was over, Lee lingered, waiting for others who wished to speak to Frances one on one. Most of them wanted to argue with her and demand that she acknowledge the primacy of Christianity. She graciously declined. A number of women had brought their copies of Frances's books and wanted her to sign them, which she did with good humor.

Finally, it was just Lee and Frances.

"What is it you wish to do with your life, my girl?" Frances surprised Lee with this deep, direct and rather personal question. But Lee liked depths and was never afraid to go there.

"I think, most of all, I want to be a Light Bearer. I'm not even sure exactly what that means." Lee looked bemused by her own admission.

"Well then, dear girl, you will need to bring light to unlit places, no matter the cost," Frances replied rather cryptically.

"There is a school, a seminary in New York City that is opening up admission for the first time to women next year to prepare for ordination as clergy. I haven't had the courage to broach this with my parents, but I want to go, I want to be a minister. Is that crazy?"

"Not crazy, my dear. But do not set even those limitations on yourself. Serve the Divine however it manifests. Be a priestess."

"Did you say, be a priestess? How do I do that?"

"She of a Thousand Names is waiting for you, Lee Hancock. Never doubt that."

CHAPTER 7
BALLINSKELLIG, KERRY,
REPUBLIC OF IRELAND,
OCTOBER 1972

Magdalena was ill. Malachi had sent word, and Frances and Alaman had returned to Ireland as fast as they could. Kwame met them at Shannon airport with a rental car, and the trip south felt like it took a million years.

"Will we make it in time?" Frances asked for the thirtieth time.

"God willing," Kwame replied.

"Inshallah," Alaman whispered.

Their flight had come in from New York at 7:00 AM, and the sky was filled with stripes of silver and coal-ash black horizontal clouds as the sun lifted higher in the sky.

"She was conscious yesterday?"

"In and out."

"Did she know you were there?"

"She lit up when she saw Sassy and began to croon when she saw Sisi for the first time."

Alaman squeezed her hand tighter and Frances wiped the single tear that had fallen off her cheek. They turned off the coast road down onto the small lane that brought them to the Kenneally cottages. Frances was moved, but not surprised, to see that the near field was filled with Traveller caravans, for the telegraph of the green roads was always faster than the speed of light.

Frances remembered coming to this cottage for the first time, pregnant, husbandless, exhausted by war and worn to the bone with worry. Magdalena had greeted her with open arms and accepting heart. Then and always.

Frances didn't wait for the car to come to a complete stop before she flew up the path to the open cottage door. It was open! Had they opened the door to let Magdalena's spirit free? Had she come too late?

Sassy appeared in the shadow of the doorway, grabbing her mother in a powerful one arm hug and led her quickly to the bedroom.

"She waited for you," Sassy said, grief ripping her voice like the tearing of a bedsheet.

Frances ran into the room and fell to her knees at the bedside. Magdalena was breathing hard, but she saw Frances and knew her.

"You came!"

"As if a herd of camels could keep me away!" And both women smiled.

It was a warm day for late October and all the windows were wide open with a soft breeze lifting the lace curtains that were Magdalena's pride and joy. Frances could smell late-blooming honeysuckle and the lingering sweetness of beeswax candles.

Sassy brought Sisi in. Without hesitation, the girl slid up on the bed and lay down with her great-grandmother, resting her cheek on Magdalena's shoulder.

"Am I hurting you, Great Grammy?"

"No darlin', you are like the brush of an angel's wing. Stay right there and let me know the scent of you."

Day dimmed into night, and Frances could hear the occasional sound of a horse whinnying as more caravans arrived. Malachi and his wife, children and their spouses and children came and went, tea was made and drunk while Frances held Magdalena's hand. One lone fiddle played outside, and the stars came out.

Sometime after midnight, when all the family except Frances and Malachi had found places to lay their heads, Magdalena opened her eyes again and looked up, seeing someone or someone's beloved. Her face took on a smile of surpassing sweetness, and Malachi and Frances watched as her spirit lifted right up out of her body to join those she saw. They sat in stillness, looking into each other's eyes in gratitude at having had the honor to witness her passing. There was no need to announce her death to anyone, for outside Young Shelta began to keen.

$$\mathbb{)} \bigcirc \mathbb{(}$$

Three nights later Magdalena was buried, without benefit of Catholic clergy. The priest of the Parish had exclaimed that "The witch woman hasn't crossed the Church threshold for forty years and she shall not do so now!" With those formalities taken care of and all the bureaucracies mollified, Magdalena's family breathed a big sigh of relief and buried her in the way she had desired.

The men had come up earlier that day to dig a grave, while the women had washed and dressed Magdalena's body and sung the old songs over her.

On Samhain Eve as twilight fell, the family carried her, wrapped in a linen cloth, up to the stone circle where the Old Ones dwelled. The procession was long and both corporeal and ephemeral. Travellers from all over the West, family and long-time friends from the village, and a spectral crowd of Grandmothers, Sidhe, and Ancestors all moved with solemnity across the upper fields to the circle. Frances felt Michael there, and Old Shelta, and others she couldn't name.

The keening was ancient and fierce as Magdalena's body, the shell of she who had once been Ni Ma of the Pleiadian Seven Sisters, was lowered into the land she loved, just inside the inner ring of stones. Frances felt a gentle pressure, like a beloved hand resting on her heart, and knew that Magdalena was right and truly at rest.

New York, New York, USA, February 1973

Frances and Alaman left Ireland mid-February for the States and another book tour. Their first stop was New York City and a fancy cocktail party thrown by her publishing house. None other than Sheldon

Stewart, Frances's CIA handler, was a guest.

"You look particularly exotic tonight," came the flat-voweled voice of Sheldon Stewart in Frances's ear.

"It felt like the right occasion to trot out my Senegalese prints," Frances responded wryly.

"Because otherwise no one would notice you?" he asked, only half joking.

Frances laughed out loud, surprising herself and drawing eyes toward them. Alaman caught her gaze and lifted one eyebrow asking if she needed assistance. She shook her head almost imperceptibly and turned to look up at Sheldon Stewart. "Because I am beginning the promotion of my book set in Africa, ya numpty!"

Now it was Sheldon's turn to startle himself with laughter. "You will be finding yourself in Berkeley, California next?" he asked.

"I would imagine that you have a better handle on my schedule than I do," Frances retorted.

He coughed into his cocktail napkin. "Well then, yes. You will indeed be going to California."

"And?"

"And, there appears to be a particular aggregation of radical ideas there that has come to our attention."

"Radical?"

"You are not going to make this easy, are you?" Sheldon snorted.

"And where would the fun be in that?" Frances said with an easy smile. It would appear to all who might be watching them that the two were engaging in social chitchat, but Sheldon made it clear that he was looking for intel on "subversive groups" of feminist, AIM, remnants of the Black Panthers, and what he labeled "ecology nutjobs."

"As always, Mr. Stewart, I live to serve," Frances said smoothly, gave him a small half-smile and glided away, her vivid fuchsia and sapphire print making her stand out amidst the muted colors and classic black dresses of the other party attendants.

Sheldon Stewart watched her go and thought to himself, "Yes, but serve whom?"

Spring in Berkeley was four seasons in one day. Frances loved it, and it reminded her of Ireland, where one needed rain-gear and layers to experience the entire year in a day.

Frances had just given a reading and lecture to a group of anthropology graduate students, some of whom found it hard to fathom that Women's Mysteries were even a thing. Frances kept her irritation in check, frequently exchanging looks with Alaman and trying hard not to grin. But finally, when one particularly insistent young man had said, "Yes, but yours are works of fiction!" adding a smirk and the insinuation that Frances simply fabricated her stories out of whole cloth, she snapped.

"I think that you might find, young man, when you leave this ivory tower and step into the real world, that turning over the rock of Patriarchy allows for all sorts of hidden things to become visible. Your assumption that just because you haven't seen it, it doesn't exist, speaks volumes about the limitations of your education."

He squirmed but didn't give up. "Well, there are no ethnographic studies that document these mysteries you speak of." As if that settled the matter.

Frances's voice got very quiet, and all the students had to lean in to hear her reply. "And why, exactly, do you think anyone would confide in one such as you?" If looks could kill, Frances would have been arrested for homicide. Alaman stood from the back of the room and walked like a panther forward to Frances.

"Beloved, we must go. You will be late for your next appointment."

Frances knew full well that she didn't have another appointment that day but understood the escape offer. She thanked the students and professor for their time and headed toward the door of the lecture hall. Alaman waited one moment and speared the young man with an even deadlier look.

When they got outside into the sunshine, Frances wanted to run and throw herself on the grass. They hurried to the nearest park and she did just that.

"The arrogance! The small-minded entitled, arrogance!"

Alaman stroked her hair, running his forefinger along the edge of the white streak at her widow's peak and replied, "In his defense, he does have 5,000 years of people telling him he is correct."

Frances pulled up a handful of grass and sniffed. Chlorophyll, sun, soil, hints of wild thyme. It soothed her soul and calmed her ire.

As they sat there, Frances noticed a group of young women sitting in a circle. They had the aura of a ritual around them, and it drew Frances's attention. It felt like watching a baby's attempts to take its first steps: fierce intention, a lack of skill, repetition and trial and error. The women stood, held hands, and began to walk in a clockwise circle keeping time to a chant that was too low for Frances to hear.

Frances felt pulled to her feet and walked over to join them. Without thinking she reached out her left hand to a woman with a full head of joyously wavy hair and started to lead the line of women out from the circle into a bigger arc, then weaving in and into a tight spiral. Each woman found the gift of looking into the eyes of the others as they passed by. When Frances reached the very center she changed direction and began to lead the line out, walking counter-clockwise in bigger and bigger circles. The women were now smiling and crying as they looked into their sister's eyes again and again. At last, they formed the full big open circle and paused in the blissful suspended space of a ritual well done.

Frances dropped the hands of those next to her and tried to slip away unnoticed. The woman to her left, the one with the riotous brown hair ran after her.

"What was that? What we just did. That was...powerful!"

"We danced a spiral. What did it feel like to you?" Frances asked.

"Like something ancient. Like I knew it, or remembered it, or..." and she drifted off, searching for a way to describe the indescribable.

"I am Frances. Who are you?"

"Miriam. Miriam Simos," the young woman replied, with her voice rising at the end, questioning.

Frances scrunched up her nose and shook her head slightly. "No, that doesn't seem to fit you. If you could be called anything, what would it be?"

The young woman's eyes widened as she opened the door to that possibility. "Something bigger. Something vast. Something with power and space around it."

"Like?" Frances prodded.

"Like...like Starhawk!"

And in that moment the fullness of who she might be and what she might do in the world rushed into Miriam Simos, and Starhawk was born.

Frances reached up and stroked her cheek. "I am very glad to meet you, Starhawk."

Jeju Island, Republic of Korea, 1972

Jeju Island in South Korea had a long tradition of women divers. These women had sustained their communities, taking over the economy initially when the male population had been decimated by war. The women had their own culture and songs and practices, celebrating rites and rituals to a number of goddesses, the highest in the hierarchy being Myoungjinguk Grandmother.

Frances and Alaman had been met by a poised young woman certified as a travel guide by the South Korean government. Her English was excellent, and she knew the lore of the island backwards and forwards. She had arranged for Frances to meet the Great Shaman of the village, and for them to stay in the guesthouse run by one of the retired women divers.

The old woman looked to be about seventy years of age or so, but as was frequently true of shamans, her life had been hard as she had carried the pains of her community for many years. Hers was a scarred face, criss-crossed with anguish and injury, but she looked at Frances and Alaman with bright eyes and an expression of eager anticipation. The travel guide translated for them.

"Great Shaman says that she knows you...from the...Before?" The travel guide looked embarrassed, as if the shaman was not making sense, and the young woman was ashamed to let that be seen by these foreigners. But Frances understood. She had seen the spark of recognition in the old woman's eyes. Here was another of the Companions, a friend from long ago.

"Please tell her that I am grateful to see her *again*," Frances answered cryptically, and the young guide nodded and repeated the thought, still puzzled.

"Great Shaman says, '*Once again* we have an important job to do.'"

Frances took the old woman's hand and clasped hard. "And as Before, we shall not turn away from our task."

Later, as they were settling into the guesthouse, Frances shared with Alaman who the Great Shaman had been. "You never knew her in the Before. She was Feyl, the leader of the Selkies. She was strong and wise with the Otherworld always clinging to her like the water of the sea. She came with Autakla to Calanais, and then she returned to her people. She was, and is, a woman of great power and leadership."

Alaman held her, wrapping his arms around her, and pulling her spine close into his belly. It was her favorite way to sleep, and she felt her eyes grow heavy with the comfort of him. Silently he said his nightly gratitudes for the blessing of the woman in his arms. "Great Goddess, Mother of All Things. Help me be worthy of this woman."

A week later they made the journey down to the beach in the darkness of night where they met the Great Shaman and several others. It had been explained to them that they would be making a short trip by boat, to get to another smaller island. They would then need to swim to get into the cave. Alaman, a child of the desert, had never learned how to swim, and he was distraught at not being able to be with Frances as she opened another Portal.

"My love, I shall know that you are waiting in the boat. I shall feel your presence. Better that than you drown trying to be at my side!"

Alaman begrudgingly agreed and held on tight to the sides of the boat as they bounced over waves in the inky black. He was not a good sailor under ideal conditions and the inability to perceive any horizon in the darkness of the moonless night was making it worse.

The motor was cut off abruptly and the rocks of their destination appeared out of the black without warning. The driver and Alaman stayed in the boat as the women slipped over the side and, taking a deep breath, disappeared under the water.

Frances was tied to the swimmer in front of her by a sturdy rope, and they made their way through a tunnel of rock, coming up into a cave-like chamber. The sounds of waves lapping and women breathing were magnified in the stone dome, but nothing was visible. It was as if they were in a womb, held aloft by salt water and the heartbeat of the Great Mother.

Someone took Frances's hand and led her to a shelf of rock where she could stand and be submerged chest deep. She could feel the other women come around her and gently slip their hands under her back and legs, holding her floating in the water. They began to tone, building sound upon sound, the music of their voices reverberating off the walls of the sea cave.

Frances became subtly aware of a vibration that was traveling from deep below her, coming up in a column of sensation, entering her body at the small of her back and exiting out the front of her abdomen. A Portal began to emerge, unlike any of those that had come before, this one channeled energy through the medium of water, carrying with it the amniotic memories of the world and all who had gone before. Frances felt all the joys, all the griefs, all the terror and all the exultations, deeply packed in each molecule of water. It was bliss. It was excruciating. It was life in a teardrop.

Above in the boat, Alaman lost all sense of time. The night sky was clouded and the few stars that broke through wavered timidly. After what felt like a lifetime, the diving group re-emerged beside the boat, startling the driver who had fallen asleep while they had waited. Alaman helped the women back onto the boat and wrapped Frances in a blanket in a vain attempt to control her shivering..

He rubbed his hand up and down her arms and legs to warm her. Frances told him all about the floating and the torrent of water and all the world's pains and joys. He couldn't find words, but let his own tears fall into the ocean.

In the morning a new sigil had emerged on the underside of her upper right arm. This one swirled in a dance like Sufis spinning in meditation, fluid and constant and hypnotic.

The women of Jeju felt the subterranean rumble as the Portal connected to the ones in America and Africa and Australia. The grid was becoming illuminated; the Portals were communicating.

In January of 1974 the Great Shaman had summoned her granddaughter back to Jeju. The girl had turned her back on the old ways and the small insular society on the island, choosing instead to go to Seoul and study medicine. She dreaded these return trips to her hometown, but when Grandmother spoke, you answered.

As she walked off the ferry she noticed a small, dark Western woman with a tall brown-skinned man. They were walking onto the ferry, holding hands, and smiling like they held all the world's joy within them. *I would like to feel like that, she thought to herself.*

Waiting for her at the ferry dock was a young man that she vaguely remembered from primary school. He had that bearing from his military service that radiated composure and confidence. He was a distant cousin of some sort, for almost everyone was somehow related on Jeju.

"Your Grandmother asked me to pick you up. It seems everyone else's vehicle has suddenly developed 'car trouble,'" he said wryly. He was well-versed in the overwhelming compulsion that the grannies and aunties had to matchmake.

They settled into the drive up into the mountain, easy with each other in a way that surprised them both.

"You went away to school, yes?"

"Yes, Seoul. Medical school after university. And you?"

"Engineering. Structural. Berkeley in California."

"Just back for a visit?" she asked.

He smiled, wide and easy. "Good God, yes! If I don't leave soon my mother will nail my foot to the floor to get me to stay!"

They chuckled. And talked. And met that night for dinner. And ten lunar months later their daughter was born.

And the Great Shaman smiled, knowing that another of the Thirteen had returned.

Yoff, Senegal, 1973

Frances had finished her next novel, *Shell Dancer*, in record time. She and Alaman had walked right past Great Shaman's granddaughter in the small airport and flown back to Senegal to rest and regroup...and to disappear for a while.

Whilst on Jeju, Frances had become aware of two men who were ominous in their ubiquity, and she was relieved to return to Yoff and safety of the village there, where everyone knew her and looked out for her. She made a visit to the American Embassy in Dakar to leave a report for Sheldon Stewart and a demand that her protection surveillance be increased. The message read,

You can keep me alive, and show me you are doing it, or our deal is off.

She handed it to the young woman at the secretary desk of the Cultural Affairs office. The young woman looked up, startled. "Do you wish to sign this?"

Frances smiled that mysterious smile she had that didn't reach her eyes and replied, "No need, my dear. He knows who this is from."

$$ \mathbb{)} \bigcirc \mathbb{(} $$

Frances and Alaman spent long easy days walking the beach, spending time with Sisi when she returned from school, talking and laughing long into the night with Sassy and Kwame. Winter in Yoff was gentle on the body. Warm days, never a drop of rain, and cool nights filled with the frequent call to prayer. Yoff was the home of numerous Sufi groups who took turns reciting the ninety-nine names of God, and the sound bounced back and forth down the narrow lanes every night, floating up though bedroom windows.

One morning Frances and Kwame headed off to the market, and Alaman and Sassy spent the hours shelling beans in the courtyard. They didn't get much time together without others around.

"Mama seems…different," she said diffidently.

Alaman paused his hands and looked up at her, his soft eyes framed by ridiculously long lashes. Sassy always thought that those eyes gave him a particular advantage as they seemed to suggest that he was docile and could disguise his inner warrior self.

"Different? How do you mean?"

"It's hard to put my finger on," she replied. "Mama has always been smart as a whip. My Da used to call her his 'clever, clever girl.' And now she seems like she is...stronger? I don't know. I feel like she has an inner structure, a grid, a lattice of steel or bamboo or..." Sassy stopped and laughed, shaking her head at what she was describing.

Alaman was thoughtful and then spoke softly. "I believe, I perceive, that with each Portal, as it opens, as she facilitates that opening, that she is *gifted* some of that energy, that quality. She is still Frances, most beloved of all women, but she is also...more."

"Yes!" Sassy exclaimed. "Exactly! She is *more*. Does she feel the change, do you think?"

"Your mother is discerning. She feels it all, I believe." Alaman reached forward and took Sassy's hand. "I do everything I can to protect her. But as you know, your mother has a will of her own. She will only allow so much protecting." Alaman smiled and Sassy responded in kind.

"I am so very, very grateful for you in our lives, dearest Blue Man."

"That is indeed good to hear. I sometimes wonder if I am some catalyst, like, how do you say...the bull in the china shop of all your lives. Perhaps it would have all been more peaceful had I never appeared."

Sassy laughed and replied, "And as my Mama would say, where would the fun be in that?"

$$\text{☽ ○ ☾}$$

In April, at the cusp of the rainy season, a messenger boy knocked on the door and handed over a message for Frances.

You shall be safe as houses, as our British cousins say.

"Is it from Stewart?" Alaman asked.

"Oh yes, I believe so. It is just pretentious enough to be his words."

"Do we trust him?"

"Not as far as we could throw him in a headwind," Frances replied, "but I do think it is in his self-interest to ensure our safety as we proceed."

"So, shall we?" Alaman bumped her shoulder with his elbow. "Shall we proceed?"

CHAPTER 8
CAPPADOCIA, TURKEY,
APRIL 1973

They flew from Dakar to Paris where they boarded a Turkish Airlines plane to Ankara. The next leg was by train to Kayseri in Cappadocia, followed by a ride in an ancient army Jeep over a potholed road, an experience in dust and jostling that surpassed all their other travels so far. They arrived into a small village at a breakneck speed that caused chickens and children to scatter. With a squeal of brakes, their driver pulled up to a small house of daub with an open door and a beaded screen.

When they got out of the Jeep, Frances had an urge to fall to her knees and kiss the ground. She caught Alaman's eye, knew he was thinking the same thing, and they started to laugh. The sound of their laughter seemed to be a signal, and people began to emerge from all the houses, children ran out from alleys, and even the chickens returned to the dusty lane. Men swept forward and grabbed their luggage, women ushered them into the house, pushing aside the beads of the door curtain, and the driver ground his gears and sped off in a cloud of dust.

"We didn't pay him for the lift," Frances said under her breath to Alaman.

"We paid in years off our lives, my queen."

The network of Grandmothers who connected through dreams and visions had notified the elder wise woman of the village that Frances and her Alaman would be arriving, so they were met with a feast and an announcement that they would "go to the power place" on the eve of May Day, just two days after their arrival.

For those days of preparation, Frances barely saw Alaman. Men and women had very different spheres here among the Yazidi, so only at night, as they nestled together in bed could they compare their experiences and what they had learned.

"Their religion is very old, and the women's mysteries are even older," Frances whispered into Alaman's chest.

"The men know that the women 'do things,' but they really seem to not have any idea what it is that they do," Alaman whispered back.

"The mysteries are really mysterious!" Frances chuckled, and then drifted off to sleep before she could say anything else.

On the day of the journey to the power place, Frances was given a ritual bath by all the women of the village. The water was scented with myrtle and rosemary, and every bit of her, from between her toes and into all the crevices of her ears, was washed and then gently dried. Frances was reminded of the ritual bathing in Yoff, the similarities in these women's mysteries, the universality of it all. If she closed her eyes she could picture herself in Senegal and in the Outback and on the Pine Ridge Rez. Step by step, the preparation to meet the Goddess was done with reverence. Frances knew that this ritual had not changed in its essence in thousands of years.

The women, and a small number of the men, walked from the village to a tumble of ruined buildings about a kilometer away. Frances was accorded the honor of riding on a donkey, and Alaman walked at her side, his hand resting on her knee. He looked as she had first seen him, face shaded from the sun by the intense cobalt of his turban, robes flowing in the hot wind. *Thank you*, she said silently to the Goddess.

At the ruins, the Wise Woman of the village led them down a stone staircase to a small cellar. Several men moved forward and removed the large stones that made up one wall. An opening appeared, an arched doorway that led into the next room and to the next room and to another staircase. Frances very quickly lost all sense of direction. Up and down disappeared. Left and right seemed meaningless. She followed the women ahead of her and let their chanting soften her bones and sinews.

They came to a stop in a large high chamber. Light filtered down from tunnels that led to the surface and made polka dots of yellow and gold on the earthen floor. In the very center of the room there was a pit that had a ladder poking out of the top. Frances was led to the ladder and motioned to climb down into the pit. By this time, she was lost in trance, and descending into a dark pit seemed to be the logical thing to do.

The walls of the pit were dry and smooth as if they had been polished and molded. The floor of the chamber was a meter or so above her head, and she reached out sideways and pressed hard against the marble-cool walls to contact the earth. She grounded her energy down, as the sound of their chant swirled and floated down to her, running along her bones, and rushing out the bottoms of her feet. She could feel the Earth's heartbeat against her palms. She felt the column of energy from the chanting running down through her crown and then she gasped as a current of energy began to flow up, through the soles of her feet, along her spine, and gush out the top of her head. It was glorious and it transported her beyond her human senses. She was the Earth. She was the living planet, Gaia. She was purely elemental. She was…Before.

For a minute or an hour she relished this state of being. Then something must have coalesced or transformed up above, for the trill of ululation bounced off the chamber walls, spun down to her, and the sound lifted her back up until she stood straddling the pit, arms stretched high and wide. Someone was beating a rapid rhythm on a frame drum and Frances felt like she had just birthed the world.

Was she the mother or the baby? It all blended together as women came forward, wrapping her in the softest cotton cloths. She was led up and through the vast array of subterranean rooms and hallways, to emerge in the tender dusk with stripes of apricot and pomegranate layering along the horizon. And while she felt that she could stride across the globe on powerful legs, she was glad when Alaman helped her mount the donkey's safe, warm back and she could dream her way back to the village.

"Is something wrong, my queen?" Alaman asked the next day. Frances was reaching into her soft slipper shoe, trying to scratch at the bottom of her right foot.

"This itch is driving me crazy. Maybe I have a bug bite," she replied. Alaman knelt down in front of her and took off the slipper.

"Ah!" Alaman sighed. "It's another sigil, beloved. And it covers the entirety of the sole of your foot. This one zig zags like the design on a Navaho blanket or Assyrian cuneiform."

"I am becoming the Tattooed Lady from the circus," she said looking a bit forlorn. She sighed.

"My Frances, why so sad?"

"My vanity has been pricked," she answered. "Perhaps the Tattooed Lady was not what you had in mind as desirable."

He took a moment to formulate his reply, sensing that though she seemed to be joking there was some hidden insecurity that was prompting her mood.

"Every single inch of you is beautiful to me," he said quietly, holding her foot on his hands and looking deeply in her eyes and then letting his eyes trail over her body. "Every single inch."

He lowered his mouth to kiss her newest sigil, then let his lips move upward along calf and thigh until he reached the juncture and her hidden well of pleasure. Waves of warmth and sensation flooded her as his breath and tongue worshiped her. Frances sighed deeply now in abandon, letting Alaman work his magic.

That same night, in a small hut far up in the mountains, the women of the village bathed the young woman chosen to be the sacred vessel. Nineteen and eager for her adult life to begin she was the great-grand-daughter of the village Wise Woman, and the seventh daughter of a seventh daughter. She was trembling with anticipation and a hint of fear, for the older women refused to tell her exactly what was going to happen. Only that she was to be the vessel of a special one who was to come.

She was led into a shallow cave in the mountain's side, and surrounded by women drumming, making a container of sound. A young man from another village was led into the cave. He was positioned down on a layer of goat skins, and the young woman came over him, lowering herself down until he filled her completely. The most ancient rhythm was begun. She rose and descended above him over and over, feeling herself taken over by a need she couldn't explain and could never exactly remember. The speed of the drums increased, the need, the urgency, and then, with a massive cry of triumph her body exploded and contracted as the young man shouted and arched. The drums beat louder and faster, and then cut off abruptly.

Down in the village, as Frances's cry of release floated thought the air, echoing the sound from high in the hillside above, the old Wise Woman, she who had once been Alama, the First Among Equals of the Goddess Nematona, felt a slip of her heartbeat, and then a settling of the pulse of life. It was good. This time she had lived. In the Before, her life had been cut short and she hadn't seen the culmination of the work. But this time she had lived, and remembered, and passed along the sacred hidden truths. She felt that Frances and Alaman had the same kind of connections to the Before that she had, as a Companion, as facilitator, as a helper to the Thirteen. And now, with the Portal opened and the ritual high up on the mountain complete, another of the Thirteen was going to make her way into the world once again.

For several months, Frances and Alaman lived amongst the Yazidi, learning their language and customs, and trying to make sense of the geo-political landscape. The Turks feared the Kurds. The Kurds saw political advantage if the outside world folded the Yazidis into Kurdistan dynamics as if they were the same thing. The Yazidis resented and resisted that. Iraq's Kurds wanted distance from the Turkish Kurds. Syrian Kurds felt like the middle child. America paid lip-service to Kurdish independence, but in actuality supported the Iraqi and Turkish claims to Kurdish territory. Armed militias of Kurds were increasing their attacks on Turkish military installations. The ancient powder keg was primed.

Within the village the tension was growing. Frances noticed that the young men were slipping away into shadows most evenings. She would wake near dawn and hear the muffled footsteps as they returned. The Wise Woman seemed distracted and had called several conferences of the mothers of the village. With only rudimentary Yazidi, Frances could catch sporadic words and phrases, but the overall gist was that danger was lurking.

One day an outsider drove into the village, was taken into the Wise Woman's house and was seen to leave some thirty minutes later. Frances was summoned.

"Sadly, our visit to the newest archaeological find has been called off."

"Grandmother, what is wrong? Is there trouble?"

"Isn't there always?" Grandmother replied cryptically.

The next day a band of Kurdish freedom fighters ambushed a Turkish army convoy just a few kilometers from their village killing several soldiers. Danger ran like ground lightning along everyone's skin. Frances and Alaman decided that this next novel, to be entitled *Drum Dancer,* could and would need to be finished elsewhere.

Istanbul, Republic of Turkey, 1973

Frances and Alaman arrived in Istanbul two days later. They checked in to a wonderfully garish and luxurious Western hotel, took advantage of unlimited hot water for bathing and soaking, and arranged to meet Sheldon Stewart in the hotel restaurant for dinner.

They found Stewart already settled at a table by the window, seated facing the door. He stood to greet Frances with a kiss on the cheek, shook hands with Alaman, and never completely took one eye off the comings and goings around them: his surveillance was subtle, but constant.

He was jovial, acting like a pal with the waiter who seemed to suffer him well. On a surface appraisal he was affable, and not terribly bright. But when the waiter had gone and he turned his gaze onto Frances, Alaman could see the sharp intellect and relentless personality of a hunting dog.

"So how was Cappadocia?" he asked.

"Dicey," Frances replied curtly.

"Anything of interest for us?" he continued in a low tone.

Frances reached under the table and placed an envelope with her notes on his lap. Sheldon slid it into his inside jacket pocket.

"It's a mess, Sheldon. There is no way to tell the players apart. No way to trust anyone's motives. And I include in that assessment the motivations and intentions of the US of A." Frances's face was flushed in frustration. "We could have been in real danger there, and I for one do not appreciate your *laissez-faire* approach to our wellbeing."

Stewart looked down at the tablecloth for a moment and then raised his eyes to hers. "Frances, what are you not telling me? I know I ask you to insert yourself in some sticky spots, but I am hearing chatter. There are other actors involved in this, possibly bad actors. Someone else is interested in your activities, and I don't get a good feeling about them…" He stopped abruptly, and for once seemed to have dropped all artifice. "Are you playing another game?"

"What chatter are you hearing?" she asked.

"Now is not the time to get icy on me, Frances!" he snapped. "I can't protect you if I don't know what you're up to!"

Frances took a breath and then said calmly, "Sheldon, you will just have to."

"You have no intention of filling me in?"

Frances didn't reply but gave him her opaque, expressionless face.

"You have an obligation to the Company, Frances. An obligation which you took on willingly. If you are dancin' with somebody else, we might feel stood up, Frances…you have to leave with the one that brung you!"

"You ask for intel. I give you the intel that seems pertinent. I can't just suck up everything and spit it back out at you."

"The powers-that-be want more from you, Frances," he said with a thread of menace in his voice.

Frances was silent. Alaman placed his hand on the hilt of the knife at his belt.

Just then the waiter brought their starters, and Stewart laughed and acted as if they were having a marvelous time. The rest of the dinner went on without a stir, but as they were leaving the restaurant, Stewart leaned over and whispered in Frances's ear, "Any particular reason why

Big Oil and Big Mining have an interest in you?"

Frances leaned back and smiled at him. "It must be my charming personality."

Stewart reached forward to shake Alaman's hand and slipped a cigar into his front pocket, "I will increase your protection, but…you need to play your parts."

Alaman looked at him, eyes narrowed, and hand at knife hilt visible, and replied, "Go with God, Mr. Stewart."

The elevator ride up to their room was taken in silence. Alaman opened the door and walked in first, as was his way, to make sure all was safe. Frances knew he was uneasy, perhaps even displeased with her, but she began getting ready for bed and kept quiet, waiting for Alaman to speak, or not, as was his wish. It was uncomfortable, this space between them, but she held her tongue as Alaman went out onto the balcony to light up the cigar he had received from Sheldon Stewart.

"Careful," Frances called out jokingly, "They tried to kill Castro with one of those!"

Alaman didn't reply, and Frances's sense of disquiet grew. She brushed her hair, hung up her dress, washed her face and teeth…there was still no movement or words from Alaman. Frances walked to the balcony door, staying in the light of the room and watching him at the railing.

"Are you unhappy about something?"

No response.

"Are you unhappy with me?"

Silence.

"Holy Mary, Mother of God, Alaman! Say something!"

She heard him draw a deep breath that sounded tight in the throat.

"I am not unhappy, Frances. I am terrified. What are you not telling me? It's one thing to keep Stewart out of the loop…but me? You are keeping something from me, and I am driven mad not knowing where the danger is."

Frances slipped out of the light and onto the dark balcony. She approached him cautiously and then, coming up close, lifted her hand to cup his cheek.

"I was supposed to be on that convoy," she said very softly.

"What convoy? The Turkish military one?"

205

"Yes."

"Why am I just hearing this now?"

"It was at the last minute. The captain approached the village head man and told him there were ruins that the government suggested I might be interested in seeing. But on the day before we were supposed to go, the Wise Woman had a visitor, a warning, that it was all a set up to harm me, so she told the soldiers I was indisposed, and they left without me. And then they were attacked…and some of them died."

Alaman was silent, and then he exploded. "You think they were planning the attack on you?"

"That is my fear, yes."

"Then why…?" He ground his teeth and snapped out an elaborate curse in his native Tuareg. "Why keep this from me? People are trying to kill you! You think I don't need to know that?"

For this first time since they had become lovers, Frances felt a gulf between them, a chasm of her own making. They had never fought. They bickered good-naturedly, but never truly argued. But now, Alaman's anger and hurt felt like a tall wall she would need to climb to return to him.

"I just thought…"

"You thought what, Frances? Please let me into your mind, for clearly I now need an invitation to be privy to those thoughts." His tone was sharp, but she could hear the sting of pain underneath it.

"I thought, if you knew about the attack, that you would try to stop me from opening the rest of the Portals."

He drew back as if slapped, turned, and walked back into the room and out the door.

Frances stared out into the night, the lights of Istanbul a flickering mosaic before her. She could smell incense, roasted meats, and cardamom in the breeze. As the minutes stretched she missed the support from Alaman that had become second nature to her. For the first time in several years, she felt that she was truly alone. She shivered though the night was warm and went back into the room.

The night was long and sleepless without Alaman by her side. When dawn was imminent and the soft pink light began to spill across the floor she heard the lock and the door opened. Alaman walked into the room and stopped when he saw that her eyes were open. It was still dim, but Frances could see that his beloved face was closed, not the open book she knew so well.

"Where did you go?"

"I walked and found myself at the Hagia Sophia. The night watchman let me in."

"For your charms?"

"For my bakshish."

Frances sat up in bed and waited until he had removed his shoes and gone to the sink to wash his hands and face.

"Did you pray?" she asked.

He turned the top half of his body toward her while he dried his hands on the towel. "Frances, since the day I met you I haven't stopped praying."

He sounded tired, defeated, but came to sit on the edge of the bed near her feet.

"What can I do?" she said softly.

He only shook his head.

"Can you bear it? Can you stay with me?" she said, trying hard not to let any pleading into her voice.

"Could you stop if I asked you to?" he wondered.

"I don't believe I could, no," she replied.

"You cannot ask me not to worry," he said angrily. "And you must trust me without hesitation, you must share everything with me, or I will lose my mind."

"Perhaps when I think about your fears, I am forced to see my own," she answered. That truth hung between them.

"So, what will it be, Frances? You must decide if it is better for you to have me with you or to be on your own... I, for me, feel, how do you say...the ice is thin beneath me." He hung his head down and looked at his hands clasped between his knees. "I should miss you like a lost limb, but tonight I felt more alone when I was with you than I thought possible."

Frances felt the tears she hadn't known she was shedding flowing down her cheeks. She wasn't sure if she had lost the right to touch him, but she got up onto her knees and leaned forward toward him. "And I did not know I could hurt so much knowing that I had hurt you."

He turned his face slightly in her direction, his profile was outlined in the early gold light of dawn. Frances placed her hand, palm up, on the bed near his hip and waited. Alaman looked down at her hand, emotions roiling inside him, and then lifted his hand and placed it in hers. She inched forward and rested her head on his shoulder, feeling like a ship reaching safe harbor after the tumult of a storm. His body lifted as he drew in a deep shuddering breath, and he tilted his head to rest it on hers. They sat like that as the sun rose, the prayers rang out across the city, and the fear of loss was eased by the relief of recovery.

Frances drifted off as Alaman watched the sunlight move deeper into the room and the white gauze curtains lift and swoop in the breeze. She woke awhile later and slipped off the bed. As she started to walk away Alaman clasped her hand to stop her. She turned her face toward him and smiled with love in her eyes. "Toilet," she said softly, and he let go of her hand.

When she walked back into the bedroom, Alaman was looking at her with starving eyes. Who grabbed whom first they never knew, but their need to connect was fierce and tempestuous. There was no time for tenderness or laughter. This coupling was desperate, forged in the fire of what they might have lost. They tore at each other's clothes, using hands and mouths and teeth and tongues to taste and claim. Their climaxes were fueled by the frantic need to have, to demand the other's response, to grab at the life of that moment in all its pain and triumph.

Limbs entangled and sweat mingling, they both fell into the bottomless sleep of soldiers after a battle. Alaman woke to the sound of fruit-sellers in the street below. He gently moved, careful not to wake Frances, dressed and slipped out of the room.

He returned with a brown paper wrapping of large peaches warm with the sun. Standing at the foot of the bed he watched her sleep. Even at rest her face was mobile, and her eyes moved beneath the lids. He undressed and straddled over her, leaning down to kiss those busy eyes. She woke to the smell of him, amber, clean sweat, and the spikenard he used to anoint before prayer.

"My Blue Man."

"Yes, yours," he replied huskily.

They had been companions now for six years, lovers and friends. But this morning was something new, some new creation of commitment, and they both knew it. This love-making was gentle and slow. They were so familiar with each other's bodies, and yet on this morning they opened up new access to soma and soul. Alaman took a peach from the package and bit into it, leaning forward to drip the juice onto her breasts, and then lapping it up slowly and thoroughly. Frances found the way down his spine with her mouth, small nibbles just short of the level of pain. Pleasure in all its forms was their universe.

Spent and at peace they lay in each other's arms whispering small snatches of thoughts and feelings.

"Was this mess in Turkey my fault?" he asked.

Frances lifted her head, but he gently pressed it back down onto his chest.

"Why? What do you mean?"

"I urged us to go, I nudged you to have another adventure. Maybe we should move more cautiously and go off the radar for a while."

He felt her nod her head.

Later...

"What if the danger is extreme and I don't want that for you?" she asked.

His hand gripped her hair and held on. "That would be my decision to make, my queen, and you must let me make it."

And later still...

"Does the Goddess ask too much of you?" he asked.

"All great magick requires sacrifice, my love. But this magick is on a vast scale. I don't think the Goddess wants me killed off before it is done!" she chuckled.

"But there are other sacrifices, my queen. Your time with your family, your peace of mind. This is taking its toll on your body too. The travel, the danger, these sigils…what do they ask of you?" He traced the design on her lower ribs with his index finger.

She rubbed her belly against him and felt him start to rise in response. "This body is doing pretty well, I think," she said coyly.

"This body is a treasure beyond price," he said and rolled over to slip inside her once again.

Saskatchewan, Canada, 1974-75

14 July, 1974

My Dearest Chicken,

My Blue Man and I are going to ground for a bit. You are not to worry. We are indeed safe, just need to not be quite so conspicuous for a time.

I love you with all my heart and think of you and Sisi and Kwame with every breath I take. This is not forever, just for now. You may write me via my publisher, and I will always be so thrilled to hear how you all are faring and what your latest adventures might be. Pictures too, if you please.

Never forget, you are the greatest gift the Goddess ever gave me.

Your Mama

15 July, 1974

Dear Sheldon,

Alaman and I are having a vacation, much deserved if I do say so myself. Please direct all correspondence along the usual channels. It was, as always, delightful to see you in Istanbul. I look forward to meeting again.

Fondly,

Frances Fletcher

Frances and Alaman flew from Istanbul and landed in New York on a blistering hot day in late July. They took a cab into the city, checked into a hotel on Park Avenue, paying in advance for five days and nights. After showering, changing clothes and adopting disguises, they slipped out the back kitchen entrance and walked to Grand Central Station.

The Amtrak train to Albany took them north where they were met by a Mohawk man driving a 1957 Chevy. He was good-natured but not loquacious, and the drive into the Iroquois Rez was peaceful. Frances watched the miles and miles of forest roll by as they drove through the Adirondack mountains, feeling safer by the minute.

Once on the Rez they piled into a pick-up that took them down to the river. A waiting boat carried them across the international border, and the Iroquois on the other side swiftly facilitated their journey west to Saskatchewan.

"Goddess bless the bush telegraph," Frances thought.

They arrived at the Cree Rez after dark the next day and were greeted with warmth and fry bread. Late that night, Frances's cousin Mica, Walter's grandson, walked them through the woods to Grandma Sally's old cabin.

"It's all aired out and we got ya enough supplies to last for a month or more. You know how to tell us if you need anything."

Frances nodded, and reached up to hug her tall, sturdy cousin. He laughed and patted her back gently with his big hands. "We got ya, Frannie. This place has always been waiting for ya."

One month became two became ten. Frances's relatives came every few weeks with foodstuffs and kerosene. Frances spent her days foraging the woods for berries and then nuts, showing Alaman the ways of the Great North Woods. He set himself the task of securing adequate firewood for winter, and when he thought he had accomplished it he proudly displayed his pile to Frances. She threw back her head and laughed.

"Three times that much, my desert fellow, and in a bad year we'd need four times as much!"

Alaman tossed down the axe and grabbed her about the waist. "I'll give you four times as much!" he threatened, and Frances laughed even harder, even as he tossed her over his shoulder and carried her into the cabin.

As the days got shorter and winter closed in, Frances got back to the work of finishing the Yazidi novel. Letters trickled in from Sassy and Sheldon Stewart, from Malachi in Ireland and from Frances' publisher, all along the circuitous route that involved several sovereign Indian nations and a lot of relatives.

January 23, 1975

Dear Frances,

I hope you are well wherever you are. We received the final draft of Drum Dancer and it needs very little editing as far as I can see. You really must leave me something to do so I can justify my salary! I'll send you the next draft by the middle of next month for your perusal.

The sales of the Dancer series are through the roof, so please don't think of stopping now. The requests for lectures and interviews keep flowing in, but I know you said to hold off on those for now. But really, Frances, this is publicity gold!

The anthropology department at Dartmouth has started a course in marginalized and aboriginal cultures based on your books, and the Women's Studies bunch at Sarah Lawrence is breathing down my neck to get you there. It feels to me as if you are the catalyst and the wave of some new ideas. Just don't go all JD Salinger on me, please.

We are re-issuing your first series with new covers. The Art department will send you some possibilities, and as per your contract, you have the right to veto anything you don't like. Why, oh why, did I agree to sign that document for an author who goes on walk-about as much as you? Other writers have agents who do all the pestering, but for you that joy is all mine. Ah yes, now I remember, I signed because your books sell like hotcakes!

In all seriousness, darling girl, I do hope you are well and that your beautiful man is right there by your side.

New York City is shit in the winter. Are you somewhere warm at least?

Affectionately,

Elspeth

March 15, 1975

Dear Ms. Fletcher,

Beware the Ides and all that. Just FYI, the situation in Cappadocia is unraveling as you foretold, though there is no happiness for you in being right about that, I believe. If you could, send me a smoke signal as to when and where you will be emerging… (Oh, I'm sorry, was that smoke signal remark insensitive? I don't care! Send some sign of life, damn you!)

Your friend,

Sheldon Stewart

May 1, 1975

Dearest Mama,

Enclosed you will see the photos from Sisi's birthday party. Nine already…how did that happen? She is shooting up: I think she'll be tall like Kwame and Daddy. I think (and I shall whisper this!) that she is as tall as you now. I can hear your shouts of outrage!

I have big news, Mama. Kwame and I are expecting. This baby, and I think it's a he, feels like a boxer, and is due in the fall, just in time for me to suffer through all the summer heat as a fat pregnant lady. I would love for you to be here for the birth. Sisi's birth and Daddy's death all coming on the same day stole that from us the last time. But only if it is safe for you to do so.

Tell Alaman to keep sending his sketches of you. He has a real talent, and we truly delight in seeing you in all sorts of moods and poses. Sisi has them taped to her bedroom wall. Who knew the Blue Man was such an artist!

You are in our hearts and prayers,

Sassy

Frances passed Sassy's letter over to Alaman and sipped her coffee as he read. The weather had warmed up nicely the last few days and they were sitting outside watching the clouds roll high and fast. He took his time, and Frances could tell he was rereading it and smiling at Sassy's news and the request for more of his drawings.

"Well?"

"I want the summer here. I *need* the summer here."

"And so you shall have it, my queen. And then?"

"And then, in September, we shall be off to Senegal 'cause I get to be a Grammy again!"

She smiled so hard her eyes almost completely shut and Alaman took a mental picture of her face in absolute joy.

Yoff, Senegal, 1975

The tangible living organism that was the Priestesses' singing filled the courtyard, winnowed its way down the corridor, slithered under the door and floated up to the rafters. With each contraction Sassy surrendered herself to the medium of sacred sound, losing her sense of self as she was held in the cosmic ocean.

The midwife had a long broad piece of fabric that was slung around Sassy's hips, and as each wave rolled through her she leaned back, putting her trust and her full weight against the cloth. Sassy was a tall, strong woman, and it took the midwife and three assistants to pull back and give Sassy the support she needed.

Frances wiped her daughter's brow with cool cloths and gave her little sips of hibiscus juice between contractions. They had walked together for hours in the early stages of labor, and now the hardest work kept Sassy standing and leaning, with deep open-throated moans joining the women's chants.

After an eternal stretch of time, the midwife led Sassy to the birthing stool and directed Frances to stand behind her daughter's head so that Sassy could lean against her mother's breastbone. Frances began a chant in a language so old that no one living knew its meaning.

"You are the Source of all life.
You are the Mother of Creation.
Vessel of Life."

Frances felt each contraction. Every woman there felt each contraction. Each birthing pang was private and simultaneously communal. The universality of giving birth echoed down through all the ancestors, each one roaring in triumph as the baby slid out into waiting hands.

The midwife blew into the baby's mouth, and he responded with a wail of his own triumph. Sassy saw her son through the veil of relief and lingering dislocation, and then she tilted her head back and looked into her mother's eyes that held ancient tears. The baby was brought to Sassy's breast, and Frances leaned forward to stroke the baby's cheek and kiss her daughter on the top of her head.

"You are miraculous my little one, and your Mama is a warrior."

The baby looked up toward the sound of her voice, and even though Frances knew that newborns didn't see sharply, she could have sworn that this baby, this newest member of the family, focused on her in recognition.

"He knows you, Mama. He knows you!" Sassy exclaimed.

And Frances knew him too.

$$\text{☽ ◯ ☾}$$

Hours later, after mother and babe had been settled and become acquainted, and father and sister had been introduced, Frances and Alaman walked to the beach and stood, watching the sun set into the ocean with a splash of crimson. Alaman stood behind her and wrapped her in his arms. She, exhausted from the day, let herself fully lean back into his strong body, just as Sassy had leaned back into the support of the women who had assisted her.

"Is it he?"

Frances's head bobbed up and down on his chest.

"Does Sassy know, do you think?"

Again, Frances nodded her head and then said softly, "Oh, I believe so. She has decided to call him Michael!"

Alaman began to chuckle, the rumble starting low then rippling out through his ribs and tickling Frances's back.

"Life with you is never dull, my queen."

$$\mathcal{)}\ \bigcirc\ \mathcal{(}$$

Six delicious months with baby Michael and his big sister, Sisi. Six months of drumming and dancing on the beach for ceremonies and celebration. Six months where Frances and Sassy had the luxury of doing the most mundane tasks together.

Alaman and Kwame would take the medical van out into the countryside for a week at a time. Alaman had spent years with the French Foreign Legion and his experience was invaluable to Kwame as they dealt with minor injuries and major health crises in the villages. These two men had always liked each other, but these forays allowed a deeper friendship to blossom.

"We wish that you and Frances would stay with us permanently. Is that possible? Does Frances have plans to leave on another adventure?"

Alaman barked a laugh as he helped Kwame unload bags of rice. "Her publisher would like her to take on another adventure. The clamor for more *Dancer* stories is quite loud, evidently."

"And you? What do you want?"

Alaman took his time responding. And, finally, he simply said, "To keep her safe." And he gave another sharp laugh. "But that is in the hands of the Goddess, not my puny self."

Kwame gave him a look of commiseration that spoke volumes. "I sometimes am envious of those of you who have these memories, this link to the past. And then I realize that my life is peacefully unencumbered by that same past. I am only in the here and now, and a very blessed here and now it is. These Standing Bear women! A passel of trouble, and worth every bit, yes?"

Alaman gave him a one-sided grin and hoisted another bag of rice onto his shoulder with a grunt.

CHAPTER 9
NEPAL AND TIBET, 1976

Frances and Alaman walked through the streets of Kathmandu, dodging the dogs that seemed more plentiful than people. The smell of incense competed with the smell of dung and butter lamps to make a cloying perfume that clogged Frances's nose. She had been having difficulty adjusting to the altitude, hoping each day that breathing would get a bit easier.

They sat along the top of a daub wall and watched the street scene before them. The people were dressed in an assortment of Western and traditional clothes. Women had long striped skirts and felted wool coats that they wore tied around the waist with the right arm loose, out of the sleeve. Men had jeans or baggy cloth pants and jackets with knives strung at the belt. Everyone wore a wide-brimmed hat to keep the super bright high-altitude sun out of their eyes. Cats sat motionless in sunny spots, children ran unwatched, and occasionally someone would squat by the side of the road and urinate. It was organized chaos, and to Frances it felt totally foreign and yet achingly familiar.

Frances took Alaman's hand. "Thank you," she said.

"For what?"

"For being you."

"I wouldn't choose to be anyone else," he replied, lifting her hand and kissing her knuckles. Two small boys spotted the gesture, pointed, and laughed. Public displays of affection were not the norm here, and Alaman grinned at the boys, and kissed Frances's hand again, smacking loudly. With that, he lifted her down off the wall and they walked toward the market with the sound of the boy's ribbing and laughter shadowing them.

Their guide was a Tibetan man who had been born in Dharamshala to parents who had fled Tibet with the Dalai Llama. He had had advantage of the English schools there, and so that was the language that they used to communicate with him.

"It is illegal."

"We know, but is it possible?"

"It is dangerous."

"How much?"

He took off the leather fedora he wore and held it over his mouth so that no one could see his lips as he quoted the price he needed to guide them across the mountains and into Chinese-controlled Tibet. Frances could see his eyes over the brim of the hat and the red rim that the hat band had left on his forehead.

"We have the blessing of His Holiness," she said very softly.

He blinked hard twice and then replied, "Well, in that case it only costs half as much."

Frances smiled wryly and Alaman chuckled. They figured that he had first quoted what in Senegal they call the 'toubab price,' the outsider price for goods and services. But if the Dalai Lama had given the okay, then suddenly they were insiders.

"It's the same everywhere," Alaman muttered, and Frances smiled widely at their new guide.

This was a journey into a lunar-like landscape. To escape notice of the Chinese border patrols they traveled at night. Frances and Alaman, both adept at riding horses, found the adjustment to yak back fairly easy to make. But the moon cast shadows along the mountain side that seemed to stretch for miles, and the eerie quiet of the highest peaks in the world were off-putting. As the sun was rising each day, they would make camp with soft brown blankets that made a roof over their heads. Dried yak dung made smokeless fires and they had a steady diet of tea and a kind of pemmican made with barley and strips of dried yak meat glued together with yak butter. They needed the calories from the fat, for at this altitude energy burned at a fast speed.

Whenever they traveled through a mountain pass they saw cairns of white stones piled high, festooned with long strands of prayer flags flapping wildly in the shifting moonlight. Frances was getting easier in her breathing, but her sleep was filled with dreams densely populated by spirits and ancestors. The air felt sharp and sparse.

Their trek took the best part of two weeks, by which time Frances had learned enough Tibetan to listen to the stories their guide told about the holy mountain.

"Tibetan Buddhists call it Kangri Rinpoche, 'Precious Snow Mountain'. Bon texts have many names, Water's Flower, Mountain of Sea Water, Nine Stacked Swastika Mountain. For Hindus, it is the home of the Hindu god Shiva and it is believed that Shiva resides there; for Jains it is where their first leader was enlightened; for Buddhists, the navel of the universe; and for adherents of Bon, the abode of the sky goddess Sipaimen."

"We are to meet a Bon shaman at the sky burial spot," Alaman said.

"I will take you near there, but I won't go all the way," their guide said. "It is not a place for those uninvited."

And so, on the morning of their fourteenth day they bade farewell to Tubten Dorgi and took off on their own for the last few miles. Frances was light-headed, and she and Alaman both struggled to be out and about in the piercing sunlight. The track was well worn, but devoid of any humans, and the only sound was the high cry of a golden eagle.

As they rounded a curve, a small person, bundled in cloth and fur stepped out from the shadow of rocks. Frances greeted her. "Tashi De-leg."

The shaman, for that is who they suspected that she was, peered up at them as if judging fruit in the market, then lifted one shoulder in a shrug and turned and walked off the path into the rocky scree. Alaman and Frances exchanged looks, scrambled off their yaks and hurried to follow her.

She was surprisingly quick and agile, even as bundled as she was. It was a difficult climb, but their shaman never slowed the pace. By late afternoon they arrived at a small level place on the mountain side. There was a ring of stones and the remains of a fire, a small bed mat and a knapsack near the rock face.

The shaman motioned for them to sit, which they did gratefully, as she stoked the fire, adding small chunks of yak dung and bending over to add tiny braids of animal hair to the embers. Within minutes the fire was steady, and she had a pot of water on for tea.

The gloaming light was gentle and expansive. As darkness was finally settling in the shaman stood abruptly, urging Frances to follow her up around the curve of rock with Alaman right on her heels. They came to a fork in the path. The shaman swept her arm out to indicate the path and made shooing motions with her hands as if to say, "Get going!"

Frances and Alaman again exchanged looks and shrugged. It seemed that that there would be no fanfare with this Portal opening, no choir of chanters, no drumming, no formality at all. Frances ask in her rudimentary Tibetan, "Which way?" And she indicated either a clockwise or counterclockwise circle.

The shaman shrugged. Frances and Alaman began to walk forward and see which way they were pulled. The shaman screeched and grabbed Alaman by the back of his jacket, shaking her head violently and making it clear that Frances was to go alone.

Frances found herself climbing higher as the darkness grew almost palpable with only the quarter moon to show her way.

When she reached the pinnacle, the wind whipped her and turned her to face the north. She waited and then began to hear the chorale of mountain wind, the hymn of air. After a time, the wind turned her to the west. Again, the music of air. Then to the south. Then to the east. Always the symphony of air. She was moved to make that circle seven times, and then, in a gust of power, the air above met the strength of the mountain beneath her feet and the Portal slammed open. Frances felt her molecules racing apart, until she became mostly space with tiny, tiny particles of matter, all held tenuously together by the tensile vibration of air. It felt like the beginning of time, the cosmic birth, the source moment.

When the peachy light of dawn slipped over the eastern horizon, Frances came to herself. She had been standing, feet planted wide, arms stretched high overhead, motionless, yet in constant divine movement for all the hours of the night. Suddenly she was exhausted, her arms ached, and she could hear Alaman calling to her from down below. Whispering a prayer of gratitude, she began her descent back to Alaman's waiting embrace and the relative comforts of the shaman's camp.

They rested there that day and night. At one point Frances looked at the shaman as a strong light hit her face, and was startled to see that this Bon celebrant was actually a very young woman. Frances had supposed she must be old and venerable, a practitioner of the most ancient spiritual tradition of these mountains. Instead, she looked to be about twenty, with a healthy unlined face and the bright red cheeks of these mountain dwellers. Frances smiled at her, for in this lifetime she looked as she had when they had known each other in the Before. She had been Yan, one of the young Companions of Tiamet, the old and cranky priestess of Lhamo, the Mother Goddess of these mountains. In the Before, even after the cataclysm that had disrupted their world, Yan had painfully missed her homeland and would speak wistfully of snow and thin air. So, Frances found it touching that in the now, Yan had chosen to come back here, to live amongst the giants of rock and cloud.

She placed a hand over her heart and said, "Celebi of Brig."

Alaman placed a hand over his heart and said, "Pel of Artemis."

The shaman had a moment of confusion and then her eyes shone bright. Memory was granted to her in their presence, and she rested her hand atop her heart and said with joy and delight, "Yan…of Lhamo."

While it was still light, the shaman led them back toward the common track. Their guide, Tubten Dyorgi, had made himself a cozy camp and was stirring something in a pot over the fire as they approached. He stood abruptly, raised a hand in greeting to Alaman and Frances, and then, when he spotted the shaman riding behind them, he froze and dropped his eyes to the ground. Frances saw him making small quick motions with his right hand to ward off evil. The shaman saw it too and snorted.

"What are you afraid of, righteous man? Does the sight of a wild woman terrify you so much?"

Tubten Dyorgi still stared at the ground but shook his head in denial. Alaman swung down off his yak and went to untie their bedrolls. Frances and the shaman also dismounted, and Frances took the young woman's hand as they walked over a small jumble of rock and out of sight of the men. They stood there for a few moments, letting the wind bring them the scents of wildflowers and stone and the high whinging sound that floated down from the sky burial site.

The shaman spotted something moving at the base of Frances's throat. She reached out to touch it automatically, as if to brush off a fly, but her hand stilled before she made contact. It wasn't an insect, but it moved as if alive. Frances saw the shaman's stare and gave a Mona Lisa smile.

"Is there a mark? A …" and she struggled for the right word in Tibetan so she moved her fingers gracefully to make patterns in the air. The shaman nodded.

Frances dragged up a pant leg and worked to lower her sock to reveal the sigil on her calf. Then she pointed to her lower ribs and the sole of her foot and said, "More marks here and here. Each time," and she pointed up the mountain toward the sky burial site, "each time, more marks on me."

The shaman gained courage and leaned in to look closely at Frances's throat. The sigil moved and appeared and then disappeared as if made like a mandala of colored sand that the wind would blow away. She gingerly touched the spot and felt her own finger tingle, looked up at Frances startled, and they both laughed.

"Power," the shaman said, looking Frances directly in the eye with admiration and a large tot of respect.

Frances nodded, shrugged her shoulders, and lifted an eyebrow as if to say, *Yes, for my sins*. Frances searched for the right words. "Only some…special people can see these marks. You have the special sight."

The shaman nodded, still staring at the sigil as it undulated on Frances's throat. "A blessing!" she said.

Frances chuckled and muttered, "And somewhat of a curse!"

They could hear the men speaking and laughing up over the ridge of rocks. The shaman shot a quick glance that way and her lips turned down in bitterness. Frances took the shaman's hand again and offered, "It is as it has been since you and I were friends before. Some people, some men make hard times for women…" Her sentence order was jumbled and she knew it, but the shaman got the gist of what she meant. "The Wheel…" and here Frances made a big circular motion with her free hand, "the Wheel is turning, and the Mother is returning."

The shaman's eyes spilled over, and tears made tracks of joy pain down her cheeks, rivulets of hope and faith washing away oppression and tribulation. They breathed into the stillness only broken by the occasional sound of a yak grunting. The two women looked at and into each other, remembering and reconnecting, making promises of friendship renewed and solidarity for what was to come. With a common nod they returned to the animals and men. The shaman jumped onto her yak's back and lifted the reins to head on her way. Alaman and Frances, side by side, put their hands over their hearts and bowed their head to her as she turned and rode off.

Tubten Dyorgi sighed deeply as he watched her ride away, only saying "Wild woman. Bon. Big magic!"

The shaman rode down toward the monastery at the far northern side of the sacred mountain. She arrived at dusk that day and set up a hasty camp for herself outside the monastery enclosure. When the moon rose she went to stand in its path of light, and she was now clearly visible to any inside the monastery who choose to look past the walls. There she stood until dawn brought the setting of the moon. It was the same the next night and the next.

On the fourth night a young monk, a childhood friend and soulmate of the shaman, slipped out past the gate and ran to her. They ran together as they had as children until the day had come when they had chosen their spirit paths, he to the monastery, she to study with the wild Bon hermit. With their shadows giant projections of their spirits, laughing as they ran, they got to a small dry gully that would flood with snow melt. Theirs was a spirit-driven coupling, fevered but not frantic, tender yet direct and purposeful. This was the first time for each of them, and somehow, they both knew it would be the last, but it was sweet and sacred and filled with all the what-ifs of all their lifetimes. Afterwards they clung together, arms and legs entwined, and they both felt the exact moment when new life was conceived. Their eyes met and their lips melted together.

With the light, they stood, arranged their clothing and exchanged one more kiss. They walked together for a short distance and then separated slowly to follow their chosen paths, clasped hands becoming woven fingers becoming fingertips touching, And another of the Thirteen had come to incarnation.

$$\newcommand{\moon}{} \text{☽ ○ ☾}$$

The opening of this Portal was the beginning of a new pattern for Frances and Alaman. Previously they had stayed with the local people for some months, learning customs and beliefs, and Frances had been able to work at a moderate pace on her novel. But the ability to stay here was severely compromised. Chinese government agents were everywhere. They had been insinuated into native Tibetan populations, and the Tibetans felt the boot on their necks. Staying inside the boundaries of Chinese-controlled Tibet was dangerous for Frances and Alaman, and also for anyone who might help them.

They followed Tubten Dyorgi back into Nepal and paid him generously. Because they had the Dalai Lama's blessing they had access to villages and groups of nomads that other Westerners would not have had. They spent the next year on the move. One week in one village, one month with nomads, crossing into India with traders, back into Nepal with pilgrims. And so it went. They felt safer as moving targets, and Frances wrote when and how she could. As had been true in the past, they found safety with those on the margins, the nomadic, the oppressed.

One year, almost to the day that the Portal atop Mount Kailash had been opened, Frances put the final period to *Cloud Dancer,* and she and Alaman slipped down a side alley in Dharamshala, brushing past chickens and goats, lifting the wet laundry hanging from lines that criss-crossed above them, and posted the manuscript off by handing it over to a monk who handed it to a nun who had a doctor friend walk it into a post office.

"What's next, my queen?" Alaman asked, reaching to pull the brim of his hat farther down over his face, the need to keep identity hidden now an instant reflex.

Frances stood still for a moment. Standing still felt really good for a change. She took stock of her physical body – strong, dusty, and to be truthful, slightly smelly of sweat and animals, and butter tea. She scanned her emotional body – satisfied, loved and loving, and missing her daughter and grandbabies. And finally, a look-see at her spiritual body – in alignment with her purpose: expanding and joyful. Two out of three needed some seeing to.

"I need, in this order: a bath, a new set of clothes, a hamburger and fries, a bed that doesn't smell of yak, and then, to see my babies."

Alaman's face split into a wide smile, his teeth startling white against the skin darkened by sun at high altitude. "I totally concur, only adding the possibility of some leisurely love-making without fifteen people listening in!"

Frances laughed loud, drawing some eyes to her and she pulled her kerchief forward. "Well then, my amorous friend, I believe we should surface, and call upon the assistance of our spy minder. Shall we then, to the American consulate?"

"Are the Americans still friends?" Alaman asked.

"Have they ever been really?" Frances responded.

)○(

When two poorly dressed nomads walked into the lobby of the American consulate one hour later, they were stopped by the Marine at the entrance.

"What's your business here?"

The Marine, twenty years old and fresh out of Norfolk, was shocked when the small woman drew off her head covering and spoke perfect English. "If you would be so kind, we need to see your Cultural Affairs officer.

"Yes, ma'am! Right this way." He turned and led them across the small lobby to the dimly lit office of one Sharyn MacLeod, Cultural Affairs officer for the US State Department and CIA intelligence operative.

She had been warned a year ago to be on the lookout for just these two who now, like apparitions, were standing before her. She pushed her chair back abruptly with a screech and stood.

"Ms. Fletcher? Mr. Sulaman? My stars, I am delighted to see you!"

Frances and Alaman walked out of the consulate forty-five minutes later with new passports, a handsome amount of US currency and a reservation at one of Dharamshala's finest hotels. And Sharyn MacLeod immediately sent word to Langley of the emergence of Frances Fletcher.

Yoff, Senegal, 1977

"Grammere!" Sisi sang out as the tuk-tuk dropped Frances and Alaman at the top of the road. Sisi was indeed tall, skinny legs flashing and wild joyous hair like a flag flying behind her. She threw herself into Frances's arms, almost knocking her over. "Grammere! When did you get so little?"

Sassy's laughter bounced off the daub walls lining the road. "Mama!" She hugged her mother hard and then did the same to Alaman. "You two look...thin!"

"Well, my sweet chicken, the mountains at the top of the world tend to burnish one down to the bone. But, who is this?"

They all looked to see Kwame walking toward them, holding the hand of a toddler who had soft brown curls and skin that was sun-kissed. As the child spotted them Frances saw his azure eyes which locked on hers.

"Michael?"

The boy let go of his father's hand and wobbled toward his grandmother with ferocity. He flung his arms around her legs, and she began to cry. She looked at Alaman as if to say, *How can one heart hold all this joy?* And he understood her completely. He knelt down next to the little boy, one knee cracking like a snapped branch.

"Hello, my dear friend! It heals the heart to see you again," he said softly as he stroked the boy's head.

Frances reached into her pocket and found the stone she had carried these last years, the stone that had held some essence of Malvu who had been Michael and was now a Michael again. She handed the stone to the small boy, and he accepted it with the solemnity of the recognition of its importance. He tilted his face up, Frances bent down lower, and they sweetly kissed on the lips.

"We'll make you a nice pouch so you can carry that wee stone around your neck shall we, boyo?" Frances asked, in the melody of Kerry.

Little Michael, known as Mick, clutched the stone and pressed it to his heart, and the deal was set.

All their laughing and exclaiming had alerted the neighborhood and soon the family was swamped with friends and neighbors. The entire crowd swept into Sassy and Kwame's compound. Food and cool fresh juices appeared in front of them and the celebration went on long into the night.

Sisi and Michael alternated between Frances and Alaman's laps, and first Michael and then Sisi fell asleep with the elders' arms around them. Sassy hadn't stopped smiling since her mother and Alaman had arrived, and Kwame felt himself release some inner fear that he had held this long time they had been gone.

As the evening wore on, the scarf that Frances had draped over her head and tossed over one shoulder fell off and Sassy spotted the newest sigil, the one at the base of Frances's throat.

"That's beautiful Mama, but harder to conceal, no?"

Frances nodded, and as Sassy watched, the sigil moved and danced.

"What next, Mama?"

"I thought we'd stay for a while, if that's alright."

Sassy smiled till her cheeks hurt and leaned over to hug the breath from her mother.

"I think we can manage to suffer that!"

And Frances ruffled her nose into her daughter's hair and thought her heart would burst.

$$\text{)} \bigcirc \text{(}$$

About two weeks later, a middle-aged white man with thinning hair wearing a pink polo shirt and khakis walked from the main highway down into the village of Yoff. Usually, the only white faces in Yoff were surfers who found the western coast of Africa a cheap place to hunker down and ride the waves. They were a scruffy and young lot, so this fellow immediately stood out as being neither young nor scruffy.

Small children began to gather around him, following him, asking him questions in Lebu and Wolof and rough French. He just smiled and kept walking as if he knew where he was going. After a few turns he arrived at Sassy and Kwame's door. They, of course, had been notified of the *toubab's* arrival within minutes of his appearance, so Sassy was ready to answer his knock.

"Good morning! You must be Sassy Kenneally Boadu."

"Must I?" Sassy responded, lifting one eyebrow.

Sheldon Stewart looked momentarily flummoxed and then he laughed. "Well, if you are, you don't take after your mother much." He lifted one hand to comment on Sassy's height.

"That totally depends to which of her aspects you are referring."

He swallowed visibly and replied, "I spoke too soon. You are, in actuality, very much like Frances Fletcher."

They stood in tableau, her with one hand on the partially opened door, him standing outside in the sun. The moment stretched.

"Might I come in? I would like to speak to Frances, if I may." He wiped his brow with a white cotton handkerchief.

"I can offer you shelter from the sun, but I cannot guarantee that Frances Fletcher is available."

"Fair enough."

Sassy opened the door wider and let the man inside the cool entryway. It took a moment for his eyes to adjust.

"Thank you. The heat always takes me by surprise."

"Mmmm." She led the way into the central courtyard and motioned for him to take a seat on the bench near the fountain.

"Something cool to drink?"

"Yes, please!" he replied in a rush, taking off his hat, wiping his face again and looking as pink in the face as his shirt.

Sassy left to go into the kitchen. A breath after she left, a small toddler wobbled into the courtyard and stopped sharply when he saw the man sitting there. The two stared at each other, one pre-speech, the other speechless.

Sheldon Stewart was used to children warming to him. He had seven of his own and in his extended family he was "Uncle Shel" to a large assortment of nieces and nephews, all who found him fun and approachable. But this small boy was not so easily won over. He stood eerily motionless for a toddler, staring with almost unblinking eyes, and giving Sheldon a case of gooseflesh.

"Hello. Are you Michael?"

No response.

"My name is Sheldon. Can you say that? *SHEL-DON.*"

If anything, the child's glare got colder.

"Well, I am a friend of your Grandma."

Cold went to icy.

Sassy returned with a tray of cold drinks, spotted Michael and the stare-down, and chuckled. She said something to the child in a language Sheldon couldn't place, and the boy looked at his mother, nodded begrudgingly, then left the courtyard with one final cutting look at the American.

"Ah, were you speaking Wolof?"

"No."

She poured Sheldon a glass of mango juice and sat across from him with a countenance similar to the one her son had given him.

"Now, Mr. Stewart, what is it you want?"

"Your mother has told you who and what I am?"

Sassy merely smiled at him with the sad and disappointed look one gives a bumbler, tilting her head to the side exactly as her mother did.

"Apple. Tree!" Sheldon retorted. And this time Sassy gave him a genuine smile.

"My mother does have some fond regard for you Mr. Stewart. Why don't you finish your juice and then take a stroll along the beach? It might be that she will join you there."

Half an hour later, Sheldon was walking in the edge of the water, shoes in hand. The bright blue fishing boats were all pulled up on shore for the day, and small clusters of men watched him walk by with non-responsive eyes. In the distance he saw a woman wearing a dress of fuchsia and sapphire pattern and an incongruent leather fedora bending down to gather shells. Frances Fletcher...in the flesh!

She turned and watched him as he approached, lifting a hand to shade her eyes, and granting him a wide, welcoming smile.

"Sheldon Stewart, in the flesh!"

Damn the woman! How did she do that? It was as if she read his mind.

He came up to stand side by side as they stared out at the waves.

"How are you, Frances? And how have you been the last eighteen months since I heard from you?" His tone turned sharper at the end of his query.

Frances tilted her head and peered sideways at him. Her thoughts were rolling. Had she reached the terminus with her CIA handler? Time for the careful hunter's soundless steps that her Uncle Walter had taught her.

"Are you troubled, Sheldon?" she asked softly.

"No! Why should I be troubled? I only have a field operative who disappears for over a year! Why should I be troubled?" His voice rose to a higher volume, and the fishermen on the shore began to move in closer. He spotted them and visibly curtailed his emotions. Frances gave a small hand wave to have them hold back.

"Sheldon, I never was *your* field operative."

"Damn it, Frances! We had a deal!"

"What we had, Sheldon, was a mutually advantageous agreement."

"And...?" He sounded quietly angry now. "Is this agreement no longer mutually advantageous? Is that what you are *not* saying?"

Frances had a calm come over her and felt all her sigils rise to visibility. She turned toward Sheldon, he saw the moving pattern at the base of her throat, and he gasped.

"What is that!" he exclaimed.

"Who I am becoming," she replied. "And you...which masters do you serve, Sheldon?"

"What do you mean?"

"Exactly that." Her gaze was unwavering, and he felt some inner unexamined walls start to crumble.

"I serve the United States of America and seek to protect her from foreign enemies. You know that!"

"And what if those masters ask you to harm innocent people, to thwart movements that would rectify injustice? What if those masters are using you, Sheldon, to do their dirty work in the name of patriotism? What then?"

Deep emotions worked back and forth over his face: stubbornness, worry, doubt, conviction, regret.

"I think I have to have faith that folks smarter than me are calling the shots, Frances."

She was quiet for several minutes and he started to fidget on his feet as they sank into the soft sand. Finally, she responded. "Misplaced faith has been the source of much human misery, Sheldon."

In exasperation he took off his hat and ran his hand through his sweaty hair. Then he slammed his hat back on his head. "Damn this heat!" He breathed audibly for several breaths and then asked again, "What is it you are *not* saying, Frances?"

"My allegiance is to the Earth, to the Mother of us all. The Wheel is turning, Sheldon, and I believe that some of your puppet masters would like to thwart that turning. You know that saying, 'the dying mule kicks the hardest?' Well, I have come to see that the powers that be, the instruments of control that you serve, that they are kickin' hard and will kick even harder in the years to come."

"I'm a patriot, Frances, not a puppet!' He was truly stung and shook his head hard as if trying to shake off a hornet. "I can't...I won't believe that. What is the world if we aren't the good guys?"

Frances reached over and took his hand, gripping his fingers tightly. "That, my friend, is what has always been so likable about you. You really believe in the White Hats, and that your team wears them. For a spook you are a very sweet man. But I have seen how very often the White Hats are willing to sacrifice good people for what they call the Greater Good. Do the ends justify the means, Sheldon?"

"Yes! Ye... I mean...Some..." he found himself floundering. He paused to compose himself. "Frances, if we part ways I can no longer protect you." His tone was urgent.

"Sheldon, I think, if you are honest with yourself, you will see that that ship has already sailed." She looked at him kindly. "I believe that my publisher has sent a letter to the address you have used to front our connection. She has acknowledged that our financial obligations have been met, my advance has been long paid off, and that we no longer need your support."

"But Frances. This...can't we find a way?"

Frances reached up and tugged his face down by the ear, giving him a kiss on the cheek. "Go with the Goddess, Sheldon Stewart. And when next we meet, may it not be as enemies."

Frances turned and began to walk up the beach, never looking back, followed by the fishermen who saw her safely home. Sheldon Stewart stood there longer, not even noticing that his pale skin was reddening. Doubts, like mosquitoes swarmed in his head until, with sheer force of will he swatted them away.

CHAPTER 10

The years rolled on and the new pattern remained the same. Frances and Alaman spent long stretches of time in Senegal with Sassy and the family, for there they could live out in the open. No one in Yoff would betray them, and outsiders were spotted before they even got into the village. From time to time Frances would feel the pull of the Earth, hear the songs of stones, and know where to go next. Her arrival would be foretold someplace where the power spot had been kept hidden for centuries. She and Alaman would travel, usually incognito, meet the Grandmother who had been guarding the place, Frances would open the Portal and receive another sigil, and someone in the Grandmother's bloodline would conceive a child, an incarnation of the Thirteen.

Increasingly they felt threats from all the forces that were organizing to stop the opening of the power Portals, to block the return of the Goddess, and then they relied on their networks of kinship and heart friends to provide sanctuary. But as resistance to their work rose, so did the support for it.

While the planet began to revive with the opened Portals flooding Her with newly freed energy, the impetus for liberation from patriarchy and colonialism also was coming to life. Women began to find one another in circles dedicated to the Goddess. Indigenous spirituality became uncovered and legal in more and more places. And Frances dropped many seeds of long-buried ideas.

Margot Adler saw Frances's books on a friend's daughter's shelf and began her research and immersion into neo-paganism. Layne Redmond saw the cover art of *Drum Dancer* on a table at the Strand bookstore and began to dream about the times when women were drummers. Kathy Jones led women in Glastonbury, England who started meeting and doing ceremony, stirring the idea that a Goddess temple could exist in the West. The Goddess was awakening. And in response, the fundamentalist aspects of established faiths began a clamor to rally the forces of fear of change.

$$\text{☽ ○ ☾}$$

In October of 1980, Frances and Alaman were nearly run off a narrow mountain road on their way to a meeting with local medicine people near Machu Picchu. They were sheltered by the villagers and four days later Frances opened a Light Portal high atop that ancient structure.

A few days after the Portal flooded light into the Andes, Sheldon Stewart saw the communique that told the details of the unsuccessful attempt by agribusiness interests in Peru to "eliminate" the irritating influence of Frances Fletcher on the local democracy organizers. He winced at how close the saboteurs had come to succeeding, but hardened his resolve to not be seduced from his own path of righteousness.

$$\text{☽ ○ ☾}$$

In April of 1983 persons working for the conglomerates that were desperate to hold onto their plantation assets slid a poisonous snake into the cabin on the island of Hawaii where Frances and Alaman were staying. The snake worked its way up the leg of the bed and onto the sheets. The sigils on Frances's legs woke up before she did. When she realized what was happening and slowly lifted her head off the pillow, she nudged Alaman in the ribs and placed her hand over his mouth. They saw to their amazement that the sigil and the snake seemed to be having a conversation. After a few moments the snake turned and slithered off the bed and out under the door.

Later that same month the volcano Mauna Loa made a spectacular display of fire and spark as Frances opened the Fire Portal there.

$$\mathbb{) \ \bigcirc \ (}$$

1989 saw tremendous change all over the planet. Freedom activists occupied Tiananmen Square. The Soviet Union began to crumble. The Berlin Wall fell. Gisela Zastrow, a native Berliner who had survived the War and emigrated to America, returned to Berlin in her fur coat to swing a hammer at the Wall. The Chinese proverb that 'when sleeping women wake mountains move' was coming to fruition. And women out-numbered men in undergraduate schools in the West for the first time ever.

That same year, men dressed as South African police stopped Frances and Alaman as they were attempting to cross the border into Zimbabwe. They held them in a small dilapidated wooden shack for three days.

"The witch woman, she has a map. You must search her!"

Frances and Alaman heard the voices outside arguing.

"I will not touch the witch woman! You search her!"

Alaman's heart filled with panic. He was tied up, unable to walk or free his hands. If anyone tried to hurt Frances, he couldn't help. He caught her gaze and the look between them spoke volumes. The door to the shack burst open, and three men hurried in.

"Witch woman, stand up!" Frances did not comply and simply looked at the men with an unreadable calm. Her lack of fear confirmed for them that she had magick, and they felt their bones weaken.

"Stand up, I say!"

If anything, Frances looked even calmer.

"Benjamin, you find that map! Maybe it is in her clothing."

The youngest of the men was pushed forward toward Frances. Alaman struggled with his bonds, but another man knocked his head with the butt of his gun. With that, Frances came to her feet and looked at

Benjamin, the young man. "Go ahead. I give you permission to touch me."

Benjamin swallowed hard but took her at her word. He gingerly approached and began to pat at her sides.

"Nothing. There is no paper on her."

"It must be somewhere. Strip her! She has it hidden!" The older man speaking had a bitter edge. He wanted the money that had been promised for the retrieval of the map.

Benjamin whispered, "Ma'am, I am sorry."

"It is quite alright, young man. Go ahead." Frances gave him a sweet smile. Alaman moaned and started to come to. He watched as Benjamin began to take off Frances's sweater and blouse.

"No! My Frances!" This was unbearable, to witness and be helpless, just as it had been when he had watched Nazis beating Michael in the prison camp. Alaman twisted and struggled against the ropes at his wrists and they started to bleed.

Frances's smile grew wider and she spoke to Alaman in his native Berber, as if she were a million miles away from what was transpiring in the shack. "My Blue Man, you must not worry. Only the pure of heart will find what these men are seeking."

Benjamin was sweating and fumbling with the buttons on Frances's trousers. He flashed her a wild-eyed look, a plea for forgiveness. In response, she began to sing a Cree lullaby. Bit by bit, piece by piece, Frances was stripped of even her undergarments until she stood bare and exposed. In the dimness of the shack she was naked and yet standing upright and valiant, like a proud crone warrior. The sigils were static and muted in the half-light, disappearing into the folds of skin and the shadows on her body.

Benjamin was trembling. "There is nothing! No map!"

The older man growled, "Witch woman! Where is it?" Frances stared at him with a look that was overflowing with disappointment. He jammed his rifle butt into her belly and stormed away as she fell to the ground. Benjamin knelt down next to her and quietly helped put her clothes back on. "Ma'am, did he hurt you bad?"

"Not nearly as much as he hurts you, young man. You must leave him before he kills your spirit."

Benjamin was startled, but nodded in understanding. He brought her water and helped to clean the wound on Alaman's temple. Come nightfall, he slipped away and made contact with people who could help.

The next day, a group of anti-apartheid fighters created a diversion and another smaller group broke Frances and Alaman out, helped them into a waiting truck, and spirited them across the border. In December, Frances opened the Water Portal while hidden in a cave alongside the roar of Victoria Falls.

Sheldon Stewart came out of a meeting about the increasing instability in the former Yugoslavia and was handed a top-secret memo. He read about the kidnapping of Frances and her subsequent escape. A few months later he received a directive to put a surveillance team onto Frances and Alaman and to regard them as "suspicious and possibly inconvenient" to the interests of the United States.

$$) \bigcirc ($$

In 1992, given the overly optimistic moniker of Year of the Woman, also saw the rise of anti-reproductive choice activism in the United States. That autumn, Frances and Alaman traveled from her grandmother's cabin in Canada, down through the Plains states, and into the Four Corners Reservation of the desert southwest. They were known as 'The Medicine Bundle' and handed on from driver to driver. They arrived in the darkest of a dark moon and were told that only yesterday a man had been apprehended by tribal police, asking questions about Frances, and pretending to be Hopi. Since his accent was atrocious, it hadn't been a hard catch to make.

Frances and Alaman disappeared into the life of the pueblo until, two months later, she descended into a hidden kiva that only a very few knew of. The Grandmother who led her down into the womb-like space whispered, "No one has been down here for four hundred years…" The Earth Portal that was opened that night created a sigil all across Frances's lower belly. The next day Alaman gently brushed a plantain ointment across the still stinging mark with his index finger.

"I am seventy years old next month. I have become an old wrinkly woman, my Blue Man." Frances said with a tiny sliver of embarrassment sliding down her spine.

He looked at her slender torso, and gently kissed all the sigils and stretchmarks and the flesh that felt the pull of gravity. With each kiss Frances felt the surge of desire rise up within her until she felt she couldn't contain it, but still he gestured her to lie back and let him honor her.

"Your body is the Earth itself, my queen, and the source of all my sustenance."

🌙 ◯ 🌙

1995 and 1996 saw an increased awareness in the Divine Feminine and a surge of resistance to Her. Hillary Clinton gave the famous "human rights are women's rights – and women's rights are human rights" speech at the United Nations Conference on Women in Beijing. Women now were the majority of students in American law and medical schools. A new play by Eve Ensler, *The Vagina Monologues,* made its debut in New York City. ALisa Starkweather birthed the Red Tent Movement and women found new safe places. Elizabeth Cunningham began a series of novels that made the Magdalene a symbol of awakened power and divine right.

And simultaneously, the Taliban came to power in Afghanistan, stripping women and girls of all access to education and public life. The dying mule was kicking harder to fight against the changing tide.

CHAPTER 11
SUTHERLAND FALLS, SOUTH
ISLAND, NEW ZEALAND,
DECEMBER 1999

As much of the world was preparing for – or mocking – the potential kerfuffle of Y2K, Alaman and Frances landed in New Zealand. They were immediately absorbed into a collection of Maori spiritual leaders, and the CIA operative who had been tasked to follow them, almost immediately lost all trace. Back at Langley, outside Washington DC, Sheldon Stewart read the report and swore in frustration. And yet part of him was secretly delighted that Frances was able to confound her tag once again.

Alaman had had a small heart attack the year before, and while he insisted that he felt "just fine, Frances!" she kept sliding looks at him to see. They made the journey to the South Island in easy stages, being warmly greeted at each step of the way. The Maori priestesses seemed particularly intrigued by Frances's sigils, and several of the young women among them had copies of the patterns tattooed onto their bodies.

For the last part of the journey to Sutherland Falls, they crammed into a Ute that had seen better days with Frances, Alaman and the driver in front, and a quorum of thirteen priestesses in the open back cargo area. When they climbed down from the cabin, the senior priestess told Alaman that he and the driver would have to stay behind.

"No men can see," she said firmly. Alaman bit the inside of his cheek but nodded, and Frances gave the priestess a look of gratitude.

As the women climbed higher, passing through dense walls of mist, Frances got the occasional boost on her behind from the younger women, and the mood was festive. They came to a small moss-covered, shallow bowl of a place that seemed hidden between three cascades of water. It reminded Frances of Ireland, the place of the three hills where the Sidhe lived, and her soul smiled. The priestesses formed a circle around Frances and began the song of the place. She stood, arms reaching skyward, until she felt the power rising beneath her feet. It came on inexorably, like the sound of a freight train drawing closer and closer until Frances shouted the true name of the place, a name never spoke in front of colonizers, a name so sacred as to cause all present to tremble. The long-hidden force within that Portal erupted, and the three cascades surged in volume and began to merge.

Frantically the women scrambled up and over the top of the mountain. Panting, they stood and looked down at the now enveloped spot where the magic had happened. Frances began to sing the new song of the place, and the priestesses joined her.

On the winter solstice, one of the young priestesses, the granddaughter of the eldest, made love with her second cousin twice removed. Her new tattoos still stung, but that pain was forgotten in the amnesia of their passion. In a different house in the same village Frances felt her newest sigil, the one that ran up her right jawline to encircle her ear, begin to tingle and knew that another of the Thirteen's souls had found a body.

New York, New York, USA, 2000

2000 saw the launch of *Mist Dancer,* the eleventh book in the *Dancer* series. Frances's publisher planned a big promotion for the book, linking it to the thirtieth anniversary of the first *Dancer* book. The entire series was re-issued with new cover art (still all subject to Frances's approval), and a big party was scheduled in New York.

Frances's original publisher, Elspeth Alcott had retired many years before, but she planned to attend and kept sending letters to Frances to encourage her to come.

Dearest Frannie,

Okay, now I'm begging. I want to see you!

I don't want to play the cancer card, but I must. It seems that the dreaded C has spread and I have chosen to not pursue those noxious treatments any more. If you can, dearest, please come. We can sit in the corner and make snarky comments about the whippersnappers while they act like they discovered publishing.

With love,

E

So, in December, Frances flew from Dakar to JFK. She came out of Customs and saw Elspeth leaning on the arm of a very handsome young man in a driver's livery. The two old friends immediately looked past the changes that disease and aging had wrought and saw true hearts still beating with love and mutual respect.

"Come, sweetness! I have cocktails in the limo!"

The party was high atop the Twin Towers at the Windows on the World restaurant. New York City was extravagantly lit up for Christmas, and the spectacular view from this vantage was like seeing the constellations upside down. The expansive room was filled with literati and 'whippersnappers' who mingled and drank and sampled delicacies gingerly like royal tasters. After Frances had stood for pictures and shaken enough hands, she and Elspeth found a corner in which to perch.

"My dear, how do you do it? You don't look a day over eighty," whispered Elspeth, who knew, of course, exactly to the date that Frances was eighty-one.

Frances threw back her head and laughed her single bark. "Clean living, Ellie. Just good clean living."

"But seriously, how is your delicious man?"

"He seems fully recovered and becomes quite cranky when I fuss. The doctors say he is as strong as a much younger man."

"But? I hear the 'but' in your voice..."

"He naps, Ellie! In all our years together I have never seen him tire, and now he naps!"

"And?"

"And, I fear the loss of him."

"He might outlast you, old woman!"

Frances gave a one-sided grin and poked her elbow into her friend's ribs. As she looked across the crowd she was startled but not surprised to see Sheldon Stewart watching her. The soft middle he had displayed decades ago had now blossomed into a pronounced paunch.

"Ellie, let me go get us some more champagne," Frances said softly. Elspeth followed Frances's gaze recognizing Stewart and nodding.

"Bring on the bubbles! But don't get out of eye-shot."

Frances walked over to the bar and Sheldon stepped in next to her.

"You look wonderful, Frances."

"No thanks to you, Sheldon."

"Frances…" he had a strained timbre in his voice. "Frances, you have a particular talent for pissing people off!"

She looked at him with genuine delight, smiling widely. "It surprises the heck out of me, Sheldon, but I am happy to see you."

"My grandkids love your books. I promised I could get some auto-graphed copies for them."

"That's why you are here tonight?"

"No, but that's the reason I gave the wife."

Frances laughed, gave a small twist of her mouth, and asked, "And why are you here really?"

"I left the Agency this year, Frances, but I still…hear things."

For Frances, the room went quiet, and her vision narrowed until only she and Sheldon Stewart were in the room. These moments of slow-motion clarity, the moments of extreme danger, were ones in which she was always thankful for the warrior in her.

"What do I need to be on the look-out for, Sheldon?"

"Your family, Frances. Watch out for your family."

"Meaning what, exactly," Frances said very quietly. Sheldon felt the hairs stand up on his arms. Frances was old but still terrifying.

"USAID has been notified that the contract for your daughter and son-in-law's Health Service is not to be renewed."

"They have been working and helping people in West Africa for twenty-some years."

"The Agency feels that they have 'suspicious contacts' with China. And China's growing influence in Africa is a worry. There are records of communications…"

"You mean the invoices for the cheaper antibiotics that they purchase from Shanghai?"

Sheldon cleared his throat. "Probably."

"And what else?"

"You granddaughter's research into global warming is making some people very unhappy."

"Will she too be seeing her funding blocked?" Frances asked.

"More like career assassination. Prepare her for the onslaught of opposition papers disputing her findings. And possibly some attacks on her honesty and ethics."

Frances felt her heart slow even more, as Sheldon could hear his pulse rapidly escalating.

"Is that all?"

"Tell your grandson to be very careful with whom he socializes."

"Meaning what exactly"

"I heard chatter about possible ways to implicate him in… in a staged rape."

Frances slipped her small knife out of its hidden scabbard in her sleeve and pushed it into Sheldon's soft middle, hard enough for him to feel the metal prick through his dress shirt. "And you, old friend?" Frances uttered those words like they were mercury dripping from her lips. "What is your involvement in these activities?"

"I told you, Frances. I retired. I didn't like what I was seeing."

"But did you do anything to stop it?"

Sheldon turned an alarming shade of crimson and pressed the heel of his hand against his breastbone. "To my eternal shame, no."

Frances pushed the tip of her knife in one more centimeter until she saw a tiny scarlet drop begin to spread across his white shirt. "The Wheel is turning, Sheldon Stewart. The old guard will lose. And you, in your remaining days must decide on which side you wish to be tallied."

Wiping the knife on her sleeve and slipping it back in the scabbard she turned abruptly and walked with an eerie calm back to where Elspeth was sitting. She had a tiny smile that spoke volumes.

"Sweetness. What is it? You look… odd!"

"The skirmishes are over, Ellie. They have declared war!"

And indeed, it did come to pass that the USAID contract for Kwame's mobile medical service was not renewed. He and Sassy scrambled to find other funding so they could continue to bring medical care and vaccines to the hard-to-reach rural areas, but every time it looked like they had found a donor, the source would mysteriously dry up. Their daughter Sisi had been scheduled to be a visiting scholar at NOAA and expand her research into global ocean warming, but that position was suddenly filled by a much less qualified scientist who had been working for Shell Oil. And young Mick, doing his graduate work at his grandfather's alma mater in Oxford, and having been warned well by his grandmother, needed to repeatedly turn down offers from young women he had never met before.

Yoff, September 11, 2001

Frances and Alaman huddled around the television with Mick, Sassy and Kwame and watched the relentless replay of the Twin Towers as they fell…those same towers where Frances had been celebrated only nine months before. They made frantic attempts to reach Sisi who was at the Lamont Doherty Earth Research Institute north of New York City. After terror-filled hours the phone lines opened up and they talked to her and could rest in the knowledge that she was safe.

"What will happen next, Mama?"

Frances and Alaman exchanged looks. "Fear will wage war over reason, my sweet chicken, and the next boogey man will be the Muslim man."

"Even old and decrepit ones such as I?" Alaman asked wryly.

"Perhaps most especially those venerable and wise ones whose long-time companion has managed to annoy the CIA," Frances reflected calmly while her mind was spinning. "We need to travel, tonight, before border scrutiny becomes too focused."

She turned to Sassy and gave her a bone-crushing hug. "My dear one, please grab the go-bag with the French passports. Alaman and I shall make our way to Ballinskellig and be safe as houses in our old cottage."

CHAPTER 12
SAINTES-MARIES-DE-LA-MER, FRANCE, AND ALICUDI, ITALY, 2008

The Roma of Europe and their Traveller cousins arrived at Saint-es-Maries-de-la-Mer for the feast of Sarah la Kali. The gathering happened every year and culminated with a procession to the sea as the statue of Sarah la Kali was carried on horseback.

This year a group of Travellers from the west of Ireland led by Young Shelta Kenneally emerged from the Chunnel in a caravan of vans and campers and drove southeast to join the gathering. They brought with them two elders who rode happily on the bench seat of one van and sang songs and recited poetry for much of the trip.

Those two elders, Frances and Alaman, took the opportunity of this festival to reunite with the descendants of the Roma family, the Levevres, who had helped them in the War. One late night, after copious amounts of wine had been consumed, Frances was enticed to recreate her tambourine dance, much to the delight of all. While the hip action was less pronounced than it had been fifty years before, her intensity and commitment to the dance was the same. Alaman had tears of laughter rolling down his face.

"Every time I think I have reached a moment of peak joy with you, my queen, I am astonished to find new heights." He was wheezing and holding his belly from laughing so hard.

Frances sat down next to him, wiping perspiration off her forehead, and giving him a gimlet glare. "I just have one question, Blue Man. Laughing *with* me, or *at* me?"

"Always with you, beloved. I am always with you."

She squeezed his hand tightly and lifted her mouth in a one-sided smile. "Right answer, *mon coeur*. Absolutely right answer!"

As the festival was winding down on the days after the procession to the sea, Frances and Alaman took advantage of the chaos to slip aboard a fishing boat headed out into the Mediterranean. After five days of a blessedly smooth and seemingly directionless sailing, they were taken ashore on Alicudi, one of the Aeolian Islands north of Sicily and embraced by the local *streghe*. The next Portal to be opened was on the nearby island of Stromboli with its ever-burning volcano, but Stromboli was popular with tourists and too crowded to stay safely hidden from curious eyes. So, they stayed high on the mountain in Alicudi for several weeks learning all the stories, songs, and green magick of the local witches. This island was a *streghe* stronghold, one of those isolated places where the Old Ways had never died. Catholicism and modernity had never shattered the community of witches up on the mountainside. And whether *streghe* or not, the entire population of the island became willing participants in the plan to help the Great Lady, the *Grande Signora,* open the next Portal.

On the night of the Summer Solstice, Frances talked Alaman into staying in that mountain eyrie as she made the trip by boat to Stromboli.

"Dearest, you know how you and the ocean are not friends. It is rough seas tonight and a very small boat. Please, stay here and watch the mountain for signs that I may be successful." She knelt before him and kissed his hands.

"I fear that I am of little use to you, my Frances. And that is my worst fear. Perhaps Sassy or Sisi or Mick should have come with you on this journey."

"Are you chickening out on me, old man?" she said cajolingly.

He smiled and gave her a little push. "Go on then. Do what She needs you to do. I'll be here when you get back."

"Promise?" Frances asked, suddenly serious.

"With all of my aged heart, stents and all."

The ride over to Stromboli was indeed rocky. Frances was in a small craft with a boatman and the eldest *stregha* of the Alicudi. She clutched the sides of the boat and willed herself not to yelp in fear. Once at the island, their small entourage of boats pulled into a tiny fingernail of a beach and Frances was guided up the mountainside atop a donkey. The constant flames and smoke made the horizon look like it was on fire. And Frances could feel that familiar tug of the power places, well known to her now, the rising tides of energy within her body doing a call and response with the currents of energy of the planet.

As she stood near the lip of the volcano summoning the Portal, she thought she heard angry voices down the side of the slope. People were coming, coming and trying to prevent the opening. A part of Frances knew that her companions were rushing down the hillside, arguing with the angry voices, fighting them, holding them off for as long as possible. And the other part of her turned to her task, feeling fire as an ally, as it swirled in her body, rushing between her cells, igniting all fire with all Fire. *Hurry! Hurry!* And in that moment, she became Fire, the spark from one synapse to the next, the explosion of the Big Bang, the first Fire. This Portal was now open and could not be closed, no matter how organized or influential the forces against it might be. Lines of energy communicated to all the other Portals all over the planet. The web was now almost complete, and the Earth rejoiced at Her awakening life.

A flare of flame and an eruption of smoke gave Frances the cover she needed to slip down the far side of the mountain, and gently feel her way back down to the beach. The boatman was pacing on the sand, looking worried.

"*Grande Signora,* I heard shouting and saw lights on the hillside. Are you alone?"

"Yes, my friend, I am here alone, and I believe we had best leave quickly!" She took his hand as he helped her over the side of the boat to sit on the cross bar.

"And the others?"

"Will do all they can to misdirect our enemies. And my friend, after tonight…"

"I never saw you, *Grande Signora.*"

)○(

The next morning, safely ensconced back in the small stone cottage on the highest peak of Alicudi, Frances looked in the hand mirror and saw her newest sigil, writhing red and orange up the left side of her jaw, encircling her ear, mirroring the pattern on the right. A young woman ran up the hill and brought the news.

"*Grande Signora!* The *streghe,* they were arrested at the volcano last night for trespass!"

"Are they alright? No one was hurt?"

The young woman laughed. "Well, several of the *polizia* were injured. My grandmother had come armed with an assortment of kitchen knives."

"Was it just the local *polizia* last night?"

"No, *Grande Signore.* There were others. Nonna said they sounded Russian."

Frances stored that away. Russians in cooperation with Italian police. Oil oligarchs allied with EU officials. Big Oil was putting pressure on every politician and environmental advocate. They must see her as a threat as well... She shook off the dark thoughts and smiled at the young woman before her who looked like a gardenia blossom ready to open.

"And you? You were not part of last night's excursion?"

"No, my Nonna said my part to play would be here. I was to take my sweetheart and go watch the sky from the highest point on Alicudi."

Frances smiled knowingly at her. "And did you? Watch the sky?"

The young woman blushed and smiled a Cheshire cat smile. "The sky, she was beautiful, *Grande Signora.*" She sighed and reached out to touch the undulating sigil on Frances's left cheek. Without being aware of why, she let her other hand drift to her lower abdomen as if to gently shelter that newest spark.

CHAPTER 13
CALANAIS, ISLE OF LEWIS,
SCOTLAND, 2012

The ancient Mayan calendar foretold the end of an epoch on December 21, 2012, the Winter Solstice, and what would be Frances Fletcher's ninety-fourth birthday. Speculation about what "the end" meant was flying over the internet. Would it be the end of times? Some started stockpiling survivalist supplies. Some thought that the end of the status quo sounded like a good idea. And the Grandmothers, those Wise Women who had been the secret keepers and had sent Alaman to summon Frances to her mission all those years ago, shared what they knew to be true: the time of the Divine Feminine was to begin.

It was foretold to be the end of the dominance of the Sky God and the beginning of healing and reparation for the Earth. It was the tipping point of change. Those forces of power-over had had their epoch, and the result had been the potential mass extinction of species, the irreversible poisoning of the air and water and soil, the escalating effects of climate change, the rise of nationalism that gripped borders and the demonization of 'the other.'

According to the Mayans, the shift would require a forty-year challenge, a period of birthing pangs between the old order and the new. But those forty years would begin on December 21, 2012, no matter what. Like two armies poised on the battlefield, waiting for the horns to blare, both sides were armoring up and preparing for this final struggle. The rise of third and fourth wave feminism, the environmental movement, the Goddess spirituality movement, the forces for racial and social justice had woken millions to the desperate needs of the planet and Her people. And the entrenched entities of nation states and international corporations fueled by fear and greed had fortified their side.

War still raged in Afghanistan and Iraq. The use of power-over to achieve desired results was more rampant than ever. A man of color, Barack Obama, was running for re-election as President of the United States where conspiracy theorists and agents of moneyed interests continued to promote 'birther' lies and fund legislation to curtail women's reproductive autonomy.

Twelve of the Thirteen had been born and were now ranging in age from forty-one to four. Their soul contracts had been written in such a way that they knew of each other and had a way of connecting that defied technology. So, while the Grandmothers shared information along astral channels, the newly incarnated of the Thirteen shared a mission that spoke to them from their DNA. They were waiting for the final Portal to be opened when the last of them would take a body. And then they would do the work they had pledged to finish millennia before.

Frances had finished the penultimate book in the *Dancer* series, *Ember Dancer,* and had spent the last few years polishing *The Book,* the treasured stories of her Granny Sally's lives from her incarnation as Atvasfara, High Priestess of Isis to her time as Sally Standing Bear. Frances and her family had guarded these stories, using some details in Frances's early book series of female heroines. But mostly, they kept the secrets until they could be revealed. Frances had made plans for this book to be published after her birthday, or after her demise, whichever happened last.

She knew that all the oppositional forces would do everything in their power to stop her this last time. And while she had ultimate faith in the wisdom of the Goddess, she was taking no chances.

Invitations to Frances's birthday party went out to family in Saskatchewan and to all those communities that she had come to love in her travels. RSVPs flooded in, and the Kenneallys, both settled and Travellers, were busy organizing the celebration. Her extended family made numerous trips to Shannon airport to pick up those coming from all parts of the globe, and every B&B and small hotel and rental from Killarney to Portmagee was filled with Frances's Cree family of blood and her adopted families of Tuareg and Maori and Tibetan and Hopi and all the other treasured friends.

The influx of so many obvious outsiders in the slow tourist winter was enough to draw the attention of a number of intelligence agencies and a plethora of global corporate entities. The chatter between the CIA and MI6 was intense. Former operatives of the KGB, funded by the extractive industries, were desperate to discover what Frances might be up to. Many individuals were notified to stop her, and the words "by any means necessary" were used. Former colleagues reached out to the retired Sheldon Stewart, and appealed for any information he might have on her motives and plans.

Suspiciously curious people kept trying to strike up conversations at pubs and restaurants with Frances's friends and relatives. Those inquisitors were all told the same story.

"I am here for a big birthday celebration on December twenty-first. The guest of honor is quite frail. She is turning ninety-four and in poor health, but she is very excited."

This cobweb of deception worked well, surrounding the Ring of Kerry with enough misdirection and obfuscation that the true plan remained hidden. Frances was indeed turning ninety-four, but in robust good health and tough as an old boot. There was indeed a big party planned…it was just that Frances would not be attending.

Early in the morning of December 15th all the invited guests began to arrive on the Kenneally farm near Ballinskellig. This thin peninsula of land had been the home of the family for decades and now sported the original three cottages and four modern houses built during the Celtic Tiger years. Malachi, Michael's brother, and his children had tended the land well and with respect for the magick that lived there.

Outdoor fires had been set up and each group of the global family was preparing the festive dishes of their culture to share. In all the hubbub a small van made its way down the long narrow lane to the secluded beach where a rowboat waited. Frances and her family exited the van and were rowed out to a trawler that sat just outside the bay.

Alaman had been well-dosed with Dramamine and given a spot near the railing so he could watch the horizon. Never good with sea or the cold, he was almost unrecognizable, so wrapped in sweaters and hats and scarves and coat and oilskin was he. Sassy came to sit by his side.

"In the Before I too felt the cold as you do. I was always wrapped and bundled so that only my nose was visible."

Alaman chuckled. "Those of us from the desert never seem to acclimatize, do we? He paused and then spoke again in a flattened tone, "This is the last Portal. Is this the end?"

They sat with that unknown. The end of the work to return the Goddess? The end of Frances?

"Whatever is coming we must hold tight and let go," Sassy replied. Alaman nodded and they leaned together, breathing in the sharp salt spray of paradox.

The rest of the group consisted of Kwame, young Michael and Sisi with her new husband of four months, Leo Tjia Ph.D.

Over the next six days, as the boat made its way up the west coast of Ireland for open seas, and then across to the Isle of Lewis in the Outer Hebrides, Frances found memories of her last voyage on these waters rushing back to her. She, as she had been as the Brighid, the High Priestess of the Mystery School at Calanais, had made an impulsive and completely non-characteristic move and raced aboard a ship headed to Egypt. In the time Before, she had only known that she was summoned on the mission by the voice of the Goddess in her heart. She, a creature of discipline and order, had left all of her responsibilities behind without a backward glance and had become a Companion of the Thirteen. These waters, these gray and agate waves, opened the cache box of her recollections. She was flipping back and forth between anticipation and agitation. She was coming full circle. It may have taken five thousand years, but she was coming back home.

"Mama, the captain says we make port in about twenty minutes." Sassy said, needing to shout over the wind. "He is choosing to not use the dock at the old fish processing plant. He says that would be too obvious, so we are heading someplace more hidden."

Frances looked into her daughter's eyes and held them. Her beloved girl, the product of all the lifetimes of love she had shared with the one first known as Malvu, and in this lifetime called Michael Kenneally. She reached for Sassy's mittened hand and clenched hard. "What a treasure you have been to me, my sweet chicken. I am so very glad you are here."

"You didn't think I would let you come back here without me, did you?" Sassy tried to quip, but the attempt was marred by the tears she needed to wipe from her eyes.

The engine modulated down to a dull roar as the boat navigated a narrow channel. The captain brought the boat to a halt and threw the anchor in a slight sandy indentation along the rocky coast. The crew lowered the rowboat, and Frances and assembly descended, precariously clinging to the ladder as the boat rocked in the swell. The sun was setting into the ocean as the group sloshed ashore and dragged the boat up onto the sand.

It was different. The shoreline had changed drastically in the thousands of years. But the land vibrated the same, the rocks thrummed the same song, and Frances felt…home. At last.

It was bitter cold. The wind off the Atlantic pushed ferociously at them and threatened their footing. They struggled up the incline, the younger assisting the older. A small van was waiting for them up on the road to take them to the stones. Alaman helped Frances into the front passenger seat and gave her shoulder a squeeze for comfort. Their driver was a woman in her mid-forties with wind-chapped skin and bright green eyes. She reached over and grabbed Frances's hand, lifting it to her lips and saying, "Welcome back, Celebi, Brighid of Calanais!"

Frances made a sound like a strangled laugh.

"You were of the Mystery School?"

"Yes, Brighid. There are many of us here along the coast. We have been awaiting your return for lifetimes."

"Then, not a minute to waste. Bring me to the stones!"

The road was narrow, but their driver knew it well and drove with speed.

"Brighid, there is a Visitor Center at the backside of the stones. Shall I take you there?"

But before Frances could answer Sisi called out from the back of the van, "Grammere! A car is following us. No, wait, two cars!"

Frances asked the driver, "Is there another way to the processional avenue?"

"Yes, there is a small lane with farmhouses."

"Let's go that way. And, shut off your lights."

The van bulleted down the road and made a sharp left turn, running dark. All of those inside the van felt the threat from those following, but Frances began a low chant in the language long forgotten, and one by one, her family and the driver joined in.

"You are the Source of all Life!
You are the Source of all Life!
You are the Source of all Life!"

All across the planet, at Uluru and Jeju Island, at the Wind Cave and the volcano at Mauna Loa, every Portal was being encircled by women and men who heard the call, heard that chant in the marrow of their bones. They were like midwives at a birth who stood vigil, holding space, protecting Her. And now was the time for those last rushes of power and pain, the last battle for life. The energy, the life force from every Portal, zeroed in on the Standing Stones as Frances and her family tumbled out of the van and raced up the processional avenue.

Frances had Kwame and Mick at her side, and Sassy and Sisi right behind assisting Alaman. The ground was uneven, and every time she stumbled one of her beloveds was there to catch her. All of the sigils on her body were undulating and emitting a frequency that called ahead to the stones, summoning their essence to this awakening.

The waxing gibbous moon was startling in the clear night sky, and it shone a path of light up the avenue to the center circle, letting their giant shadows spill behind as they moved quickly to the rings of ancestors. The temple of rock was not empty. Local people, those who knew and had waited for this night, slipped out of the shadows to make a large ring of protection and homage, each one standing in the embrace of the outer ring of stones. Frances was deep into her past and the needs of the future and didn't hear the slamming of car doors in the Visitor Center parking lot or see the movement of some of the women and men of Calanais who hurried off to block the intruders.

The battle for and against the new world order and the raised voices and the sound of fists hitting flesh became sharp and frantic, angry and desperate, the background for what was to follow.

Frances ran to the center of the Stones as she had millennia before, as she had in a much younger body. She felt the thrum of the Stones and absorbed the energy hurtling toward her from all the other Portals. It was a surge of power, a fusion of Light and Fire and Water and Earth and Air that blew apart the final lock. All the glory of She of a Thousand Names was again alive as Frances, surrounded by her family, by those incarnated friends from loves and lives past, stood, feet wide and arms stretched over head, and allowed it all to flow through her and become her and transform her. Her physical body trembled with the force of it all, and for one sliver of a moment Frances wondered if she and this body would survive.

The Stones woke up. They shimmered with a rainbow light and began to sing. All of the assembled began to weep as What Had Been became What Is once again. Light shot up and out from the Stones forming a grid of power that was mirrored in the ground below. The land, the very soil, remembered what it was like to be fully alive and in connection to all things.

All over the planet, every ley line responded, all the Portal power lines were surging at full capacity. The full potential of Mother Earth was awake. And Frances was the key that had opened the locks. Her heart was beating ever more slowly, and in the space between heartbeats she could hear the voices of all who had been awaiting this moment. She saw the women who held circle in their backyards. She felt the pain of children and women and men who suffered under patriarchy. She heard the Elders of the ancient peoples praying their prayers and chanting their chants as they participated in the fulfillment of prophecy.

And just when Frances thought that she would disintegrate in the fullness of this power, all the sigils on her body intensified and grew. They began to twist and spread like the tendrils of magickal plants until they joined into one large sigil, one symbol of Mother Earth, one visualization of Gaia, making a cohesive web that embraced all that Frances had been and was and would be. Her body became the unified map of the planet. The Stones sang louder and louder. All standing stones across the globe sang along. Volcanos sputtered, wind whipped across mountain tops, tides rose higher than ever. The new epoch was begun and the wisdom of the Goddess, the wisdom of balance and respect for all beings, and the connection of all things was the rising voice. All of creation sang the ancient song, born anew:

She is Here!

EPILOGUE

I n a gated golf community in Scottsdale Arizona, Sheldon Stewart chuckled as former colleagues began to send emails about how he must have been misinformed.

"Nobody fitting the description of Frances Fletcher has shown up at Stonehenge. Just a bunch of hippies and pagan freaks. Some fat fucks from Nebraska fell off a tour bus and started crying. But nothing actionable. The intel you sent us was bad, Sheldon."

"I'm at Sedona and it's just a bunch of crystal lovers and white kids with dreadlocks. And one guy in a kilt playing the bagpipes. I don't see Frances Fletcher. Bad intel, Stewart."

"I see some old women here on the beach in Bali, Stewart, but they all look Scandinavian or Chinese. No Frances Fletcher. If I hear any more Tuvan throat singing, I'll shoot myself. Your intel was garbage, Stewart."

"I did it, Frances. I finally made the right choice," he muttered.

And the hippies and soccer moms and pagans and migrant workers and witches and accountants and shamans and marine biologists and medicine people and brick layers and rainbow children who had gathered at Glastonbury and Ephesus and Philae and the Paps of Anu and along the banks of the Ganges and in all the other spots where She had been remembered – they knew. They felt the synthesis of elements. They opened to the stirring of Her wisdom. They knew and all rejoiced.

She is Here!

$$\text{)} \; \bigcirc \; \text{(}$$

Ten lunar months later Frances held her new great-granddaughter in her arms. Conceived on the night of that last Portal opening, as Frances and her family had recuperated in Margaret Curtis's small cottage near the Stones, this baby was that final piece of the beautiful mosaic. Twelve other people across the globe felt the 'click' of that threshold being crossed.

"Hello, long-awaited One," Frances whispered to the small bundle.

The baby, who would be called Sally Standing Bear Boadu Tjia, opened her eyes and looked with full awareness at her great-grandmother who had been her granddaughter. The final one of the Thirteen had been born.

"You, you Thirteen, are all here on this green beautiful Earth at the same time, Atvasfara. I have done what you asked of me, what She asked of me. And my reward is to see you again."

Frances felt the stone that she had carried for over eighty years, the stone that had held the essence of the first Sally Standing Bear, turn to soft dust in her pocket, she kissed the baby's cheek, and shared a smile with Sisi, propped up in bed, looking and feeling victorious.

She is Here!

In loving memory of my PawPaw,
Herbert Dow Martin,
who taught me the sanctity of stillness.

ACKNOWLEDGMENTS

This book has had a mind of her own – or should I say, a mind of Her own. I began this creative journey with an intention to write book three of a trilogy that would be set in the year 2032. That was fine and dandy until Sally Standing Bear demanded to be heard, and the rest, as they say, is speculative history.

There are a number of real-life women in this book, and their appearances are purely the result of my goddess-fueled imagination. I love to dwell in the 'what ifs', and we all have had the experience where some chance encounter or overheard phrase has opened doors that we hadn't known we wanted opened. So, I am grateful for the multiverse options that I have written for Marija Gimbuta, Carol Christ, Lee Hancock, Starhawk, Lane Redmond, and Margot Adler. I have shamelessly stolen Gisela Zastrow's swing at the Berlin Wall, and paid homage to Kathy Jones, Eve Ensler, Elizabeth Cunningham, ALisa Starkweather, and Hillary Clinton. There are also some folks whose names I have pilfered, from my great-grand and my nine-times great-grandmother

Magdalena to the brilliant Celtic scholar Sharynne MacLeod NicM-
hacha to my goddess daughter Leonore Tjia and many more. It is with
love and respect that they may find characters in this book who sport
them. I was inspired by the gifted artist, Hamish Douglas Burgess
whose 'Dragon Protecting the Goddess' graces my office wall.

I have made every effort to honor the indigenous peoples that I mention in these pages. I have had the great benefit of the wisdom and
generosity of two cultural advisors, Dr. Marie Nazon and Dr. Lush-
anya Echevarria. Mistakes made in this story are mine alone. I offer
descriptions of ceremonies and rituals and have been cautious to not
expose details of rites that are not mine to share – sometimes purposefully changing specifics to allow for the mysteries to remain mysterious. A percentage of profits made with this book will be shared with
the following charities and organizations that are doing the good work
to protect marginalized peoples, our planet, and the life on Her. Living
Stories Landscape, bit.ly/livingstorylandscapes; Kunsikeya Tamakoce,
kunsikeya.org; Redes Ecovillage, redes-ecovillages.org; Cork Traveller Women's Network, facebook.com/Cork-Traveller-Womens-Net-
work-752270951645072

I have eternal thanks to my Monday Night Scribes – Judi, Linda,
Naaz and Jess – the writing group of gifted, heart-led women who held
me and this story as it emerged. I love us!

My dear friend and brother from another mother, Scot An Sgeulaic-
he led me to Calanais and the mysteries there. I got to experience Tibet
because of Tashi Dolma, Egypt because of Dalia Basiouny, and Senegal
because of Marie Nazon. Beverly Little Thunder graciously showed me
the Lakota Inipi lodge and taught me how to pray in that way. I have
been blessed by the presence in my life of many magickal women and
men – so very blessed.

The very fact that there is a Womancraft Publishing is a miracle, and
that they decided to help me birth these books is a divine gift. Patrick,
Leigh, Sarah and the inestimable Lucy. Words fail me, but the heart
pours over.

And then, the Home Team. I have support and love and gentle rib-
bings from three of the best humans ever. Rick, Eliza, Malcolm – how
did I get to be so lucky?

ABOUT THE AUTHOR

Gina Martin is a founding mother and High Priestess of Triple Spiral of Dún na Sidhe, a pagan spiritual congregation in the Hudson Valley. She is a ritualist, teacher, healer, mother, wife, lover of Irish Wolfhounds, and writer of sacred songs. She has helped to create RISE (Revivers of Indigenous Spiritualities and Eco-systems), an organization dedicated to protecting and promoting indigenous and pagan belief structures and the lands that support them.

Gina is a practitioner of Classical Chinese medicine and a Board certified licensed acupuncturist having been a longtime student of Dr. Jeffrey Yuen, 88th generation Jade Purity sect.. She has served as chair and board member of the NY State Board of Massage Therapy. As a Shiatsu Sensei and head of the Eastern Studies department at the Swedish Institute College of Allied Health Sciences she helped design the degree-granting curriculum and wrote the text "The Shiatsu Workbook". She has acted as a consultant to national accrediting bodies and state boards to enhance the professional standards for somatic therapies.

She lives as a steward of the land that previously held a village of the Ramapough Lenape where people can come together now to remember the Old Ways. She is kept company by her husband and dogs, as well as the Sidhe who live in the hills.

ginamartinauthor.com

Other Books by the Author

Sisters of the Solstice Moon
Walking the Threads of Time
WomEnchanting

ABOUT THE ARTIST

I ris Sullivan was born in Australia, lived in the UK and finally settled in California to raise her 4 children. Iris now lives on Maui teaching art therapy, and the understanding of color in relation to the soul to international groups. Iris strives to reveal the invisible transparent soul movements through her art.

movingthesoulwithcolor.com

SISTERS

of the

SOLSTICE MOON

GINA MARTIN

BOOK 1 OF THE
WHEN SHE WAKES SERIES

O n the Winter Solstice, thirteen women across the world see the same terrifying vision. Their world is about to experience ravaging destruction. All that is now sacred will be destroyed. Each answers the call, to journey to Egypt, and save the wisdom of the Goddess.

This is the history before history.

This is herstory, as it emerged.

An imagining… or is it a remembering… of the end of matriarchy and the emergence of global patriarchy, this book brings alive long dead cultures from around the world and brings us closer to the lost wisdoms that we know in our bones.

Sisters of the Solstice Moon is a story of vast richness and complexity, in the tradition of speculative historical novel series, *Clan of the Cave Bear* and *The Mists of Avalon*.

WALKING
the
THREADS OF TIME

GINA MARTIN

BOOK 2 OF THE
WHEN SHE WAKES SERIES

I n lifetime after lifetime, she who was Atvasfara, High Priestess of Isis, seeks the others of the Thirteen as they appear – and disappear – in different configurations, genders and moments in human history from ancient Egypt and China, through medieval Europe, the Cree community in Canada, via Ghana and the battle fields of the First World War.

In this gripping sequel, the thirteen vision carriers first introduced in *Sisters of the Solstice Moon* face death and danger to serve the Goddess in the times when She is forbidden. Travel with them as they navigate through patriarchal history, seeking to save Her wisdom in the darkest of times.

"This is magic realism at its most sacred feminine."

ABOUT WOMANCRAFT

Womancraft Publishing was founded on the revolutionary vision that women and words can change the world. We act as midwife to transformational women's words that have the power to challenge, inspire, heal and speak to the silenced aspects of ourselves.

We believe that:

+ books are a fabulous way of transmitting powerful transformation,

+ values should be juicy actions, lived out,

+ ethical business is a key way to contribute to conscious change.

At the heart of our Womancraft philosophy is fairness and integrity. Creatives and women have always been underpaid. Not on our watch! We split royalties 50:50 with our authors. We work on a full circle model of giving and receiving: reaching backwards, supporting Tree-Sisters' reforestation projects, and forwards via Worldreader, providing books at no cost to education projects for girls and women.

We are proud that Womancraft is walking its talk and engaging so many women each year via our books and online. Join the revolution! Sign up to the mailing list at womancraftpublishing.com and find us on social media for exclusive offers:

(f) womancraftpublishing

(⊙) womancraft_publishing

(𝕀𝕟) womancraftpublishing.com/books

USE OF WOMANCRAFT WORK

Often women contact us asking if and how they may use our work. We love seeing our work out in the world. We love you sharing our words further. And we ask that you respect our hard work by acknowledging the source of the words.

We are delighted for short quotes from our books – up to 200 words – to be shared as memes or in your own articles or books, provided they are clearly accompanied by the author's name and the book's title.

We are also very happy for the materials in our books to be shared amongst women's communities: to be studied by book groups, discussed in classes, read from in ceremony, quoted on social media…with the following provisos:

+ If content from the book is shared in written or spoken form, the book's author and title must be referenced clearly.

+ The only person fully qualified to teach the material from any of our titles is the author of the book itself. There are no accredited teachers of this work. Please do not make claims of this sort.

+ If you are creating a course devoted to the content of one of our books, its title and author must be clearly acknowledged on all promotional material (posters, websites, social media posts).

+ The book's cover may be used in promotional materials or social media posts. The cover art is copyright of the artist and has been licensed exclusively for this book. Any element of the book's cover or font may not be used in branding your own marketing materials when teaching the content of the book, or content very similar to the original book.

+ No more than two double page spreads, or four single pages of any book may be photocopied as teaching materials.

We are delighted to offer a 20% discount of over five copies going to one address. You can order these on our webshop, or email us. If you require further clarification, email us at: info@womancraftpublishing.com